I0573656

The Keepers of Éire

Jordan Bernal

Dragon Wing Publishing
California, USA

ISBN: 978-0-9910134-0-1
ISBN: 978-0-9910134-1-8 (ebook)
THE KEEPERS OF ÉIRE
Copyright © 2013 byDeborah 'Jordan' Bernal

Cover Design: Christine McCall, Christine McCall Designs
Interior Format: Patricia Marshall, Luminare Press

Library of Congress Control Number: 2013952321

Dedicated to the memory of my parents Lee Bernal and Sandra Bernal-Davis. While writing is a solitary endeavor, I felt their loving guidance. I learned my dad was a writer after I started this project. He passed away long ago, but I know he would be proud of me. My mom always encouraged my dreams and started my dragon fascination with my first dragon figurine. I thank them both for their unconditional love and miss them greatly.

In dreams begins responsibility.
— William Butler Yeats
1914 volume of poems *Responsibilities*

The Keepers of Éire

Jordan Bernal

One

Christian Riley clicked the safe closed and gave the tumbler a quick spin. He picked up the portrait showcasing the politico eejit, careful to re-hang it level. He stuffed what he came for in his rucksack. His head snapped up, his focus on the locked door leading to the hallway beyond as several sets of heavy-soled boots slapped on the marble tiled floor, echoing louder until they halted outside.

Bloody fecking hell, he thought, Gardaí. Christian shoved his thick, black hair into a knit cap and risked a glance over his shoulder at the boom of a battering ram. He slipped his arms into the straps of his rucksack and rushed to lift the partially opened window. The scream of approaching sirens filled the room.

He snagged the length of rope he left anchored from the roof when he broke in not five minutes ago. Christian clamped his carabineer in place as another boom from metal slamming into wood sounded. The door behind him splintered and he leapt into the rain-soaked abyss.

Rain stung his eyes as he landed hard on the puddle-riddled pavement.

"Damn close call, that one," Christian muttered, his gloved hands shook as he unhooked himself. He flung the rope, then ducked into the shadows and away from the crowd of Gardaí vehicles surrounding his latest job. He doubled back several times to make sure he hadn't been followed.

Christian darted past the neighborhood patrol into the least rundown of the North Dublin tenements and dashed up a dim narrow staircase, avoiding the creaky fourth step. He entered his flat and locked the door behind him. A quick scan confirmed there was nothing out of place in the sparse living area. He crossed to the bedroom, reached in, and flipped on the wall switch. His gaze flicked to the paperback extending over the nightstand by the length of his thumbnail. He stepped over the threshold and found the single strand of his hair on the rumpled bedclothes. His breath eased and his fingers relaxed on his clenched knife. His luck was holding. No one had caught him—yet.

Christian tucked the weapon under his pillow and tossed his rucksack into the corner. He stripped out of his damp clothes and fell face down onto his oversized bed. The clock blinked three forty-five and he hoped exhaustion from the heist and the adrenaline drain would keep his recurring and disturbing dreams at bay. Sleep overtook him.

Cold tendrils of fear slid down Christian's back and swept over his face, chilling him. He grabbed at the covers, his legs thrashing in the tangled sheets. His heart pounded and his breathing labored, as though he was once again that sixteen-year-old street urchin running from the orphanage through Dublin's run-down shipping quays.

Christian knew in his sleep-shrouded mind it was 'the dream.' He wanted out before it could grab him, but nothing stopped it. The dream reached out its sinewy fingers, clutched him, and catapulted him over the precipice.

Watery sunlight broke the boundary between night and day. A steady rain highlighted the eeriness of the hour. He crept past a whitethorn tree pregnant with white and colored ribbons marking the remembrance of loved ones. Mocking him.

Ten meters ahead, a stone circle with another whitethorn on the northern side stood in silent memorial. The mists swirled and parted. A figure, dressed in a dark hooded coat and black Wellies, making the gender indistinguishable, emerged from beneath the tree and walked to the center of the upright stones.

He stole through the wet grass toward the lone silhouette. A twig snapped like gunfire ricocheting in a tin can. The figure spun toward him, the hood fell back with the sudden motion, revealing a petite woman. She sported blonde hair that frizzed with the rain, dark eyes, and a small mouth twisted into a snarl.

"What are you doing here?" Her cheeks flushed and her eyes narrowed. "Haven't you done enough?"

His jaw slackened, his mouth fell open. No sound emerged.

The wind caught and shredded her next words. Hot bloody rage roared through his body, drummed in his ears, clouded his vision red. He forced an unsteady hand to pull a jewel-handled dagger from its sheath at his belt.

Get it over with quick, the thought thundered in his mind.

The woman glanced up as a shadowy dragon swooped down to land between them.

"Now," his mind screamed, "before the creature transforms completely and kills you."

Feet planted wide, he stood transfixed unable to wretch his gaze from the apparition. He gulped air into starved lungs like a firestorm consuming oxygen.

The dragon grew in density, a gray shadow changed to iridescent burgundy. It stood on scaly hind legs, thick as juvenile oak trunks. Spikes erupted from the top of its triangular head. A red, forked tongue flicked between gleaming razor teeth. Sapphire eyes whirled under lowered ridges. The bat-shaped wings extended from its back, hiding the woman. Its chest, devoid of diamond-hard scales, lay exposed.

He tightened his fingers around the jeweled handle of the dagger, flipped it until he pinched the tip of the blade between his thumb and forefinger, drew back his arm, and hurled it.

A strangled cry escaped the woman's lips.

He braced to absorb the dragon magic he knew would be released. The dagger passed through the still shimmering body of the dragon, and embedded into the woman's chest.

Wave after wave of power buffeted him. He staggered. Wild, fiery, it tore through him, drove him to his knees. He gasped and fought to lift his head.

The dragon vanished like fog caught by a ray of sunlight. The woman slumped to the ground in slow motion. Rain continued to fall, cooling his face. The magic dissipated.

He pulled his exhausted body to his feet, his head and shoulders slumped and made his way to the woman. He gathered her in his arms and carried her lifeless body toward the growing light of day.

Christian moaned and thrashed his head from side to side. He was aware the location in the dream had shifted, but still couldn't break free.

The rain slowed to a drizzle as he leaned the woman against a spiral and circle engraved boulder the size of a small car. The boulder blocked the entrance to a rock structure surrounding an enormous round earthen mound.

Sunlight glinted off something between the hilt of the dagger and the woman's chest. He reached down. The air exploded with noise like thunder. Blinded by a burst of white light, he careened back as if lightning had struck his fingertips and burned him all the way down to his toes. More magic than anything he had ever felt raced through him. Much like the River Liffey divided the city of Dublin, his heart split in half. Joy at the power the magic provided him warred with his grief.

Christian awoke to afternoon sunlight dappling his pillow. Its warmth bathed his face. Yet, the chill of the dream remained. He rubbed his chest where his pendant lay hot against his galloping heart. Was the pendant somehow triggering the dreams? He untangled himself from the sheets, rolled to a sitting position, and pressed the heel of his hand between his eyes. His headache speared like the jewel-handled dagger.

He'd seen a woman and a dragon inside his head. Heard her and the killer—the words, the tone. More disturbing, he'd experienced it all from within the murderer—his anger, his grief, and his intentions.

Christian stumbled from the bed to the loo to hunt up some aspirin, gobbled four tablets, then splashed cold water on his face. He scrubbed away sleep and the dregs of the dream. This one had been different. In the six months since the start of the dreams, the other three murder victims had never spoken to him.

Was he responsible for the death of another human being? Christian wondered. His breath shuddered out between trembling lips and his hands shook. He clenched them into fists, pounding the countertop over and over and over. In the mirror, dark blue eyes glinted back at him. A night's beard growth couldn't hide the pallor of his face. He gritted his teeth and opened his fists. One bruised hand reached for his dragon-embossed silver pendant. He felt the words engraved on the back.

Gaelic, he thought, but what did they mean? *Dílseacht, Fáil, Saoirse.*

He clutched it and wondered if his life was at stake—perhaps his honor as well—and his very soul.

Devan Fraser pressed her forehead against the pressurized airplane window. She gazed as the white-capped ocean crashed into the cliffs of Ireland's rugged coastline. She wondered for the hundredth time if she was do-ing the right thing. Had she really just packed up her life and traveled six thousand miles from her home in San Francisco on a whim? Or was she following the predestined path alluded to in her great-grandparents' letter?

The green fields past her window spread out like a chessboard, each square bordered by stone walls. Devan glanced down at the letter in her trembling hands. She closed her eyes and battled back the threatening tears. Chanel No. 5, her deceased mother's scent, wafted out from the paper. Devan let the memory of the day she found the letter, and much more, assault her.

Devan meandered her parents' long-shuttered master suite, her hand lingering over her father's monogrammed cufflinks. She cradled her mother's porcelain figurine of Dagda—the mythical Irish god. With their funerals over, Devan started the emotional task of sorting through her parents' things. She had returned from bereavement leave to discover her position at the university eliminated by the latest round of budget cuts. Her life had stopped, shattered into shards that continued to slash her into pieces.

Her parents had died in New York, celebrating their anniversary. Theirs was the only love she could ever count on. Her relationship with Rick had ended in disaster. She shuddered, dislodging the unwelcome images that crowded her mind. No, Rick's manipulation and possessiveness was not love. Better to concentrate on her family's love.

The mahogany bureau door hung ajar and Devan sighed as she opened it. Framed photos of both sets of grandparents, her parents, and her Uncle Gabriel in his Army uniform lined the shelves like gravestones.

The top shelf held a porcelain collection of castles, fairies, and other magical figures her father had given her mother. One for each anniversary. Devan wondered if there would be a new one in the suitcases she knew waited in her father's study.

Devan placed Dagda on the shelf. Her hand skimmed other Irish mythical heroes. Tucked at the back of the shelf, her hand whispered over a warm wooden box. She brought it down. Her fingers traced the carved dragon on the lid.

"Why, when Mom knew of my fascination with dragons and my Irish heritage, had she never shown me this before she died?" Inside the red velvet lined box lay a silver ring with the same dragon engraved on it. She took the ring to her mother's side of the bed, set the box down, and turned on the lamp. Peering at the ring under the light, she noticed the foreign words engraved inside.

"Dílseacht, Fáil, Saoirse," she stumbled over the pronunciation. "What does that mean?"

She turned the ring over and over in her hand. "I've never seen Mom wear this." She picked up the box. "I've never even seen this before."

Something white peaked through a corner of the box, from under the lining. Carefully, Devan peeled the lining and lifted it out. It was a letter. She closed her hand around the ring. Perhaps, it was a birthday present for her. It was perfect: the ring and its box matched her collection. Suddenly, she felt like a six-year-old who had stumbled into a secret cache of Santa presents. Her hands shook as she unfolded the letter and read. It was addressed to her grandmother, Brinna. Brinna's mum and da hinted of a destiny and family to be found in Ireland.

Devan opened her hand and again looked at the ring. Her legs trembled and she was glad she was sitting so she couldn't fall. Not a present from her parents, not directly. But as she pushed the ring onto her right middle finger, she knew it was hers. She could almost hear the echoes of the foreign words as her finger tingled under the ring. She was the only living offspring of Patrick and Brinna Gallagher, therefore heir to the ring, and possibly to a new destiny.

Refolding the letter, Devan returned it to the box. Her gaze returned to the bureau, alighting on the pictures of her Irish grandparents. She knew Patrick and Brinna Gallagher were born, schooled, and married in Ireland. They immigrated to New York in the late 1940s when they were both in their early twenties and looking for work. Devan's mother, Meghann, was born in 1955, six years after her brother. Uncle Gabriel had been the one to die for his country in the Vietnam War, before he could marry and start his own family.

Devan took the photos from the bureau, along with the mahogany box, the Dagda figurine, and her father's handkerchief and cufflinks. In her room, she upended her gray backpack, emptied it of old notebooks and papers left over from her now defunct job. She wrapped the photos in a T-shirt and placed them carefully in the backpack along with the box, which held the letter, her father's cufflinks, and his handkerchief protecting the figurine.

Turbulence jostled her and the memory ended. Devan opened her eyes, returning her gaze to the Irish landscape speeding past. She was on the first leg of a journey to discover her hopes, her dreams, her destiny. The tears came and she couldn't stop them. Her lips trembled, and she bit down on her lower one to hold back her cry. She gulped down unsteady breaths. For the first time in her life, she was alone. No family, no one to love, no one to love her.

Two

S ean O'Shea, the Tuatha Dragon Clan leader, hunched his six-foot-three trim frame and leaned his forearms on the windowsill to peer at the withdrawing clouds. He stared out without seeing his red dragon, FIONN, land in the smaller of two cobblestone courtyards. Sean should be preparing Loughcrew for the céilí to celebrate the spring equinox. The enclaves at Lough Gur and Beaghmore were due to arrive shortly. Yet the murders of three of his clan mates over the last six months invaded his thoughts. Fear for the clan's survival mingled with frustration at his impotence in finding the killer.

His thoughts dissipated as the great doors of the communal dining hall opened. Aisling, his wife of twenty-seven years, strode toward the natural cavern that housed the dragons. Sean's gaze followed. The exterior of the cavern resembled a grassy knoll with standing stones atop—typical of over a thousand hills dotting the Irish countryside. The only difference: the interior opened into a lair large enough to house eleven wings-folded dragons.

Sean turned from the office window and paced.

"What are you brooding about?" FIONN'S question reverberated in his mind.

"I'm not brooding. Just formulating safeguards. I'm not sure the clan is safe, even though the killer didn't strike on Imbolc," Sean bespoke silently as he scratched his ginger and gray-bearded chin and rolled his shoulders to ease knotted muscles. Something was wrong, his gut warned.

Meara Callahan stepped out of her clan mate Padrick Nolan's office at Lough Gur into the midday sun. The last of next week's scheduling was finally done. Since they were shorthanded, there was little down time. She shoved her hands into her armpits as a cold wind swept in. Her nostrils flared at the muddy scent carried southeast from the Shannon.

"Meara!" Braeden Boyle yelled as he ran toward her from the cottages fifty meters down the dirt road.

She turned.

"Have Mary and AALYSIA returned?" He skidded to a stop less than two feet from her. He bent at the waist, huffing air.

"No," she said. "Slow down and tell me what's going on."

"Th…they haven't returned," Braeden stammered. "Mary woke me before dawn. Said to go to the celebration ahead of her, as she had an errand to run. But I thought she'd be back by now. I'm supposed to help set up for the music and all. I need to leave soon, I wanted to ride together."

Meara placed a hand on his shoulder. "Why don't you go on? I think I know where she went. I'll go get her. She's probably on her way back and we'll run into each other." *Lord, let Mary be safe,* she prayed. For Braeden's sake, she pushed away her growing fear.

She turned him, slipped her arm around his shoulder, and led him back to the cottage he shared with his wife. "Go on now. Don't forget your guitar, I want to hear the new song you wrote. Mary and I will see you at the céilí later."

"Thanks," he said as he opened the cottage door.

Meara returned to her house to retrieve her riding gear. She clasped her hand over her dragon pendant and bespoke her compeer. *"We need to go to Carrowmore, Love. Mary and AALYSIA have not returned. I'm getting my coat, meet me in the courtyard."*

When Meara approached, CARRIGAN bent her pale green foreleg. Meara stepped onto it and settled between her dragon's neck ridges. Once Meara was secure, CARRIGAN spread her wings, took two quick steps, and launched herself into the air.

They flew north. Meara searched for Mary and AALYSIA as she urged her compeer faster.

I should have called Sean, she thought. Mary shouldn't have come this way alone.

A trickle of cold sweat rolled down her back. Carrowmore lay one hundred and eighty kilometers from Lough Gur as the dragon flew, but Carrigan pressed for speed and arrived in just over an hour.

"Can you hear Aalysia?" Meara bespoke her dragon.

"Nigh." Carrigan landed in the tall grass, as close to the megalithic rock formations as her size allowed. Meara leapt to the ground.

"Mary," she called. "Are you here?"

When no response came, Meara streaked through the jumble of boulders, some taller than herself, searching for Mary and her burgundy dragon.

She slipped on wet grass and landed on her knees beside a two-foot rock tomb. She steadied herself on the stone and her hand came away smeared with blood. She hadn't slipped on grass, but on blood. A lot of blood.

Mary's, she thought as she inspected her hand and knees. "Oh, God!" she cried aloud. "It's happened again."

Meara wiped the blood from her hand on the grass, then stumbled to her feet. As quickly as her shaky legs could carry her, she returned to Carrigan, mounted, and directed her dragon back to Lough Gur with haste. Their return journey was a blur.

Carrigan landed in the inner courtyard. As Meara dismounted, Padrick, his salt-and-pepper hair disheveled and his lips pulled down in a frown, rushed out of the Great Hall.

When he saw her tears, he took her hands into his. "Mary?" At Meara's confusion, Padrick explained, "I saw Braeden before he left."

Meara's hands trembled. She swallowed past the lump in her throat and nodded.

"Was her body there?"

Meara shook her head, then managed in a weak voice, "I'd better get cleaned up, we'll need Sean."

Padrick released her one hand but kept the other firmly entwined in his. "Everyone left half an hour ago."

She changed into clean, black trousers and a pale green jumper that matched the color of CARRIGAN's wings. After she washed the tears from her face, she joined Padrick outside. Together they donned their riding gear and mounted their dragons.

Padrick nodded to her, pointing up, signaling her to launch first. Except for the whooshing of their dragon's wings, they flew in silence. Goggles protected her eyes from the wind, but Meara's tears still formed. She willed them away. She needed to be strong for the clan, but mostly for Braeden.

The sky darkened over Loughcrew as Sean once more searched the skies. Most of the clan had already arrived to celebrate the spring equinox, but Sean awaited the stragglers with apprehension. The céilí was in full swing, tables overflowing with food and drink. Chairs sat haphazardly around the dining hall built for fifty. Musicians tuned their instruments in the far corner, the cacophonous notes bouncing off the high oak-beamed ceiling. From the open double doors, Sean was cheered by the sight and sound of his clan mates. Maybe all would celebrate the spring, as they were meant.

From the West came the unmistakable outline of only two dragons.

CARRIGAN with Meara and AALYSIA with Mary, he thought. Finally. Had Padrick stayed in Lough Gur?

The dragons, backlit by the moon, loomed in the sky as they neared. Sean noticed one was too large and too dark to be Mary's AALYSIA. Dust swirled as Meara's CARRIGAN landed softly next to Padrick's black DECLAN in the outer courtyard. Both riders dismounted and approached Sean. When Padrick shook his head, Sean shifted his attention to Meara.

Tears glistened in her eyes. She forced them back. "I found blood."

Sean rubbed the knot of tension in his neck. "Where?"

"On the standing stones at Carrowmore."

"Maybe she's running late?" Sean asked. "Slipped and cut herself."

"Not with the amount of blood I found. Braeden said Mary had something she needed to do. I told him to come ahead, I'd track her down."

Padrick soothed Meara's shoulder. His sorrowful gaze sought out Sean. "When Meara told me what she found, we came straight here."

Meara glanced at both men. "She still mourned her sister, Anne. That's why I checked Carrowmore first. She told me once that she felt the reassurance of the stones there. Tied prayer ribbons."

Sean winced. "I forgot. How long has it been?"

"Anne and her unborn son were killed in a car accident last June. Her husband was the only survivor and he blamed himself," Meara said. "I don't think Mary ever forgave him for bringing Anne, in her condition, on his work assignment."

"He caused the accident?" Sean asked.

"No, but Anne was near full term and shouldn't have been traveling so far from Dublin."

Sean glanced at the room full of festive clan members. "We should make sure, before we interrupt the céilí. Let me contact Assistant Commissioner Byrne of the Gardaí and the coroner to meet us there, then we'll go." He telepathically summoned FIONN.

The lounging red dragon—the size of a two-room cottage—rose as Sean approached. He slipped his riding coat and gloves on, settled onto FIONN's neck, and urged his compeer to take flight.

Padrick, straddling DECLAN, flew behind and to the right. Meara, on CARRIGAN, completed the arrowhead formation on Sean's left. They flew southeast forty kilometers into the already dark sky and toward the giant earthwork mound of Newgrange at Brú na Bóinne—where the three previous murdered clan members had been found.

The dragons circled, then landed at the entrance of the rugby pitch sized earthen mound. With the low mists swirling around them, Sean, Padrick and Meara slid down from their dragon's backs. Their boots sank into the damp grass. They approached the waist-high boulder blocking the tomb entrance.

They found Mary just as the previous three dragonriders had been found. She was propped in a sitting position against the Threshold Stone of Newgrange with an eight-inch gem-handled dagger piercing her heart. One edge of the Tuatha Dragon Clan pendant worn around her neck was chipped. As with the other deaths, the dragon's body would never be found—a byproduct of the dragon magic that ensured that outsiders would not learn of the existence of dragonkind.

Sean's legs turned to jelly. He bore down, locking his knees. It wouldn't do for Meara or Padrick to see their clan leader falter. But, oh how he wished he didn't have to be stoic. Even though Mary was the fourth clan member murdered, he couldn't get used to the sight of a dead person, a clan member. Someone he considered a friend. Mary was not much older than Sean's own son, maybe a year or two. What would he do if it had been Matthew? He shuddered.

Meara knelt down in front of Mary's body, crying. "I should have insisted she take someone with her. It's my fault," Meara said when she'd caught her breath enough to speak.

Sean clasped a hand on Meara's shoulder. "No, no it's not. The fault lies with the killer, no one else. Everyone, even a dragonrider—especially a dragonrider—should feel safe going about their daily lives."

A.C. Gardaí Byrne and the coroner joined them. After the coroner's assessment, Sean crouched down and carefully slid the dagger free with his gloved hand. Wrapping it first in cloth, then plastic, he slipped it into his coat breast pocket.

"I'll file the report like the other three, accidental deaths," the Gardaí said. "I'm sorry for your troubles." Sean nodded his thanks.

Padrick flanked Meara's other side. "You couldn't have stopped her. The killer could have stalked her, known when she was most likely to be alone. Mary followed the rules, but she needed her privacy. Her time for grieving."

"I know." Meara's voice cracked. "I just don't understand why this is happening. She would never hurt anyone."

"None of us would," Sean said. "We took an oath. That oath means not only loyalty to the clan and dragonkind, but also Ireland and its inhabitants. We can't give up our beliefs. Then Mary and AALYSIA's deaths, and the others, would serve no purpose."

He lifted Meara's chin with one hand and Mary's nicked and bloodied pendant in the other. "She was one of us. A dragonrider. She endeavored to fulfill her destiny. All we can do is honor them both and redouble our own convictions." Sean's voice rose with emotion. "We will find the killer, I promise."

Padrick nodded. Together, the two men pulled Meara to her feet.

Once Padrick and Meara stepped away, hand-in-hand, Sean lifted Mary's body into his arms. He gathered her close and walked to his compeer, his grieving friends trailing behind.

They would need to return to Loughcrew, and the clan. Sean dreaded having to break up the céilí. There hadn't been much to celebrate over the last six months and the spring equinox was supposed to be a joyous time. Would he ever feel joy again? Surely not the innocent joy that had been such a part of his life with the dragon clan before the killings.

Sean gently laid Mary's body across Fionn's neck. He seated himself behind, then signaled Padrick and Meara to lift off. The dragons returned to Loughcrew. Each rider lost in their own thoughts.

As they neared, he heard Fionn bespeak the gathered dragons.

"Aalysia and her rider are no more."

Keening rose from the twenty-five dragons scattered around the outer courtyard. The three dragons landed, Fionn in the inner courtyard, Declan and Carrigan in the outer. Clan members emerged from the Great Hall.

"What's happened? Who's that? What's all the commotion?" Voices shouted from the growing crowd.

Sean took Mary from Fionn's neck. Several riders gasped in horror. The music halted mid-song as more people rushed out. Sean placed Mary's limp body on the dolmen and horizontal capstone that divided the two courtyards. Murmurs passed through the crowd as Braeden shoved people aside.

"Is it Mary? Is she okay?" Braeden's hazel eyes widened and the rosy hue on his cheeks faded when he reached for his wife. "No! She can't be dead. She was to meet me here. No. Someone help me." Tears rolled down his now mottled face.

Sean stopped him from climbing on top of the monument. Padrick flanked Braeden's other side and guided the distraught young man to his sand-colored dragon waiting on the edge of the cobblestones.

"Let me in." Dr. Shelby's baritone voice cut through the mass of crying people. He reached Braeden and Padrick. "Someone get me my kit."

Sean's wife, Aisling, brought the black leather case. "What can I do to help?"

"I'm going to give him a sedative," the doctor said, rummaging in the bag. He pulled out a glass vial filled with a milky fluid and a syringe.

Braeden knocked the items from Shelby's hands. "No." He wiped his nose on his shirtsleeve. "I need to be there for my Mary. She deserves that much. The fecking gobshite should have killed me, not her. I'll see the murderer drawn and quartered, scourged by FAOLAN'S fire." He weaved his way back to the monument and Mary's body.

"I'm sorry." Sean rested a hand on Braeden's shoulder. Anger swirled at the thought that he hadn't prevented another murder.

"Why didn't you protect her?" Braeden jerked his shoulders, dislodging Sean's hand. "If you can't stop the bastard, I will."

"We don't even know who the murderer is. Are you going to demand FAOLAN flame anyone not associated with the clan?" Sean's tone hardened. "Will you risk the entire clan? Is that what Mary would want?"

Braeden bowed his head at the mention of his dead wife. "No. But she wouldn't sit idle and wait for the killer to pick us off one by one. Mary's death can't be in vain. We have to take action."

"We will. We need to narrow down the possibilities. Find what Conor, Shannon, Dylan, and Mary had in common, besides being dragonriders. Track down where the daggers came from," Sean said. "The other leaders and I are working on keeping everyone safe without putting Éire in danger."

"I want to be there when you find the murdering son-of-a-bitch."

Sean nodded. "Right now, we need to honor Mary. Can you do that?"

"Aye." Braeden's chin came up. His eyes blazed.

The clan gathered around the monument with hands joined. Dragons of every size and color stood wingtip to wingtip behind their riders and the other family members, forming the clan's circle of life.

Sean's voice rang crisp as he called out to friends and family. "*A Caras, A Clan.* Today we honor another fallen clan member. Mary was murdered as she visited Carrowmore to mourn the loss of her sister." How he longed to never have to give another eulogy. He cleared his throat. "We swore to serve Éire. I call on each of us to renew our commitment." He recited the oath. "*Dílseacht, Fáil, Saoirse*—Loyalty, Destiny, Liberty." Each word was a promise emblazoned on his aching heart for revenge.

He drew a deep breath and led them in a prayer. Then he turned to Braeden. The young man stepped up to his wife's body.

"*A ghra, mo chroí*, I will hunt down the one who murdered you. *Tá geall*, I promise." Braeden kissed her, then collapsed.

Sean and Padrick rushed to his side. They carried him to a chair retrieved from the dining hall. Meara and Aisling joined Braeden as each clan member paid their respects. When the last human stepped away, FIONN, CARRIGAN, and Braeden's FAOLAN formed a triangle around the monument. Dragon fire consumed Mary's body and melted the Tuatha Dragon Clan pendant—ensuring no residual dragon magic escaped.

An anguished rumble emanated from the dragon circle, like the torn lonely cry of the wind, as the dragons paid tribute.

The clan members scattered to clear away the party remnants. Sean watched helplessly as Dr. Shelby led Braeden away. FAOLAN keened softly as his compeer trudged after the doctor. With one last look at the bowed head of the young man, Sean beckoned Padrick, Meara, and Kiely, the Ulster Province leader, and Padrick's mother, to join him in his office.

The leaders assembled around Sean's desk. He called the meeting to order. "It's obvious we can no longer protect our counties individually. Until the killer is apprehended, no one rides alone."

Kiely lifted her eyes to Sean. "We're stretched thin as it is. Now we have four counties without a dragon and rider. How can we cover these counties and our own, yet ensure no one works alone?"

"Perhaps now is the time to push young ROARKE and DOCHAS into selecting riders," Meara suggested. "We need all the dragons available and there's no time to waste searching for the perfect compeer."

Sean set his jaw. "No! We can't pressure the dragon youngsters into accepting someone not of their choosing."

"So, not only are we shorthanded during the critical spring plantings," Meara began, "but we must spend time searching for likely candidates. How do you propose we do that and protect ourselves while still on patrol?"

"We compromise," Sean decided. "We conduct a search while we do our daily fly overs. But the priority *must* be the safety of the dragonriders."

"Safety?" Kiely sneered. "You've wasted time. We could have had another dragonet pair hatched by now if you'd got off your arse after Conor and DONOVAN were killed, or even Shannon and TARA. Two pairs if you'd mate two dragon pairs at a time."

Sean leaned forward. "When Conor and DONOVAN were killed, we didn't know they were to be the first in a string of murders." He ticked off his points on his fingers. "Next, how was I to know ROARKE and DOCHAS would balk at selecting partners? We don't have a grasp of what a winter mating flight would do to the eggs. All mating flights have taken place on Samhain. We've no precedent here." He rubbed his neck. "Besides, new hatchlings require lots of attention. Attention we are in short supply of. We need everyone flying, and we need *time* to determine who is out to destroy us.

Silence followed.

Padrick glared at his mother, then broke the strain in the room. "I'll see if there is anything written about mating at different times of the year, find out if there are dangers."

Three

S till shaky from his latest dream, Christian weaved his way around the bustling tourists along Grafton Street. He nicked a fat wallet from an unsuspecting man arguing with his wife. The man looked longingly at the corner pub.

Christian smiled, following the mark's gaze. His eye caught the jerky movements of a filthy street urchin grabbing at a spiky, brown-haired woman's backpack. The woman stood in the middle of the richest shopping district in all Ireland with a large-lensed camera covering her face, oblivious to the young thief behind her. The eejit pickpocket would ruin it for the rest of the working grifters if someone didn't stop him.

Without another thought, Christian sidled up to the young boy, at least he thought it was a boy, clasped a hand around the back of his dirty neck, and propelled him away from the woman.

"What the bloody hell are you thinking?" Christian hissed. "She'd have felt that."

"I don't know what you're blathering on about. Let me go. I'll call out to the Gardaí." The youth twisted and pulled, trying to break Christian's hold. "I swear." The boy's voice broke.

"Call out and the Gardaí will be only too interested in the wallets you have hidden on you," Christian said.

"Do not. You don't know nothing."

Christian lifted the soiled jumper away from the boy's back and pulled two wallets from the waistband of his jeans. "What are these?"

The boy grabbed them and shoved them into his front pockets. "None of your business. You shaking me down? I gotta come home with something or my old man is gonna beat the shite outta me. Let me go."

"Your da or your boss?

"Either," the boy said, then lowered his voice. "I can let you have ten percent."

Christian shook his head. "Keep your spoils. You earned them. But you need to get yourself into another line of work. You're too jittery. You're going to get nabbed." He let go and the boy scuttled away and disappeared around a corner.

"I am too old for this bullshit," Christian said aloud, then searched for his drop partner. He found the woman and passed on the lifted wallets.

Silently he vowed that this job would be the last. Logan, his childhood friend was getting sloppy. Hitting too many marks, too quickly. Christian felt he had paid back the debt owed and then some. Besides, the dreams were coming nightly now, pulling at him with more clarity. Something needed to be done, and soon.

His long legs carried him north toward the O'Connell Bridge. He passed the crowds of shoppers, tourists and Dubliners on their way to work. He scanned the musicians arranged along street corners playing their tunes for coins. The view never seemed to change. The city did have a few redeeming qualities with some central areas renovated. His favorite was Grafton Street with its smart shops and architecture featuring red brick and gray stone.

The busy River Liffey split the city in two, north and south. From the O'Connell Bridge apex, he stopped to take in the ships moored at the quays and the majestic dome of the Four Courts building glistening in the sun. These waterways and bridges had once been home to a sixteen-year-old who used his wits and talents to claw his way out of the alleyways of his youth.

He knew he would have hooked up with the devil himself to escape the "families" of foster care. Often used as a pawn for the adults to make ends meet, violence ran rampant. If the daily take didn't meet expectations, discipline was meted out with fists, boots, belts, even a bat a time or two. Whatever was handy. It's no wonder he'd hooked up with Logan. The thug always had something up his sleeve, working some con.

By the time he had turned nineteen, Christian craved a different life. So they had parted ways, business-wise, yet still mates. Now he knew the friendship had also run its course. He already told Logan he was through, today would even the debt. Logan was pissed and claimed he would make him pay, but Christian was no longer a lad and afraid of threats.

Looking up from his wandering thoughts, Christian saw Logan in deep conversation with a slightly older man with shrewd-looking eyes and a mouth set in a hard line. Logan finished his meeting and hurried the man away.

"So, what's the take boyo?" Logan scratched the jagged scar on his chin.

Christian ignored the not so subtle insult. "You should know, as your girl was quick for the pickup. We're square now, Logan. I'm done with this penny-ante stuff."

"You always thought you were the better, smarter than the rest of the gang. Don't expect to be welcomed back when things don't go smoothly for you. We're as much done with you as you are with us." Logan sneered.

"Aye. Even, then." Christian turned to cross back into the south side of Dublin, and thought he heard Logan mumble 'not bloody likely, boyo'.

No way was Christian falling into a trap. He'd ditch the tail Logan was sure to put on him, then head back to his flat. He shoved his hands into his pockets and whistled a carefree tune, glancing at the shop windows until he spotted one of Logan's runners. He grinned and ducked into the corner pub his earlier mark had found. Sure enough, the mark was spitting mad, throwing up his hands, and calling for the Gardaí.

Christian scooted out as two Garda entered. Logan's tail was detained long enough for Christian to disappear into the crowds. He crossed the Ha'Penny Bridge, heading north and entered the glass front doors of the office building he had vacated late last night. The lift clanked and scraped its way up to the top floor. Christian rapped his knuckles on the doorless jamb and entered without permission.

"Had a bit of trouble last night?" His client shot a quick glance at the fingerprint-dust covered window, then smirked.

Christian didn't answer. He tossed a manila envelope onto the desk and inclined his head.

The client opened the packet, pulled out its contents, and frowned.

"I see." He grabbed his checkbook.

"No. Cash," Christian said. "You know the rules."

The client paid Christian from a briefcase filled with bundled euros.

"I'll be in touch." Christian slipped two bundles into his inside coat pocket, allowing the client to see the handle of a blade tucked into his waist.

At the client's wide-eyed stare, Christian nodded and left.

He meandered the streets, making sure he was not followed. At the working class neighborhood cemetery, he took the crushed stone path that curved through a rose garden. Not for the first time since he left the orphanage, Christian wondered who his parents were. Could they be buried here, so close to his flat, without his knowing it? Would he sit at their graves like that sorry, blond-headed sap and pour out his heart, his grief, to them? Or would he demand to know why they left him?

Four

Robert Smyth reached for his blanket and found it on the floor. He pulled it over him, shivering in the afternoon warmth. Would he ever be warm again? He'd arrived back in Dublin late last night to an empty flat.

Rubbing sleep from his eyes, his gaze rested on the oak and blackthorn display case. A wedding gift from his beloved Anne, two and a half years ago. Before opening the lid, he traced his thumb over the raised outline of Ireland and the engraved *September 20*. Tears welled at the sight of two remaining jewel-handled daggers among six slots. Four daggers used, four murders committed, and still the deeds had not brought his family back.

The memory came unbidden. Anne, dressed in her white satin gown, smiled under fluttering lashes that brushed her rosy cheeks as she presented the handcrafted box and its contents to him.

"For you, my love." Anne rose on her toes and pressed rich red lips over his. "To remember our vows to love, honor, and cherish each other. Forever."

Robert recalled the promise spoken together, each taking turns kissing one of the jeweled daggers at the juncture of haft and tang, a quick slice of the blade across their left palms, then clasping hands to mingle their blood for the oath. He believed their love was the greatest magic in the world.

His vision wavered, then cleared to show Anne one year later laughing as they walked hand-in-hand along the shoreline. He had taken her back to Ardmore, the tiny village nestled at the base of the Celtic Sea in southern Ireland, where they had married and honeymooned. Back to the romantic sounds of the waves lapping the shore, away from the pressures of living in a turbulent Dublin, to cherish each other and conceive their first child. They enjoyed roaming the rolling hills above the village, seeing the conical stone tower stand guard over the roofless ruins of Saint Declan's Oratory, and strolling the cliffside path to Saint Declan's Well.

The memory shifted to when he first learned of Éire's greatest secret—dragons. Another year had passed and Robert stood alone on the hilltop overlooking Ardmore. He trudged along the path leading to the well; head down, hoping to ease his devastation. In a sheath next to his heart lay one of the jewel-handled daggers. Earlier that morning, he repeated the vows spoken two years ago and kissed the blade. The coolness of the steel contrasted with the heat from the late September sun.

Robert ducked under the stone archway and spotted a man kneeling before the well. Gray edged his eyesight until all he saw was the intruder. Robert and Anne had spent hours at this special place, sharing dreams and making wishes for their future. Why had someone invaded their sanctuary?

A feral scream penetrated the silence. Robert realized the cry came from his lips. Without forethought, he unsheathed the dagger and threw it. A misty dragon shimmered in front of the man and a shriek emanated from the beast. The man slumped over, the blade embedded in his heart. The dragon vanished. Power swept over Robert like the wind, stormed within him, boiling.

Robert found himself back in the empty flat, kneeling on the floor, gasping for air. He clenched his teeth, his fists, until the hammers of panic slamming against his chest eased. Minutes went by, yet it seemed like days. When he could stand, he gathered the blanket and folded it over the back of the couch, just the way Anne had countless times before. He needed a drink. Finding no whiskey, he settled for tea. After placing the kettle on the stove, he toasted the last piece of bread. Stale. Just like his life without his wife and son.

He blundered out of the kitchen, down the hall to the tiny, brightly painted nursery. When he crossed the threshold, he remembered when Anne, in loose pants and one of his worn T-shirts, splashed paint on the walls as she prepped for a mural. She wore more paint on herself. Her laughing voice raised in song. *"Come away! O, human child!"* He had smiled at

W.B. Yeats's poem sung off-tune by his wife.

He blinked and Anne faded from his vision. Instead, he faced the mural of famous Irish landmarks and dragons painted on the nursery walls. His eyes followed the progression of damage to the colorful painted dragons above first Saint Declan's Well, the Poulnabrone dolman, on to Ballynahinch Lake, and finally the stone circle at Carrowmore. The dagger slashes grew to burned out holes the size of his hand, completely obliterating the painted dragons.

Did Robert's spoken vow of love infuse the daggers with magic? He wasn't sure, but he continued the practice, even after hiring the gypsy, Bridget to cast a spell over the remaining daggers. Running his fingers over the two holes above the Stone of Destiny at the Hill of Tara, Robert felt like he touched something alive, breathing. He imagined the heady surge of energy might be akin to what Anne experienced having their child growing inside her.

The sound of a car horn outside snapped Robert back. He pounded his fist against the doorframe on the way to his and Anne's bedroom. "I will bring you back. Both of you."

The silence in the apartment was deafening.

Robert dressed in black as somber as his mood. Careful to keep his gaze averted, he passed the nursery and left the lifeless flat. He walked down the tree-lined street to a local, family-owned market. Mixed amongst the canned goods, household supplies, and fresh baked scones sat bunches of colorful floral arrangements. The blooming spring flowers he bought did nothing to lift his bleak disposition.

He left the store and pulled his coat collar up in defiance of the steady drizzle. Anne would have called the day 'soft', with a fine mist to keep the grass the luminous green famous in Ireland. The filtered sunlight opened the flower petals dappled with moisture. Robert hustled north three blocks and passed through iron gates. A sneezing fit seized him at the smell of fresh-cut lawns. He sat with hunched shoulders at his customary bench overlooking the rolling landscape dotted with inscribed stone and flowers. Alone.

An anchor weighed heavy on his chest and he forced himself to breathe in and out, in and out.

"Soon, my love. We'll be reunited, you and I and our son. I promise."

"Hey, Robert." June called out to him. She was the white-haired, stoop-shouldered grandmother who joined him every Sunday. She ambled around the bench, resting a hand on his shoulder. "How are you? I'm sorry I missed you last week. Ethan, the youngest, came down with the sniffles."

"He's better now?"

June sat next to him. "Oh, yes. Back in school, which he hates."

"Hmm." His gaze drifted past her, into the distance.

"The flowers for your wife are lovely. A cheery spring mix."

He dropped his eyes to the forgotten bouquet. "She loves the smell of a soft rain on flowers. Says the wet brings the scent to the surface and springs from the petals."

"Well, those remind me of rainbows after the rain. I think your choice is perfect." June stood. "I best be saying hello to my Charlie, then I'm off to prepare for my domino game. It's at my house tonight. I'll see you next week. Take care of yourself. You're looking a little peaked."

Robert lifted his head and forced a smile. He pitied June, knowing her husband would not be returning. Not like his Anne and RJ.

After June left, Robert shuffled over to his wife. "These are for you, my love. You light up my world as these flowers do a garden."

He knelt on the moist grass, ignoring the wetness seeping into his trouser knees. A sigh trembled from his lips. He arranged the colorful blooms in the cement vase at the base of an etched headstone. A small red fire truck nestled next to the flowers. He read the words engraved on the stone.

"The love of my life. Who gave such meaning to this world. Much too young to die, my lovely wife. And my newborn son, his life not yet unfurled."

A breeze rustled the flower petals. Robert blinked back his tears as the words blurred.

"Why? I just don't understand. Why couldn't it have been me?" Sobs racked his body. He no longer cared who might see him. "I should have died. You're so good, so perfect. It's my fault. Why did I put you in jeopardy?"

He pressed his palms over his eyes. He saw Anne, the seatbelt snug beneath her bulging belly, giving him directions to Ballynahinch Castle. The summertime photo assignment was supposed to launch his career, display his talents with light and dark, sun and shadow. Anne was his sunlight. In a flash, he saw the other vehicle cross into the wrong lane. The crunch of metal screeched in his ears. The impact threw him sideways into the door. His head smacked the window and he saw nothing but blackness. Only the memories of his Anne, and his wedding day promise to her, kept him from utter madness.

The silence of the graveyard drew Robert back. He narrowed his eyes and concentrated on Anne's and RJ's headstone. He felt their spirits, trapped under the dirt and grass and stone.

"Now I have nothing, no one. I'm lost without you." He shuddered and took a deep breath. "Oh, Anne. What am I missing?" He traced her name with his fingertips. "I believe the magic of our love and the dragon power will bring you and RJ back. I can feel the power grow with each killing, but I can't harness it. Every time, I get stronger and it lasts longer. I thought your sister Mary would be the one, the key—"

A light breeze wafted cool upon his face and birds sung in the trees.

"Please, Anne, don't be mad at me. I'll do whatever I have to for the chance to have you with me again. I'm sorry Mary's sacrifice wasn't enough to exchange your lives for hers. The release of the dragon power and the human offering should have freed you from death."

He reached out, pushing the toy fire truck back and forth over the headstone. With his fingertips he conveyed a kiss to each name engraved.

"Perhaps it's your bodies that must be brought to Brú na Bóinne. Yes, the two of you and, I think, two sacrifices." Robert's gaze lingered over Anne's birth date. "The next Celtic holiday is Beltaine. Oh my love, on your birthday. It must be fate."

He stood and rubbed the wet from his knees. "I can't go on without you. I'll never stop loving you. I promise."

Five

Sean sipped his morning cup of tea while watching the billowing white clouds meander across the brightly lit blue sky. The rains of the last few days were gone. He turned to his desk when the phone rang and sighed, wondering who was backing out of the meeting.

"It's Kiely. I'm not going to make the council session."

Sean lifted his right brow, but she continued before he could respond.

"I'll send a delegate in my place. Not sure who yet, but they'll have full authority to speak on my behalf, for the good of Ulster province."

"That's fine. I hope you're not ill, or something." He hoped for a clue as to why the Ulster leader would not be present herself.

Kiely only answered, "No."

"Then I will talk to you soon and look forward to greeting your representative."

Sean replaced the receiver into its cradle. He rubbed the back of his neck, speculating on whom Kiely would send. The wait wasn't long as FIONN bugled a welcome to the dragon and rider flying from the north. Sean watched from his office window, a warm smile spreading over his face, as a young brown dragon landed close to the lake on the eastern border of Loughcrew. Sean emerged from the building happy to see his son, a clone of himself at the age of six and twenty, alight from his mount. He jogged to the pair.

"I'll just walk from here," Matthew said aloud to his dragon, KIERAN. "Go ahead and eat something, but don't overdo. Remember you ate two days ago. The meeting will probably take most of the afternoon."

KIERAN ducked his triangular head, butting his snout against Matthew's shoulder.

"Well, you're both looking fit. How are you, Son?" Sean clasped Matthew's right forearm and brought him close for a hug.

"I'm good."

"KIERAN is a good size for two years old. How's his appetite?"

"He's always hungry."

Sean laughed. "Yes, FIONN was the same at that age. Come to think of it, still is."

FIONN snorted. *"I am the largest dragon in Éire."*

Sean relayed FIONN'S response. Both men laughed.

Father and son strode across the grassy knoll, through the cobblestone courtyard, and greeted Aisling. Matthew gave his mother a long hug. The trio watched KIERAN as he lifted his great wings preparing for flight. He launched himself.

KIERAN flew west toward the sheep pens, picked out a plump candidate, swooped down to pluck it from its fellows with his talons, and circled back to land next to the lake to eat his meal. He snapped the sheep's neck. With surprising neatness, he stripped the meat, ligaments, and tendons, leaving a pile of clean, white bones.

Sean, Aisling, and Matthew entered the main dining hall when KIERAN lumbered to the lake. Sean walked to the back of the room as Matthew removed his warm riding gear and stowed them in a cubby along the left wall.

Leaning against a large, round table with seating for eight, Sean laughed at something one of the serving women said then shooed her away with his hands. The smile stayed on his face as his wife and son walked arm-in-arm toward him. Lord, the sight of his family brightened his day.

"Am I the first to arrive, then?" Matthew asked.

"Yes," Sean said. "The others should be here shortly. I'm glad Kiely sent you, because I wanted to discuss something with you." He gestured to the table and chairs behind him, indicating they should sit and get comfortable.

Matthew nodded, sat and waited for him to begin. Stalling, Sean poured a glass of water for each of them.

Aisling walked toward the kitchen. "I'll check on lunch."

Sean took a long drink, not comfortable with the topic he needed to bring up. He turned in his chair. "I don't know any delicate way to phrase this, so I'll just ask straight out. Do you think one of the Northern drag-onriders could be behind the slayings?" Before Matthew could respond, he continued. "It's no secret there are tensions between the Republic and the Northern members."

"Why ask me?" Matthew shrugged.

"You're assigned to the Ulster compound at Beaghmore, along with Ryan and Maggie. Since you're younger than either of them, I figured your political views aren't as set in stone. Maybe you heard something, someone complaining, or saw someone acting strange."

"No one comes to mind. There's always grumbling about positions and responsibilities within the clan. You know how the Northern Six never command the respect or the plum assignments that the Republic dragons and riders get."

"I don't want to believe any dragonrider is behind the treachery, let alone outright murder. But I need to look at the situation from every conceivable angle. Keep your eyes open. And keep this conversation between us." Sean pinched the bridge of his nose to ease the forming headache. "The North-ern Six have legitimate complaints. Padrick and I are working to fix the slights from the past, but these things take time."

"I understand." Matthew sipped his water. "I'll do whatever you need. The clan is my priority, my family. But I don't think the killer is a clan member. No dragon would ever allow another dragon to die, let alone four. A rider would need to be highly skilled at keeping their thoughts from their compeer, or just plain crazy so their dragon doesn't pay any attention anymore."

"Those are my feelings too, but I need to eliminate the possibility." Sean looked toward the entrance as several riders came in, shedding their riding gear. Standing up, he clasped Matthew's shoulder in a gesture of love and respect, before he strode toward the newcomers.

As tradition dictated, Sean first greeted Padrick, his right-hand man, fol-lowed by Meara of County Mayo. Matthew and Aisling joined the group as he finished the formal greetings.

"Thank you for coming." Sean gestured to the table set up for the meeting.

Padrick caught Sean's arm discreetly. "My mother didn't come?"

"No. She called this morning." He rubbed the back of his neck. "I don't like it. She's up to something. She wouldn't quit an opportunity to steal away my leadership."

The smile formed quick and cocky on Padrick's face. "Oh, to be sure. Watch your back, and I'll do the same."

The clan members shuffled to seats around the table. Sean rang the bell on the serving table behind him before he took his place. The head serving woman ducked out from the kitchen alcove and nodded acknowledgment. Three servers delivered platters of food and pitchers of drinks. With plates full of steaming meats, fresh cheeses and fruits, and warm rolls, the members ate.

Sean began the meeting. "Thank you all for giving up your day of rest to attend this meeting. As I said at the spring céilí, we are living in dangerous times and we need to protect the clan. While I would like to have all the dragonriders present to voice their concerns and ideas, that would be unwieldy and unproductive."

Everyone agreed.

"I'm asking you to join me in this new council and to represent the clan members of your province in these meetings. To protect the Tuatha Dragon Clan, ensure the bounty of all Ireland, and stop the slayings of our brethren." With his right hand fisted to his heart, Sean spoke the promise of the dragonriders—*Dilseacht. Fáil. Saoirse.* Loyalty. Destiny. Freedom.

Each member at the table mirrored the clan leader's gesture and pledge.

The rules and responsibilities of the council were laid out as the remnants of lunch were finished and the table cleared.

Padrick leaned down from his chair, rummaged through the backpack next to his foot, pulled out a map of Ireland, and spread it out on the table. Padrick again dug into the pack and produced a pad of sticky notepaper. He took one of the pens from Aisling and wrote 'St. Declan's Oratory, September 20, Conor and DONOVAN.'

"We know the first murder took place here." Padrick attached the note to the bottom of the map in County Waterford. "We believe Conor and

DONOVAN were at the monument to celebrate the equinox. I found blood near the Holy Well and a trail suggesting his body was dragged to the Oratory. Conor must have been transported by car to Newgrange where his body was found." With his finger, Padrick traced the northern route and stopped northeast of Dublin. He placed a new sticky note on the spot.

Matthew spoke from across the table. "Why would the killer transport a body from the southern tip of Ireland so far north, through half the country? Why not just leave the body where he was murdered?"

"Good question," Sean said. "Let's keep it in mind and continue with the others, until we map it all out."

Padrick continued. "The second killing was about six weeks later. This time at the Poulnabrone tomb in the Burren, County Clare. Blood was found at the scene and Shannon's body was propped against the entrance of Newgrange. Just like Conor."

"Murdered on Samhain—summer's end, according to the ancient Celts," Aisling said.

"Yes." Padrick recorded the location, date, and Shannon and TARA'S information and placed the note on the southwestern section of the map.

Meara took the sticky pad and pen from Padrick. "We have at least one pattern here. The third slaying also took place on a date significant to the Celtic calendar. December twenty-first, the winter solstice."

"Interesting," Sean said.

"Dylan was killed at Ballynahinch Lake in Connemara." Meara wrote this on the sticky note. "Since he regularly let TIERNEY fish the lake for a snack, this was the first place Sean and I looked for evidence after his body was found at Newgrange. We found blood and matted grass near the cannon aimed at the ruins on the island in the lake." Meara stuck the square note on the map farther north than the second note.

"Okay. Now Mary has been found, again at Newgrange, and again on a Celtic holiday—the spring equinox," Aisling said.

Meara prepared the fourth note and stuck it northeast, just before the land mass curved inward to begin its northern top of Ireland and the province of Ulster. "Her blood was found at Carrowmore, on several stones of one of the megalithic tombs."

Sean rubbed the back of his neck. "Each murder took place on a Celtic holiday, and all four bodies transported to the Entrance Stone at Newgrange. What else?"

Matthew cleared his throat. "All were found with a dagger in their chests, buried to the hilt. The dagger pierced the heart, so the killer must have been up close. Also, the daggers are all identical, including the same gem-handled adornment."

"Two riders from Munster Province and two from Connaught," Aisling said. "I don't know if it's significant, but maybe the killer is from one of these areas."

Padrick pondered the information posted on the map. "That may be true, but all four riders' bodies were found at Newgrange at Brú na Bóinne in Leinster Province. So he, and I'm assuming the killer is male as we believe each body was loaded into a car and that takes strength, could live just about anywhere."

Matthew lifted his hand to interrupt Sean before the clan leader could speak. "I know what we're all thinking." He glanced around the table into the faces of his peers, but these were also his elders. "Nothing has happened in Ulster, specifically in any of the Northern six counties. And Kiely, leader of Ulster, isn't here. The other three provinces are represented by their leaders, why not Ulster? I cannot answer that, but I don't think the killer is one of our own. What purpose would that serve?"

Sean agreed. "Also, dragons and riders have sworn their allegiance to the clan. Dragons would not kill dragons, nor would they let their riders kill."

Two hours later KIERAN woke to find his mother, golden BRIANNA, Padrick's black DECLAN, and Meara's green CARRIGAN curled around each other in a loose sleeping circle. Not wanting to wake them he silently queried his rider. *"How goes the meeting?"*

Matthew answered. *"The meeting will probably take another hour. Did you have enough to eat, without making a nuisance of yourself?"*

"I limited myself to one sheep," KIERAN bespoke sulkily. *"I will continue to enjoy the warm sun."*

BRIANNA stirred. Her movements awoke the others. KIERAN greeted each of them.

"Young one," BRIANNA replied. *"How faired the plantings in the North?"*

"The seeds are in, the soil is moist and rich. I believe the harvest will be bountiful. At least in County Monaghan, I cannot say for Derry or Antrim. How does it go for you?" KIERAN asked.

DECLAN turned his triangular head toward the west. *"With four of us gone between Munster and Connaught, the harvest will suffer. We are hoping the yearlings* ROARKE *and* DOCHAS *choose compeers soon."* He turned his gaze back to BRI-ANNA. *"Have you and* FIONN *spoken with them?"*

"We have. At length." BRIANNA stretched her wings, then repositioned them across her back.

"Have you explained the urgency of the situation?" CARRIGAN asked, her head spikes bristling with impatience.

BRIANNA rumbled. *"Of course. They know what has happened. They grieved for the losses, as we all did. However, neither of them has felt the touch of their compeer's mind yet. These things cannot be forced."*

"I remember the joy and completeness I felt the day Matthew and I mind-touched." KIERAN'S eyes swirled with fondness at the memory. *"I do not think it would be the same with another human as it is with my Matthew."*

DECLAN walked to the lake and drank deeply. *"It shall happen for* ROARKE *and* DOCHAS *as well. When it does, the Clan will be closer to full strength. Until then, we endure."*

"Wait a minute," Aisling muttered. She addressed Meara. "How old was Dylan?"

"He just turned thirty a few months before he was killed. Why?"

"That would put all our victims from ages of twenty-six to thirty. All fairly new dragonriders with young, inexperienced dragons," Aisling replied.

Padrick tapped his fingers against the table edge in a staccato pattern. "So they were caught unaware? I could see that with Conor, but after the first murder every rider should have been wary."

Matthew paused before taking a sip from his cup. "How was anyone to know that Conor and Donovan's deaths were the beginning of a series? Their deaths could have been an isolated incident."

"Let's get back to what we know," Sean said. "Each murder took place on a Celtic holiday, so we probably have until the next major one, which is May first…Beltaine."

Meara pulled a thin, book-sized calendar from her bag and thumbed quickly through the pages. "If the killer is devout about Celtic holidays, then why did he skip Imbolc in February?"

"Maybe he's not well versed in Celtic lore or his calendar doesn't show the newest festival as yours does," Aisling said.

Padrick laughed.

Sean raised his hand for silence. "We can speculate on that another time. I want every dragon and compeer to be extra vigilant on patrol, and we will continue to fly in pairs."

"That puts a heavy burden on the dragons and compeers from Munster and Connaught." Meara pointed to the map. "We could use some help, maybe from some of the smaller counties in both Leinster and Ulster. Twice a week would keep our teams fresh."

Sean nodded. "Aisling and I will work up a schedule that will give you and Padrick three dragons and their compeers every other day, starting tomorrow. You can rotate them as you see fit. Matthew, can you work with Kiely to provide one team a couple days per week as well?"

"Yes. We'll coordinate with you, Meara."

Sean pointed to the map. "I'll talk with Moira to see what she knows about Newgrange, since it's in her county. There must be something special about the place, other than being a burial chamber. I'll also check with the curator at the National Museum. He's a personal friend, and the docent at Trinity College, a friend of the clan."

"You should take one of the daggers with you," Padrick said. "They may have seen one like it, or know where they come from."

"Good idea." Sean stood. "Let's meet again next week. Get the other riders' ideas. I'll have Moira brief us on Newgrange."

Padrick rose from his chair, rolled the map, and handed it to Sean. "You should keep this in your office. We can add to it as we learn more."

"Tapadh leat." Sean thanked all and walked them to the entrance.

Padrick, Meara, and Matthew donned their riding gear and strolled out into the afternoon sunshine. Padrick and Meara stepped onto their dragons' offered foreleg, swinging up into their neck saddles. DECLAN and CARRIGAN spread their mighty wings and launched into the air. They flew southwest toward their home in Lough Gur.

Matthew shook his father's hand and hugged his mother before he settled himself on KIERAN. He nodded to them and directed his dragon compeer homeward.

Sean drew his wife close to his side. "He has grown into a strong man. I'm proud of the way he handled himself during the council session. He could have easily deferred, you know."

"He takes after his father."

"Yes, but in my case you call it stubborn." He leaned down and kissed her temple.

"Was he receptive about the Northern Six?"

"He'll get back to me. Something is going on in Ulster. And Kiely was hiding it when she called. If anyone can ferret out the information, Matthew can."

Aisling sighed. "I hope he's careful."

Sean fretted over the Celtic holiday timing. Beltaine was in five weeks. Could he ensure Ireland's prosperity?

"Can I keep the clan safe?" he wondered aloud.

Six

The pub door opened. A dark-haired woman rushed in with the wind and rain. Christian stared at the woman. He had seen her before, but he couldn't remember where. She hung her coat on the rack near the entrance door and sat on the stool at the far end of the bar. Her jeans and jumper revealed an athletic build. She raked her hand through her hair, sprinkling droplets over her shoulders and onto the hardwood floor.

Christian frowned as he concentrated on her face. She wore no makeup. The brown of her eyes reminded him of Irish whiskey. Her mouth hinted of sensuousness. She reminded him of someone. That must be it. Why else would he have such a strong reaction to a stranger?

He watched her across the rim of his pint. Her brown hair rioted with streaks of sun-bleached reds and golds. It stood out in short spikes. When the publican leaned in her direction, she ordered quickly. While her Guinness was being built, she nibbled on the mix of nuts in the wooden bowl on the bar.

Though the crowd grew as the musicians warmed up, Christian's view of the newcomer remained unobstructed. When she lifted the half-pint to her lips, he saw the glint of silver from the ring on her finger. Her eyes closed at the first sip of the dark stout. She said something to the publican that made him throw back his head in a raucous laugh. He took her free hand, kissed her knuckles, then stepped away with a gleam in his eyes.

She turned on the stool and observed the room. Her eyes took in the postage stamp-sized stage before locking onto his intense stare. A shy smile tugged up the right corner of her mouth. She broke eye contact, retrieved a menu and skimmed through it. She flagged the jovial barman, and gave her order. Settled more comfortably, she again took up her glass.

The musicians played a lively reel that set toes to tapping. Conversations hushed as the vocalist sang about Captain Farrell's robbery. Soon the pub regulars joined the chorus of *Whiskey in the Jar*. Requests were yelled out and the music slowed to a ballad. The rebel song *Patriot Games* brought a rousing cheer from the younger crowd.

Christian signaled the publican for another round for himself and the woman. She glanced up from her bowl of Irish stew at the fresh half-pint. Her eyebrow raised in query of the publican. He pointed to Christian as he departed to fill another order. She lifted her glass in salute. He returned the gesture. Amusement lit her eyes. The music changed tempo.

He moved to the vacant stool beside her. "Hello, I'm Christian Riley. You looked very familiar when you walked in. Do I know you from somewhere?"

"No. I don't think so. It's my first trip to Ireland. First trip outside the United States. I'm Devan, by the way. Thanks for the beer." She saluted again.

"So, you're here on holiday?" At her blank look, he remembered. "I mean, vacation?"

"Yes, something like that." Her hand lifted to her hair. "I'm here looking for some family. I guess you get a lot of people searching for their Irish heritage, especially around St. Patrick's Day."

"Some, I suppose. Whereabouts are you from?"

"My Irish grandparents settled in New York, but my mother met my father in college and moved to California for his career. So I'm from California, near San Francisco. That's on the West Coast. I'm rambling, I always ramble when I'm nervous." She laughed. A rich, full laugh. "What about you? Are you a Dubliner?

Lifting his Guinness, he nodded. "How long are you here for?"

She hesitated briefly, but he caught it. "A couple of weeks or so."

"All in Dublin?"

"No, I'll be traveling. I want to see as much of Ireland as I can. This may be my one and only trip, so I'm going to make the most of it. Have you been to the West Counties?" She tasted her stew.

"Sorry, no. I haven't been much outside Dublin." He stared at her hand.

"What would you recommend I see here?"

"What?" He was fascinated by the ring on her hand. "Oh, the most popular are Dublin Castle, Trinity College, and since you fancy Guinness, go to the Guinness Storehouse. And you mustn't miss Grafton Street." Remembering his earlier escapades, he bristled. The image of a tourist with a camera pressed to her face and the boyo ready to cut the strap of her backpack emerged. "I could show you around tomorrow, if you'd like. Grafton Street is wonderful, but can be costly to a tourist. Pickpockets and such."

"Thanks for the tip. I'll be careful."

The publican gestured at their drinks. Both of them nodded for more. The music swirled around the room. Conversations ebbed and flowed. The door opened and closed as more people streamed in. When the fresh drinks arrived, Christian stared into his pint. Silence hung between them for several heartbeats as she worked on her stew.

He looked up. "I couldn't help but notice your ring. It's quite unusual. Is it a family piece?"

"Belonged to my mother and to my grandmother before her. Now it's mine. I'm hoping it's the key to finding more of my family."

"How's it going to do that?"

"My grandparents came from somewhere in County Clare. I'm going to visit jewelry stores for anything similar. I'll start here then try County Clare."

He sipped his stout. "Hmm, that's a good idea. Except you said it belonged to your grandmother, right?"

"Yes, why?"

"That would make it what, fifty years old? Do you think anyone is still making that design?"

"I don't know, but it's all I have to go on, other than their names. Gallagher is fairly common. Hopefully someone will know of them by narrowing down the search with the ring." She toyed with her ring, then slid it off her finger and handed it to him. "See the words inscribed on the inside. They're Gaelic for 'loyalty, destiny, freedom'. That doesn't sound like a romantic vow, does it?"

"No." He inspected the ring. The dragon design matched his pendant, right down to the inscription. His fingertips grazed his chest where the pendant lay hidden. "How do you know what the words mean? Do you speak Gaelic?"

"I researched the words. It's what I do. Research, I mean. I tried to find out about the design, but no luck. It's not the Gallagher's family crest. Which is why I'm here in person." She held out her hand and he reluctantly returned the ring.

He felt a tingling on his fingers as their touch lingered. How was it possible to feel a bond with her? He was just interested in how her ring and his pendant were linked. But he felt the spark. Did she feel it too?

"I should probably get going." She signaled for her tab. "Thanks for the company and the Guinness."

The publican waited until she counted out the proper euros, thanked her for coming into his pub, and invited her back. She finished the last of her Guinness.

"Wait a minute and I'll walk you out." Christian tossed several bills onto the bar.

She hesitated and shied away, then lifted her chin and nodded.

He grabbed her coat from the rack, helped her into it, then shrugged into his own jacket. Opening the door, he guided her out of the boisterous room and into the brisk Dublin air. The rain had stopped. The streets were still wet and the lights from windows shimmered their reflections in puddles. They walked to the corner and turned right.

A man dressed black as the night brushed against her. He grabbed her arm and pulled, thrusting a broken bottle under her chin.

She muffled a scream as the jagged edge nicked her skin.

"Step away from the woman. Toss your wallet and watch to her," the mugger said. He released her arm, grabbed her hair, and yanked her head back. The glass pressed against her neck. "Don't be a hero, I just want the cash and jewelry."

Christian vowed that as soon as the makeshift weapon cleared Devan's throat, he'd take back what was theirs. He pulled out his wallet and tossed it. Removing his watch, he repeated the toss, sliding closer. "There's five hundred euro in there. Take it and let her go."

"Not yet. Now Miss, your wallet and jewelry." He shoved Christian's wallet and watch into a pocket, then grabbed her hair again. She whimpered. "Let's go, I don't have all night. Where's your purse?"

"I don't carry one. My money's in my front pocket." She dipped her left hand in and withdrew euros. "That's all the cash I have." She held up the bills.

"Give me your jewelry." He tucked her money away.

She removed her earrings and watch. "It's not valuable." She shielded her ring.

Christian drew closer, knowing she wouldn't give up her ring, not without a fight. He tilted his head. She seemed to understand his signal and flung the jewelry at her attacker's face. As he brought his hands up to protect himself, she pivoted out of his grasp. Christian barreled into the thief. The impact slammed the attacker into the wall. The bottle shattered on the ground. Before the attacker could catch his breath, Christian was on him. Two quick jabs to his nose, a knee to the groin, and he slid unconscious to the pavement.

Devan picked up her watch and sighed. "Broken." She pocketed both earrings along with the watch and returned to the men.

Christian blocked her view of the bloodied attacker. He stood and rushed to her as he noticed blood on her neck. The faint twang of copper wafted from the handkerchief he pressed to the wound.

"Are you okay?" He removed the cloth to check her cut. "It doesn't appear to be very deep, just a nick." The bleeding had stopped. "Let's get you to your room. We can clean it there."

"I'm fine, just a little shaken. Shouldn't we call the police and report what happened?"

"We got our stuff back. I'd prefer not involving the Gardaí."

She looked back. "We can't just leave him there, can we? You worked him over pretty good. Besides, he might try that with someone else, then I would feel responsible."

"He'll find his way home soon enough. He won't be attacking anyone else." He stopped in front of her hotel. "I'll come with you to check that cut."

"I'm fine, really. I don't let strangers in my room, even someone that defended me from an attacker. But I'd like to take you up on your offer as a guide tomorrow, if that's okay. Can we meet here at nine a.m.?"

Christian held her hands in his. Her fingers trembled. "I'm not going to hurt you. I just want to make sure you're okay. Get some antiseptic on your cut; we don't know where that bottle's been." He squeezed her hands, then let go. "Pick you up at nine. Dublin's a walking town, so wear comfortable shoes. Good night."

He waited until she entered the building. Slipping into the shadows, he saw a second floor room light up and Devan twitch the window curtain open. Satisfied that she couldn't see him, he leaned against the opposite building, and waited for the light to go out. Then Christian turned and headed back the way they had come.

Seven

At nine o'clock sharp Devan left the hotel. She didn't expect to see Christian, the stranger who befriended her and thwarted the mugger from last night. Yet there he stood under the lamppost, dressed in jeans that emphasized his height, a sweater, and the same jacket from the previous evening. When he smiled, a dimple appeared at the left corner of his mouth. His strong, angular face was framed by jet-black hair that brushed at his collar, sharp cheekbones, a not-quite-straight nose, and a poetic mouth. But it was his eyes that held her. Their intense blue reminded her of Lake Tahoe, back home.

She had given a lot of thought to him last night as she tossed and turned, then fell into a dream-filled sleep. What did he want? She knew herself to be naïve about many things outside of the academic world, but she was not a woman that attracted handsome, dangerous-looking men. She was a tomboy, and comfortable with that. What could he want from her?

Devan returned his smile as she watched his gaze sweep from her head to her toes then back up to rest on her face. Her confused thoughts and feelings from last night vanished when he grinned.

"Well, I see you're ready for the walking tour."

"Yes, I'm really interested in finding out about my ring." She twisted it around her finger. "I thought we could start at Trinity College, check out a couple of jewelry shops, then end at the National Museum as they have the most complete collection of medieval metalwork."

"Determined aren't you? Have you left room for a meal in there somewhere?"

She laughed. "Yes, I'll feed you. As a thank you for last night."

He reached to zip her coat. She took a quick step back and zipped it herself. Then chided herself. *Relax, not all men are like Rick.*

"Well, at least you'll see a bit of Dublin with your itinerary. Can I see a list of the shops you want to visit?" He held out his hand. His right eyebrow quirked up as he perused the list she give him. "Did you know that Trinity College and the National Museum are this way?" He pointed east. "Several of the shops here are either in the opposite direction or across the river."

She frowned at him. "They look fairly close on the tourist maps I have."

"They're not so close when you're walking."

"Okay, can we start at Trinity and see where we are by lunchtime?"

"Sure."

He turned and led her north on Great George's Street. The brisk morning air cooled her face. A few white clouds billowed against the azure sky.

She glanced up at his profile and wondered how to phrase her question so as not to put him off. Although she could probably find the answers she was looking for alone, with his help and knowledge of Dublin, the search would be faster. Certainly more interesting. Straight forward was usually the best policy, she decided.

"I'm curious. Why are you helping me?"

He studied her as they walked. "Why not? You're an attractive woman and I find myself drawn to you. I don't know why, but I feel I'm to help you."

"I'm not, but I appreciate the lie." Heat rose in her cheeks. She shook her head. "It's a weekday, don't you have work or something?"

Christian guided her right when they reached Dame Street. "I work for myself, so I can decide which days I work and when to leave off to help a lady with a problem."

Nervous, she ran her hand through her hair. "Okay. As long as I'm not impeding the hands of business or stopping the government from running."

He laughed. "No, I'm sure businesses and the government will get along fine without me for the day."

When they reached the end of the street, she stopped and stared slack-jawed at the Victorian architecture of Trinity College. She realized this city, this country, and part of her heritage went back centuries.

He passed a hand in front of her face. "Hey, what's wrong? Where'd you go?"

"What?" she mumbled. "Sorry. It's just that for the first time since my parents died, I feel connected to…if not someone, at least something. Ireland. My ancestors. And I can relate to a college campus."

"When did they die?" Concern etched his words.

Still rooted, she turned her head to look at him. "Last month. They were killed in an auto accident on their anniversary."

"I'm sorry."

"That's what started me on this journey. I found the dragon ring amongst my mother's things. Along with the ring was a note written to my grandmother, from her parents here in Ireland. The note spoke of destinies, a clan, and the ring being part of my grandmother's heritage. Now it's my heritage, my destiny."

They started walking again. She remained silent until they arrived at the building that housed the Old Library. He opened the door and motioned her inside. She gasped in awe as she stepped over the threshold.

"It might be wise to take a guided tour," she said after she caught her breath. "Otherwise, we could live here a month and still not find any reference to the ring's meaning."

He shrugged. "Okay. This is obviously your specialty, since you do research. I wouldn't know where to start."

They paid for the tour and gathered with several others to await their guide. The group included an elderly couple with English accents, a young woman carrying a notebook and pen, and a blond-haired man in his early thirties with slightly red and swollen eyes. Their guide was a middle-aged man with thinning hair who spoke in the soft lilt of his country. The first stop was the Colonnades Gallery with a viewing of the *Book of Kells*.

As they approached the glass display cases, she grabbed Christian's hand and pointed to the first case. "I never thought I'd see it."

His gaze wandered to the passageway away from the artifact. He said nothing.

"Sorry. I'm a little excited. This is one of the oldest books in the world, you know."

He glanced at the displayed page, then lifted his eyes to hers. "I'm not really religious." His voice dropped to a whisper. "I had enough pounded into me from the sisters."

As they walked away from the display cases, she glanced up at him, not sure if she should respond or if he meant for her not to have heard. She decided to ask him about it when they stopped for lunch. For now, she needed to concentrate on the tour.

They left the Gallery and climbed the stairs to the Long Room.

This time Christian gasped, but not in awe. "How are we ever going to find what we're looking for? There must be two dozen rows on each side, two stories high filled with books." He whistled low. "Just look at that ceiling—it's barrel-shaped."

She patted his arm in reassurance. "We'll ask about books on Celtic history. The dragon in my ring is clutching a Celtic knot of protection in his foreclaws." She held up her hand for him to see. "Also, we'll cross reference books on Gaelic sayings, look for the inscribed words." He stared at her. "What? Do you have a better idea?"

"No," he replied. "I don't know much about libraries, but this one is huge. You were right, this could take weeks."

They strolled along with the tour group. The tour ended with no mention of a Celtic section. She approached their guide. The blond-haired man was talking with him and she thought he was a local.

When he stepped away, she asked her question. "Can you tell me where the section is on Celtic history? Also, do you have anything about Gaelic oaths or sayings?"

The guide paused. "There are a couple of sections on Celtic folklore and history." He pointed upstairs. "However, the books here are off-limits to tourists. They are very old and the pages are fragile."

"Oh well, thanks for your help and the tour." She started to rejoin Christian.

"Miss," the guide said.

She turned back. "Yes?"

"You had a question about some Gaelic?"

"Oh. Yes, thanks. I forgot. I wanted to look up a phrase I heard recently."

"I speak the old tongue. Perhaps I can help."

She looked around to see if anyone was within earshot. The blond man appeared engrossed in a marble bust of a famous Trinity graduate. "I'm not sure of the pronunciation, but it sounded like: deel-shockt, fall, sear-sha."

The guide's body stiffened and his left eye twitched. He reached up, pressing his hand near the offending eye. "That's not a phrase. Those are individual words that mean loyalty, destiny, freedom." He regarded her for a long moment. "Those words used together are not common. Where did you hear them?"

She hesitated and sighed in relief as Christian joined them. The guide studied them both.

"Are you ready?" Christian asked. "I could do with some food and a pint."

"Yes, I was just thanking our guide." She smiled at the man, linked her arm in Christian's, and they walked to the exit.

Once outside, she pulled him to a bench near a grassy area. "I found out a couple of things. First, the Celtic section is upstairs, but not accessible to the public. Second, I asked about the phrase on the ring—"

"You didn't show him the ring, did you?" Christian interrupted.

She raised an eyebrow at the vehemence of his question. "No. He offered his help and I played it as if I had heard the phrase somewhere. He said it wasn't a phrase, but three individual words. He gave me the same translation. The interesting thing was, he tightened up and developed an eye tic as if the combination of the words spooked him. He wanted to know where I'd heard them. You saved me from having to tell him."

"Okay." He sounded relieved. "Sounds like he may know something. Maybe we'll find it in one of those books."

"We can't even search, no one is allowed to open them." She shook her head at the loss of the knowledge in books that couldn't be read.

Christian groaned. He stood up and pulled her to her feet. "We'll think of something. Besides, can't do all that research on an empty stomach. Let's go."

After they ordered in a nearby pub, her curiosity got the best of her. "When we viewed the *Book of Kells*, you said something about your sisters pushing religion on you. How many siblings do you have?"

Christian narrowed his eyes. "I didn't say I have sisters. What does it matter anyway?"

"I thought since we're working together on this, it might be a good idea to get to know each other better. Last night I told you quite a bit about me, or at least what brought me here. I know next to nothing about you, except your name and you're handy to have around during a mugging."

"Well, there's really not much to tell."

The server brought their Guinness.

"Tell me about your family."

He didn't answer right away which only piqued her curiosity.

Finally, as if debating whether or not she could be trusted, he looked at her with those piercing cobalt eyes and sighed. "My life isn't as pretty as yours. I don't..." He paused as the server delivered their lunches. When the server left, he continued. "I don't have any siblings, that I know of. I don't even know who my parents are."

He took a bite of his sandwich and washed it down with a long draught of stout. She watched him, not daring to interrupt.

"The sisters at the orphanage found me on their doorstep one chilly morning in late March, twenty-six years ago. I was no more than a week old." His hand lightly touched his chest. "They named me Christian—as it was a Catholic orphanage. I don't know where Riley came from."

She reached out and laid her hand over his. "I'm sorry."

"What for?" He pulled his hand away. His voice roughened. "I got through it."

Looking down, she concentrated on her sandwich. He must've been beautiful with the black hair and dark blue eyes of the black Irish. Who would have given him up? What circumstances brought his parents to do it? She knew that some orphanages treated their charges well. Just as many didn't. She wondered which type he grew up in.

"You turned out to be a knight in shining armor, saving the damsel in distress," she said to break the disquiet.

He snorted out a laugh. "Just shows what you know. I'm none of those things. I don't appreciate getting dropped on, and you happened to be with me."

"Well, you were my hero last night." She touched her neck where the broken bottle nicked her.

"You're not too shabby yourself, with the distraction."

She sipped her stout which was black as peat. "I'd like to check out a few craft stores near here after lunch. I want to question the guide again, but since I can't research there I'll need to come up with another idea. He knows something. His demeanor changed when I asked about the inscription."

"I noticed, which is why I interrupted. Also, the blond guy was eavesdropping. He tried to act casual, but I could tell. He kept staring as if he knew you."

She frowned. "I don't know him. Anyway, we may find some answers at the shops or the National Museum."

Christian finished his pint. "If you want to do all of that this afternoon, we'll need to hop a taxi. I meant what I said earlier; many of the shops are quite a distance from here. Walking will eat up valuable time."

Devan pulled her money out for the bill, but he stopped her with his hand.

"I've got it. After all, I need to keep up my gentlemanly image." He laughed.

Eight

Robert needed more research. Even though he knew dragonriders existed, he knew next to nothing about them. Only that they existed in secrecy and utilized old magic to keep them hidden from humankind—the Tuatha Dragon Clan and a few select others knew of them. He was after the old magic. He held it within him, briefly, after each sacrifice. There must be something else he could do to retain the dragon magic and enhance it to serve his needs. He had come too far to fail now. His high school friend Cliff, the history professor, was meeting him in the library at Trinity. As he waited, his mobile rang.

"I'm glad I caught you." Cliff's voice wheezed through the phone. "I'm held up here, a last minute staff meeting. I'll need a rain check, okay?"

Frustration pounded at Robert's head. "No problem. Talk to you soon." He disconnected. Might as well see what he could learn on his own.

Once inside the Old Library building, he sought the information desk. The young woman behind the counter with bright red and purple hair pushed a wad of gum into her cheek. "What can I do for you?"

"Do you have any books on dragon lore, in particular, dragon magic?"

"I'm not sure. There sure are a lot of books in here. Could be some about dragons. This is my first day. I just sell tour tickets. You could join the next one. Eight euros, please." He pulled the money from his wallet as the clerk blew a bubble larger than her mouth and popped it. "Here's your stub. You can wait over there." She pointed toward an elderly couple and a school-aged girl.

He nodded, took his ticket stub, and joined the tour group. He hoped the guide had more information than the clerk.

A couple minutes passed and a young couple joined the group. The tour guide, a middle-aged portly man, stepped from a door to the right of the information booth and announced the start. The group moved at a leisurely pace giving everyone a chance to view the *Book of Kells*.

Robert's attention strayed to the young couple. The spiky, brown-haired woman talked to her companion in hushed tones, but used her hands extensively. With his concentration focused on them, he sensed power. He pried his eyes and mind away. Could they be the key? Or was he projecting his needs onto them? Wanting to be sure, he concentrated on the elderly couple in the group. Nothing. No twinge of power emanating from them. He checked the guide and the younger girl. Again he felt nothing from them.

The young couple held power. Both of them. He sensed individual power, but together they were stronger than any of the dragonriders he had matched against so far. He needed their power and a way to capture it. His research became doubly important, for he intended to use their power to bring his Anne and RJ back. Perhaps today, the fates guided him here. To this place, at this time.

During the tour he studied them, only half-listening to the guide as they toured the first room. He climbed the stairs and entered the library on their heels. The man stopped suddenly at the threshold and he blundered into him.

"Sorry," Robert mumbled and stepped around him.

The man stared into the room, not moving until the woman touched his arm and murmured something. Robert tried to eavesdrop, but the tour guide interrupted his concentration, pointing out the sculpted marble busts at the ends of each stack of books. By the time the guide moved on, the couple had wandered down the center of the room.

"Excuse me," Robert said to the guide as the tour wound down. "Do you know if there are books about magic here? Specifically dragon or Irish magic?"

The guide inclined his head. "There are Irish fairy tales, not here of course. *Draiocht,* or magic is prevalent in them. Although, I don't recall any stories about dragon magic. You'll need to try a bookshop for that type of fantasy. Waterstone's Booksellers has a good selection of fiction, as well as Hodges and Figgis Books."

"Thanks. I'll check there."

He wondered again if he would find any book to help him. Yet, he dared not call attention to himself by pressing the issue of dragon magic with the guide.

As he stepped away, the power-infused woman approached the guide. Robert hung back, straining to hear the conversation.

The woman turned to leave, but the guide called to her. When she looked back, Robert edged closer. She scanned the library quickly while he feigned interest in a marble bust several meters from them. He still could not hear them. Before he could get closer, the woman's companion joined her. The couple left arm-in-arm.

He exited in time to see the couple saunter through a grassy area, heading south toward Grafton Street. He quickened his pace to keep them in sight.

When they entered O'Brien's pub and didn't come out right away, he glanced at his watch and noted the time. They were probably having lunch. Should he go in? Would they think he was trailing them? Better not, he decided. He spotted a cafe with outside seating down the block. He settled himself in view of the pub entrance and ordered tea and a fish sandwich.

Not long after he finished the sandwich and drank a second cup of tea, the pair left the pub. They turned onto the street in front of him and hopped into an arriving taxi.

Robert threw twenty euros on the table, not caring that he overpaid. He ran into the street and searched for a taxi. Nothing. Only red taillights of their cab as it turned right, a few blocks away.

"Damn it." He pounded a fist into his palm. "I need them. I need their power!"

Nine

Christian opened the taxi door and motioned Devan in. "How many more shops do you want to waste our time in?"

"Just one more."

As the taxi pulled into traffic, Christian leaned back into the faux leather seat and closed his eyes.

"You didn't have to come with me," Devan said.

He opened his eyes. "Yes, I did. I'm your tour guide, remember? I just didn't know we'd be spending so much time shopping. Also, I'm supposed to help you."

She sighed. "It's the middle of the day. I can stay out of trouble by myself."

"I'm not so sure. You know your way around a library, but you aren't experienced in the pitfalls of Dublin." Laughter lightened his voice. "Besides, the help I mean is finding out about your ring, your destiny."

When the taxi stopped at the craft shop, Christian paid the driver, then escorted her to the curb. A bell clanged as they entered the brightly-lit shop crowded with merchandise. Cases with jewelry sat along the right wall surrounding an old-fashioned cash register. Shelves of uneven heights and depths lined the left and back walls. The center aisle held racks of clothing and three mannequins displaying warrior garb and weaponry.

They headed to the store clerk standing near the jewelry. The woman's back was to them as she changed the CD in the music player behind the register. She pushed her gray hair away from her face as she turned.

"Afternoon. What can I show you?"

Devan stepped to the glass case, removed her ring, and held it out for the clerk to see. "I'm looking for any information you may have about this ring." She knew she sounded annoyed, but couldn't help it. They had been to every other craft and jewelry shop in her tour book. This was the last one. Devan laid the ring in the clerk's palm.

To her left, Christian was inspecting the jewelry in the cases. His gaze lifted and he gave a slight shake of his head. The display held nothing close to her design.

The clerk raised the ring to the light. "'Tis a beautiful piece, it is. We don't carry this design. May I ask where you got it?"

Devan told her about her grandmother and the ring.

"Well, I can understand why you thought my shop might have produced it. The workmanship is excellent. There is an inscription here." The clerk held a magnifying glass to the inside of the ring. "It says loyalty, liberty, destiny—in Gaelic." She frowned. "Interesting. It was your grandmother's? You are American, no?"

"My grandmother left Ireland when she was young."

Devan held out her hand. The clerk returned the ring and watched her slide it onto her right middle finger. Christian checked the cases to the right and shook his head a second time.

"I've been to several shops here and no one had anything similar. I was told that you design most of your stock. If anyone knew anything, it would be you."

"'Tis true. I design the jewelry I sell here, as well as commissioned pieces, but not your piece." The clerk hesitated. "If you leave your contact number, I'll ask some of my associates and let you know."

Devan again saw the barely perceptible shake of Christian's head. "I'm going to be traveling about for a bit. Can I just check back with you when I get a chance?" She took a business card from the tray near the register and stuffed it in her back pocket.

"I didn't get your name."

"It's Devan. Thanks for your time."

Christian linked his arm with hers and they strolled out into the afternoon sun.

They passed the shop windows before he turned to her. "She knows something."

"What makes you say that?" Devan raised an eyebrow.

"She frowned when she translated the inscription. Then she glanced at the phone when she said 'interesting'."

Devan shrugged. "I repeat, how do you deduce she knows something?"

"Her face, her eyes. When people lie, their gaze drifts away—usually up and to the right. And, she looked at the phone, indicating she wanted to call someone. My bet is she's calling right now." He pulled her close and pointed back to the window. "See?"

"Okay. What do we do about it? It's not like we can rush in and demand to know who she's talking to."

"We do nothing for a few days. We give her time to get in touch with whoever she's calling, then we come back and hope she sets up a meet."

Devan laughed. "You make it sound very double-o sevenish."

Christian hailed a taxi, helped her in and glanced back at the shop before climbing in after her.

"I think we can still make the National Museum," Devan said.

"Sure. Why not." He nodded to the driver. "National Museum."

They arrived an hour and a half before closing. Armed with her tour book, Devan led Christian through exhibits on the first floor. She headed for the second floor gallery, which held display cases of Irish silver, coins, glass, and jewelry. They searched the entire collection in under an hour.

In a dim alcove, Christian faced her. "I didn't see your ring, but there were some pieces that included dragons."

Devan hesitated. "I'm not sure this was such a good idea."

"Are you giving up?"

She raked her hand through her hair and huffed out a breath. "No. It's just that everything here dates back centuries. I don't think my ring falls into the same category."

Christian lifted her chin with a finger and held her gaze until she began to squirm. "The note to your grandmother spoke of heritage and destinies. That sounds like something passed down for generations, so your ring could easily be a part of Ireland's history."

"I suppose you're right." She looked back at the gallery.

"What are you thinking? I can almost see the gears turning in your head."

Devan smiled. "Two things. First, why are you so fired up about my destiny? Second, since I've had no luck in the shops, I want to see if the museum docent might know something."

"Well…maybe."

"You don't seem enthused. And you haven't answered my first question."

"I've never trusted people in authority."

"Is that why you didn't want me to show the ring to the guide earlier?"

Christian grunted an affirmative.

Devan pulled him back down to the ground level and toward the information desk. "A docent doesn't really have authority, they're just knowledgeable volunteers."

A round-shouldered gentleman with thinning white hair looked up at them. "May I help you?"

"I hope so." Devan held out her right hand to him. "I was wondering if you have seen anything with this design on it?"

The docent stood, took her hand into his own, and inspected her ring through round, wire-framed spectacles that slid down his nose. After a thorough study, he peered into her face. "It is highly crafted. We have several dragon pieces in our collection, but nothing with this design."

"Could this ring, or this design, hold significance in Irish history?" Christian asked.

The man blinked at him. "What makes you think that?"

Before Christian could answer, Devan removed the ring and held it out to the docent. "It's engraved with 'loyalty, liberty, destiny' in Gaelic."

The docent's watery blue gaze snapped back to hers then dropped to the ring. Pushing the spectacles back up the bridge of his nose, he studied the inscription. "Hmm." Abruptly, as if it burned his hand, he handed it back. "I have not seen a ring like it. Did you purchase it here in Dublin?"

"No." Devan returned it to her finger. "It's a family piece."

"I'm sorry I couldn't be more helpful, Miss." He shuffled to his chair. "I could ask the other docents, if you want to leave your name and phone number." He inclined his head at a notepad.

She jotted her name and her hotel. "I don't have a phone. But you can reach me here, for a couple more days."

The docent tucked the slip of paper in his shirt pocket and nodded. "I'll see what I can do. The museum is closing now, so you'll need to be going."

"Well, don't let the door hit you on your way out," Devan mumbled as they left.

"What?" Christian asked.

"He couldn't get rid of us fast enough, once he saw the inscription."

"True."

"He's hiding something too. I don't know what it is with my ring, but several people who have seen it are being very secretive. Why can't they just tell me? It can't be that bad, can it? It's not as if we're mass murderers.

Ten

It had been hours since Christian left Devan at her hotel. He hadn't lied when he told her he felt compelled to help search for her heritage. He just hadn't told her everything. That somehow they were linked. He didn't know how—yet.

His gut told him his disquieting dreams were somehow tied into all of this. His dragon pendant and her matching ring were pieces of the puzzle. The solution, he hoped, resided in the restricted books at Trinity. That was why he was here in the dead of night.

Christian's gaze darted left then right, always on the lookout for the Gardaí. His long, nimble fingers held the pick steady while twisting a second tool until he heard the soft click of the lock spring open. He glanced at his watch—less than two minutes. Not bad, he thought. He slipped inside and turned on his pocket torch.

Dressed in black from his jacket to his boots, he blended into the darkness. Entering the Long Room, he paused to control his breathing. Silence permeated the room like a tomb, a tomb that held over two hundred thousand ancient texts. Satisfied, he mounted the spiral stairs.

This would be no easy task. Where to start? He walked to the first row. He played his beam of light over the bindings, starting from the top. Engrossed in the task, he almost missed the footsteps below. When the crepe soles of the security guard's shoes squeaked on the flooring, Christian doused his torch. He held his breath and waited for any sign of discovery. The guard's pace never wavered. Slowly, Christian let out his breath, walked to the end of the row, and peered over the railing. The guard's own torch swung in a steady rhythm—left, right, left, right.

Christian heard the clomp, clomp as the guard ascended the staircase. Christian ran through the opening in the bookshelf, ducking his head to avoid smashing his skull. Twelve sections separated him from the other end. He quickened his pace and slipped through the last opening as the guard topped the stairs. Christian dove under a heavy oak table and pulled the chair snug. The chair legs scraped over the floor. He held his breath. Hearing footsteps approaching, Christian hunkered.

After several minutes, the guard departed, plunging the room into darkness. Christian crawled out, switched his torch back on, and checked his watch—twelve forty-five a.m. Starting where he'd been interrupted, he pulled down several books, flipped through the pages. He continued removing and replacing books from the shelves. Just before three thirty he stumbled across a passage in a large volume on Celtic history that baffled him.

When he heard the guard this time, Christian took the book with him to hide. He was impatient to be away, but he felt this passage was key. Time crawled by. Finally, the guard left. Sitting at the table, Christian opened the book.

OVER ONE MILLION DEAD AT THE HANDS OF THE GREAT FAMINE. MOST FROM THE POTATO BLIGHT, SOME FROM THE RICH LANDOWNERS' CAVALIER ATTITUDE TOWARD THE MASSES. BETWEEN THE START OF THE FAMINE AND 1870, ANOTHER THREE MILLION EMIGRATED TO AMERICA, AUSTRALIA, CANADA, AND OTHER LANDS. HUMAN COMPEERS NEEDED TO HELP THE KEEPERS IF ÉIRE IS TO SURVIVE, LET ALONE THRIVE.

Christian copied the passage word for word in his notebook, though he didn't understand several words. After searching the remainder of the book and finding no further mention of the odd words, he returned it to the shelf and descended the stairs. Halfway to his escape, he heard the unmistakable clop, squeak of the guard's shoes. Shite, why was the guard back so soon?

Christian ran for it. He slipped outside and into the shadows created by nearby shrubs. After taking several deep breaths, he strode away. His shoulders sagged and his steps slowed as the adrenaline swept out of his body.

He would need to tell Devan, of course. How much was the question. Undoubtedly, she could help understand the passage. The bigger issue was: should he show her his pendant? Would she be furious he withheld something from her—something so tangible that linked them? And why didn't he tell her when he first saw her ring? Now she wouldn't trust him, and he couldn't blame her. He had his own questions and he needed her to find the answers.

Letting himself into his flat, his thoughts turned to the dreams. He couldn't tell her about those. Not until he knew more. Not until he knew for certain he wasn't the killer. He fell into bed fully clothed. The clock on the nightstand illuminated the time—ten after five.

Christian dreamed. This one differed from the last—dusk in this version, not morning.

Standing on a hill surrounded by undulating tree-studded pastures, he watched and waited. There was not a hint of rain as the dying sun warmed the grassy knoll. In the center he saw an enormous bonfire ringed by scores of people. Dozens of dragons in every size and color imaginable interspersed among them. He crept closer. The shooting flames illuminated the faces of those gathered. Then he saw her—Devan.

He gasped. As quick as a bullet, a jewel-handled dagger flew toward her.

Before the dream could continue, before he could witness Devan's death, Christian forced himself awake. His soaked shirt plastered to his body and sweat gathered on his brow. His skin turned clammy and cold. His hands trembled.

"No!" He cried out. "No, she can't die."

Eleven

When he arrived at Devan's hotel, Christian still hadn't decided what to tell her. Would he sound crazy warning her she was a potential murder victim? Not any crazier than if he told her he saw dragons materialize, cry out in agony, then dissipate like mists torn to shreds. Would she trust him if he told her about his pendant? He couldn't be sure.

As he contemplated his choices, Devan walked out of the hotel, map in front of her face, and collided with him. She yelped. He steadied her and stepped back.

"Sorry," she said. "I wasn't watching—oh, Christian? What are you doing here? Did we have plans today?"

He waived his hands to slow her down. "No, but I need to talk to you." His eyes dropped to the map. "Where are you going?"

Devan folded it before answering. "I'm off to breakfast. I want to try a full Irish. Then I'm heading back to the library to see if I can learn anymore."

Christian patted his coat. What he had tucked away would be his opening, he decided. Then he could gauge her receptiveness before he told her the rest. "How about I take you for breakfast and we can talk? Kill two sheep with one stone."

"Thanks, I'd appreciate the company. I heard O'Brien's, where we ate yesterday, cooks up a full Irish breakfast."

"They're respectable." Christian guided her down the street. Once they found a secluded booth and had placed their orders, Christian pulled out the neatly folded paper.

"Last night I went back to the library and found something."

Devan gasped. "What? How?"

"I have my ways—that's not important now. What I found isn't much, but it might be relevant."

"What do you mean, you have your ways? Did you break in?" She waved her hands at him. "No, don't tell me. I don't want to be an accomplice."

Christian shook his head. "You want to know what I found or not?" Before she could answer, he continued. "In one of the many tomes of Irish history, I ran across this." He read the passage he had meticulously copied earlier that morning. When he finished, he asked, "Have you ever heard 'compeer' or 'Keeper'?"

"No. Have you?"

He shook his head. Devan tugged the paper from his fingers.

While she studied the passage, their server brought two large platters heaped with steaming potatoes, sausage, rashers of bacon, hot buttered pancakes, and fresh fruit. Christian's included scrambled eggs. A fresh pot of tea replaced the one that had turned lukewarm.

Christian smiled at the server and nodded his thanks. Then he dug into his meal. He pointed a strip of crispy bacon at her. "What do you think?"

"'Compeer' sounds Irish, but 'keeper' isn't. Keeper is a protector—as in the keeper of the keys being a jailer, or the keeper of my heart being some-one who cares for me." She refolded the paper and returned it.

They ate in silence. Christian drank his tea and watched her. Again, he wondered how much to tell her. He should tell her something about his dreams. Maybe leave out certain details—the parts about the dragon, and about him possibly being the killer.

He cleared his throat. When she looked up, he said, "There's something else."

"More?"

"Not exactly." He waited for the server to clear away the empty dishes. When the server left, he continued. "I've been having dreams. For the last six months. Bad dreams—nightmares or premonitions. Although that's hard for me to admit. There are people killed by a thrown dagger. So far four different dreams, four people dead."

"Premonitions?" Her skepticism showed on her face.

He frowned. "Within a week after each dream, the death is reported in the paper, along with the victim's picture. The picture matches the dead person in my dreams. There isn't much detail in the obituaries, but all four victims were young—twenties to early thirties. All were listed as accidents."

"Maybe you dream after you've seen each obituary."

Taking a deep breath, Christian reached for her hand. "No. The timing is as I said. Last night, I had the dream again." He gently squeezed her hand until she looked him in the eye. "Last night, I saw you—the blade flying to your heart."

Devan jerked back into the cool leather booth, snatching her hand from his grasp. Her eyes widened as she scanned the restaurant. Fear crossed her face. When she looked at him, he held his hands in front of him, palms up.

"I didn't see you murdered, I pulled myself out of the dream before the end." Christian lowered his hands, careful to place them on the table, in plain sight. Smooth, he thought, you couldn't have broken it to her gently?

"Who's throwing the knife?" Devan's voice trembled. "Where are you and what are you doing in the dream?"

Christian's heart pounded in his chest. He took a couple deep breaths to calm himself. How could he explain? As close to the truth as possible, he decided.

"I don't know who's throwing the dagger. I can't see the person, only the dagger sailing through the air toward…anyway, I'm not in the scene. I can't see myself."

Devan exhaled as she leaned forward, her shoulders relaxed. "That doesn't make sense." She ran her hand through her hair. "Why would somebody want to kill me? I only know a couple of people here in Ireland, including you—and not very well, I might add."

Slowly, Christian tapped her ring. "I think this is the connection."

"Someone wants to kill me for my ring? We don't know it was crafted here. No one wants to even talk. Oh! There's something special about it, enough to kill?"

"I'm not sure, but I need to tell you more." He pulled euros from his wallet and placed them on the table next to the bill. "Let's get out of here and

I'll explain. What I have to say can't be overheard—not by anyone. Do you trust me? I want to go somewhere private, either my flat or your hotel room."

"Well—" Devan hesitated.

"Just talk, I promise." Christian chuckled. "Of course, if my motives weren't pure, I'd say the same thing." He waved a hand, brushing the thought away, and looked up at the graying skies. "The park's out, since we're going to get rain soon. It'll clear by afternoon, but I'd rather not wait." He could see her debating. "Your hotel's more public than my place. We can find a private area without having to use your room."

She shuffled her feet, then nodded.

On their way back, he considered what he could get away with omitting. He would keep his pendant from her as long as he could.

A block from the hotel, the rain started and they ran for the door. Her hotel was small, but that worked in their favor. Few guests were about and the staff left them alone in a secluded alcove next to a window, not far from the entrance.

They sat facing each other. "Okay. This is going to sound strange. Please, just let me get it all out before you respond. Okay?" Christian took her right hand, holding the ring up to the waning light from the window. "See the dragon?" She nodded. "In each dream, just before the killing, a shadowy dragon coalesces in front of the victim. It roars with unspeakable pain and anguish. I'll never forget that sound. It chills my blood." He shuddered, as if to prove his point. "Then the dragon just vanishes—it doesn't fly off. It's just gone."

Christian stopped. He'd leave out his role in the dream. She was already freaked out enough, without thinking him a murderer. "Then the scene shifts. The victim is leaning against an enormous rock mound, some kind of hilly structure. And then I see the dagger. Embedded."

She studied him, waiting for more. "Are you done?"

He released her hand and rubbed his face, wiping away his fatigue.

"Okay. Let's say I believe you—and I'm not sure I do just yet. Are you saying that the place where the murder happens and where the body is found are different?"

"Yes, but that's not all. Sometimes the weather is different too. What I mean is…" Christian closed his eyes to concentrate on his memories. "In the last dream, before the one last night, the murder happened at dawn, in a rainstorm. But where the woman's body was found, the grass was only damp from a light drizzle. If it were the same place, the rainwater would have puddled. In the first dream, the sun was shining overhead when the victim, a man, was killed. When his body was left at the stone hill, it was dark—after nightfall. Stars lit up the sky and the temperature dipped enough to need a light jacket."

Devan held up her hand. "Hold on. Did each murder happen at the same place? Or, were the bodies just placed at the same rock mound?"

"Each murder happened in a different location. I saw different land-scapes, but…I think you're right, the rock mound is always the same."

"Can you describe it? Wait." She jumped up. "I need to get something. Be right back."

As Devan headed to the lift, Christian slumped in the chair and closed his eyes. He was as tired as if he had relived each dream again. The telling drained him. Was he drawing Devan into trouble? Or was she headed there anyway, with or without him? What would he say if she asked why he was involved? She would—sooner or later. He hoped for later. Much later.

Devan returned with a palm-sized notebook, pen, and her guidebook. "There are questions zipping through my mind right now. I'm going to get to them soon, but first I want you to describe the location where the bodies were found."

Christian leaned forward as she opened the notebook and used her guidebook as a writing desk. "Okay. The lighting and the weather are dif-ferent each time. Each body is leaning against a meter high stone as thick as the length of my arm. The stone blocks the entrance into the round, rock structure. It's a grassy mound, the size of a rugby pitch or a horse track, quite tall with rocks that match, pressed into the sides of the mound. There are designs, circles, and spirals and squiggly lines, carved into the gigantic stones. Even the one blocking the entrance has designs carved into it."

Devan stopped writing. "Hold that thought." She flipped through her guidebook. When she found the page, she turned the book around so he could see. "Is this the place?"

Christian grabbed the book. The picture he held in his hand was exactly the same as the one in his head. Shock hit him first, then amazement. She found it based solely on his description. Yet, she had only been in Ireland for less than a week. He lived here his entire twenty-seven years—granted only in the city—but he hadn't recognized the place. Newgrange at Brú na Bóinne, he read. He must've been taught about it in school; but then, he had avoided school whenever possible. When he looked up, Devan was staring at him with expectation or confidence, he wasn't sure.

"Yes, that's it," he murmured. "It must be well known if it made it into a travel guide. I…don't get out of Dublin much."

Devan recovered the book before he dropped it. "I had some time on the flight over. This is one of the places I wanted to visit." She studied the photo. "It was a burial or passage tomb. Maybe a thousand years older than Stonehenge." She raised her gaze to him. "Perhaps the killer was trying to bury them, or save them. One legend has…" She scanned the page quickly. "Here it is, Aengus, the God of love, bringing the fatally wounded Diarmund's body to Newgrange, in a failed attempt to save him. It also serves as a type of calendar." She turned the book so he could see where she pointed. "During the winter solstice, the rising sun's rays shine through this opening and illuminate the burial chamber."

Christian nodded, trying to take in everything she was saying. His thoughts jumbled. He couldn't possibly be the killer; he had never been there before. Relief flooded through him. Unless. Unless he'd been in some kind of trance—where he didn't know what he was doing or where he was. Was that even possible? His head ached. Devan said something about needing to go there, making a plan.

"What?" He rubbed his throbbing temple.

She looked at the guidebook again. "It's too late to go today. How about tomorrow?"

"Why do we need to go there? We know that's the place." His voice pitched higher with growing anxiety.

Devan raked her fingers through her hair. "Because it's the only solid clue we have. If your dreams are related to me and my ring, I need to follow every lead. Which brings me back to my questions." She waited for him to lift his gaze. He'd known it was coming; he just wasn't sure how he would answer.

"How do you know it's a dragon? When did you correlate your dreams to my ring? You said you've been having them for half a year, why didn't you say so yesterday?"

Christian held up his hands. "I wasn't positive you were tied into them—until the dream last night. At first I thought you were in the dream because of all the time we spent together yesterday. Also, we don't know each other very well. Why would I tell a stranger something like this? Most people would think I'm insane—a dragon, really? Anyway, your ring caught the firelight in the dream, just before the dagger flew your way, and I woke myself up before the dream ended." He narrowed his eyes, recalling more details. "I remember a bonfire with people, and about two dozen dragons interspersed in the crowd. Some dragons were huge—big as my flat. Some were smaller, like a van. Their colorings were fantastic. I didn't recognize any of the people." He took a deep breath. "That's all I can remember."

"Okay, maybe more will come back to you. I still don't understand how you're connected. Why you're having these dreams? It's a mighty big coincidence that I ran into you the other night—let alone talked. I don't usually speak to strangers, and I certainly don't spill my life story to them."

"Is that your life story?" Christian laughed, trying to steer the conversation away from why he approached her in the pub. This was boggy ground and he could get sucked under. His finger grazed the pendant snug against his chest, hidden. Would she forgive him for omitting his connection? Bugger it—he still didn't know how the two of them were connected.

"Are you trying to evade my question?"

He quirked an eyebrow. "Was there a question in there?"

"How are we connected? You started our conversation the other night, as I remember." She frowned. "You noticed my ring." Her voice took on a sharp edge.

"Okay." Christian desperately hoped to avoid the truth, the whole truth anyway. He saw the impatience and something more. Was it fear? He knew he would have to confide in her. He should have done so earlier, but he couldn't change that now. He inhaled a deep breath, and again took her right hand. "I don't know how we're connected…exactly. You have to believe that. I'm still trying to puzzle it out. To be honest, I wasn't going to tell you about my part in this, until you appeared in my dream."

Slowly he tugged the leather cord and pendant from beneath his shirt. He gripped her hand tight and leaned forward, until the pendant dangled beside her ring. The same in design and engraving.

Shock, then anger, and finally suspicion crossed Devan's face.

She opened her mouth then closed it. Her gaze darted between him and the twin dragons. "What? How could you?" She nearly yelled. "I was such a fool, trusting you."

"Please, let me explain," he pleaded.

"You've had all kinds of time to explain." Devan pulled her hand away. "What do you take me for? You've been hanging around, for what? So you could steal it, have the matching set?" Her voice lowered now, more dangerous than derisive. Her brown eyes darkened as she abruptly stood up, the books falling from her lap.

"Wait!" Christian stood as well. "Calm down. Let me explain."

"No! I need to…to go." She sprinted for the front door.

"Good going, Riley," he muttered, berating himself as he retrieved her fallen items. "Couldn't have fecked it up any better." He headed for the same door, hoping no one noticed her outburst.

He should leave her alone, let her think things through, but he was afraid something would happen to her—that his nightmare would come true, like the others. He reached the sidewalk, but couldn't see her. The rain had gone and the sky was a brilliant blue with puffy, white clouds.

Calm down, he told himself. She's in Dublin, it's midday. In the dream she's in the country, on top of a hill. There's nothing like that here.

Twelve

Sean couldn't get away from Loughcrew until noon. He didn't mind going into Dublin—in fact he enjoyed the bustling city. He just preferred not to risk detection by arriving during the middle of the day. The rambling cover of trees at St. Stephen's Green would help shield his arrival from the mass of students and tourists of Trinity College. The dragon magic rendered the red dragon and himself invisible, even against the blue sky. Once he disembarked and FIONN flew ten meters away, Sean would be vulnerable.

He directed FIONN to land at the southern edge of the green. Removing his riding gear, he stepped into the grove of trees and waited for FIONN to take flight. The downdraft from the heavy beat of dragon wings ruffled the trees and nearby bushes.

FIONN circled overhead and flew southwest toward the outskirts of Dalkey to await his compeer's summons. Sean emerged from the trees. He glanced at several students nearby to gauge their reaction to his sudden appearance. They didn't even notice, so he set off at a brisk pace to Trinity.

William had been frantic over the phone, Sean remembered.

"I need you to come. A young couple were here asking questions about the oath," William had said in a rush. "They were insistent, asking about Celtic lore and then springing the oath on me."

If that had been the only call, Sean would have sent Aisling. His wife had a way of calming people that he couldn't match. William sounded overwrought—his eye probably twitched for the rest of the day. Sean would find out what the guide knew about the couple and calm the man down. However, William's was not the only summons. Kate, his sister, and Brian from the museum had also called. Each told him of a young couple asking questions. The woman owned a dragon clan ring.

None of the current family wore a signet ring. He remembered a story his grandfather, the clan *seanachais*, told about a member with the gift of hearing all dragons—not just her own. That member had worn a ring instead of the clan pendant.

Before leaving that morning, Sean had searched the clan records for any mention of the ring, or a rider with special gifts. He found planting and harvesting schedules, border disputes, skirmishes between neighboring families, and birth, marriage, and death records dating back a hundred and fifty years. Not a single mention of a signet ring—or the pendants worn today for that matter. He did notice entries when a dragon and rider were pressed into service in a county not their own. Maybe these compeers possessed a special talent, but nothing specific was recorded.

After his meeting with William, Sean walked by a woman sitting on the bench across from the library door. She looked like the woman William described, but she was alone. He hesitated.

Any number of women could fit that description, he thought. Yet, he sensed something. Was it the dragon magic? No, it couldn't be. He was just out-of-sorts having to placate the twitchy William. Shaking his head, Sean continued on the path toward Dame Street. He caught a taxi and directed the driver to the west end of the upscale Temple Bar section of town.

The day was cool and had cleared from a morning shower, the clouds scattering with the light breeze. Sean wished the tension in his shoulders would dissipate as easily. He drew a cleansing breath before going into the shop.

"Well, well, well. Look what the wind blew in," Kate said in a melodious voice. "Is this the only way I get to see my youngest brother? Clan business?"

Crossing the threshold, Sean stepped into her waiting arms. Their hug was fierce.

Kate drew him back, her gaze long and searching. "So, what I've heard is true. There's been another murder. Who?" She locked the door and flipped the open sign over.

"Mary and AALYSIA. She was at Carrowmore, paying respects to her sister." Sean walked with her to the office in the back of the store. "Oh, Kate. That's four dragons and riders in six months. What kind of leader am I? I can't even keep everyone safe, for pity's sake."

Kate fisted her hands on her hips. "Now wait just a minute." She pointed her finger and prodded it into his chest. "What was Mary doing going off by herself? I know you. You would've warned clan members to keep their guard up. No one should've been alone outside the compound."

"I had to make it a direct order. Patrols must be flown in pairs. No flying solo."

"Except for my indestructible brother," Kate teased. They sat together on a bright, floral patterned couch. Kate held his hands in hers. "You are doing everything you can to keep them safe and still uphold the oath. Speaking of which, the couple that came in the shop yesterday—"

Sean held up a hand. "Wait." He pulled the notebook from his pocket and flipped to a page. "The woman was American and the man was Irish, right?"

When Kate stared at him incredulously, he shrugged, and related what William had told him earlier.

"Well, the woman, Devan was her name, was American. Her grandmother was Irish. I'm not sure about the man. He never uttered a word, just let the woman lead."

Sean nodded.

"She wore a ring. Silver, with the clan emblem and the oath inscribed inside." Kate leaned forward and drew Sean's pendant out from under his shirt. "Exactly like this—the dragon clutching the knot of protection." Letting go of the pendant, she watched it settle against her brother's shirt.

"Did you tell her anything?"

"No. Yes." Her gaze lifted from the pendant. "I mean, I gave them the translation from Gaelic. It surprised me. The whole incident. I've never made a clan ring, only pendants. Who is she? Who was her grandmother?"

Sean tucked his pendant back under his shirt. "Did you get anything else from her?"

"Tried to, but she said she'd be traveling and would check back with me.

I told her I'd check with other jewelers. Right after they left, I called you."

"Describe her."

"My height. Brown eyes, short, spiky brown hair with blonde streaks from the sun, or a clever hairdresser. Mole on her upper lip, left side. She wore jeans, a jumper, and a black leather jacket. The man was similarly dressed. A touch shorter than you with black hair. I didn't pay much attention to him."

Sean stood and pulled Kate to her feet. "If they come in again, give me a call. I'd like to meet them—if they agree."

Kate pulled his face down and kissed him. "You know I love you. You'll find the killer. You're as tenacious as a hungry dog with a bone. Keep in touch."

"I will. You do the same. Keep safe." Sean walked through the shop. He opened the door and signaled for a taxi before looking back to see Kate turning the sign to reopen. He waved to her as he got into the back seat. Closing his eyes, Sean directed the driver to his last destination.

Christian strode quickly past taxis lining Dame Street. Would Devan turn him in to the Gardaí? Christian hoped not. He thought she would seek refuge where she was most comfortable. That would be the library, most likely. Hadn't she said she was going there earlier? Scanning the pedestrians and bicycle riders on the path ahead, he spied her sitting on the same bench they had shared yesterday. Had he only known her for two days? It seemed impossible. In the short time since their meeting, his life had changed. He couldn't explain it, but he knew his destiny, his future, his very life was tied with hers—the American with Irish roots.

Should he approach her, or remain unseen and just make sure she was all right? Would she cause a scene with the crowd around? He thought not. For all her chatter about her ring and family, he had been the initiator. She was reserved and alone. He took a different bench.

Devan twisted the ring round and round her finger. A man walked between them, his heavy, brown duster flapping with each long stride. His red hair and the duster's movement caused her to glance at the man who had paused briefly, and she spotted Christian. He caught the weariness in her eyes and in the firm set of her mouth. She didn't run.

Christian stayed where he was. Around him the crowd noises faded. The scent of fresh-cut grass drenched in the recent rains soothed him, and the warmth of the afternoon sun bathed his face. In his exhaustion, he closed his eyes. When he opened them, Devan sat beside him. The sounds of the city returned.

"I'm sorry. I should have told you from the beginning. My only excuse is…I don't know what's going on either." Christian scanned the tourists and students on the pathways dividing the verdant lawn. They sat publicly isolated on the busy university grounds. Carefully, he took her hand. "You know that I grew up in an orphanage. I rebelled, ran with the wrong crowd. Anyway, when I was ten years old, Mother Superior called me to her office. I'd been caught stealing sweets with some other lads. I expected to be handed over to the Gardaí, in shackles."

He waited for her to say something. She remained silent. "I dragged my feet going to see her. It was only the two of us. She sat behind her desk, tapping an envelope in the palm of her hand. I took the only vacant chair. She stared at me as if trying to determine who I would become. I was scared as hell. Finally, she opened the envelope and withdrew this pendant."

Pulling it from beneath his shirt, he continued. "She told me how I came to them, that the pendant came with me. No one knew anything about it. She said I was old enough to have it now. The next day I was sent to live with a couple who couldn't have children of their own. It was okay for about six months, until they found out she was pregnant, and I was shipped back to the orphanage." Christian kept the revolving door of the foster care system and the multiple beatings to himself. He held her gaze. "So you see, I was stunned by your ring the other night. All I could think was to learn as much as I could from you. The more I learned, the more confused I became. How could we be connected? Could someone from your family be related to me?"

Devan stopped him. "You could've told me. Trusted me." She shook her head. "But I suppose it's not in your nature."

"No, it's not. The more I was around you, the more jealous I became."

"Jealous? Of what?"

Christian shrugged. "Here you came from America to learn about your ring. I have done nothing in seventeen years to find out about my own pendant. You have courage and determination. I—"

Devan interrupted him. "Our circumstances are different. I come from a loving family, one I recently lost. I have nothing to lose in this quest. You don't know who your parents are, and grew up in an environment of distrust and God knows what else." She shoved at her hair. "Is the rest of it true—the dreams? The dream about me?"

"Yes." He wouldn't tell her of his role in the dreams. He couldn't.

"Where do we go from here?"

He smiled. "Thanks for not thinking I'm crazy. How about something to eat? We missed lunch."

"How about we research 'keepers' and 'compeer' first? I don't think I want to go back to the library here though." She indicated the building he had broken into. "So we'll need to get my laptop."

As soon as Sean entered the museum, Brian ushered him into a small antechamber to the right of the information booth. Motioning Sean into the visitor's chair, Brian leaned his elbows on his desk and steepled his fingers in front of him.

"So, what's going on, Sean? Riders and dragons murdered. I've read about it. Oh, not the dragons, mind you. And no one knows the victims were dragonriders. I guess you can't keep everything from the media. Now two strangers are walking around Dublin with what appears to be a clan signet ring, asking questions. Could they have stumbled onto something and used the ring for murder?"

Sean pulled out the jewel-handled dagger from his coat pocket and placed it on the desk between them. "The ring isn't the murder weapon, this is."

Carefully, Brian lifted it. He turned it over, inspecting from tip to pommel. Whistling through his teeth, he looked up at Sean. "Sure is a beauty.

More ceremonial than functional. The jewels on the hilt disrupt the balance. The killer would have to be highly skilled to throw it. Or get close enough to thrust it into someone." Brian reached into the top drawer and pulled out a jeweler's loupe. Again he inspected the dagger, focusing on the jewels. "They're real. Emeralds, sapphires, and rubies. Hard to believe the killer would leave it behind."

"The killer left four identical knives. One for each murder. Pierced each rider through the heart. There are no prints, so he must have worn gloves," Sean said. "Have you seen anything similar?"

Brian returned it, handle first. "I've seen daggers aplenty. To have four identical, I would guess that's a set. Specially made. Could be only four in the set, but more likely six. If you could spare that one, I'll ask around."

Sean nodded and laid it on the desk. "What can you tell me about your visitors yesterday?"

"A couple. American woman wearing a silver ring with the clan symbol and the oath engraved inside. Said it was passed down from her great-grandparents. The young man is from here, Dublin by his speech. Wanted to know if the ring held historical significance." Brian pushed his glasses back with a finger. Reaching into his shirt pocket, he handed Sean a neatly folded piece of paper. "Her name and hotel."

Unfolding the paper, Sean read. "Devan Fraser. Scottish or American." He tucked the paper away. "I'll look into this. Thanks." He nodded toward the dagger. "Let me know what you find out."

They stood and walked from the room. When they reached the information desk, Sean shook Brian's hand. "I'll be in touch."

What should he do? Go to the woman's hotel, demand an explanation? The couple had done nothing wrong. They could be the killers, but somehow he didn't think so. His priority was stopping the killer before he struck again. The killer's timetable—if he held to the pattern—gave Sean five weeks. He shouldn't waste any of it on this Yank and her companion. Yet there must be a connection between them and the clan. Why else would she have a clan ring?

He clasped his hand over his pendant. Immediately Fionn's presence entered his mind.

"Are ye ready? I can be there momentarily."

Sean looked south toward where his compeer waited. *"Not quite. I need to make one more stop. Check on someone. I shouldn't be more than a half-hour. I'll get back to you when I'm close to our rendezvous spot."*

Turning west, Sean squinted into the slowly setting sun. He wanted to clear up this matter quickly, and hoped the last person on this visit would not throw any daggers.

Devan and Christian returned to her hotel. While she retrieved her computer from her room, Christian stayed in the lobby and observed the hotel security. He wanted her safe. The place was designed more as a bed and breakfast, small and not very secure. Maybe he should get a room for the duration of her stay. Before he could inquire at the front desk, the elevator opened, and out spilled Devan, chatting with a mohawked and heavily pierced couple.

Definitely not secure.

Devan directed Christian to the alcove where they sat earlier. "The place has Wi-Fi." She worked the computer for a few minutes. "Compeer means partner. Can I see that passage again?" He gave her the paper. "Human compeers, partners, needed to help the Keepers if Éire is to survive, let alone thrive," she read softly. "I think the keepers are the dragons. That means humans and dragons, working together, living together, surviving together."

Christian nodded. "I still don't understand why we have a pendant and a ring. Are we compeers, or descended from them?"

"It would make sense, at least from my great-grandparents' letter." Devan pulled it from her backpack and passed it to him.

Christian read quickly. "The letter says your ring, your heritage, your destiny are tied in with some clan. Destiny—it's part of the inscription on both our pieces."

Devan looked up from the laptop. "For as long as I can remember, I've been fascinated with dragons. There's a ton of stories and myths about creatures that supposedly don't exist. Here it is."

She read the passage aloud.

The ancient Druids believed Earth was like the body of a dragon, and they built their sacred stone circles upon the power nodes of this body. Power nodes, ley lines, dragon lines, they all mean the same thing. The Celts believed the dragon's power and their presence influenced the ley of the land. Dragons were considered guardians of knowledge and wisdom, protectors of birth and all living things.

Guardians, protectors, keepers—that fits." Devan tapped a key. "I'm going to save all this."

Christian stroked his pendant. "We need to eat, then decide what to do."

Devan nodded and stuffed everything in her backpack.

They left and flagged a taxi. As the cab pulled away from the curb, Christian's eye caught the heavy, swooshing brown coat of a man entering the hotel.

Thirteen

Hidden amongst the greatest cluster of stone circles anywhere in Ireland stood Beaghmore, the dragon clan's compound for Northern Ireland. Over one hundred kilometers separated it from Loughcrew and Sean, the clan leader. Kiely, the Ulster Province leader, cherished this physical distance, which afforded her autonomy.

Kiely dug out the last fist-sized chunk of lamb from the twenty-liter bucket her husband, Ronan, had brought earlier that morning. She dropped it into Tullia's hungry maw. Ever since the plum-colored dragon laid her egg two weeks ago, the nesting mother only ventured away long enough to relieve herself. That left Kiely to attend to her needs: meals, clean bedding, and oiling and polishing.

Tullia's forked tongue licked the juices from her meal. She arranged her ten-meter body with the egg snuggled against her leathery chest and her tail wrapped around it. Her body heat and the peat fire in the hearth kept it at a constant forty-one Celsius, optimal for incubation.

Attentive to her dragon's needs, Kiely softly crooned as she scratched Tullia's eye ridges and continued down her neck to the shoulder muscles. Tullia leaned into the caress and blew warm air over her egg and over Kiely's dyed blond tresses. The seventy-three-year-old mother of two and grandmother of three adhered to the philosophy that you are only as young as you look—and she certainly didn't want to look her actual age.

It had been pitifully easy to keep Tullia's condition a secret, even from Kiely's own province mates. As the elder dragon in Beaghmore, no one dared question her growth or her increased appetite. By day, the pair ostensibly patrolled County Derry. In reality, they stayed in their personal quarters, caring for Tullia's egg.

Kiely whispered to her beloved compeer. "*A ghra*, you have done a wonderful job seeing to your egg. It's my turn to care for you. I think you'd enjoy a dip in the lake and I could freshen your bed. Then I will oil your hide and wing joints and polish your scales. We don't want cracking in the wing membrane when you next fly, and the rate of egg hardening tells me that will be soon. You must be ready to show your little one how to spread its wings after hatching."

With one last puff of heated breath over her egg, Tullia relinquished it to Kiely's care and left her chamber—flying northeast to the lake for a quick bath.

After the dragon had gone, Kiely summoned her grandson, Peter, to rake the top layer of hay and lay a fresh batch over the sleeping pallet. Kiely gently rolled the egg, positioning it within the new hay. When she was satisfied, she dismissed Peter and retrieved a jar of her special blend of oil along with several soft rags.

Another week or two at the most, and the secret would be out. The entire Beaghmore complex would care for the dragonet after it hatched and for a year until it matured enough to bond with its chosen compeer.

Once it was known they had defied the clan leader and the council, Kiely would be punished. With the clan shorthanded, she was willing to risk it. After all, she should have rightfully been clan leader, not Sean. The young upstart should have deferred to his elder. The succession of leadership brought another blight to the Northern Six, as far as she was concerned. Even her firstborn, Padrick, had voted against her.

So what if the clan already had a plethora of young dragons—with two still not choosing compeers. She knew Roarke and Dochas had been bred as replacements for herself and Ronan and their compeers, but she wasn't ready to retire. Not with so many of her plans unrealized.

She rested a hand on the curved egg. Now that the dragonet was soon to hatch, she thought the event would bolster the clans' spirits. She would be revered and her bravery praised. After all, Tullia had managed to fly her post, perform her duties during the past three months—mostly. And the county hadn't suffered much.

Kiely could have timed it better, but that wasn't her fault. It was in the dragon's nature to give birth in the spring. Something about spring signaling birth and renewal of life, she couldn't remember exactly. She had forgotten more than that upstart, Sean, would ever know.

It grated that Sean denied her appeal for more dragon matings, and the rest of the council agreed with him. It had been a risk to mate TULLIA and CALHOUN, as they were two of the oldest dragons in the clan. No one knew for sure if TULLIA's egg was even viable—a single egg, not the usual two. TULLIA had borne the mating and gestation well, but the egg was smaller and mottled a sickly yellow. It was nowhere near the size and color that DOCHAS's and ROARKE's shell had been.

Hearing her compeer enter, Kiely dismissed her negative thoughts. She didn't want her beloved upset.

TULLIA shook water from her body and wings before settling into the refreshed pallet. She sniffed the repositioned egg then placed her forelegs to one side of it and curled her body and tail around it.

Kiely dried her compeer's scales and oiled the shoulder joints down to the foreleg elbows, then shifted her attention to the hips, knees, and talons of the hind legs. An hour later and she had yet to do the chest and wing membranes. Not to mention polishing the scales across the back and tail.

Massaging her tired muscles, Kiely leaned against TULLIA's forelegs and rested. Outside, several dragons landed noisily in the courtyard. Had the day passed so quickly? The demands of dragon care were more than Kiely had expected. This was definitely a drawback in keeping the egg a secret. She only trusted a few—Ronan and his dragon, CALHOUN of course. And Peter, her oldest grandson and personal stable hand. His most fervent desire was to be a dragonrider. His best chance would be with TULLIA's and CALHOUN's offspring. Kiely took advantage of Peter's devotion to ensure his silence.

As she worked, her thoughts drifted to her family. Her husband was weak and pliable, like putty for her to mold. Not so her daughter, Tess. Peter's mother left to marry outside the clan. But Padrick, her firstborn, was a dragonrider and destined for greatness. Twenty-seven years ago Kiely directed her son's romantic notions away from that girl, Erin. He couldn't be allowed to marry an outsider. Not if he was to be clan leader. A common village chit would ruin Kiely's aspirations for her legacy.

When Ronan entered the lair, Kiely was more than ready to hand over Tullia's oiling and polishing duties. The wing membrane, being the most delicate part of a dragon's anatomy, took the longest time and the most patience. Something Kiely was in short supply of.

"Just in time." She extended the oil pot to Ronan. "I've oiled all but her wings, could you finish? I swear there's more to rub every day. She wants me to hand feed her when she would benefit from picking her own food and flying more often."

Ronan shed his coat and riding gloves, tossing them on a bench near the entrance. His snowy white hair was tied in a short queue at the nape of his neck and his deep blue eyes twinkled as he accepted the pot from his wife. He began oiling the dragon's outstretched right wing. "You knew the commitment. Why don't you have Peter do more of the chores? He needs to learn if he's to be a dragonrider, and it would free you to do neglected clan duties."

Kiely snorted. "The lad is in a constant daydream. Tullia gets impatient. Besides, I can't be sure he won't tell Matthew or one of the other riders in his excitement. Better to keep him busy caring for the livestock and away from his friends—at least until the hatching."

"Okay, but you're going to have to put in an appearance in the main dining hall for dinner. People are missing you and there are murmurs of your or Tullia's health failing, especially since the céilí. You and Tullia must fly Derry. She needs to rebuild the magic. There are problems with the spring plantings."

"What is troubling ye?" Tullia bespoke.

Kiely glared at Ronan as she soothed the dragon. *"Sorry, my sweet. Nothing to worry about."*

Ronan shifted to the dragon's left wing and continued his ministrations. "I'll finish up here. Why don't you relax in a long, hot bath and then we'll go to dinner together? Calhoun can keep an eye on his mate for the evening."

"Sounds like heaven," Kiely said as she rolled her neck to loosen the knots.

An hour later, Kiely and Ronan walked arm-in-arm across the courtyard and mounted three stone steps. Ronan opened the heavy oak door and Kiely preceded him into the oblong dining hall. Already, several dragonriders and their families were spread amongst the wooden tables and chairs. The raucous chatter and children's laughter quieted as Kiely and Ronan wound their way to their customary table opposite the door.

"Has it been so long that I am made a spectacle in the hall?" Kiely murmured as she sat.

"You've not taken your dinner here since TULLIA laid her egg. Except for the céilí, which turned into a funeral for Mary and AALYSIA, you've been absent. The members need to feel your leadership, now more than ever," Ronan said.

Others arrived, Matthew and Peter included. Matthew paused when he saw Kiely, then continued to a table that seated half a dozen young singles.

Kiely requested Peter join them.

The noise grew as conversations multiplied and the meal was served.

An hour later, as the evening wound down, Kiely stood to address the crowd. Talk became murmurs that faded to silence.

"*Dia daoibh*," Kiely intoned the traditional greeting. "I'm sorry, I've been remiss in my duties for the evening meals. As you can see, I am in good health, as is TULLIA. I have been extremely busy with clan business. It has taken all my time over these past weeks. Soon, I hope to show you the fruits of my labor." She closed with the clan oath and after the customary reply, strode from the hall.

Had she tempted fate in her arrogance? Would a clever rider figure out her secret before the dragonet hatched? She hoped not. Adulation and respect, along with surprise, would be hers.

Fourteen

Devan and Christian left Dublin early the next morning, heading north to Drogheda, then west to Newgrange. They left the city behind and in twenty minutes entered the rolling hills and meter-high rock walls that separated estates. Sheep and cattle grazed in the fields. The only sounds were the car engine and the wind racing past the open windows.

It felt weird to Devan to be sitting in the left seat with no steering wheel in front of her. She turned from the pastoral view to watch the wind messing Christian's hair, scattering stray strands from the leather band holding it.

He glanced away from the road. "What do you make of the man that asked for you at the hotel last night?"

"He was probably sent by the museum curator, since that was the only person I gave my hotel information to. I just wish the man had left his name or a message. How do we know what he wants or if he has information for us? Maybe we should phone the shop to find out what the jeweler knows. At least she was friendly."

"I don't trust any of them." Christian frowned. "If I belonged to a secret clan with dragons, I wouldn't tell outsiders anything. I'd be suspicious as hell."

When they reached the Brú na Bóinne Visitor Center, they looked around the two-story building, not seeing the earthen mound.

Devan slung her camera around her neck. "Let's see about tour tickets. Maybe we can figure out why the killer put the bodies here, instead of leaving them where he murdered them."

They boarded a bus with other tourists for a short drive to the monument. Sunlight glinted off the dew-tipped grass on the top of the flattened, four-story mound, and reflected off the white quartz and granite kerbstones. They approached the tomb, their eyes never leaving the sight before them. Christian halted, facing the semicircular courtyard and the oblong guardian stone with its ornate carvings. Devan, not noticing he had stopped, bumped into him.

She apologized, then took a deep breath. "Wow. It's more impressive in person. The pictures don't do it justice—just can't capture the feelings and atmosphere."

Christian nodded; his eyes did not leave the Neolithic tomb.

Devan paused at the entrance. With the guardian stone filling her viewfinder, she captured the double and triple spirals and concentric semicircles carved into the granite. She counted the upright stones lining the passageway as she squeezed past—forty-three. At the end, the burial chamber held three recesses, each with a large basin stone that once may have held human remains and funeral offerings. She moved trancelike toward the rounded-out stone.

Christian startled her by grabbing her arm. "I wonder why the bodies were left outside, not brought in here," he whispered. "They'd have been discovered quicker out in the open."

Devan nodded and kept her voice low. "I don't think the killer could navigate this corridor carrying a body. Faster too, especially if the place was crawling with tourists. He'd have had a finite window of time to leave the body and not get caught."

They made their way back to the entrance with the other tourists. Devan continued taking pictures, capturing the guardian stone from every angle as well as the area leading to the tomb.

"Let's walk around it. Maybe you'll get a better idea of the dream's location."

They circled the pear-shaped mound. Continuing to take pictures, she counted a ring of twelve tall stones encircling the mound about ten feet away. A decorated kerbstone squatted at the back of the mound.

"Are you sure the bodies were placed at the entrance? This stone is also carved, maybe the bodies were here?" she asked.

"No. It was at the entrance. Once I saw it, I knew. It's weird. The more I see the entrance, the clearer the images, but they flash by so quickly. It's hard to concentrate, to separate them."

"Let's see the visitor's center, learn what we can, then go. This place has an overwhelming sadness about it—more than a centuries-old burial tomb."

They wandered the exhibits for over an hour, but other than the history of the passage tombs and prehistoric Ireland, they learned nothing new.

"I think better with a full stomach," Christian said.

Devan laughed.

They drove to the small town of Donore a few miles farther west and found an open pub.

She marveled at Christian's appetite as he plowed through a bookmaker sandwich, fries, and a cavernous bowl of lamb stew. She ate a smaller serving of stew. Both washed down lunch with a pint of Guinness.

"I think I can handle going back now." Christian leaned back in the booth. "I need to recall each dream, separate them, pick them apart, see if there's anything I missed."

"Are you sure about this? You blanched when you saw the entrance."

"I need to do this. Now, while the dreams are fresh in my mind. Besides, if I concentrate on this one place, get that aspect over with, maybe the murder sites will become clearer."

They waited until the last tour of the day finished, then returned to the monument. Christian spread a blanket close enough to the entrance for him to ignore the wooden steps on either side, and sat.

Christian shuddered and wrapped his arms around his middle. He closed his eyes. His breathing deepened. He opened his eyes, focused on the entrance stone, and recalled the last murder.

"A blonde, curly-haired woman with dark eyes wearing pants tucked into Wellingtons and a long, black coat. A light drizzle fell. The morning spring sun's rays reflected against the dampness on the woman's face. Silver glinted beneath the protruding dagger in her chest. A thunderous noise, coupled with a burst of white light." Christian toppled over on the blanket as the vision reverberated in his skull.

"We should stop." Devan helped him sit up. "You aren't well."

He waved his hand. "No. Let me catch my breath. I want to get this over with." He looked away from the entrance stone until the pounding in his head eased.

"Are you sure?" Devan's voice shook. "We could come back. Do this another day."

"Being here once is enough. I don't want to come back." He squinted at the carved stone, let the previous visions return, and recounted the details.

"One took place in winter. Sleet fell. The victim was a man wearing heavy wool trousers with fur-lined boots and coat. His hair was dark brown, curled under a wool cap. Same dagger embedded in his chest, but no additional noise or lighting. Another victim was a redheaded woman with bright green eyes. A steady rain fell as the sun set."

He ran a hand over his clammy face before continuing. "In my first dream, it was a man propped against the stone while the stars twinkled in a clear sky. The night air had just turned cool. He wore a white billowing shirt, brown cargo work pants, and short black boots. No jacket. His black hair was shorter than mine and his blue eyes lighter."

"Is that all?"

Christian hunched forward and nodded. "See what I mean? Four distinct people, four different times of the day, four seasons. They all were brought here, with a dagger embedded in their chests."

"In the last murder, you said you heard a loud noise and saw a burst of light. Was that lightning?"

"No. The weather was soft, not stormy. Just a drizzle, with patches of sunlight."

"Did that happen in all the dreams?"

Hair fell into Christian's eyes as he shook his head. "Only the most recent, when a spot of sunlight shone through and sparked on the dagger."

The sun dipped low in the sky as Christian folded the blanket and stuffed it in the trunk. "Let's head back to Dublin. I'm tired and hungry."

Devan chuckled. "You're always hungry."

"No, it's just I eat whenever I am. I don't have to worry anymore where the next meal's coming from, or when."

"Oh." Devan felt abashed, remembering the circumstances of his youth. As they got in the car, she said, "I can drive, if you're tired."

"Have you ever driven on this side of the road? With the steering wheel on the right?"

She shook her head. "No, but it doesn't look difficult. And I'm an intelligent person. I'll figure it out."

"Not in my car. Not at night. Not on these roads." Christian turned the key and the engine roared to life. "I want to live to figure this out."

"You don't have to be obnoxious. I was only trying to help."

While Christian drove, Devan watched the landscape fade into the growing darkness. An hour later, she saw city lights in the distance. They entered Dublin as a light rain fell.

She turned to face him. "Yesterday, when you told me about the dreams, you said you read about the victims in the obituary. Do you remember the dates they died?"

"Better than that." Christian glanced at her. His lip curled toward a smile. "I saved the newspaper articles. I'm not sure the dates are listed, but the articles are dated."

"Maybe there's something—"

"I know what you're thinking," he interrupted, "but there's nothing about where any of them died, or where their bodies were found. Believe me, I read them so many times I practically memorized them."

Devan nodded, then realized he couldn't see her in the darkness. "Okay, but now we know more. Something might stand out that didn't make sense before. Besides, you have a fresh perspective—me."

"I'll swing by my place and get them."

Before she could object, he parked the car on a street with several run-down-looking buildings north of the Liffey. He looked past her, to the tan and brown building across the street.

Devan whipped her head around, but saw nothing except the concrete steps leading to the three-story building. The bare bulb over the entrance showed a well-worn oak door with rusted iron hinges.

Christian touched her arm. "This neighborhood may not look it, but it's fairly safe. Since it's dark, why don't you come with me? We'll only be a minute and then we'll have something to look over while we eat."

Hesitating, she stared into his cobalt eyes.

Could she trust him? He had confided his childhood and his dreams—neither shiny nor comfortable. She knew they were linked, somehow, just as he said. He had been nothing but a gentleman to her. She opened her door and stepped out, trusting him with her life.

Fifteen

Robert trudged up to the seedy hole-in-the-wall. There was no sign over the door, just a yellowed bulb that flickered. Off, then on, then off, as if it couldn't decide whether the place was open or not. He'd never been to this part of Dublin before. Just a few blocks north was the trendy section called Temple Bar, a few blocks east, the upscale shops of Grafton Street. While the Liberties had undergone a startling transformation, there were still pockets like this dive that catered to unsavory characters. People for hire that could blend in, not draw attention to themselves, who could seek out and follow the couple he was interested in. People like Logan, or one of his thugs.

Pulling the door open with a sweaty hand, Robert took one step inside. He let his eyes adjust to the dim haze of low-level lighting mixed with smoke. A scarred oak bar dominated the left side of the room. Standing behind it pouring drams of whiskey, the burly, carrot-topped publican narrowed his eyes as he looked Robert up and down. Three of the five square tables scattered around were occupied. Four dingy red leather booths lined the right wall. The noise level dropped slightly as patrons watched the newcomer with interest.

A lone man sat in the shadows of the far booth. Robert made his way past the groups seated at the tables and slid into the booth opposite Logan.

Robert glanced back at the men whose conversations resumed. "Um." He cleared his dry throat and started again. "I'm Rob—" Logan raised his hand, cutting off Robert before he could provide his full name. "I'm looking to, um…hire someone to find and trail someone, a woman. I'm told you're the man to talk to."

The mousy-haired man lifted a ratty eyebrow. "She your wife? Because I'm no P.I. looking to catch infidelities."

"No, no." Robert waved his hand. "It's nothing like that. I just need her followed, so I know where she goes and who she's with. I'd do it myself, but I have business I must attend to and can't afford to lose her." He'd been told Logan would not ask too many questions. He hoped that was true, because he didn't know how to explain why he needed the woman followed.

"So, you want a twenty-four hour tail." Logan smiled, showing uneven teeth as a jagged scar deepened on his chin.

Robert shuddered. A thin line of sweat trickled between his shoulder blades.

"That'll cost you. How long?" Logan shifted.

"At least a week. Maybe longer."

Logan took a long draft from his pint, studied him. "Five hundred euros for the week, plus expenses if my man needs to travel. Cash up front. What's her name and where's she now?"

Robert winced. "Um… I'm afraid I don't know that."

"Where she is, or her name?"

"Both," Robert said as he took an envelope from the breast pocket of his coat. He removed a photo of a woman with short, spiky brown hair talking with a middle-aged man. Rows and rows of books framed the duo. He handed the picture over. "She's American, probably staying near Trinity. She was with a man in his mid-twenties, just over six feet, with shoulder length black hair. They were very interested in the library at the college."

Logan looked at the picture. "The man here isn't mid-twenties."

"No. That's the guide from the library. I didn't get a clear shot of the person she was with, but I think he's from Dublin. He knew his way around Grafton and where to catch a taxi down there with all those one-way and closed-off streets."

"Having to find her first will cost extra. Another five hundred, unless you can narrow it down."

Robert swallowed, hard. He hadn't expected the price to be so steep. But he had to find the woman. He needed the power he sensed within her, and he still needed to find how to capture and contain the dragon power. What else could he do?

Glancing around to make sure he was not being watched, he nodded, reached into the envelope again, handed over the money, and a card with his phone number on it. He carefully pocketed his remaining euros.

Logan folded the cash, placing it and the card in his shirt pocket. "I'll keep the picture and call you when she's spotted."

Robert hesitated. He wanted assurances, but knew Logan wouldn't give any. So he nodded once more, slid out of the booth, and hurried from the smoke-filled pub.

He had to get away. Fast. He felt dirty, unclean—not from the smoke and alcohol. Could he trust Logan? It was too late now, he'd already paid him, so he'd see it through. With an hour before his next meeting, he walked north two blocks before finding a taxi. When he arrived home, he shucked his clothes, tossed everything into the hamper, stepped into the shower and scrubbed. Scrubbed himself pink. Twice.

Logan placed a phone call. He wanted his old mate for this job, but Christian had bailed on him last week, too good for the life anymore. Christian was the best pickpocket Logan had ever seen, the smartest and most resourceful. Yes, he could have used the boyo on this one—not for his quick fingers, but for his cool, level head under pressure. Oh well, Kelly would have to do. He wasn't very subtle, but he was persistent.

Ten minutes later, Kelly strolled nonchalantly into the bar, saw Logan in the booth, and held up two stubby fingers to the bar. Kelly sat in the spot vacated by Logan's newest twitchy customer. The publican brought two Guinness.

Lifting the fresh pint, Logan nodded his thanks. "I got a job for you." After tasting the dark stout, he explained the assignment and handed over the photograph.

Kelly rubbed a beefy hand over his crew cut. He studied the woman in the picture. "You're sure she's a tourist?"

"She's American." Logan smirked. "The client said she was keen on Trinity. Start there. Let me know when you find her. Here's two hundred. Full payment upon completion."

"Right." Kelly pocketed the money. "I'll be in touch." He downed the rest of his drink in one swallow. Then he left the pub in the same casual way he had arrived.

Satisfied, Logan nodded to his man tending the taps and departed.

An hour later, Robert met Cliff, his history professor friend, at the tiny tea shop in FitzWilliam Square.

"What can you tell me about Ireland's history as it pertains to mythical creatures?" Robert dove right in.

Cliff polished his thick glasses on the tattered hem of his V-neck jumper. "What? You, interested in history? Since when? You're the artistic type, always have been. Photography."

"I'm photographing Ireland's mythical places for a book." The lie came easily.

"They are certainly thousands of sites to choose from. Stone dances throughout the countryside," Cliff said.

"Yes, I know." Robert struggled with his impatience. "I'm interested in mythology that has to do with dragons specifically."

Cliff leaned back and stroked his bare chin. "Most of the dragon lore is of the Celtic variety. Dragons signify power. Power over the land. It was believed that where dragons frequented, power could be found. Similar to the Chinese idea of Feng Shui."

That caught Robert's attention.

"Also, dragons were strongly associated with water," Cliff continued. "Many took the form of sea serpents like Loch Ness. St. Patrick was credited with ridding Ireland of these monsters. The symbology is that dragons were the devil and when Christianity came to Ireland, the devil was banished."

"That doesn't help me much. Tell me…if dragons roamed Ireland today, where would they go?"

"They'd stay away from symbols of Christianity. Probably flock to the old Celtic strongholds. So again, stone circles and ancient Celtic ruins. Places like County Clare's Poulnabrone and the like. You'll need to get out of Dublin to find what you're looking for."

Robert jotted Cliff's speculations in his pocket-sized notebook.

"Of course, this is all academic, as dragons don't exist. Humankind has expanded. Where could dragons hide? Surely, nowhere close to humans, or they'd be seen," Cliff said.

As they ate, the idea of old Celtic sites occupied Robert's mind. That might explain why he encountered the dragonriders at the Burren and Carrowmore. But why at St. Declan's Well? That was a Christian place of worship. And what about Ballynahinch Lake? That wasn't associated with Celtic lore, was it?

The power had been strongest at Carrowmore's cemetery. There must be a connection with these Celtic places and the dragon power. Maybe it truly was his destiny to resurrect his wife and son.

Cliff interrupted Robert's thoughts when he scraped his empty plate on the table. "I better get back, I have class in twenty minutes. By the way, how's Bridget working out for you?"

Robert blanked for a moment, then recalled Cliff giving him the gypsy's number. "Fine. She knows about spell casting and other bits of oddities."

"Thanks for lunch. Let me know how the assignment works out."

"I'll be in touch. Maybe bounce more ideas off you when I decide on some sites."

"Call anytime," Cliff said. "You could come to dinner, you know. The wife would love to fuss. I realize it's been a bad time, but I'm glad you're getting back to living. Anne would've wanted that for you."

Sixteen

Sean pulled on his riding coat and gloves, absently pondering what Kiely was trying so hard to hide. Matthew called yesterday to relay the bizarre scene two nights ago—after days of not seeing the Ulster leader at the communal meal, she finally put in an appearance and left with an unusual statement as a parting shot. Matthew then tried to get his friend Peter to discuss Peter's grandmother's claim of working on clan business, but the lad was uncharacteristically mute on the subject.

Fionn, saddled and eager to fly, awaited his compeer. Sean mounted his dragon's offered foreleg and swung into position at the base of Fionn's neck.

"Let's be away," Sean bespoke. He waved to Aisling who had emerged from their house to see them off.

Fionn spread his blood-red wings to their full extension, bent his powerful legs, and leapt into the air with one swift down stroke. The next wingbeat increased his height off the ground by several meters and allowed him to catch an updraft and veer east, away from the livestock pens. Fionn gathered the magic around his body, allowing it to surround him for ten meters. The magic left no sign of their passing, no gust of wind, no shadow on the rolling hills below.

The countryside shimmered green with scattered patches of purple heather. From Sean's height, the land looked well tended, but he could not make out the size or condition of the crops. Part of this land was Matthew's responsibility, so these crops should be plentiful.

He knew he had to approach Kiely with care. Yes, she was his elder and the mother of Padrick, his right-hand man, but he was the clan leader. He would have to be firm, but not upset her in front of the other Ulster members. Like handling a spirited horse, he thought.

The woman was up to something. When she had a mission, she was tenacious. He'd witnessed her deviousness firsthand, when she campaigned against him for the leadership of the clan. She'd dug up everything she could to use against him—every infraction from his youth. When that failed, she demanded her family vote for her. Ronan had complied, though Sean couldn't really blame him. Padrick had defied his mother. Kiely had not forgiven her only son. The woman held a grudge and that made her dangerous. Sean didn't believe she would hurt the clan. Not intentionally. But Kiely didn't always grasp the whole picture. She wanted instant gratification and hang the consequences.

When the standing stones of Beaghmore came into view, Sean reined in his negative thoughts and concentrated on appealing to Kiely's vanity—her elder status and knowledge.

Fionn landed in the courtyard without circling first to avoid stirring up the livestock to the northwest. As Sean swung his leg over the saddle and slid down his compeer's polished scales to the ground, Kiely stepped out of her house. She signaled to her grandson and he hurried into the house with a glance back from the threshold.

Sean schooled his face into a smile—one he didn't feel in the least. He strode toward her. "Ulster Leader."

Kiely greeted him. "*Fáilte*, Clan Leader. To what do I owe the pleasure of your visit?" She gestured toward the Great Hall, away from her house. "Let us have some refreshments." Her sweet tone piqued his curiosity.

Sean opened the heavy wooden door and Kiely preceded him. Halfway to the back of the room, she stuck her head in the kitchen and requested snacks. She led him to her customary table along the back wall. Apparently, she didn't want to meet in her office, or anywhere near the house. Were the rumors true? Could Tullia be ill or injured?

Almost as though she heard his thoughts, Kiely said, "You caught us returning from our patrol. Almost everyone is still out, including Matthew. He'll be sorry he missed you."

One of the kitchen staff arrived with a tray of tea and sandwiches.

Sean waited for the server to leave before helping himself to a small, triangular cheese sandwich. He poured tea for both of them, adding lemon to Kiely's, then cream to his own.

"Thank you for sending Matthew and KIERAN to the council meeting last week. I hope all is well here. We missed you." Sean hoped to lure her reasons for not attending the meeting herself. She was not forthcoming. "How are the spring plantings?"

Kiely sipped her tea, her eyes narrowed. "We're right on schedule here in Ulster. I know the duties required of the clan better than you."

Sean bristled inwardly at her condescension, but gave her a neutral expression. Appeal to her experience. Keep calm.

"I just wanted to offer assistance, if needed. With our provinces lending help to both Munster and Connaught, I didn't want anyone feeling shorthanded or overburdened."

"Of course we're overburdened." Kiely slammed her hand on the table. "We're lacking four dragons and riders, and the two youngsters still won't take compeers." She huffed out a breath. "We wouldn't be in this predicament if I was clan leader, or if you'd listened to me about breeding more dragons."

Sean sighed. "You know the reasons for waiting. I was elected clan leader—for better or worse. I hope I can rely on your knowledge and ideas to help us through these difficult times. Just because I don't always agree with you, doesn't mean I don't value your opinion. Besides, the clan will need you and Ronan to continue flying. At least for another several years."

"We will do our duty. As always."

"I know you will." Sean needed each province leader on his side, especially the Ulster leader. Kiely must be kept busy so she would stay out of trouble. "Could you look at one of the murder weapons? Between you and Ronan, maybe you know someone who could provide a clue to the killer. I'm checking with the curator of the museum in Dublin, but your contacts could be invaluable."

"I repeat," Kiely said, "we will do our duty. Rest assured, Ronan and I will be discrete."

Sean pulled a dagger, sealed in plastic, out of his coat pocket. He handed it to her. "All four are identical."

Kiely turned the weapon over and over, viewing it from every possible angle. "You wiped off the blood."

Before Sean could respond, the front door burst open and several young riders entered, Matthew leading the way. The others stopped to remove riding gear at the cubicles near the door. Sean stood and skirted the table as his son strode toward them. Kiely rose as well, leaving the dagger on the table.

Even at six and twenty, Matthew embraced his father with a lopsided grin. "Da, it's good to see you. How's Mum?" Matthew crammed the last two inquiries as his brow furrowed.

Sean clasped his son's shoulders. "She's fine, sends her love."

Matthew's gaze drifted to the table and the item left at its center.

Kiely's lips thinned into a slight frown.

"We were just discussing some clan business," Sean explained. "I'm asking for help with the murder weapon." He swept his gaze over the approaching riders. "How's Kieran?"

Matthew glanced between the Ulster leader and his father. "Growing bigger every day, it seems. He would leave us with no cattle, no sheep, if I didn't rein him in."

Kiely laughed—a rough, halting cackle. "It's true. The young one is always hungry."

Sean chuckled, too. "All young dragons are until they reach maturity."

"You mean he'll eat like this for another two years?" Matthew's eyebrows rose.

Both leaders nodded and Matthew groaned. Sean placed his arm around his son's shoulder, squeezed, held him.

Matthew rolled his eyes. "I'm done for the day, except for monitoring Kieran's food intake. Are you staying for dinner? It's in about an hour. Besides, you could impart your wisdom and self-control on my compeer. He'll listen to the clan leader."

Kiely interrupted them, addressing Sean. "I need to see to Tullia and check on the returning teams. Spend some time with your son. We'll talk again during the meal, and I'll bring Ronan up to speed." She grabbed the dagger from the table and strode from the dining room, leaving Sean and Matthew staring at her retreating back.

Father and son left the hall. They stepped out into the fading light of day, in time to see Ronan dismount from his pearl-white dragon, CALHOUN. Not bothering to greet the clan leader, Ronan retreated into his and Kiely's house.

Matthew glared at the closed door.

"I have to trust they won't put the clan in danger." Sean sighed. "But I know they're up to something."

Seventeen

Over a late dinner, Christian and Devan dissected the four obituaries. Details were sparse. Each took less than three inches of space, including a picture of the deceased. Just the facts were listed: name, age, county of residence. Christian found it interesting that the four were from different counties. None from Dublin.

After he walked Devan to her room, he strode back to the lift, his hands closed into fists and his jaw clenched in frustration. They hadn't found any reason why these people had been murdered or how he was involved. At the reception desk, he inquired about a room for the night. No luck. The hotel was full from a convention.

Christian returned to his flat. Sinking into the worn cushions of the couch, Christian studied the obituaries, his gaze alighting on the first victim. He stretched out, his head on the rounded sofa arm. He'd rest for a few minutes, then study the papers again. His breathing slowed, his chest rose and fell in a steady rhythm, his eyes twitched behind closed lids. He slipped into the dream.

A light breeze drifted from the sea bringing a salt tang and fish smell up the gorse-covered and boulder-strewn slope. White billowing clouds floated lazily overhead, breaking up the azure expanse of the sky. An autumn sun warmed his face as he lifted it, breathing deeply. Feelings of love surged in him. Coming here again brought closure, he thought, as the binds around his heart loosened. Waves slapped the shoreline in a steady cadence that beat in time with his lightened heart.

At the crest of a hill, he came upon the cylindrical tower that loomed over the village tucked at the feet of the sea. The slender stone tower stood ten stories tall with its conical roof still in place. Cathedral ruins lay nearby. He climbed over hills of grass and purple heather that swayed in the breeze. He continued on a well-worn path leading through a shrub-covered stone archway.

The sounds of the sea faded as he passed under the green and gray arch, even though the waves crashed against the rocks below and to his right. He continued on the path toward another stone structure, this one topped with three stone crosses standing guard and two open rock entrances. Peacefulness settled over him.

As he approached the structure, he saw a man in a white button-down shirt, sleeves rolled to his elbows, mud-colored work pants, and scuffed black boots crouched down in the larger entryway. The dark-blond-haired man filled a bottle from the well. The serenity he felt moments before dissipated like a stiff breeze, and anger tinged with remorse took its place. He was not alone in his sanctuary. There would be no closure today. At the sound of footsteps, the man spun around, staring with his mouth open, ready to form words.

Without warning, a dagger hurled through the stillness toward the man attempting to stand. The glass bottle slipped from his hand to the ground, the liquid turning a small patch of dirt to mud. The air between the blade and the target shimmered. A washed-out yellow dragon with outstretched wings materialized, shrieked once, then vanished. The man slumped against the stone structure between the two openings as the dagger quillion and haft protruded from his chest. Jewels from the haft sparkled in the sunlight, shooting a rainbow of color across the man's white shirt. A pool of deep red spread outward from the wound. Gurgling emanated from the gaping mouth, reddish-pink foam trickled out of the corners. The man breathed no more.

Power, joy, and hope surged, electrifying the air. He swayed, falling to his knees on the trampled dirt and grass. His fingertips tingled. The short hairs on his forearms and the back of his neck stood on end. A roaring like the crashing of waves pounded in his ears. His heart beat fiercely in his chest until he thought it would burst.

Christian bolted upright. The dim light and the coolness of the pre-dawn air jolted him from the dream. The doum, tekka, tekka, doum of his heart, like a bodhrán master plying his trade, was the only sound. His hands shook as he reached for the blanket on the back of the couch.

Calm down, he thought, it was only the dream. Again. But, this one was more intense, more vivid, more real.

Rubbing the back of his neck, knowing he wouldn't get back to sleep, he rose to start a pot of tea. Might as well put the time to good use and record everything he could remember. With several biscuits balanced on the rim of his cup and the full pot of steaming tea in his other hand, he returned to the couch.

Christian's gaze drifted to the obituaries scattered on the low birch table in front of him. As he shuffled the papers into a neat stack, the murdered man in his dream stared up at him. Conor Flannigan. Conor from County Waterford had been twenty-nine at the time of his death. Not much older than himself.

The man sported a goatee on a square face. His pudgy nose hooked slightly left of center, drawing attention away from his eyes. In the photo Conor smiled, showing white, even teeth—not so in the dream. Christian had seen Conor's back muscles straining under his shirt when he whipped around, just before he died.

Christian wrote Conor's name and pertinent information down, then noted both the victim's description and the location of the murder. To the best of his recollection, this was the first time the dream started without the victim already in sight. Maybe that fact was significant. He also recorded what he could remember of the feelings and emotions that slammed into him from the beginning until the end.

He thought Devan could decipher the location from his description. As he sipped a fresh cup of tea and polished off the last biscuit, his mind drifted to her. He marveled at her courage and her unerring ability to look at each situation in a positive light. In so many ways they were opposites. They shouldn't get along as well as they did. But they complemented each other. He liked her logical nature. She could have bolted with all he told her, but she stuck. Even contributed, as he now knew more about his pendant and his dreams than ever before.

At half seven, he could wait no longer and dialed her hotel, asked for her room. She answered on the third ring, out of breath.

Christian's heart leapt into his throat. "Are you okay? Is someone with you?"

"I'm fine, you caught me coming out of the shower is all. What's up?"

"Nothing." His heart slowed to normal. "That's not quite true. I had another dream. Very intense."

"Are you okay?" Devan's voice softened. "Want to talk about it?"

Christian smiled. Definitely an optimist, he thought. "Yes, but not on the phone. Can I come over?"

"Sure. I'll see you when you get here."

Before she could hang up, he said, "Devan. Do me a favor, stay in your room until I get there. Ten minutes." He hung up and bolted.

Nine and a half minutes later, he requested the hotel clerk ring Devan's room.

She exited the lift looking relaxed. Tension drained out of him. Her smile made his heart beat faster.

Christian returned the smile. "Good morning. You look rested."

She reached for his hands. "You, not so much. Bad?"

"Not really, just…intense. Very detailed this time." He squeezed her hands before letting go. "Let's sit and I'll take you through it."

Devan headed away from the alcove they had occupied several times already, toward the lift.

He raised an eyebrow in question as they waited for the door to open.

Devan grinned then pulled him inside the chrome and faux wood paneled car. "My laptop and guidebooks are in my room. I trust you. Besides, the way you look, I could take you down with both hands tied together." A brief frown marred her face, then disappeared so fast he thought he imagined it.

When the lift door opened, they stepped out onto carpet the color of stormy skies, stopped at the second door on the right, and entered a standard-sized hotel room. A double bed took up most of the space in the center. To the right, a small secretariat snugged under the open floral drapes of the room's only window. The left wall held an oak bureau with a television on top and a door leading into the bathroom.

Christian disregarded the tidied bed with its functional white sheets and pillows smoothed under a forest green comforter. He sat on the lone chair with Devan's laptop humming on the desk, a photo of a stone circle as the screensaver. The smell of soap faded into the humidity emanating from the bath. Light, clean, the scent of fresh rain.

She sat on the bed facing him, her hands clasped tight in her lap, betraying her earlier bravado.

Christian unzipped his jacket, pulled out the folded obituaries and his notes. He breathed deep to calm his thoughts. "I was reviewing the obituaries and must've been more tired than I thought, because I fell asleep and into the dream. I dreamed of Conor, the first murder victim." His hands trembled when he handed her Conor's obituary. "It was September of last year."

His voice was no more than a whisper as he recounted the dream. His gaze focused on the middle distance between them as he experienced the vision again, the notes in his hand forgotten. As the telling drew to a close, Christian's heart drummed in his chest and he gasped for breath. He couldn't get enough oxygen in his lungs. Sweat beaded on his forehead. Blackness crept inward as his vision blurred.

Devan shoved his head between his knees and he closed his eyes. The roaring in his ears slowly dissipated, the nausea bubbling up his throat subsided, and the shaking stopped.

Her voice broke through. "You're okay now. Deep breaths, that's it. A few more. Slow and easy." Her breath warmed the top of his head. Denim-covered knees crouched in front of him. Her hand held him in place. His notes lay scattered at his feet. "Can you sit up?" When he nodded, she lifted her hand and sat back on her heels. Lines etched her face with worry as she pushed a hand through her hair. "You scared the crap out of me. Has that ever happened before?" She didn't give him time to answer. "*Don't* do it again."

"Water." He managed to croak through dry lips.

Water splashed from the loo as Christian wiped his face with both hands. He pushed his hair away. Two deep breaths and Devan shoved a glass in his unsteady hands. He sipped. The cool liquid quenched his raw throat, soothed his upset stomach, and cleared the turbulence from his mind.

"Thanks," he said after draining the glass.

"What happened?" Devan took the empty glass from his now steady hands. "One minute you're describing the dagger shimmering through a silhouette of a yellow dragon and impaling this Conor fellow, the next you're hyperventilating and on the verge of passing out."

"Immense power. I tried to tell you earlier, but I felt it again. Very strong.

Then…a feeling of joy and hope, of stumbling upon an answer of some kind." Christian shook his head. "It doesn't make sense, there should be shock and remorse and disgust at taking a life. But, whoever committed this heinous act feels thrilled and alive." He retrieved his notes. "I wrote it all down. The obituary listed County Waterford as his last known residence. We should start there."

Devan nodded and returned the glass to the loo.

Christian thumbed through the guidebook on her desk until he found the section on County Waterford and Southern Ireland.

"Can I see your notes?" Devan asked as she sat. She skimmed the pages, mumbling about a tower and roofless stone cathedral, a stone arch covered in greenery, and a well with three worn stone crosses. "Look for a village along the coast with a conical round tower and cathedral on a hill above the bay."

He held the book out to her. "I found it. Ardmore, the Celtic Sea, and Saint Declan's Oratory and Well."

Taking the guidebook, Devan flipped between several pages. "I guess we know where we're going next." Before he could protest, she held up a hand. "I'm following any clues that connect my ring with these events."

"A man was murdered there, right between those openings in the well. A sacred well that offered no protection…"

Devan touched his arm. "This isn't the place you saw me in your dream. I'm not killed there." She sighed. "We'll take precautions, but there might be a clue to the killer's identity. We could go to the police—"

"No Gardaí." Christian rubbed perspiration from the back of his neck. "They'll think I'm crazy, lock me up, toss the key into Dublin Harbor."

She smiled. "You're probably right. Let's go find ourselves a killer."

Eighteen

Devan packed in thirty minutes and they drove south, down the coast, to Waterford City. She had hoped to see parts of Ireland, not just the big cities, but she hadn't envisioned doing so on the heels of a killer. Why she trusted Christian she couldn't say, only that she did.

She contemplated what little she knew of her ring and how she and Christian were connected. It was obvious the same person crafted the two pieces of jewelry. Was it the shop owner in Dublin? The woman definitely acted suspicious after their visit.

When Christian turned inland, Devan broke from her musings. Rain splattered the windows. Christian turned on the wipers and slowed to check each road sign. At Waterford City, the rain moved on and a brilliant rainbow crossed from the low mountains in the north to the sea in the south.

"Let's stop and eat. I don't know how large Ardmore is, or if they have lodging and a pub," Christian said.

"We can ask about Conor, find out where he lived."

"How?"

"At the library here. They should have some records—I hope," she muttered.

Kelly hurried to his car to follow the woman. He would update Logan when he had the chance. For now, he didn't want to lose his quarry. Not after everything he went through to track her to the hotel. He stayed two cars behind until they were out of Dublin. Once outside the city limits however, traffic lightened and he was hard pressed to remain inconspicuous. Two hours later, when the blue Audi stopped in Waterford City, he circled the street the couple parked on, then saw them enter a pub. He filled up with petrol and called in his report and location. After the pub, the couple visited the library. Kelly ate a cold lunch in his car.

Devan dragged a hand through her hair in frustration. "How can there be no record? The obituary listed Waterford as his place of residence, right?"

Christian pulled out the clipping. "It says that he lived in County Waterford, not necessarily here in Waterford City."

"There should at least be a birth certificate and a record of his death. It's odd. Like somebody doesn't want us to find out what really happened. I think after we visit Ardmore and Saint Declan's Well, we better investigate the other victims' counties of residence."

"Let's get to this murder site first."

"Maybe I can ask for Conor at the local police station. Say I'm a friend, a pen-pal that heard he died and wanted to pay my respects to his family."

Christian shook his head. "Too dangerous. If it were a conspiracy, then we'd just alert them to our interest. Besides, he may not have family living. How would you explain that you don't know much about him?"

Devan glared at him. "Do you have a better idea?"

"Not really, but yours is risky. We'll continue on to Ardmore, then see where we go from there."

Christian glanced north to the grassy hill above the village of Ardmore. The clouds loomed overhead, the skies gray and streaked with fading blue, the sun lowered toward the western horizon. If the rain held off, the sunset would be spectacular with bold reds and oranges layering over the blue ocean and green outstretched peninsula.

Through the windscreen, he viewed the tower with its three horizontal stone bands that separated the imposing height into unequal measures. The windows below the conical top gave it the appearance of a rocket, ready for takeoff.

Dread filled him. Would he find the place familiar? Had he been here before? Was he the killer? A cold sweat popped out on his forehead at the thought. He wiped his face with unsteady hands and looked to see if Devan noticed his unease.

Her attention centered on the hill and its stone inhabitants.

He sighed. "No time like the present. Looks like we hike from here."

As they exited the car, Devan grabbed her camera and a notebook. At his raised eyebrow, she responded. "We should document the site. Also, we'll look less suspicious if we act like tourists."

Ardmore Bay stretched out like a blue-gray swath under layers of storm cloud-filled skies. What sunlight existed was weak. The air turned damp and the wind kicked up to blow Devan's short hair into disarray. Christian heard the crashing of the waves and zipped his jacket to his chin. The beat of the Celtic Sea kept time with his heart.

Devan wandered into the roofless ruin and stepped in front of a carved pillar stone. Christian leaned on the entrance as she ran her hand over the symbols from long ago. This place didn't hold the same recognition for him as Newgrange. He hoped that meant he'd never walked here physically, only in his dreams.

Rough stones broke the ground to mark burial sites. Flowers waved over the rolling ground. Devan strolled out, looked at the carved images on the three archways of the cathedral that the passage of time had faded. Christian was sure she knew whom the images portrayed, and would tell him if he asked. He didn't want to know.

Christian left her and inspected the adjacent gravesite. Conor Flannigan had been killed here, but his body placed elsewhere to be discovered. Would he be buried here, where he died? Christian saw the markers of the dead, but not one new enough for a recent burial. Nearly all held flowers. The dead lived here once, and Christian knew they were still remembered. He thought of the cemetery near his flat and an ache welled in his chest. He headed back to where he left Devan.

They took the curved path toward the ocean leading to Saint Declan's

Well and its stone crosses. Emerging under the vine-covered archway, they stood in silent contemplation as if honoring Conor—the man they knew almost nothing about. Devan reached for Christian's arm and held it tight. They crossed the distance to the well.

Christian stared transfixed at the well front with its two openings: a meter and a half tall by a half meter wide on the left and a blocky meter by meter square on the right. The scene was exactly the same as in his dream, including the scent of the grass and dirt and stone. Christian couldn't breathe, just couldn't get enough air to fill his lungs. He gasped, sucked in the life-saving oxygen in greedy gulps.

Devan squeezed his hand until he looked at her. He forced a twitch of his lips he hoped resembled a reassuring smile and nodded. She let go and surveyed the surrounding landscape.

He crouched, avoiding the muddy ground in front of the right entrance, where Conor had knelt six months ago. Christian gazed at the spot where he stood in his dream, expecting…expecting what? A dagger hurling through space? A dragon to materialize?

Instead, the dream sequence sprang clear in his mind. Would Conor have felt fear or terror when faced with someone brandishing a dagger? Why would he? He had a dragon, a beast the size of a two-room flat covered in scales, to protect him. And yet, Conor had died. The dragon had vanished—possibly dead.

Christian pulled himself out of the fatalistic vision. Even with the area clear of everyone but Devan and himself, he shuddered.

She joined him, leaning into the second opening. "It feels sacred. How could anyone take a life here?"

"Anger." Christian stared, sightless. "The killer came here to remember, to memorialize someone he lost. Someone special. Someone he loved. He was angry to find another person here. All he wanted was absolution for his part in the loss." Christian's voice strengthened with certainty. Relief replaced the apprehension. He took several deep breaths, then looked at Devan. "I don't think the killer planned this murder. The unexpected circumstances, confused feelings, all helped push him over the line."

"That doesn't explain the other three murders, all with a similar weapon."

"No, but remember the feelings of power I felt? Maybe once he got the taste for it, he needed to keep feeding his appetite."

Devan mussed her hair. "Why kill at four different locations? Why move the bodies to Newgrange? If he really wanted to help the dead into the afterlife, that one act seems like remorse to me."

"Perhaps the Gardaí was on to him and he had to get out of Waterford County."

"So many questions, and no real answers. I'm going to wander, take some photos."

Christian nodded, but stayed where Conor lost his life.

They may not have all the answers, but he had arrived at an important conclusion. Today was the first time he walked over this ground, laid his eyes upon Saint Declan's Well and Oratory in person. He felt relief at the knowledge that he wasn't the murderer.

Christian found Devan taking pictures of the village. He peered at the clouds amassing overhead. "We should start back, it's going to rain soon."

The sun played hide-and-seek as they retraced the path to the car. They reached the shelter of the vehicle just as the skies opened. The rain battered the metal roof. Lightning flashed over the distant mountains. Thunder shook their sanctuary.

Devan shuddered. "That came on fast. Ferocious, too."

"Better find a place for the night. I don't fancy driving in this."

"I think there's a hotel overlooking the bay."

Christian nodded, then started the engine. Within minutes, the car's headlights illuminated the three-story, white hotel.

Lightning continued to slash overhead with thunder only seconds behind. The rain increased until the wipers couldn't keep pace. As he parked, the rain turned to marbles of hail.

"Let's run for it," he said. "Leave the bags, I'll come back after this blows over."

They exited the car and bolted for the safety of the hotel entrance.

No sooner had they crossed the threshold, than thunder boomed, and the hotel plunged into darkness.

Kelly again followed the late model Audi as they continued southwest into the tiny town of Ardmore. He played the role of tourist, snapping pictures of the town and the tall tower while the couple hiked the trail. Kelly stayed far enough back to remain unseen.

Nothing about the woman struck him as exceptional. This didn't stop him from speculating, however. She wasn't beautiful, with her hair cut short and spiked up around her head. The pair seemed comfortable with each other, yet they weren't lovers. He focused his attention and his camera lens, on the man. So familiar, but he couldn't place where or how he knew him.

He hid behind some shrubbery when the couple started back, then followed close behind. He was still ten meters away when the downpour began.

"Shite. Where'd that come from?" He stuffed his camera under his wet jumper and hunched his shoulders. "Hurry up and leave already."

Lightning flashed in the distance and instinctively he ducked. He knew they couldn't see him. Their car's engine roared to life on the heels of the next thunder boom. The Audi crawled into the roadway heading to town. A sodden mess, Kelly scrambled into his own car. Stopping on the road near the hotel, he watched the couple dash for the entrance. The building went dark.

Several minutes passed with no motion at the hotel entrance. Only the pounding rain and hail. Kelly approached the Audi on foot, stopped at the rear, and bent, pretending to tie his shoe. While hunched, he popped the lock, and rifled through the woman's suitcase and the man's smaller weekender. Clothes and toiletries, nothing more. He set the boot to rights and closed the lid with a thud. A quick flick of his wrist and he attached a magnetic tracking device to the bumper, hidden from view. He glanced into the back seat and discovered a backpack. Before he could pull out his tools again, the hotel door opened.

His quarry emerged, heads bent against the heavy rains. They headed his way. Quickening his stride, Kelly passed them.

He heard the woman say, "I just want my backpack, all the research is in it."

As Kelly pulled the entrance door open, the hotel lights blazed bright, blinding him momentarily. The backup generator must have kicked on. While his eyes adjusted, he wiped rain from his face and ran a hand over his crew cut, scattering droplets.

People milled about infusing the lobby with noise. Kelly wandered through the crowd at the restaurant entrance. He faced the lobby just as the couple re-entered, backpack slung over the woman's shoulder. They climbed the stairs at the far side of the reception desk.

Kelly approached the receptionist to procure a room and noticed the couple had signed in as Mr. and Mrs. Michael Collins. Fancied themselves rebels, did they? Regardless of their alias, they had been given the last room, number 214. Kelly didn't relish the idea of sleeping in his cramped car with a storm thrashing its wild temper down on him.

Several minutes later the couple returned to the lobby, empty-handed. They took a table in the restaurant and Kelly waited until the server took their orders before heading upstairs.

The lock clicked open and Kelly slipped into the darkened room. A narrow beam from his torch swept left then right, stopping on the backpack sitting open on the breakfast table. He rummaged through the main compartment finding a camera, tourist maps, and several notebooks with papers folded neatly between the pages. In the front compartment he found three framed photos wrapped in a worn, UC Berkeley T-shirt. Studying the faces, he realized they must be the woman's relatives. He rewrapped the photos, then reached deeper until his hand grasped a wooden box. He pulled it clear. The mahogany glowed deep red under the torchlight. Warm and smooth sides contrasted with an engraved design on the lid.

Kelly traced the dragon engraving with the pad of his thumb. He opened the lid and found cufflinks and a godlike figurine wrapped in a white handkerchief. Nothing of value, he thought in disgust. Even the cufflinks would bring no more than fifty euros. The engraved box was interesting, but again wouldn't bring much coin. He replaced the wrapped figurine in the box and stuffed the cufflinks in his pocket.

He rifled through the notebook pages and read each folded paper. Four obituaries? Why were they interested in four dead people? Kelly flinched as he heard voices in the hall. Shutting the notebook, he shoved everything back in the pack, and doused his torch. He twisted the lock and scrambled through the glass balcony door into the rain, just as the room door jiggled. The door locked behind him.

Despite the pounding rain, Kelly's breath sounded harsh in his ears. He shifted away from the glass, into a corner. The darkness would hide him from the couple, but nothing could hide him from the storm. He huddled there, cursing the weather, cursing the couple in the warm, dry room, cursing his ill luck. He vowed the woman would pay.

"Stop!" Christian grabbed Devan's arm before she reached for the door handle. "Someone's been here."

She stumbled back a step as he bent to examine the lock and pick something from the floor.

"What? How do you know?" Her voice lowered to a whisper.

"The telltale's not where I left it and the lock's scratched."

As she peered over his shoulder, Christian pointed to the knob and then a fine, black hair that lay on the hall carpet. "I stuck the hair across the knob. Only someone opening the door would cause it to fall."

Stepping past him, Devan opened the door and flipped the switch to illuminate the room. "I'm not sure I want to know how you learned that or why you felt the need, but it could've been the housekeeper to turn down the beds." She stared dumbstruck at the bed. One bed. *Where's the other one?* She collided with Christian as he stepped into the room. Feeling the heat rise in her cheeks, she gasped as he reached to steady her.

"What's the matter?" Christian pulled her behind him. "Who'd you see?"

Before she could answer, he moved to the bathroom door, his finger pressed over his lips, a silent warning, and pushed open the door. Empty. He whirled to the closet and repeated the search. Dropping to the floor, he checked under the bed then stood and checked the balcony door. Locked.

From her vantage point, Devan only saw the room reflected back. When Christian's gaze returned to her, she shook her head.

"I didn't see anyone. But…"

"What?"

"There's…there's only one bed."

Christian chuckled. "I hadn't noticed. Besides, it was the only room available. Shelter-seekers can't be picky. That's not the most urgent issue. The maid wasn't here. So who was? And why? Check your pack."

Devan sprinted to the table, opened the pack and pulled out the pictures, then the mahogany box. A sigh escaped her lips. Opening the box lid, she removed the wrapped figurine, gasped, then looked at Christian with tears in her eyes.

"They're gone." Her voice trembled, then broke on a sob.

"What's gone?"

The wooden box shook in her hands. "The cufflinks. My father's favorite. I gave them to him for Christmas last year."

Christian took the box, set it on the table, then lifted her chin. "Is anything else missing?"

When Devan continued to stare, he nodded toward the backpack.

The movement broke her trance. She pulled out the notebooks, maps, and finally her camera. "No, it's all here. Except the cufflinks. Why take them and not the camera? It's more expensive." Tears fell down her cheeks.

Christian gathered her in his arms. Devan tried not to stiffen, then finally relaxed into Christian's warmth as he soothed her.

"The camera would have been noticed right away. The cufflinks, not so much. How often do you open the box?" Christian asked.

She shook her head. "Not often," she admitted. "I just wanted something of my parents, to carry with me, to feel close to them. I know it's crazy. It's not them, but…"

"It's okay." He patted her back, then released her. "Can you describe the cufflinks? I'll talk with the manager, find out if they've had other thefts."

Devan sat and peered at the now empty box. "They were silver with an oblong, onyx stone at the center. His initials were inlayed in silver within the black stone—JF, Joseph Fraser."

The rain slowed outside. Lightning flashed in the distance and several seconds passed before the rumble of thunder arrived.

Christian knelt before her. "I'll get our bags and check with the front desk. Will you be okay here?"

"Yeah, just hurry."

"We don't have to stay." He wiped a tear from her cheek. "The storm's heading out to sea. We could go somewhere else."

She laid her hand over Christian's on her cheek. "No. It's late. I'm tired and you are too. There may not be anywhere else for miles."

"I'll be right back." Christian stood.

When the door shut behind him, Devan stabbed stiff fingers into her hair, then rose to wash her face. The crying jag drained her. A thick robe hung on the back of the door. She ran a bath and lay in the luxurious warmth. Memories of her parents flooded her mind. She let the memories come, wrapping them around her as she did the robe—soft and close.

Kelly rose stiff and wet from the terrace corner. He peeked into the room, saw no movement, and considered his escape. The squish of his soaked shoes brought him up short. Could he risk walking through the room, leaving a trail? Before he could fumble his lock pick out of its case, the room door opened and the man re-entered. With the choice taken out of his hands, he moved back into the shadowed corner, and looked down. The long drop didn't bother him. It was the darkness, not knowing what lay below.

Just do it before you get caught, he thought.

He scaled the rail, lowered himself as far as he could, then dropped into the dying storm. His shoes cushioned the impact but the tough rosebush thorns pierced his clothes, carved grooves in his legs and arms, drew blood.

Oh yes, he thought, this woman will suffer.

When Devan came out of the bath, Christian stood watching room service set the table. Devan's suitcase and backpack rested on the low dresser opposite the bed.

Christian tipped the waiter, walked him to the door, then motioned Devan to the table. "Since we only had tea downstairs, I'm starved. Let's eat." He lifted the cover off two orders of fish and chips. "The manager says she's had no reports of theft. She vouched for all her people." Christian savored a forkful of beer-battered fish. "With the weather and the hotel having a backup generator, the place is packed—guests, diners, and anyone looking to dry off. Said it could be anyone. Could've gone missing before we arrived, for that matter, as we weren't away from our room for long."

Devan looked up. "But you don't think so."

"We can't be sure they weren't stolen before tonight, but that doesn't explain the lock and my tell." He shook his head. "So, no. They were taken from this room. What do you want to do about it?"

She toyed with a French fry. "They weren't expensive, just held sentimental value. I want them back. But since we aren't staying and I don't know where we're headed, there's no point going to the police."

"We could backtrack to Waterford City to check with pawn and jewelry shops. Go to Cork, as well, as it's the largest nearby town."

Devan pushed her half empty plate away. "I appreciate it. We'll inquire if there are likely shops wherever we end up, but the cufflinks aren't my dad, and whoever stole them can't steal my memories of him. My love for him." She blew her nose.

Christian stacked the plates. "Why don't you rest, you look knackered."

"Knackered?" She lifted her lips in a wobbly smile.

"Tired, exhausted." He raised a brow. "What?"

"Nothing. I haven't heard that word since my grandma used it. I was six or seven. Where are you going to sleep?"

"The bed." He chuckled. "Don't worry, I'm too knackered for anything more than sleep." He grabbed his bag, went into the bathroom, leaving her standing with her mouth agape.

Not wanting to smell fried fish first thing in the morning, Devan placed the dinner dishes outside the door, and pulled her pajamas and toiletry bag from her suitcase.

As Christian emerged attired in another hotel robe, she swept by him to ready for bed.

The nerve of the man, she thought. Then laughed softly. Just because you're attracted to him, doesn't mean he wants you.

Devan felt a blush rush up her throat and fill her cheeks with color. Splashing cool water over her face, she finished dressing, then returned to the darkened room. The dim light of the moon illuminated Christian's six-foot frame on the far side of the bed. The double bed that now looked smaller than a twin-size. Could she sleep with him so close?

Coward, she thought, just sleep. She climbed in, curled on her side facing away from him—the devilish smile, deep cobalt eyes, and ink-black hair of the infamous Black Irish.

In the morning, Devan awoke warm and curled around a pillow. Except the pillow smelled like a man, had an arm holding her, and was kissing her. Still sleepy, she kissed him back, sliding her tongue in when his mouth opened. Her body softened against his hard, angular one. He was hard all over and she moaned with the sensations sweeping through her.

The kiss intensified as he rolled her onto her back and his weight pressed her into the mattress. When his lips traveled down her neck, she sighed and opened her eyes. The black hair startled her. That's not right, she thought, Rick was blond. And he never kissed like this, never let her feel his desire rest heavy between them.

Her memory returned. With reluctance, she dislodged Christian.

He opened his eyes, blinking away the dregs of sleep.

Devan blushed. "Sorry." Her face flushed with embarrassment, her body flushed with desire. She scooted backward and fell off the bed. The quilt fell with her. Mortified, she scrambled to cover Christian.

He lay exposed in snug, black underwear. Very snug. His muscular chest, his flat stomach, and about a yard of leg was exposed.

Where's his robe? He was obviously comfortable wearing so little. Before Devan could escape, Christian grabbed her arm, and pulled her down. Caught off guard, she overbalanced and fell against him.

"I'm not." Christian's voice, Irish and smoky rough as a peat fire, was as sexy as the rest of him. "I've wanted to kiss you since that first night, after the attempted mugging." He lifted his hands to her face and kissed her again. Long and deep. "You're such a contradiction. Strong and sure, then vulnerable. So compelling. So attractive."

Regaining her balance, Devan tried to break free, to no avail. "If it's one thing I know, I'm not compelling or attractive."

Christian ran a finger across her jaw. "I don't know who told you that, but they're wrong. Or maybe they didn't take time to get to know you. Since I've met you, you continually surprise me. I said before, I'm jealous of you—your drive to find your place, your heritage. I'm also envious of your honesty, your willingness to show your emotions." His finger lifted her chin, his eyes capturing hers. "Tell me what you're feeling now."

Through her thin cotton pajamas, Devan was acutely aware of the heat of his body, the minuscule boxer briefs he wore. The heat rose up to her face as she remembered the passionate kiss.

"I've embarrassed you." Christian released her.

She sat up, leaned against the pillow. "I thought you were too knackered for more than sleep."

He sat across from her. "That was last night. Besides, you're the one who curled into me."

"You kissed me, while I was still half asleep."

"And you responded, intimately." Christian smiled as he reached for her hands, kissing one then the other. "I know you're attracted to me, as I am to you. So why stop?"

Devan pulled her legs up to her chest, wrapped her loosened hands around them, and laid her head on her knees. "This is too fast. I'm not good at relationships." Lifting her head, she stared into his eyes. Eyes that reminded her of the blue depths of Lake Tahoe. "I don't know you very well. Yes, I'm attracted to you, but I'm a mess. I just lost my parents. I'm in a foreign country searching for answers. And now the two of us are on the trail of a killer. Not just a killer of humans, but of dragons—a creature that isn't supposed to exist. That's a lot to handle all at once. I need time. Time to know you. Hell, time to know myself."

Christian smiled. "Okay, that's fair. I don't force myself on women. I'm not going anywhere and I can wait."

"While you wait, can you get dressed?"

"Distracting you, am I?" He quirked a brow as the corner of his mouth lifted into a wicked grin. "No, I think I like making you nervous, flustering you. It puts a glow on your face."

She sighed. "We have more important things to worry about. I'd like to see if there are public records here. And then I think we should head toward the hometown of the second victim."

"I asked the manager last night if they have a library or Town Hall for records. She said Waterford City or Cork are the closest." Christian rose and headed for the bathroom. Leaning on the door jamb he asked, "Can you get the obituaries and the notes?"

Devan waited until he closed the door before retrieving her backpack. She heard the shower start. Closing her eyes, she rubbed her lips. She could still feel the heat of his kiss. "Get a grip," she told herself. "You can't start anything with him, you don't know how long you'll be here."

The shower shut off. Devan scrambled off the bed, rummaged for clean clothes, then placed the notebook and obituaries on the table. She wanted out of her pajamas and into something that would ease her vulnerability.

Christian stepped into the room, looked at the items in her hand, and motioned her through the door.

Devan skirted past. "Obituaries are on the table. I won't be long." She closed the door behind her.

When she re-entered the room, Christian stood over a map spread on the table. He traced a finger along its western edge.

"Did you dream last night?" Devan peeked over his shoulder. Lord, he smelled good. She took a quick step back, seeking distance—physical and emotional.

Christian faced her. "Actually, for the first time in quite a while, I dreamed of pleasant things." He pulled her to him and kissed her.

Her eyes closed. The heat of his lips on hers, his body against hers, his hands intertwined with hers, warmed her as the shower could not. She moaned as he deepened the kiss. With the sanity she still possessed, Devan broke contact, and stepped away before she did something she might regret.

Nineteen

The white daffodils Robert held didn't lessen his trepidation, his guilt. He heard the cooing before he saw the gray dove next to his customary bench. Anne would have had crumbs handy for such a chance encounter. He had nothing.

"Sorry." He held his hand open to show the bird it was empty. "She's the one who would've fed you."

The dove tilted its head, listening. It cooed again, then darted away.

June shuffled by, patted his shoulder, sat next to him, and studied his face. "You look better than last week."

"Thanks, I think."

The old woman chuckled. "Your lady would like the simplicity and purity of your choice in flowers this week. They're a pleasing contrast to the brightness of the sky this morning." She tilted her head. "Your artistic side's peeking through. It's lovely to see you starting to live again."

Robert's temper flared. He tamped it down. There was no reason to share his thoughts, his feelings, his devotion with this virtual stranger. She was a lonely old woman whose only commonality with him was a dead spouse. Her Charlie was never coming back, but his Anne would. He'd do anything to bring his beloved wife and prematurely-born son back to the living. He'd even sell his soul.

Smiling at the thought, Robert pressed the flowers to his nose and inhaled. He sneezed, twice. The warmth of the air, the pollen of the flowers, and his allergies reminded him spring was upon him. He felt the press of time, like a runaway train nearing a precipice. He had to find the answers to control the dragon power. The young American woman would be his conduit. The power raged in her. He would strike on Beltaine, May first. That would be his best chance as it was Anne's birthday.

June continued talking. When he didn't respond, she rambled on. Robert disregarded her voice, her presence. So far, luck was not on his side. He found nothing in his research that mentioned controlling the dragon power. Perhaps he had been too hasty in his last attempt. He should have kept Mary alive long enough to question her, have her spill what she knew, how she worked with her dragon. But she had been belligerent, accusatory in her tone and look.

In truth, Robert was afraid of his sister-in-law. She reminded him of Anne—not so much in appearance, but in her demeanor, her strength, her ideals. He was afraid if he didn't act quickly, she'd figure out his plan. Thwart him, overpower him, defeat him.

He blinked out of his reverie to notice June no longer sat next to him. Her white curls dipped with her head as she stood over her husband's grave.

Guilt arrowed to his gut. He should've talked with her. Spent ten minutes out of his day to partake of her life, the world. Robert sighed as she turned to leave. "I'll see you next week. Sorry, my conversational skills are lacking today. My mind seems to wander."

June smiled. "Don't worry yourself over much. I do the same. Next week."

Robert bowed his head. What should he tell his wife? He still hadn't found any answers, but he wasn't giving up. After his visit, he would do more research. The birdsong brought him out of his stupor. He knelt at the headstone and ran a loving hand over the engraved names.

"I brought you flowers. They're white for purity, the purity of my love."

Twenty

Devan glanced at the map, silently calculated distances, then scanned the horizon as the sun ducked behind a layer of clouds. They wouldn't be touring the second murder site until tomorrow. "We better find a place for the night. It'll be dark soon, too dark to go traipsing around a barren wasteland—if the guidebook is accurate."

They found a two-story bed and breakfast in Ennis. Over dinner in the pub next door, they discussed the events of the day.

"That's two shops with two not-so-subtle dismissals, two phone calls on the heels of our exit." Devan sighed. "Those aren't coincidences."

Christian nodded. "The question is, what do they know? And if they're so secretive, are we stirring the pot with our inquiries?"

"This is frustrating. All I want is information on my ancestors, my ring. I thought the Irish were a welcoming sort."

Christian shrugged. Devan's mind wandered. At least tonight she'd sleep. She had her own room. The clatter of a plate hitting a wooden table brought her back. "You're awfully quiet. What's up?"

Christian sipped his Guinness. "Something's not right. My gut tells me that trouble's brewing. I've learned over the years to trust my instincts."

"Are you trying to scare me?" Devan looked over her shoulder at several couples, a family of four, and a lone man. "It looks like a typical crowd enjoying dinner."

"You're probably right. Still, I have the feeling we're being watched. I don't like it."

They finished their meal in silence and made their way back to their rooms.

At her door, Devan turned to bid Christian goodnight and bumped into him. His chest was solid as granite. He steadied her. His lips brushed over hers once, twice. When hers parted, his tongue swept over hers, delving into her mouth. He gripped her waist. They stood hip pressed to hip, center to center. Heat to heat.

Devan buried her fingers in Christian's thick hair and pulled him tighter. Heat gathered in her core, spread until she thought she'd explode like a dying sun. She heard a moan and wasn't sure who it came from.

The kiss intensified. Tongue stroked tongue, teeth rasped against teeth, lips warred for dominance. Christian bit her lower lip, then used his tongue to soothe. When Devan thought they'd ignite the hallway, Christian broke off.

He stroked her jaw. "You are potent." His breath labored through his lips. "I need to kiss you again. A little too much for your own good, and for mine. You better go in before I forget my promise to give you time." He stepped back. "Goodnight."

Devan entered her room, closed the door, locked it, then leaned against the cool wood—surprised her body heat didn't set the door ablaze.

In his room, Christian rubbed his hands over his face. He'd be lucky if he got any sleep. He forced himself away from the door, away from Devan, away from the temptation.

The feeling of being watched hung with him until he fell into a fitful sleep and the dream started, once more.

A midmorning sun streamed through the clouds, sparkled off still-falling rain, and turned the light as luminous as a pearl. The vast, rocky landscape mirrored the colors of the sky. Yellow, purple, and white flowers, their faces lifted to drink in the liquid sunshine, littered the deeply-fissured limestone floor. Wind whipped at his back, slanting the rain.

Bundled in a bright red raincoat, a woman knelt under the stark outline of a T-shaped stone monument. Her braid swayed, glistening with shades of brown and red as she rose to a crouch and swung around to face him.

The jewel-handled dagger sailed toward her like lightning to metal. At the last instant, a shadowy copper-colored dragon leapt from the horizontal capstone to block the weapon. The blade shimmered, continued through the dragon and impaled the woman's chest. A high-pitched shriek exploded the silence. A strangled gasp escaped the woman's lips. She collapsed.

Power rippled from her in waves, buffeting him as he absorbed the invisible force. Should he remove the dagger? Better not, he thought, as it might disrupt the dragon power transfer.

When all fell quiet, he gathered the woman in his arms, careful not to jostle the dagger loose, and walked away from the ancient stone tomb.

Christian awoke, tangled in sweaty bed sheets in an unfamiliar room. He switched on the bedside lamp. Running a hand over his face, he remembered the bed and breakfast in Ennis and that Devan slept in the next room.

Funny, he thought, the dreams haunt me every night. Every night except when Devan shared his bed, when he held her in his arms, when he wrapped his body around hers.

Twenty One

Aidan sat astride his pale blue dragon, Sebastian, and felt the warm spring winds tousle his brown hair. Last night's storm blew the clouds away so the sky was several shades deeper than his dragon's scales. He surveyed County Waterford, not his normal territory, with a critical eye.

The clan leader had dictated each dragon and rider pair was to fly with another pair. Aidan scoffed at the order, but found himself and Sebastian teamed with Liam and Rory from Kilkenny to fly their normal patrol and the additional territory today. The two men were of an age, had partnered their dragons a year apart and underwent training together over eight years ago. They worked well together, although Liam complained at the extra workload.

"Who does the clan leader think we are, some wet-behind-the-ears lads who can't look out for themselves?" Liam shouted. "It's not like I'd be caught without protection." The sun glinted on the blade he pulled from his coat pocket.

"What the blazes are you doing with that?" Aidan steered his dragon closer. "Put that away; we'll not need it on patrol. I don't plan on landing." He urged Sebastian ahead and led the way.

As they approached the southern coast where the land butted against the Irish Sea, Aidan felt a sharp blast of power. It knocked the air from his lungs.

What the hell was that? Dragon power? He directed Sebastian to circle the hill that anchored a tall cylindrical tower and stone ruins. Yes, he thought, the power emanated from somewhere nearby.

They hung in the air twenty meters above the sea and waited for Liam and Rory to come into view. Aidan signaled his intent to investigate. His desire to remain airborne was forgotten.

Sebastian set down on the far side of the ruins from the village nestled below. He folded his blue and silver wings as Aidan swung out of his saddle and slid with a soft thud in the moist knee-high grass.

Rory and Liam followed. Liam hurried over to Aidan. "What's up?"

"Didn't you feel it?" At Liam's negative reply, Aidan continued. "Dragon power."

Liam pulled off his gloves and goggles. "Probably residual from Conor and Donovan. They died here. This is Saint Declan's Well and Oratory."

"It can't be them. They died over six months ago. This power is fresh, strong. Besides, no one mentioned noticing residual power at any of the murder locations. And the death ceremony and funeral pyre destroys the clan pendant and the dragon power. This is new. I'm going to look around. See where I feel the power most. Stay with the dragons."

"Are you crazy? Sean said to stick together."

"I need you to watch my back, alert me if anyone approaches. Perhaps it'd be best if you and Rory circled overhead."

Aidan waited until Liam was airborne before he left the safety of Sebastian's dragon magic. He kept a running dialogue with this compeer—not only for company, but to ease the wariness he felt. He searched the area to make sure he hadn't been noticed. That was all he needed, to have someone see him appear seemingly out of nowhere.

The power was everywhere. It seemed weaker in the graveyard and around the tower, stronger at the Ogham stone within the oratory ruin, stronger still on the path leading to the stone well. At the well entrance, Aidan staggered. The force drove him to his knees.

Through the roaring in his head, he heard Sebastian. *"Aidan, converse with me. Let me know ye are well. Otherwise I will come for ye."*

"I'm okay. Shaken is all. The strongest power is at the well. Give me a minute and I'll be back. Tell Rory." Aidan passed an unsteady hand over his face, then on shaky legs, made his way back to his dragon.

Rory and Liam waited with Sebastian.

Liam ran to help his friend. "Are you okay? You're whiter than a bloody Englishman."

"Aye. The power's strongest at the well—where Conor and DONOVAN were killed."

Liam whirled around. "Do you think the killer's come back?"

"I don't know, but we'd better tell Sean."

Liam cupped his hands, hefted Aidan into his saddle aboard SEBASTIAN. Aidan's legs had turned to mush.

Even though the sky held no clouds, they flew to Loughcrew as if lightning bolts crashed at their backs—with no more than five meters separating their compeer's wingtips.

Aidan lifted his clammy face, allowing the wind to clear his fogged brain. Blood suffused his face and hands. The numbness ebbed from his fingertips.

SEBASTIAN landed in the inner courtyard near Sean's office while RORY landed in the customary outer courtyard.

Aidan fell out of his saddle and landed with a thud on the cobblestones.

Sean rushed out of his office. "What happened?"

Aidan lifted his head, his face drained of blood, and whispered, "Dragon magic at Ardmore."

"Thank you all for coming so quickly." Sean nodded to the riders that made up his new council seated in his office. "Aidan and Liam made a discovery today."

Aidan stepped forward to stand by Sean's chair. With no room at the table, Liam leaned against the wall behind. Aidan cleared his throat. "Liam and I patrolled Waterford. I flew lead and as I neared the town of Ardmore, I felt it. Dragon power. Emanating from the hill overlooking the bay. SEBASTIAN felt it as well."

Padrick raised an eyebrow at Liam. "Did you share the experience?"

"No," Liam said. "Aidan and SEBASTIAN hovered until I caught up. We landed and Aidan said he felt something. He wanted to explore the area, so I flew cover overhead. RORY and SEBASTIAN maintained contact."

Sean tilted his head toward Aidan. "Please continue."

"I went to investigate, as Liam said. I could feel wisps of power, like mists swirling over the ground, at both the conical tower and graveyard. It intensified inside the ruins, at the Ogham stone, as well as the path to the well. At the well's entrance, where Conor was murdered, the force dropped me to my knees." Aidan gulped air. His white knuckles gripped Sean's chair back.

Meara's eyes widened. "You think it was Conor and Donovan you felt?"

"No," Aidan said. "Liam thought that too. This felt different. It was fresh, no more than one or two days old."

Voices bounced off the walls, colliding with each other.

Sean's voice rose above the cacophony. "It could be the murderer, but I have another theory." He waited for everyone's attention. "We may have found…new dragonriders. With Roarke and Dochas not choosing from within the clan, we must entertain the idea of outsiders."

Voices rose again.

"Let me explain," Sean said when the room quieted. "Several days ago, while I was in Dublin, I too sensed power. I was at Trinity surrounded by people, and couldn't pinpoint the source."

"That doesn't rule out the killer," Padrick said. "We already decided he could be anywhere."

Sean lifted his hands for quiet. "That's true, but there's more. While in Dublin, I saw several people. Each told me of their encounter with a couple—an Irishman and an American woman. The woman, Devan Fraser, asked about the clan oath, and she wore a silver ring. A clan ring."

The stunned silence stretched out as the impact of his statement seeped into the riders' minds.

Aisling spoke first. "A clan ring hasn't been worn or made in over a hundred years. I don't even remember who wore one last." She turned to Sean. "Do you?"

He shook his head. "I searched the archives, but found no mention of the ring. I do remember my grandfather's stories of ring wearers having special abilities—specifically, being able to hear all the dragons."

Meara sighed. "That would be handy right about now. Even better six months ago. Maybe we wouldn't have lost four dragons and their riders."

Padrick squeezed her hand. "I don't think anything would've stopped Conor's and DONOVAN'S deaths. We never thought ourselves vulnerable. Perhaps we could have prevented the others."

Matthew leaned his elbows on the table, steepled his hands, his fingers intertwined. "Is there some way of tracking the power source?" He looked up at Aidan. "Could you get a sense of the power anywhere else?"

Aidan stroked the stubble on his chin. "To be honest, I was a little dazed. My mind was clouded. When I could mount up with Liam's help, we headed back here to report the incident." His eyes unfocused in the way most riders' did when communicating with their compeers.

Moments passed and Aidan refocused on the people at the table. "SE-BASTIAN didn't notice either. As I said, we flew straight back." Color rose in his cheeks. "Didn't even finish our patrol."

"You did the right thing," Sean said. "Go take care of your dragons. Eat. Rest."

Aidan nodded. He and Liam left.

Sean waited for the door to close behind them. "I asked Moira here today to expand our knowledge of Newgrange. And I have some information on the daggers." He nodded his head to the golden-haired woman seated across from him.

Moira held notes as she read. "Newgrange is a megalithic passage tomb, part of an enormous Stone Age cemetery. It was built around 3200 BC and is older than both Stonehenge and the pyramids of Egypt. In times past it was believed to facilitate the passage of souls from death to the new life." She lowered her notes. "Considering my research and the placement of the bodies, I believe the killer had some desire to help the souls of his victims into the next life. For what reason, I don't know."

"We still don't have any solid answers, just more questions," Meara said.

Sean nodded. "I talked to Brian from the National Museum about the daggers. He's seen similar ones in a boxed set. Each laid out with six blades in a starburst pattern. He knows of two specialty stores in Dublin that sell them and will talk to the owners for us. Hopefully, there haven't been many sold."

Padrick blew out a breath. "Six! That means the killer may have already selected his next victim."

Twenty Two

Devan awoke unsettled. Her dreams involved Christian and the events of the past few days. A niggling feeling intruded, keeping her from sinking into a deeper sleep. Maybe it was jet lag. After all, she had flown across one whole continent and an ocean only to barely settle into Dublin. Now she travelled around the southern half of Ireland and into the West.

Yesterday she thought she heard voices—whispers really—just south of Limerick City, as they drove toward County Clare. She chalked it up to being tired and upset at the loss of her dad's cufflinks.

"You're letting your imagination run wild," she said aloud as she swung her legs over the side of the bed. "Might as well get up, as you'll only think of Christian and your encounter last night anyway."

At breakfast, Christian relayed his dream in hushed tones to Devan. They agreed to visit the site as Devan again found information in her guidebook.

"Poulnabrone Portal Dolman." She read aloud. "A wedge tomb consisting of four upright stones supporting a thin capstone. The remains of adults, children, even a newborn were uncovered during excavation. It's also known as the Portal of Sorrows." She shuddered. "I can understand why."

The road narrowed to allow room for one car in each direction, barely. A car park and brown tourist sign on the right signaled their arrival. They were the only visitors. As they clambered over the broken limestone, the portal dolmen speared up—a lonely monument on the rocky landscape.

They approached from the back and circled around to the east-facing opening. The capstone stood less than six feet off the ground here. No wonder the murdered woman never stood up.

"It's easy to feel the solitude and sorrow in this place," Devan said.

Christian stepped over the rope barrier intended to keep people away from Poulnabrone and crouched under the protruding capstone. "Aye. The killer was drawn here in his own grief. I think he hoped the slaying of the second victim would relieve him of a portion of his sorrow."

"His sorrow?" Devan's right eyebrow raised in question.

Christian nodded. "Remember the feelings I had at Saint Declan's Well? That the killer sought to memorialize the loss of someone he loved, a wife perhaps. What I feel now strengthens that theory, but I believe the bulk of the sorrow here is directed at the grief of losing his child."

"A child? Are you sure?"

"Reasonably sure. In the dreams, it's as though I'm him. In his body, thinking his thoughts, feeling his emotions. Things are jumbled. His desire for the power he feels is only one aspect." Christian touched the left up-right slab to keep his balance as he experienced a surge of energy and grief. "When I'm here, in the exact spot of the attack, the emotions are clearer. The killer's thoughts are centered on his baby, his son, his namesake."

Devan gasped. "What's his name? We can go to the authorities and stop him from killing anyone else."

Christian rose. "I don't know, his thoughts don't mention the name, just confusion over why he had to lose both of them—his wife and son."

"Can we go to the police? Tell them what we know and be done with it?"

Distant voices carried on the wind, interrupting Christian's answer.

They stepped back over the barrier and walked to the car park, nodding acknowledgment to the group of four strangers they passed.

Christian started the car and headed away before answering Devan. "We don't have enough to involve the Gardaí. At this point, all we know is four people have died. We believe they were murdered, but the authorities either think differently or they are already actively investigating the murders and don't want anyone knowing. Whatever we can tell them is based on my dreams and conjecture. We would only draw attention to ourselves." And I'd be the prime suspect, he thought, shuddering.

Devan reached out and held his hand. "Sorry. I know this is difficult for you, especially since it's your dreams. I'm just along for the ride."

"You're not, you're linked to this. Perhaps in danger yourself." At her blank look, Christian continued. "Remember, I dreamed of a dagger flying toward your heart."

"It's not likely that I'd forget. But I thought you'd mixed me up with one of the other victims."

"No. In the dream with you, there are dozens of people and dragons gathered around a bonfire. With the other murders, the victim's alone, or at least appears alone. The dragon partially materializes at the last moment."

Devan ran her free hand through her hair. "So what do we do now?"

"We follow the dreams. Find the locations of the last two murder victims. Maybe we'll get lucky and find out the killer's identity. Let's concentrate on the third victim."

Later that night, Christian forced himself to concentrate on the third victim. He studied the obituary until he could describe every feature on the young man's face. Weariness dragged him down. The dream rushed into his mind, into his senses, into his very soul.

The soft, white castle-like structure sat on the other side of the gray expanse of a rapidly-flowing river. The scene unfolded as if he peered through Devan's camera viewfinder. Ice huddled in patches near the shore, the branches of trees sprinkled with fluffy snowflakes, rocks and tree roots poked up amongst the white coat crusting the ground.

To the right of the three-story dwelling, a wood plank footbridge spanned the river. Past the bridge, the water expanded into a lake. As though adjusting the distance of the viewfinder, a stone ruin anchoring an island in the middle of the lake came into focus.

The place looked deserted, tranquil. He heard splashing halfway between the shore and the island, yet saw only ripples on the water's surface. Had a fish jumped, or a bird swooped down for a mid-afternoon meal? Movement in the yellow grouse part way down the left bank drew his attention. He zoomed in with the camera viewfinder and spotted a man, standing near an ancient cannon trained on the island, casting a line in the lake. Aha! The source of the concentric circles. But the fly line was not cast nearly as far as the phenomenon he spotted moments earlier.

Could this fisherman be the dragonrider? He couldn't feel the dragon power from this distance, if indeed the man was a rider. In any event, he would need to be closer to ensure accuracy with the dagger.

He stole through the winter silence, skirted broken twigs and icy patches on the path, and arrived within ten meters behind the man as he cast his line into the water again. A curly shock of brown hair peeked out at the knit cap and brushed the man's coat collar.

Faint dragon power shimmered around the fisherman. Would it be enough? Where was the dragon? Filled with trepidation, he glanced over his shoulder. Could he have miscalculated the date? No, he thought, today was the winter solstice—six months to the day when his beloved wife and son were killed. Perhaps his information on the dragonrider's habits was incorrect. He couldn't be sure this fisherman was a rider. True, he felt power here, but not as strong a force as at the two previous slayings.

He must've made a sound because the man whipped around, causing his fishing line with the green and black fly tied to the end to sail in a graceful arc overhead.

He was caught by surprise before conscious thought formed. The dagger nestled warm in his palm moments before, slid to his fingertips, bounced lightly to balance the weight properly, then split the air between the two men. A sky-blue shadowy dragon landed to guard the rider. Too late. The jewel-handled blade shimmered through the dragon and stopped dead in the man's chest.

A burst of dragon power exploded outward and slammed into him. He staggered backward until he rammed his hip into the cannon. A yelp of pain escaped his lips as he fell.

Christian awoke wind-milling his arms to break his fall. He lay in the middle of a bed, warm and unhurt.

Calm down, he told himself, 'twas only the dream. The dream of the third murder.

Twenty Three

TULLIA'S panicked rumblings woke Kiely. She rushed to her compeer dressed only in her bedclothes.

"What is it, love?" Kiely rubbed TULLIA'S eye ridges to soothe the anxious dragon.

"Something is wrong. My egg…" The plum-colored dragon's blue eyes whirled like pinwheels in a hurricane.

Ronan stumbled bleary-eyed to the doorway. "What's happened? You need to keep her from shouting, even mentally. She'll roust the entire compound. CALHOUN is awake and agitated."

"I'm trying to calm her. Help me, bugger it." Kiely huffed. "Let me check the egg. She says something's wrong with it."

Ronan replaced Kiely at TULLIA'S head. Kiely ran her hands over the meter-length mottled egg. She felt no discernible flaws. The only alarming change was the color—from a yellow to a dingy gray.

"Nothing is wrong, *mo chroi*, my heart." Kiely crooned aloud. "I think it's close to hatching is all."

"I can sense a presence, yet there is a defect." TULLIA'S eyes swirled faster as she grasped the egg with her clawed forelegs.

The bitter, iron taste of fear rose in Kiely's throat. She swallowed hard, then surged forward as the dragon's claws chipped a fist-sized chunk of shell away.

"What are you doing?" Kiely pulled at TULLIA'S powerful forelegs, to no avail. "It's too soon. The dragon hasn't fully formed yet. It will break the egg on its own in another week. Please stop."

"I must see what is wrong." TULLIA tore at the shell.

Kiely jumped clear as frantic ripping sent shell pieces flying. She stumbled backward into Ronan, staring at TULLIA through her tears. Could a dragonet survive if born this early?

Cradled in the remaining half shell, a gray body lay curled and still, covered in scales with none of the soft, leathery hide of a newborn.

TULLIA nudged the newborn with her muzzle, once, twice. *"Breathe, little one. Ye must draw oxygen."* TULLIA blew hot air into the dragonet's nostrils until its chest rose and fell on its own.

The dragonet squawked with indignation, stretched its legs, and bristled its neck spikes. Blue eyes spun clockwise in the gray triangular head.

TULLIA shrilled, a harsh keening note. CALHOUN'S anguish joined his mate's from outside the chamber.

Kiely covered her ears against the sorrowful wails of their duet. "What is it?" She yelled. "You've rousted the babe out of its shell, you can't expect it to be happy. Let me help. We need to spread its wings to dry."

TULLIA ducked her head to capture Kiely's attention. *"The dragonet, my offspring, has nigh wings."*

"Don't be ridiculous. They're just translucent and pressed to its body. Oh, for heaven's sake, what is your babe's name?"

"His name is GRAYSON. He has nigh wings, translucent or otherwise."

The quiver in the dragon's mental voice alerted Kiely to the truth. GRAYSON had indeed hatched without wings. A hot fist of guilt slammed into Kiely's solar plexus, stealing her breath. Was this the price she'd have to pay for her defiance of the clan leader? A wingless dragon? Perhaps the wings were the last to form and would grow now the dragonet was outside the egg. There was still a chance for GRAYSON to be whole. Kiely took a steady breath, moved to soothe her tormented compeer.

"It is my fault." TULLIA'S mental voice wavered. *"I am too old to fly long enough to mate properly."*

Kiely's throat closed and squeezed her comforting words back down. Only a sob escaped.

"Nonsense." CALHOUN'S mental voice flowed from TULLIA'S mind into Kiely's as CALHOUN pushed his way into the crowded chamber. *"There is nigh fault."*

TULLIA stretched her neck over GRAYSON and puffed warm air across the dragonet's wingless body. *"The clan needs flying dragons to make up for those killed."*

CALHOUN's baritone continued. *"Perhap, we were not meant to provide them. After all, it is the duty of FIONN and the younger ones to see to the survival of the clan."* CALHOUN nuzzled his mate's head. *"Our offspring is a treasure. He may not have wings to fly, but he will do his part to keep Éire safe and prosperous."*

TULLIA turned distressed eyes to Kiely.

Kiely rubbed her dragon's eye ridges again. "Don't worry, *a ghra*. Everyone will love your son, just as he is." Or they'll answer to me. She buried the thought deep to keep any hint of her worry from her compeer.

Boots slapping on stones startled Kiely back to their situation.

"The entire compound is awake," Ronan said.

CALHOUN helped TULLIA chip away the remaining eggshell.

"Come GRAYSON, wade clear of your egg. It is time to meet your clan mates, dragons and humans alike."

GRAYSON warbled. *"Hungry, hungry, HUNGRY."* He teetered out of his shell and sprawled on the hay-covered floor.

TULLIA conveyed her offspring's demand to Kiely.

"We better feed him," Kiely said. "Before he decides to eat someone."

Ronan chuckled, then retrieved a bucket with fresh meat chunks and shoveled the food into the newborn's ravenous mouth.

A half hour later, with a sated GRAYSON, Ronan threw open the outer double-doors. Clan members milled about, straining to see into the dragon's chamber. Their voices rose in question of TULLIA's earlier keening. A gaggle of children halted their game of tag.

Murmurs rippled through the growing crowd. When they spotted TULLIA and CALHOUN flanking the newborn dragonet, parents gathered children to their sides. Their chatter escalated when Ronan and Kiely joined the dragons as they emerged into the watery morning sunlight.

Peter approached from the stables. "What's this, grandmother?" He gestured to GRAYSON, but addressed Kiely.

Clan members converged around them. Matthew and his compeer, KIERAN were among them.

Kiely pitched her voice to encompass the crowd. "This is GRAYSON, the newest Tuatha dragon, offspring of Tullia and Calhoun."

Shouts erupted between some of the clan members. Grayson cowered behind his parents. Tullia growled at the bickering clan members.

Peter gawked at the dragonet. "But, he…he doesn't have wings."

The terse words from the crowd dropped to whispers.

"What have you done, Kiely?" Michael, Seamus's rider and protector of County Tyrone snapped accusingly. "Obviously Sean doesn't know. He wouldn't condone a dragon of Tullia's advanced age mating. Where did you pull off this abomination?"

Kiely thrust her chin up, narrowed her eyes. "As Ulster leader, I made the decision to save the clan. We need more dragons and riders. Sean didn't want the responsibility, so I took it."

Matthew began to protest. Kiely cut him off. "Your father's not ready to lead, and this proves it. I should have been elected clan leader. I'll do whatever it takes for the good of the clan." And I have, she added to herself.

"For what you deem right for the clan?" someone shouted. "The council, under Sean's leadership, decides these things, not some renegade rider."

Kiely surveyed the crowd for the insolent speaker. "Sean would not act, so I did. I'm not sorry for it and I won't apologize."

Ronan sidled to his wife, brushed her arm, and whispered, "Don't antagonize them, we're going to need their support in caring for Grayson, if for nothing else.

"Where's the other one?" Matthew asked. "Every mating flight produces two eggs, two dragons." He let the question hang for five heartbeats. "Is the second one deformed too?"

"Tullia only produced one egg." Kiely thrust her chin up at the hurtful remark.

"How's he to fly?" Someone shouted. "He'll be nothing but a burden to the clan. And at a time when we are already short-handed."

Angry words at her disregard for clan leadership reached Kiely's ears.

"Enough." Kiely cut off any other comments. "As long as I am Beaghmore's leader, you will do as I say." She stormed away, leaving Ronan to deal with the incensed crowd.

Twenty Four

Sean hustled into his office carrying his steaming cup of tea and snatched up the ringing phone. "Hello."

"Da…I mean, Clan Leader." Matthew rushed the words.

"What is it, son?" Sean rubbed the furrow between his rust-colored eyebrows.

"You need to come. Kiely has done something awful."

Sean waited, counted five heartbeats. "Tell me."

"Kiely mated TULLIA with CALHOUN. They…they produced an offspring. One male named GRAYSON, and—"

"Son of a bitch!" Sean sank into the chair behind his desk. What else? he thought. Don't I have enough to deal with, without a renegade rider? "Sorry, you started to say something else?"

"He has no wings." Matthew's voice rang hollow. "TULLIA only dropped one egg, not the normal two. Kiely and Ronan kept everything secret. Maybe Peter knew. He's been solemn recently and stuck close to his grandparents."

Sean's sigh echoed in the room. "Where is this newborn now?"

"In TULLIA'S chamber. When will you arrive? KIERAN and I will meet you."

Sean scanned the stacks of unfinished duty rosters, supply lists, and scraps of paper littering his desk. "I'm buried here. If the dragonet is in no eminent danger, and it doesn't sound like he is, then I'll be there in the morning." He paused, then added, "Matthew, does Kiely know you're calling me?"

"I'm sure she does, I wasn't quiet about my feelings. Several riders agreed with me. She claimed you were negligent in your duties as leader and that she was only doing what was best for the clan."

Sean pressed his throbbing temple. "I'm not surprised; I knew she was up to something. I just hadn't a clue what. Please be careful. If she can't get me out of the way, she may try to hurt you."

"I'll be all right. Michael and some older riders are upset too. I'll stick close to them tonight."

"Okay. I love you, son."

"I love you too. Tell Mum."

Sean hung up, then rested his head in his hands, elbows propped on the desk. *Fuck, what more could go wrong?*

"Aisling, are you busy?" he called.

His wife's curly, brown-haired head poked into the open doorway. "You need me?"

"Yes." He gestured her in. "Let me call Padrick and Meara, that way I'll only have to explain it once."

Sean relayed everything Matthew told him over the phone's speaker, then made plans to meet Padrick tomorrow at dawn for an official visit to Beaghmore.

The sun rose over the forest east of Loughcrew. Sean mounted FIONN, and sketched a quick goodbye nod to his wife. As he flew northwest to the rendezvous point with Padrick, he turned Kiely's outright insubordination over and over in his mind.

FIONN circled the waiting black dragon and rider, then landed within a wingspan of the pair.

"*Dia duit.*" Sean fisted his right hand over his heart with the greeting.

"*Dia's Muire duit,*" Padrick replied.

Sean shaded his eyes with the flat of his hand. "Let's audit Kiely and Ronan's territories before we continue to Beaghmore and the newborn. There's no telling what duties they let go between the time TULLIA mated and the hatching."

Padrick nodded and gestured for Sean and Fionn to lead the way. The dragons flew a circular pattern extending to the North Channel. The riders surveyed Derry County from west to east.

"Damn." Padrick pointed to the blighted fields. "You were right. Tullia couldn't fly before dropping her egg, or while awaiting the hatching. Chalk up one more dereliction for my mother. How could she jeopardize Éire this way?"

Fionn and Declan back-winged, and landed in one of the troubled fields. The two men dismounted, inspected the withering crops and scruffy, thin beasts, then returned to their compeers.

Sean's nose twisted into a sneer as he rubbed his neck. "Someone will need to work double to fix these crops. Not Kiely. I don't trust her to perform her duties. I'd like to relocate your parents to Leinster so I can keep my eye on Kiely, but I can't right now, no time to train riders to swap counties. I think Ronan goes along with Kiely's schemes because he loves her."

Padrick snorted. "Love? My dad is blinded, besotted, and bedazzled with the witch. I don't understand his devotion. He won't stand up to her, even when he knows she's wrong. I call that whipped." He pinched the bridge of his nose. "You know my history with my mother. I can't be objective where she's concerned."

"Well, they produced you and your sister and partnered with Tullia and Calhoun. So there must be some redeeming qualities." Sean smiled.

"Not according to Kiely. Tess is a failure because she didn't partner a dragon, never mind that she and her husband are happy. Or that she, at least, provided grandchildren. Me, I've not chosen the right women, I'm not ambitious enough, I'm not clan leader. Oh, she wants the position herself, don't think otherwise, but if not her, then it should be me. And after Erin disappeared, I waited too long with Meara, so I have no heir. There'll be no glory from the family. Unless it's from Mother."

It was Sean's turn to snort. "Notoriety, you mean. You have nothing to be ashamed of. You're one of the best men I know, and a hell of a dragonrider. Did you think I chose you as my second because of your looks?" Sean laughed to lighten his friend's sullen mood.

Padrick chuckled. "Got you beat any day of the week and twice on

Sundays. Just my bad luck Aisling preferred an ill mannered, redheaded brute."

Sean threw back his head and laughed. He wiped his eyes, then stroked a hand through his beard. "Better see this dragonet and confront Kiely." They mounted their dragons.

"Whom will you put in charge?" Padrick asked.

"Michael. He's experienced enough to lead the younger riders without being too old, he's prudent enough to evaluate a situation without being steamrolled, and he's diplomatic enough to keep an eye on Kiely without her bristling at his leadership."

"Good choice, then."

Sean nodded at Padrick's confirmation. "I should have overruled Beaghmore compound's election of Kiely's continued leadership when I ascended to Tuatha clan leader, but I didn't want to be heavy-handed."

"You'll keep them in their assigned counties?"

"For now, unless Kiely does something else to force my hand." Sean urged FIONN into the thin morning air. "Ronan wouldn't neglect his duties, so we don't need to check Antrim County. In fact, he's probably the reason Derry is not in complete ruin."

They flew directly to Beaghmore.

Matthew awaited Sean and Padrick in the outer courtyard. The men dismounted and greeted the young man.

Sean bespoke his dragon. *"Go ahead, A Storin. Get your take from the other dragons. Be circumspect with TULLIA and CALHOUN, however."*

"I understand. Are ye settled on Michael and SEAMUS to lead Ulster? Matthew and KIERAN are better suited," FIONN bespoke.

"They would in the long term, but are too young to lead just now." Sean patted FIONN's neck.

"What does number of years from the egg have to do with ability?"

"You're right, of course," Sean said. *"But humans have the notion, right or wrong, that age equates to experience and leadership skills. Also, as Matthew is one of my blood that would smack of nepotism and would undermine my ability to lead the entire clan."*

FIONN blew hot air through his flared nostrils, expressing his disgust with human politics.

Sean rubbed his compeer's eye ridges. *"You know, dragons have their own prejudices and cliques."*

"As ye say." FIONN dipped his head in acknowledgment. *"I shall endeavor to ferret out the sentiments of each dragon."* He lumbered with DECLAN toward the lake and the Ulster Province dragons.

Matthew fidgeted beside Padrick.

From the corner of his eye, Sean spied Kiely and Ronan's front door opening and he turned to confront the renegade pair.

"Kiely, Ronan." Sean inclined his head. "We need to talk."

"Talk, that's all you do. Not one for action until you've dissected every scenario. Well, I'm not afraid to act." Kiely sneered.

Padrick's blue eyes shot icicles at his mother. "To hell with the consequences, not only to the entire clan but to the innocents affected by your dangerous impulses. You go too far, Mother." He whirled to face his father. "What about you? Don't you have a scrap of a brain cell, or does she do all the thinking for you?"

Sean laid a restraining hand on Padrick's forearm. "Not here. We'll discuss this in private."

As Kiely and Ronan headed for their office, Sean turned back and asked Matthew to find Michael and pass along the request to have him join the four leaders.

Sean entered the office to find Padrick and Kiely glaring at each other. Ronan busied himself pouring tea at the side table. At Ronan's inviting gesture to the food and drink, Sean shook his head.

"I'll get straight to the point," Sean said. "Kiely, I'm relieving you as Ulster leader."

Kiely sputtered. Her face flushed red as she narrowed her eyes at him. "You can't do that."

"I can."

"I've been selected by the riders here at Beaghmore." Kiely fumed. "You can't dictate who leads the other clan compounds."

Sean raised his eyebrows. "As clan leader, I can and will remove anyone who is a detriment to the clan. That includes the leadership."

Michael knocked on the open door and ducked his head in Sean's direction. "You wanted to see me, Clan Leader?"

"Yes, please come in and shut the door." Sean nodded to Matthew standing outside before the door closed.

"*FIONN, please relay to KIERAN to tell Matthew that I will catch up with him when I'm finished.*"

"*KIERAN and the other dragons are disgusted with Kiely's thoughtless behavior,*" FIONN informed his partner. "*By the by, TULLIA and CALHOUN have not engaged the others, either socially or duty bound. They spend their time with the dragonet.*"

"*Thanks.*" Sean broke the mental contact with his dragon.

He gestured everyone to sit. "As I've just informed Kiely, I'm replacing her as Ulster leader. Michael, you'll take over. Effective immediately."

Michael's eyes widened and his mouth dropped open in his broad face. He seemed to realize his mouth hung open and snapped it closed.

Sean turned to Kiely. "I'm sorry, but you've left me no choice. The members have chosen me to be clan leader, and you can't do whatever you bloody damn well please. I have clearly stated my reasons for waiting to breed more dragons. You defied that decision. You endangered not only the clan, but the whole of Ireland." He paused to smooth the sharpness out of his tone. "We're already shorthanded, you restricted TULLIA for the gestation and hatching, and now other clan members and dragons will be required to care for this newborn."

Kiely thrust out her chin. "My grandson, Peter, will care for GRAYSON. No one else needs to be pulled from their duties."

"Disregarding the newborn's condition for the moment," Padrick interrupted, "what if TULLIA had produced the standard two offspring? How were you going to manage the care, feeding, and training of two flying dragonets without involving the entire compound?" His cheeks suffused with blood as his temper lashed out. "Now we have a wingless newborn and Derry land untended. If we weren't down four dragons and riders already, I'd demand Sean relieve you of *all* your duties, not just leadership here."

Kiely scowled at her son. "You don't have command over me. I can't believe you're even my flesh and blood. You'd side with this one," she flicked her hand in Sean's direction, "over me. Where's your family loyalty?"

"Right where it belongs, with the clan."

"TULLIA and I won't fly if you do this," Kiely threatened Sean. "Neither will Ronan and CALHOUN."

"No, Kiely." Ronan's quiet voice melted the anger in the room. "CALHOUN and I will do our duty, just as we've always done. And you and TULLIA will fly. You've both sworn an oath to protect Ireland. Now you'll abide by Sean's decisions as Tuatha clan leader."

Kiely folded her arms over her chest and glared at her husband.

Sean rose and nodded to Ronan. "I'll see the newborn now."

The group left the office and entered TULLIA's chamber through the courtyard door. FIONN and DECLAN joined their human compeers.

TULLIA reared back and bristled at the intrusion, but submitted with an encouraging nod from CALHOUN. The gray ball nestled against TULLIA's belly snored.

"Awake, GRAYSON," FIONN bespoke to both Sean and the dragonet. *"The clan leader is here to meet ye."*

Baby blue eyes peered out from the triangular head that lifted clear of the curled form. *"Who are ye?"* The newborn's voice quivered in Sean's head as FIONN directed the dragonet's direct communication to him.

"I am FIONN, compeer to Clan Leader Sean."

"Is not TULLIA and Kiely clan leader?"

FIONN snorted and shook his head. *"Nigh, they are one dragon and rider pair stationed here in Northern Ireland. There are many dragons and riders that encompass the whole of the Tuatha Dragon Clan. We protect all of Ireland. Sean and I lead the entire clan."*

"GRAYSON," Sean spoke aloud. "I understand FIONN has been explaining clan structure to you, and I'll let him continue in a minute. First, I need to evaluate you. Please stand so I can gauge your size."

The dragonet unfurled his body, bristling his neck ridges.

Sean inspected the newborn, running his hands over flanks, chest, and legs before gentling his touch across the back and shoulders where the wings should have attached.

GRAYSON dipped his head in TULLIA's direction.

"Yes, you appear to be strong." Sean inclined his head toward Padrick and his black dragon. "This is Padrick and his compeer, DECLAN. If you would like, the dragons will stay for a while."

At GRAYSON'S nod, the humans returned to the office.

"I didn't feel any knobs or growth where the wings should be," Sean said. "I doubt they'll grow. GRAYSON is a drake, a wingless dragon."

"Are you sure?" Ronan asked.

"After I heard—" Sean began.

"From your meddling son, no doubt," Kiely interrupted.

Sean returned Kiely's piercing glare. "Yes, from Matthew, a protector of Ulster lands and one of many kept in the dark with your schemes." He waved a hand to dismiss the subject. "After I learned of GRAYSON, I reviewed the clan archives. I found one reference to a drake. One hatched during the first partnering with humans after the famine rebellion in 1848."

"What became of it?" Michael asked.

"It seems our ancestors had no use for a flightless dragon. I asked FIONN if he ever heard stories from the elder dragons about a wingless one. He remembers the humans cast out such a creature. FIONN thinks the drake survived by inhabiting the many loughs around County Galway."

"So, the drake could have lived a normal lifespan," Padrick said. "The question is, what do we do about our drake?"

"He'll not be cast out. TULLIA and I, with Peter's help, will tend to him." Kiely lifted her chin. "After all, he's my responsibility."

Sean stroked his beard. "For now." He addressed Michael. "The transfer of Ulster leadership happens today. I'll expect weekly progress reports on both GRAYSON and Derry County. At the first hint of Kiely's neglect of Derry, I will remove GRAYSON from her care. Make no mistake."

Twenty Five

Christian sat at the breakfast table across from Devan. "I forced my-self to dream last night." He sipped his tea, grimaced at the bitter-ness, and added a spoonful of sugar. "Dreamed of the third victim, Dylan from County Galway."

Devan rested her hand over his. "Tell me."

"It was December. Snow coated tree branches and ice formed on the banks of the loughs." He ignored his breakfast as he told her the details. "The interesting part was, the whole dream laid out as if I viewed it from behind your camera lens."

"Do you think that's a clue?" Devan buttered her toast. "A house near a lough, a lake? How are we going to find the one you described? County Galway has over seven hundred."

"There can't be many with a cannon."

"I don't know. I doubt this place will be in any guidebook. We'll have to ask around."

Christian nodded and lifted a rasher to his mouth. "Let's head into Gal-way. And don't forget, I saw a mansion on the banks of the lake."

Devan widened her eyes in mock surprise. "Oh, that's right. A mansion or castle. There can't be more than one or two in the whole of Ireland." The sarcasm left her voice. "Sorry, it's just the only thing more prevalent here than thatched roofed dwellings are castles."

"You have a mean streak I hadn't noticed before." Christian tilted his head and narrowed his eyes. "I like it." He brought her hands to his lips, first one then the other. The kiss caressed her knuckles and whispered down to her fingertips.

"Yeah." Kelly answered his mobile as he tossed clothes into his overnight bag.

"It's Logan. I haven't heard from you. Where are they?"

"In the West Counties, at some farmhouse or other in—Hold on." He fanned through the tourist brochures on the nightstand. "In a town, and I'm using that term loosely, called Ennis in County Clare."

"Okay. Stick with them. The client is very specific. Like molasses, you understand?"

"I've got it covered. I put a tracker on their car." Kelly zipped up his case.

"No. Follow them personally, not just with electronics. Report back to me every evening."

Kelly limped to his car. His knee ached like a busted tooth. Where were they going now? So far, they'd played tourist. They visited stupid stone monuments and tiny fishing villages, driving all over the country on the smallest and most pitted roads possible. They never stayed in one place more than a single night. One night in the hotel-from-hell where he'd re-injured his knee when he was forced to jump from the balcony or risk being discovered. Others were spent in family homes touted as bed and breakfasts in tiny towns or villages.

This job was rubbing on his last nerve. How long must he endure this torture? Couldn't Romeo seduce Juliet in a civilized place, a four-star hotel or a castle? Maybe she was playing hard to get? Meanwhile, he had to forgo decent food, decent lodging, and female companionship of his own. He'd make the woman suffer.

If Kelly grabbed her now, took her back to Dublin, he could keep her locked up. That would solve all his problems. Then he'd hand her over when the boss's customer wanted her. No more muss, no more fuss. Maybe he'd have a little fun with her, show her what a real man was capable of. He laughed.

Kelly lifted the gray-black Citroen's boot to toss his bag in when his quarry exited the latest run-down house and headed for their car. He needed to get the woman away from her friend. Today.

At the tourist office in Galway, Christian and Devan hit a snag. The old woman at the desk couldn't pinpoint the lough they described.

"She did say there are a few shops nearby that bought and sold jewelry. We could ask about your father's cufflinks and your ring," Christian said.

"Thanks. I'd like that." Devan twisted the dragon ring around her finger. "I'd also like to check out the library to see if we can narrow down the location of the murder site."

They visited several jewelers with no luck on either the cufflinks or her ring.

Devan ran a hand through her hair and sighed. "At least we weren't given the evil eye in any of these shops."

"No," Christian agreed. "But we didn't learn anything either."

"Let's check out the library." Devan unfolded the city map she acquired from the tourist office.

"After lunch. I'm starved."

Devan laughed. "How can you possibly be hungry? You ate enough for a week not three hours ago." At Christian's hangdog look, she relented. "Okay, but let's find a place near the library. I can start the search while you eat."

They found a pub down the street from the public library. Devan left Christian and walked the two blocks. She entered the building and approached the front desk. The librarian retrieved several books and magazines at Devan's request. She sat surrounded with research materials.

Kelly strolled into the library behind his prey. She struck up a conversation with the librarian at the counter, so he wandered to the floor-to-ceiling shelves. When the Yank took books to a nearby table, Kelly grabbed a random volume from the shelves and sat in the chair beside the window that gave him a clear view of her.

What was the couple up to? They had crisscrossed the city, stopping at no less than five jewelry shops. Now the woman was in a library? At least she was alone. This would be his best chance to grab her. To hell with Logan's orders, Kelly was tired of following her and reporting in. He wanted action and it was time to repay the woman for all his suffering.

Devan found several houses that might fit the murder location, but none matched exactly. None boasted a cannon facing a castle on an island in the middle of a lake. About to give up, she opened the Connemara booklet from the tourist office. The cover showed Connemara National Park and the Twelve Bens above a mist-shrouded bogland.

This was the Ireland Devan imagined as a child, when her mother read bedtime stories to her. Paging through, her eye caught an advertisement offering guided walks of Ballynahinch, a castle hotel and estate. The photo showed the three-story structure at the base of the hill, with mountains in the background and a lake in the foreground. Another possibility, she thought.

Armed with information on several possible sites, Devan stowed her research in her backpack, returned the borrowed materials, and made her way out. Just beyond the library windows, someone brushed her arm. She stepped left to let the person pass.

The next thing Devan knew, a man yanked her into an alley, away from the main road. Devan opened her mouth to yell.

"Don't, or I'll hurt you," a gruff voice spewed into her ear.

Fighting panic, Devan struggled. Her first thought was that Rick had somehow found her. But this man was rougher, not as refined as Rick. The attacker tightened his grip, yanked harder. Something popped in Devan's arm and pain speared in her shoulder. She moaned. The man swung her around to face him. All Devan saw was his cruel mouth.

She didn't think, only reacted. Her knee jerked up and connected with the man's groin. He released her, hissing. One hand cradled his injury as the other grabbed her.

Run, Devan screamed in her mind. Her trembling legs wouldn't cooperate. The man's beefy hand circled her throat and squeezed. Devan's eyes bugged wide. She kicked out; her right foot connected with a bony knee, slid down his shin, and stomped on the top of his boot. Pain shot up her leg. The attacker howled and released her throat.

Now Devan ran, stumbling out of the alley. She had to get away. Her left arm hung limp at her side, her foot sang with each step, and she still felt the pressure of those sausage-fingers closing off her windpipe. She would not cry, would not give in.

Find Christian. He'd know what to do. Where was that pub? Devan tried to scream, get someone's attention, but only quiet sobs escaped.

Limping, Devan pulled open the door and slammed into Christian's chest.

"Christ Jesus!" He held her up. "What happened?"

"I…I." Devan lifted her arm to point to the alley and the attacker. Stabbing pain ran like lightning from her shoulder to her fingertips. She gasped and everything went black.

Devan opened her eyes to find Christian leaning over her. She was laid out on her back. His brow creased as his eyes narrowed. A frown tugged the corners of his mouth. Devan started to push up.

Christian held her down. "No, stay here. You'll just pass out again."

They were in a small, windowless room. The only furniture, besides the couch she occupied, was a chair and a battered desk that held a computer, papers, and a phone. Christian rose and paced between the desk and the door.

Devan closed her eyes against the sharp overhead light. "What happened?"

"That's what I'd like to know."

The couch gave way next to Devan's hip. She opened her eyes a sliver and Christian was seated again. "Where are we?" she asked.

Christian feathered his fingers through her hair. "We're in the snug. The publican's private office." He ran an unsteady hand over his face. "I think your shoulder's dislocated. We're waiting for the medical van and the Gardaí."

"You called the police? I thought you stayed well clear—"

He waved her concern away. "You were attacked. They need to find the bastard. Do you remember anything?"

"Yes." Devan tried to sit up.

"Here, let me help." Christian wrapped his arm under her uninjured shoulder and lifted her. He slipped from the couch, knelt on the floor so she could rest against the back. "Try not to move your arm. What can you tell me?"

Devan winced at the pain radiating up her arm. "He grabbed me, at the library. The alley—"

A brisk knock on the door interrupted. A uniformed man entered, while two medics hovered in the doorway.

"Ma'am, I'm Sergeant Finley." He narrowed his eyes at Christian. "What's the trouble?"

Christian leapt up, placing himself between Devan and the cop. "She was attacked. What kind of city is this? That a person can't walk down the street in open daylight without fearing for her safety?"

Devan leaned to see the policeman, which made her dizzy.

"Calm down, Sir." Finley held up both hands. "I'll ask the questions here."

"She's hurt. I want the medics to treat her, get her to hospital. Then you can ask your questions." Christian waved the medical personnel forward.

"Now, just one minute." The sergeant grabbed Christian's forearm. "You're obstructing an investigation."

Devan tried to stand, but fell back. She cried out.

Christian yanked his arm. "You're going to be free to arrest me for assault in about two breaths. She gets treatment. Now!"

Sergeant Finley moved to the desk, allowing the medics to enter.

"It's her left shoulder," Christian said. "I don't know what else."

The taller medic nodded. "Okay. We're going to immobilize your arm, then we'll get you checked out and fixed up."

The second medic maneuvered into the tiny room. He bound her left arm to her side with a swathe. "There's no room for the stretcher. Can you walk if I help you stand?"

Devan nodded and bit her lower lip to keep from crying. Once outside, she lowered herself to the stretcher with the medic's help.

Christian and the sergeant glowered at each other. "Christian, are you coming?"

"Yes." He faced the medic with the same hard expression he showed the cop. "I'm going with her."

"Let's ride."

Inside the ambulance, Devan watched Christian as the medic inserted an IV. Christian slammed the door on Finley's livid face.

In the hospital exam room, Christian paced. When the door opened, he whirled. The young man in the scrubs and lab coat retreated one step.

"Um, Ms. Fraser?"

"Yes." Christian answered for Devan and gestured for the doctor to enter.

"I'm Doctor Crowley. I have your X-rays." He slapped the film under the clip on the light box. "Your shoulder is dislocated, not separated, so there's no ligament damage. We can anesthetize the area and pop it back into place. You'll be sore for some days, but we won't need to operate." He replaced the first X-ray with another. "There are no broken bones in your foot, just a severe bruise. Again, you're lucky. You'll need to rest it. We'll give you something for the pain and inflammation. I'd like to keep you overnight for observation."

Devan swallowed the lump of fear in her throat and looked at Christian.

He held her right hand. "She's been through enough today. If I swear to keep to your instructions, can I take her out of here?"

The doctor raised his eyebrows.

"If she's in too much pain, I'll bring her back. I promise," Christian said.

"Okay, but I need to reduce the shoulder. You'll have to wait outside."

"I want him to stay." Devan's voice shook. "I was attacked."

Dr. Crowley nodded. "I see. I'll get Nurse Emily and we'll proceed."

"What about the police?" Devan asked when the doctor left.

Christian squeezed her hand. "Not until they're finished attending to you."

"Where's my backpack? I have some possibilities for us to check out."

"Not a chance. You'll be resting, doctor's orders."

Devan tried to glare at him, but the pain… She wouldn't let Christian see her weak. She looked away to blink back the tears.

"I'll look over what you've discovered, once I'm satisfied you're comfortable and safe."

"But—"

"Or I'll let the doctor keep you overnight. Your choice," Christian said.

Devan sulked until a nurse bustled into the room, followed by Dr. Crowley. The nurse helped unbutton Devan's shirt and uncover her injured arm

At the sight of a gigantic needle in the doctor's hand, Devan averted her gaze and fixed on Christian's blue eyes. For the first time, she noticed a slender scar running lengthwise through his right eyebrow.

Dr. Crowley interrupted her contemplation. "Take a deep breath and relax your arm."

Devan breathed through her nose, let it out through pursed lips to a slow count of ten, then sucked another breath. She felt a quick tug and heard a pop that sounded like a shot from a BB gun. "Bloody hell!"

Christian laughed. "Well, it looks like Ireland's winning you over. You're swearing like a true Irish lass."

Devan glared at him through teary eyes. "Not the time to be funny."

Nurse Emily's eyes twinkled as she placed Devan's arm in a sling and helped button her shirt.

"Since you can't use crutches to keep off your foot, I'm placing you in a walking boot," Dr. Crowley said. "I'll be back with medication and instructions."

Ten minutes later Devan sat on the edge of the exam table with a black boot cushioning her foot and wrapping her leg to just below the knee.

"You have a visitor," Dr. Crowley said when he returned.

Devan gave him a blank stare.

"The Gardaí?"

"Oh, right."

"Her medications and instructions." Dr. Crowley handed Christian a stack of papers and two bottles. "Any problems, any pain that can't be controlled by the meds, I want her back here. Your word."

"My word." Christian nodded, folded the papers and stuck them in his back pocket.

"The boot stays on for a week. The sling for three. Keep it on, except for sleeping and bathing. We'll get you an ice pack for your shoulder. Twenty minutes on, every hour for the rest of today. Then several times a day for the next three weeks. I've included some shoulder exercises to start after you remove the sling." His instructions complete, Dr. Crowley left.

A brief knock on the door and Sergeant Finley entered. "Ms. Fraser, I'd like to get an accounting of the attack, if you're up to it."

Devan relayed everything she remembered, careful to leave out why she was at the library.

"Where can I reach you if I have more questions?"

"We just got into town, so we'll have to call you when we know where we're staying," Christian said.

"So, the two of you are visiting Galway. Mister…?"

"Yes." Christian didn't provide his last name.

"May I inquire as to your relationship with Ms. Fraser?"

Christian stared daggers into the sergeant's eyes. "That's between us. It's not against the law."

"No, it's not." Finley inclined his head. "Just curious."

"I don't like seeing her hurt, or harassed."

Finley closed his notebook. "Neither does the Galway City Gardaí. Tourism is one of our largest industries. We take all assaults seriously. You might want to try the Harbour Hotel near Eyre Square and Quay Street." At Christian's blank look, Finley continued. "Hotel, place to stay. The staff is exceptional and there's easy access to stores and restaurants nearby. I'll give you a lift back to your car."

"No need." Christian wrapped his arm around Devan's waist and eased her off the exam table. "We can manage and we wouldn't want to keep you from your job."

"I'll be continuing the investigation." Finley opened the door and waved them through. "So, I insist."

Upon returning to the pub, Christian led a hobbling Devan to a corner booth.

She raised her brow. "What are we doing here?"

"You need to eat. You're shaking like a leaf; you need food and pain medicine. In case you haven't noticed, it's past tea time and you've had nothing to eat since breakfast." Christian signaled for two menus. "I also want the sergeant to leave before us, so he can't follow or figure out who I am."

After they ordered, Devan leaned her head back and closed her eyes. "Why would Finley be interested in you?"

"I've not had good experiences with the Gardaí. I don't want them tailing us. We don't know where my dreams are leading, or what the Gardaí knows of the murders."

"Okay, but I think the sergeant was just helping." Devan ate her fish and chips in silence, trying to remember more details of her attacker, to no avail.

Christian gave her a pill from each bottle. "I'm going to settle the check and see if Finley's car is still around. Then we'll go." He came back minutes later. "Finley's gone. I asked the publican about lodging. He confirmed the Harbour Hotel is our best shot. There are bed and breakfasts around, but their guest rooms are on the second or third floor with no lifts. At least the hotel has easy access, so we'll go there."

"Sounds good to me." Devan winced as she slid out of the booth.

Christian grabbed her waist with both hands and lifted her to a standing position. Devan swayed.

"Lean on me." Christian wrapped his arm around her. He nodded to the barman as they exited.

They walked out into the late afternoon. Clouds gathered on the horizon and Devan thought they would have a nice soaking by the morning.

At the hotel, Christian helped her from the car. "We'll check in, get you comfortable, then I'll come back for the luggage."

Devan laid back on the cushions Christian propped against the headboard of the bed. When he left, Devan slid her left arm out of the sling, and cried.

Stupid, stupid, stupid, she told herself. You should've handed over your money. Now she was injured and would slow Christian down. He might even leave her here to investigate on his own. She wiped her eyes, reached for a tissue to blow her nose, and gasped at the pain that stole her breath.

More tears fell. Devan clenched her teeth. She swung her legs off the bed, pushed up with her good arm, and stood with her legs shoulder width apart until the dizziness abated. Lurching like Frankenstein, she made it to the bathroom. She was washing her face one-handed when someone pounded on the door.

"Bloody hell." Christian swore. "Why didn't you wait for some help? I thought you were abducted when I didn't see you where I left you."

Devan opened the door.

Christian scowled. His gaze dropped to the sling still loose around her neck. "Why'd you take it off?"

"I wanted to lie down and the doctor said not to use it in the shower or for sleeping."

"But you're not lying down. Must I take you back to hospital?"

"No." She glared at him. "I can't wear this thing for three weeks. Besides, Doctor Crowley popped my shoulder back into place. I'll be careful."

"That you will. Because you'll be wearing the damn sling."

"Maybe for a day or two, but not for three whole weeks."

"We'll see. I'm bigger and stronger." Christian pulled her toward him.

Devan stiffened briefly and opened her mouth to protest. Christian claimed her mouth with a searing kiss. He feathered kisses over her cheeks, down to her throat. Framing her face with his hands, he touched his lips to her brow.

"You've got guts." His eyes darkened. "It's one of the sexiest things about you. I want you, whole and healthy. I want to feel your arms holding me, both arms." His mouth returned to hers. He guided her back to the bed.

Before Christian broke contact, Devan cupped the back of his neck and deepened the kiss. She tasted his desire and poured her own into the flames that leapt between them. Laid back against the pillows, her eyes closed. She drifted, and thought of nothing but Christian.

Twenty Six

Devan awoke to the plink, plink, plink of rain hitting metal gutters. Her head rested on Christian's shoulder. She realized she was still propped up in a sitting position. Her shoulder lay tucked against his side, protected, but the pain made itself known.

Christian slept soundly in the awkward slouching position.

With as much care as she could, Devan inched away. Despite her efforts, when her head left Christian's shoulder, he stirred.

His arm pinned her against the pillows. "Where do you think you're going?"

Devan tried to push him away. "To the bathroom."

"Let me help." Christian released her, rolled from the bed, and helped her to stand. When she swayed, he said, "Take a minute to get your legs under you."

Limping, Devan reached the bathroom. She found her toiletry bag on the counter, where Christian must have unpacked it. She washed her face, brushed her teeth, and brushed her hair. When she opened the door, he was ordering room service.

"Maybe I wanted to go downstairs to eat."

"You're hurting. This is easier. Afterward, I'll help you with a bath."

Devan snorted. "I can handle that myself." She rummaged in her suitcase for a clean outfit. "I'll need to do laundry soon." She struggled with her clothes single-handed.

Christian took them from her and placed them on the counter near the tub. "We can send the dirty stuff to the hotel laundry after you've cleaned up."

When the meal arrived, they ate in silence. Devan swallowed her medications with her tea and pushed up to head to the bath. Christian followed.

"I can do this. I've been bathing alone for many years now."

"You've not been shorthanded before, I'll wager." Devan scowled and Christian laughed. "You don't have anything I haven't seen already. Besides, we'll be lovers soon. You know it as well as I."

"Not if I don't wish it." Devan narrowed her eyes. *But you do wish it,* she thought.

"And do you?" Christian broke her train of thought.

"Do I what?"

"Not wish to be lovers?"

Startled that Christian seemed to read her mind, Devan stuttered. "N-no."

"Liar." Christian's eyes swept from her face, down her shirt and jeans, to the one booted foot, then up again to rest on her face. His mouth covered hers.

Heat spread from her center. Devan melted against Christian and tried to remember that she didn't really know him. *Liar,* her mind whispered. Christian closed the distance, until not even a hair separated them. His tongue explored her mouth, urged hers to do the same.

Then the world shut off. All that remained was the wonder of mouth against mouth, body against body, until Devan heard twin moans: his and hers. She wanted to stay wrapped in Christian's embrace forever. God, he was so solid, so hard. Devan was baffled that he wanted her. But he did. She could feel his desire.

Christian lightened the kiss, nibbled on her lips, then eased back. He held her hips, gentle yet firm. His lips twitched up. "Your body betrays you. I could have you now."

A blush rose over Devan's cheeks and she knew he was right.

Before she could respond, Christian said, "I don't want that. When we become lovers, it won't be just sex. We'll make love, the two of us. Equally. I may be many things, but I'm not a rutting beast."

Devan nodded and noticed the deep blue of his eyes had darkened to midnight.

"Now, let me help. I'll wash your back." Christian unbuttoned and slipped her shirt from her injured shoulder. "Sit and I'll take off the boot." He knelt, lifted her foot to his thigh, and unstrapped the cushioned boot.

Devan sighed, wiggled her exposed toes, and rotated her ankle. "No pain. Maybe I can skip the boot."

"Let's see how it feels when you put weight on it. How's the shoulder?"

"Better." Devan grimaced when Christian lifted her arm past her breast.

"Better than what?" He lowered her arm and helped her to stand.

"Better than before Doc Crowley popped it back." The arch of her foot ached.

"Hmm." Christian unsnapped her jeans.

Devan covered Christian's hand when he grabbed the zipper. "I can do it."

"Stubborn woman." He sighed. "I'll start the bath. Don't try to walk."

Devan frowned and waited for him to leave.

"I mean it, Devan." Christian's voice echoed from the bathroom. "I'll take you back to hospital if you're naughty."

"You've got a mean streak as well." Devan sat down and finished removing her jeans. "And I don't like it."

Christian laughed over the splashing water. Swallowing her nervousness, Devan called out to him. "It seems I need help after all."

A smile lit Christian's face when he returned. He sat next to her on the bed and unhooked her bra.

The heat of a blush started at her breasts, rose over a throat that squeezed closed, and continued to her hairline. Devan risked a glance. Christian was aroused. He bent, put her jeans on the bed with her shirt and bra.

"Now your knickers." Again, Christian helped her stand and pulled them off. He skimmed her naked body, then diverted his eyes and guided her to the bath.

Everywhere his fingers touched, heat flowed to Devan's core while shivers of desire brought goosebumps to her flesh. Though Christian remained fully clothed, the vulnerability of Devan's nakedness disappeared. He was right, they were linked. Sharing this intense moment felt more intimate than anything she'd experienced with Rick. Devan sank into the sweet, honeysuckle-scented bubbles, tucking her left arm snug against her body. Christian watched her.

"It doesn't seem fair that I'm naked and you're not." Her voice rose with her nerves.

"Christ, Devan. Are you trying to kill me?"

"No, just evening the playing field."

Christian's eyes darkened and he let out a strangled chuckle. "You're covered with bubbles, I say that makes us even."

"I am now, but your eyes drank their fill before. Mine should get the same privilege. Come on, you can't be shy."

"If I get naked, I won't stop there." His right eyebrow rose.

Devan curled a lip at his implication, displaying a confidence she didn't quite feel. "We'll deal with that later. Besides, how else are you going to help wash my back?"

Christian pulled his T-shirt over his head and dropped it. Devan stared at his smooth muscular chest, shades lighter than his arms. A single fine line of black hair started at his navel and disappeared toward the bulge in his dark jeans. Her mouth went dry, then saliva pooled at the corners. Devan swallowed.

Am I ready for this? she wondered. We've only known each other a short time. What does time have to do with the depth of your feelings?

Christian toed off his shoes. "Last chance." His hand went to the snap of his jeans. "These come off and we'll be lovers today." His gaze held hers.

Devan wiped perspiration from her lip, then bobbed her head up and down.

A dimple formed on Christian's left cheek as he smiled. Lord, he looked like a Celtic god with those chiseled cheekbones, a touch too-long black hair, and those deep, lake-blue eyes.

Christian removed the last barriers then climbed into the claw foot tub, straddling her, his chest against her back. He kissed the nape of her neck and her shoulders, gentle with her injured side.

"What's this?" With his finger, Christian traced the tattoo on her left shoulder. "A bit of a wild streak. Did you rebel against your parents?"

Devan led out a shaky breath. God, the heat of the bath had risen. "No," she said as his open-mouthed kisses fluttered over the tattoo. "They didn't necessarily agree, but there was no rebellion. I wanted it, no…I needed it, craved it like an addict craves heroin. I've been captivated by dragons for as long as I can remember."

Christian soaped a washcloth. "It's perfect, destiny even. And you have another." He rubbed his thumb over her right biceps. She couldn't speak. He tilted her head to the side, and rubbed his lips against hers.

The heat made Devan lightheaded. She tried to tell herself it had nothing to do with a gorgeous, naked, aroused man stroking her, kissing her senseless. Christian washed her back, her arms, and swirled his soapy fingertips to her breasts. He circled her nipples until they pebbled hard under his thumbs. Devan gasped as more heat spread from her center. His erection hardened against her soap-slicked back, smooth as velvet. Christian caressed her belly, lifted her right leg, washed her foot, her calf, the back of her knee, then her upper thigh. When she reached to block him, he started on her other leg.

"Relax," Christian bit her ear lobe, then soothed the ache with his moist tongue. He reclined and pulled her with him.

Devan closed her eyes, pressed her back to Christian's chest, drifting as he drew lazy circles over her breasts and down. He dipped a finger into her, and groaned. His thumb stroked her, working in tandem with his finger. Devan's eyes flew open. She shuddered and arched against his hand. "Lord, what are you doing to me?"

"Pleasuring you, pleasuring me." He picked up the pace.

The tension at Devan's core grew, almost painful as Christian continued his assault. His breathing matched her own. A moan escaped before Devan could bite her lip. She wanted him to stop, she wanted him to never stop, for this vicious need he brought out in her to end.

"Let go," Christian whispered, his voice husky.

Devan shook her head. "I can't." She fought the wonderful sensations rushing through her body.

"You can. Just feel. I've got you." His finger pressed against her insides. "Fly, I'll catch you."

The orgasm ripped through Devan. She'd never felt anything like this, not in any of her romantic, youthful dreams. Her moan trembled and her body quaked as warmth flooded through her.

Christian kissed her neck, nuzzled, and dipped his tongue into her ear.

"Oh, God," Devan said as another shiver overtook her.

"You're welcome." Christian chuckled. He pulled the tub stopper, pushed up and out of the tub.

Devan watched, fascinated as Christian slung a towel low around his hips. His erection was evident. He tossed a second towel over his shoulder, then bent over the tub.

"Mind your shoulder." Christian scooped her into his arms and carried her to the bed. He sat with her in his lap and began to dry her with the second towel. When he was done, he tossed the towel away. Christian lifted her into his arms again, knelt in the center of the bed, and laid her down. He covered her mouth and kissed her slow and sweet.

Devan's eyes fluttered closed as lips and tongue explored. She ran her hand up his muscled arm, over his shoulder, and into his hair. Christian deepened the kiss before pulling away to sit back on his heels and look at her naked body.

In his eyes, Devan saw a hunger she had never seen before. Was she ready for this? She'd had sex before, but did that unpleasant experience measure up to the challenge she now faced? She trembled with apprehension.

Christian's eyes gentled as he whipped his towel to the floor. He picked up her right foot, ran his fingers from the bruised arch to the top of her foot, then trailed up to the back of her knee. His lips followed, nibbling and soothing the tiny flames his fingertips had incited. When he reached the notch of her thigh, Devan thought she would die from bursts of pleasure. She shuddered.

"Are you cold?"

"No." She could never be cold again. The heat tore through her. "No."

Christian repeated his attention on her other side. Devan lay steeped in sensations. The world spun, but they were the only people in it.

When Christian's mouth clamped over her moist core, even the world stopped. His tongue drove into her, into the heat. She pressed him closer, her fingers threaded through his silky black hair as she cried out her pleasure. Christian's kiss tasted of desire, dark and pungent, as he moved over her. His erection pressed against her for two heartbeats, then he plunged deep. He held himself there as her body convulsed in another orgasm.

Together, they moved in the ancient mating dance. Christian's mouth roamed her face, then settled on the pulse in her throat. He quickened the pace, returned his lips to hers. This time, Devan was ready to make demands of her own. Her tongue met his as she lifted her body to his. Christian groaned and pressed Devan deep into the mattress. They flew off the edge together.

When Devan could draw a steady breath, she saw the watery sunlight seep through the window, casting small circular rainbows over the bed. Christian's heart beat a staccato, identical to hers. He started to pull away, but Devan held him with her good arm.

"I'm heavy." His breath tickled her neck.

"No, I like it."

Christian raised his head and looked at her. "I would roll us until you're on top, but I don't want to hurt you. How's the shoulder?"

"Can't tell." Devan wiggled her fingers. "It's throbbing to the same drumbeat as my heart." A smug grin lit Christian's face. Trailing her hand over passion-slicked skin, Devan squeezed his butt. "Mmm, nice ass."

Christian reached under her, lifting her hips until he could duplicate the action. "You too." He nipped at her chin.

When he moved inside her, Devan moaned. She felt him harden, fill her. This time, Christian slowed into long, deep strokes. As the orgasm began to shimmer through Devan, Christian whispered words in a language she didn't understand, and followed her into the magic.

When Christian felt the need for her surge in his groin, he slipped out of bed. He didn't want to risk re-injuring her shoulder, though he wanted to make love to her again. Scooping up their used towels, he tossed them into the tub, and rubbed his hands over last night's stubble. He pulled on a fresh pair of khakis, leaving his chest bare. Gathering their dirty clothes in a hotel laundry bag, he dialed the concierge, requested service, then placed it outside the door.

Christian sat at the small, round breakfast table and watched her sleep. What was it about her? He'd lain with women before, but he'd never felt the desire to have a woman after he'd just finished making love with her. With Devan, it seemed the more he quenched his need, the higher the flames of his desire leapt, until he couldn't catch his breath. Unless he was mistaken— and he wasn't—he'd taken her further than she'd ever been before. A grin spread over his lips.

It wasn't just her body. Christian wanted all of her. The grin shifted to a slight frown. Forcing his thoughts away from Devan lying cozy and flushed from loving, Christian opened her backpack. Her notes of the third murder were stuffed into the brochures from the tourist office. He spread them over the table. Before he could sift through them, someone knocked on the door.

Christian pulled a T-shirt over his head, glanced to make sure Devan hadn't stirred, then answered the polite knock.

"Afternoon, Mr. Riley," Sergeant Finley said as his gaze swept over Christian's attire, down to his bare feet, and back to his face. "Am I interrupting?"

"No." Christian noticed Finley's use of his last name. He probably checked with the registration desk. "Devan's resting. Have you found the bastard who hurt her?"

"I'd like to discuss that with Ms. Fraser."

"Christian?" Devan's sleepy voice drifted to where the two men stood with the door partially closed.

"I'm here, love. The Gardaí's here to see you." Christian narrowed his eyes at the sergeant. "Wait here."

Christian returned to Devan, helped her sit up, and dressed her in one of his button up shirts. It hung loose over her naked form. He pulled the bed covers over her waist, kissed her once, then strode to the door.

"Don't tire her out," he warned Finley.

Sergeant Finley removed his hat as he entered the room. Droplets of water fell to the carpet. "Ms. Fraser," he said with a slight nod. "I wanted to see how you're faring."

"I'm fine. Have you any news on my attacker?" Devan cradled her left arm against her body.

Finley glanced down at the carpeted floor, then back at Devan. "No, not yet."

Christian sat on the bed beside Devan, took her hand and linked fingers. "What have you been doing?"

Gesturing to a chair at the table, Finley sat when the pair nodded. "We've been combing the streets for a man fitting the description you provided. We've also checked at the hospitals. No luck. I think he may have gone to ground. Went into hiding, maybe even left Galway."

"Oh." Devan sighed, stared down at the shirt buttons.

"Not to worry, we'll keep our eye out. I don't think he'll try for you again." Finley smiled at her. "You probably put him out of commission for a while." He stood and looked at the colorful advertisements of the Connemara brochure on the table. "You two planning on doing some fly fishing? I hear Ballynahinch Castle is the best spot around. They regularly pull eight kilo fish from that lake. Anyway, you staying here for a few more days?"

"We'll be here at least until tomorrow, maybe longer." Christian walked Finley to the door.

"She'll be safe. I really think the perp took off," Finley said.

"Damn right she'll be safe…with me. I'll not let her out of my sight. Find him. I'll be in touch." Christian closed the door. When he came back into the room, Devan was struggling to get out of bed. "Oh, no you don't. Where do you think you're going?"

"I need to get up, move. I can't stay in bed all day."

Christian pressed Devan back against the pillows. His mouth descended on hers. The kiss spun out, wrapping her scent around him, until he couldn't think of anything but her and making love. He lifted his lips. "Wanna bet?"

Twenty Seven

Matthew O'Shea removed the riding harness and rubbed Kieran's neck scales. He thought about his friend Peter being overwhelmed with new responsibilities. Caring for a newborn dragon entailed a lot of work, even with help from other dragons and members of the compound. Peter had none. Kiely had foisted Grayson on Peter and still expected him to attend to his other duties with the horses and livestock. Matthew squinted into the late afternoon sun as Kieran flew off to the pens to eat. Matthew headed to the large open doors of Tullia's chamber where he hoped to find Peter.

With hands tucked into his back pockets, Matthew leaned against the open doorway. "What can I do to help?"

"Nothing." Peter whined. "Unless you can magically sprout wings for this beast." He inclined his head toward Grayson. Peter slopped a water bucket in the near corner. The water sloshed over the edge to turn the dirt and hay into a muddy mess. Matthew held his tongue at the careless treatment his friend showed the dragonet.

Grayson lay curled in a mound of hay, far from his caretaker.

Matthew retrieved a rag and oil. "I'll start oiling Grayson while you get his food, then we'll get something to eat ourselves. We haven't had much chance to hang out since—" He stopped, not wanting to bring up Peter's not partnering a dragon.

"Thanks, Matt." Peter grabbed the empty food bucket. "I'd like that. You're the only one who understands what I'm going through."

When Peter left, Matthew linked to his compeer. *"Kieran, has Grayson complained about Peter's attitude or care?"*

"I have not heard one thought from the little one since the clan leader left several days ago. Do ye want me to inquire?"

"No, it's not necessary. I'm going to oil his leg joints. Just let me know if you pick up any disturbed thoughts." Matthew broke the mental contact.

"GRAYSON, I'm Matthew, the clan leader's son. I'm going to work some oil into your legs, okay? We don't want your hide to crack as you grow. Let me know if I'm hurting you, you can bespeak my dragon KIERAN. He'll listen for you."

The dragonet uncoiled his body, looked at Matthew, then stretched his hind legs. Matthew worked in silence. He oiled all four legs and started on the underbelly before Peter returned. Peter plopped the bucket full of fresh meat next to the water. Matthew opened his mouth to speak. Peter turned to him, sighed, then retrieved the bucket and brought it over to the waiting dragonet.

"Do you mind if I feed him?" Matthew asked. "It's been a while since KIERAN was young enough to need my assistance. I miss it."

Peter shrugged. "Be my guest. I don't know why you'd want to, it's bloody messy."

Matthew suppressed a retort. He didn't want to lecture Peter on the difference between caring for a dragonet and other newborn animals. Instead, Matthew decided on another approach.

"Did Kiely give you the rundown on GRAYSON's care?"

"No." Peter sulked as he slouched on a stool by the door, his feet outstretched, crossed at the ankles. "She volunteered me in front of Sean, Uncle Padrick, and the entire Beaghmore clan, then she and TULLIA left. Each day, while everyone is out on patrol, I'm expected to be here morning and evening. Grandmother tells me nothing. She just complains about your father and being replaced as Ulster leader."

Matthew wiped his hands clean, and lifted a chunk of meat to GRAYSON. The dragonet nipped the morsel from his fingertips.

"Grandfather told me the beast would be moved to the barn in a couple more days," Peter said. "Then he and Grandmother would pack up their stuff from the office, so Michael could use it."

Nodding, Matthew fed Grayson another chunk of raw, bloody meat. "That's about right, newborn dragonets go to the dragon lair when they're about a week old."

"You heard Kieran right away, didn't you? I can't hear this one at all."

"No, I heard Kieran when he selected me as his compeer. He chose earlier than the usual one year, but still I didn't hear him until then. Kieran talked to the other dragons, though. And I spoke to him aloud whenever it was my turn to care for him. You should talk with Grayson. I think it helps with the partnering."

"Maybe. I'm so pissed off at my grandmother for what she's done. Sorry for not confiding in you about Tullia's mating. Grandmother made me swear not to say anything, especially to you. She threatened to drive me from the clan. Said she'd keep me away from everyone I cared about. She'd done it before and would have no trouble doing so again."

Matthew wanted to ask what Peter meant, but decided to loosen his friend's tongue over an early supper. Finished with Grayson, Matthew rubbed the dragonet's muzzle affectionately and stood.

"Let me wash up and I'll meet you in the dining hall."

In the food line, they bumped shoulders like they had when they held each other's secrets as school mates. They heaped fried chicken, potato salad, and slaw on their plates. Each grabbed a pint of Guinness.

"What do you say to eating by the lake?" Matthew asked. "We'd have some privacy."

Peter handed Matthew his pint. "I'll get us a full pitcher."

Hands brimming with food and Guinness, the two found a spot under a whitethorn tree and set to filling their stomachs.

"What did you mean when you said Kiely would run you out of the clan? She can't do that. You have every right to be here." Matthew took a large bite of his chicken.

Peter shrugged, took a long drink from his dark stout, then refilled his glass. "My mom isn't here."

"But she and your da chose not to live with the clan," Matthew said. "They weren't prevented from staying or from moving to another clan compound."

"We don't know that for sure. They've never said anything to me or my siblings about their decision. But I know Grandmother's passion for Northern Ireland." Peter ate some potato salad and washed it down with another long drink. "I heard she was livid at Uncle Padrick when he chose to leave Beaghmore for Lough Gur. She saw it as an affront, choosing the Republic over Northern Ireland, his best friend Sean over his family." Peter wiped his mouth with a napkin. "Around that time, his fiancée left without a word. I wasn't supposed to know about that, but I heard my mom argue with Grandmother about it when I was near on ten years old. Shortly after, Mom and Da decided to move away from here. I never understood the tension between Uncle Paddy and Grandmother, until now. She's a controlling old hag."

Matthew pointed his half-eaten chicken leg at Peter. "You think she can make you leave?"

"She knows I want to be a dragonrider. Grandmother's in a position to give that to me, or take it away. It's her greatest weapon. She finds your weakness, then exploits it." Peter drained his remaining Guinness and poured another full pint. "I want this more than anything, so I'll need to stay on her good side. And she knows it."

"Kiely has no influence on who becomes a rider. Each dragon picks their own compeer." Matthew took a casual sip from his own pint. "You said she told you she'd run someone off before. Do you know who?"

"I don't have proof, but I think it was Uncle Paddy's fiancée."

Matthew stared across the lake. "Have you thought about bringing all this to my father's attention, as clan leader, or at least Padrick's?"

"No, and I can't complain. Grandmother brought me back here when I was floundering after secondary school. I owe her."

"You don't owe her anything, you're family. Besides, you perform a valuable service to the clan." Matthew punched his friend's shoulder. "You'll always have a place here, even if you're not a dragonrider."

Peter rubbed his shoulder, then shrugged. "I asked Uncle Paddy once about his fiancée. His face clouded over like he was angry and sad at the same time. He asked how I heard about her. When I told him I heard Mom and Grandmother fighting about it, Padrick said it was his business, adult business, and not to be concerned about something that happened before I was born. I never asked again."

Finished with his meal, Matthew stood and searched the nearby shore for stones. Finding several round, flat ones, he notched the first between thumb and forefinger, crouched low, and threw horizontal to the surface of the lake. Matthew counted the skips—one, two, three, four, five. He was pleased when Peter joined him in their favorite schoolboy activity. Several rounds later, Peter's stone skipped eight times before sinking into the placid lake. Matthew declared his friend the winner and vowed a rematch.

"You know, you can talk to me anytime," Matthew said. "If Kiely makes any more threats, veiled or otherwise, you should talk to Padrick or your folks. I think they'd understand."

"Thanks." Peter laid a hand on his arm. "I was feeling down and you let me vent."

Matthew turned from the lake. "I better get back, I have some stuff to do before my night patrol. Let me know if you need help with GRAYSON." He gathered his dishes and headed off to the dining hall.

Surveying the tables in the room, Matthew found Daniel, his patrol partner, finishing his meal. Kiely and Ronan's table stood empty.

"We can leave for our evening patrol in an hour," Matthew told Daniel, then he left the dining hall and checked on GRAYSON. He saw the dragonet alone and sleeping in a corner of TULLIA'S chamber.

Perfect, Matthew thought. *KIERAN, are TULLIA, CALHOUN, and their riders on patrol?*

Yes. They left when ye were oiling the little one. Are we off as well?

Damn. Kiely and Ronan would be back soon.

I just need to gather my riding gear, be right there, Matthew bespoke his compeer.

During his short night patrol with Daniel and LORCAN, Matthew mulled over his conversation with Peter. He agreed with his friend. If Kiely had forced someone from the clan, it made sense that it was Padrick's fiancée.

Hours later, Matthew crept from his quarters. Outside, the sliver of moonlight wavered in and out of the clouds, hiding his approach to the building farthest from the dragon cavern.

Pressing the flat of his hand like the bill of a cap, and his face to the window, Matthew saw nothing but black. He tried the doorknob and found it locked. What should he do? He didn't know how to pick locks. Looking around the courtyard, he thought of waking Peter. Maybe he… No, Kiely wouldn't trust Peter with a key to her office.

Matthew heard a snort, followed by a cough. Was someone awake? He bolted around the corner of the office. His heart pounded in his chest like a bodhrán drum. Straining to hear, he couldn't make out anything over the bang, bang, thump, thump of his own heart. As he leaned against the wall looking out to the lake where he and Peter had skipped stones earlier, Matthew's head smacked the protruding frame of a half-opened window.

An old-fashioned crank raised the window open from the bottom. Matthew grasped the wood frame and applied steady but firm pressure up. Centimeter by centimeter the window rose until he had enough space to pull himself up and over the windowsill. He slid across the top of a metal file cabinet that fit under the window. His hand brushed something in the dark room. Panicking, Matthew rolled, grabbing the object before it crashed to the floor, then tucked it to his body like a rugby ball. His momentum somersaulted him the meter and a half to the carpet. On the way, his left foot hit a chair, which rolled into its mate with a thud.

Dazed, splayed on his back, with water drenching the front of his shirt, Matthew fingered the object he held. A vase. He sat up, pulled his torch from his pocket, turned it on, and saw flowers littering the floor. Water seeped into the carpeting.

"Feck," he whispered. Matthew knelt on hands and knees, gathered the crumpled blooms, and shoved the stems into the vase. Standing, he placed the vase on the file cabinet. He doused his torch and studied the bottom of the door leading into Kiely and Ronan's house. No light seeped there.

Finding the door unlocked, Matthew opened it. He could make out a den furnished with a sofa, two chairs, and a television. One wall was dedicated to floor-to-ceiling bookshelves. He sighed. The evidence could be anywhere, or not even exist.

Matthew maneuvered to the far door, pressed his ear against the cool wood, and listened. No sound penetrated.

Where would Kiely hide evidence? Someplace others wouldn't have access. He remembered Peter saying Kiely would be cleaning out her personal items from the office in the next few days, so perhaps Matthew should start there. But when Michael took over, the door between the office and the living quarters would be locked. Better start in here.

Turning his torch back on, Matthew scanned the bookshelves. He searched the family albums first and found one picture of a young Padrick, perhaps mid-twenties, with a young woman. Willow slim with light brown hair, she stood in the man's encircling arms, a look of complete rapture on her face.

Matthew flipped through the entire album and four others, but found no more pictures of the woman—or Padrick, for that matter. When nothing turned up in the photo albums, Matthew stared at the hundreds of books lining the shelves. His gaze swept over titles on multicolored spines. Tired, he rubbed his eyes and pinched the bridge of his nose. Opening his eyes, Matthew noticed the black binding of a book among several tomes on the history of Ireland and the Troubles. There was no title on the thin spine.

He pulled it from the shelf and opened to the first page. Reading with rapt fascination mixed with anger and horror, Matthew learned of Kiely's treachery and why Padrick's fiancée left without a word. Matthew whispered the offending entry.

"...so easy. The tart has no backbone. She won't ruin my son's chance for clan leadership. I've seen to that. Erin bought the whole story of Padrick sowing his oats before he settled down with a dragonrider of my choosing. I told her it was clan law and she fell for the lie. I will never allow my son to take a bride that doesn't belong to the clan. Besides, I framed the chit's father. Told her he'd go to gaol if she came back."

Several pages later, Matthew read aloud the last passages that mentioned Erin.

"...my hired man tracked the girl to Dublin. She must've spied the tail, because she gave him the slip. I paid off the incompetent wretch and dismissed him. Five months have passed and still no sign of the chit. Padrick has left Beaghmore for Lough Gur. He won't listen to reason. Thinks I drove off his precious Erin. If he only knew."

Matthew closed the cover. Furious, he shoved the book into his back pocket, retreated to the office, and closed the door. Then, he heard the shout.

"Stop!"

Matthew launched himself over the file cabinet and through the open window. He rolled to break his fall. Without looking back, he ran for the trees near the lake. His heart pounded in time with his scrambling feet. Matthew stopped when he reached the safety of the whitethorn tree where he and Peter had dined. Bent at the waist, hands on his knees, he sucked oxygen as if he would never breathe again.

Was it Kiely or Ronan that had almost caught him? It didn't matter. He had the evidence. Matthew tapped his back pocket to make sure it was still there. Yes. Now he needed to sneak past the office and house he had just escaped and wait until he was out tomorrow morning to contact his father.

Matthew peeked out from his hiding place. Lights burned bright in the office and several windows of Kiely's house. In the glare, he saw Kiely march toward the livestock pens and the barn. Toward Peter.

Without a second thought for his own safety, Matthew hid the book in a bole at the base of the tree, then strode toward the tack room attached to the barn and the advancing dragonrider.

Matthew and Kiely arrived together, steps from Peter's door.

"What are you doing here?" Kiely's face was red. The lines of her mouth were drawn tight.

Matthew shrugged, tried to look casual. "I couldn't sleep and went for a walk. I saw lights from your house come on and someone heading here. Is GRAYSON all right?"

"Of course, why?" Kiely's eyes narrowed as she studied him.

"You seemed in a rush. Peter is caring for the dragonet, right?"

"Yes. But that's not why I'm out here." Kiely peered beyond him toward the darkened lake.

By her hardened expression, Matthew could tell she didn't believe his alibi. He only hoped she didn't take out his transgression on Peter. Matthew lifted his chin in defiance of her silent accusation. "I'm going in. I think I can sleep now."

"I don't think so," Kiely said. "You were in my office, my house. I demand to know why. Are you spying for your father now? He's taken my position away, what more does he want?" Her voice rose in the still of the night.

Why hadn't Matthew thought of Kiely's hatred for his father? He wasn't sure how to divert her attention. Matthew was a poor liar.

The tackroom door whipped open. A disheveled Peter stood looking at Kiely through sleepy eyes. "Grandmother, what are you doing here?" He rubbed his hand over his face. "Matthew, is that you? What time is it?"

"It's late," Kiely said. "After two."

"What's up?" Peter shifted his gaze from Kiely to Matthew.

"He broke into my office and rummaged around in the den." Kiely fisted her hands on her hips. "I thought it was you." She spun around, her glare hard on Matthew. "I want an answer, you little bastard." She pointed her finger at him.

Matthew took one step back when he realized his shirt was still damp. "I told you, I was out for a walk." His mind latched on a whisper of a thought. "But if you must know, I couldn't sleep because of a woman. I was sorting out my feelings."

"Who?" Kiely demanded.

"I'm not saying." Matthew looked at Peter, then back to Kiely. "I'm going to bed now, if you don't mind."

"Me, too," Peter said.

Kiely waved her hand, dismissing Peter.

The closing door plunged the area into darkness.

"I know you did it." Kiely's voice grew cold. "You can't hide from me. You're just like your thieving whoreson of a father. Know this, you ingrate, breaking and entering is a crime. I'll make sure you're punished." She cackled. "That'll teach the clan leader that I hold the real power."

Twenty Eight

By the second night, Devan was tired of herself and the restrictions Christian imposed by way of doctor's orders. She demanded a stroll after dinner and rebelled on the walking boot, but compromised on the shoulder sling. They meandered the quays. Devan searched faces for the scowling snarl of her attacker. Once, she thought she saw him standing across the street in the reflection of the store window. She whirled around but the sidewalk was empty.

"You're jumpy tonight," Christian said. "Perhaps this is too soon."

"No. I was going stir crazy." Devan glanced sideways at him. "No offense."

Christian chuckled. "None taken. I know what you mean. Finley hasn't tracked down any more clues."

"You spoke to him?"

"He's okay for Gardaí. He's kept me informed."

"But…" Devan raised an eyebrow.

"Nothing. Your attacker is laying low, hasn't been to hospital around here."

"That's good."

"I'd rather he showed himself. We don't know if this was a one-time act, or if he's waiting us out." Christian guided her back to their hotel. "I'd like to know which."

They entered the lobby and Devan found herself scanning the groups of people. How long could she keep up the façade? When would she stop trembling at the slightest stare from an unknown man? And they were all unknown, except for Christian and Sergeant Finley. Devan couldn't even describe the paramedics who had treated her. She was jumping at shadows and she hated the feeling of being a victim. It reminded her too much of her ex.

"Tell me we're leaving tomorrow," Devan said as the elevator doors nicked closed.

Christian nodded. "We'll go, but at the first sign of fatigue from you, we'll tuck in somewhere. You're still recovering and I'll not have you suffer a setback." When the doors opened to their floor, Christian slid his left arm around her. His right hand drummed his hip as he glanced up and down the empty corridor. He did a quick study of his tells, opened the door, then motioned her inside.

"All clear?" Devan asked.

"We're good. I'm not taking any more chances. We'll be extra cautious from now on."

"Yes, sir." Devan saluted.

"Let's get you into bed."

She smiled. "Now there's an idea I can get behind."

"You need to rest," Christian said, though he didn't stop her from unfastening the top two buttons of his shirt.

The next morning, Devan waited in the room while Christian stowed their bags in the car. She studied the map.

They drove northwest in a light rain, arriving at the long gravel drive of Ballynahinch Castle near lunchtime. Several cars dotted the lane and Christian parked across from the immense double-door entrance.

"Let's see if they have room for us. You're looking a little pale. How's the shoulder?"

Devan unfastened her seatbelt, readjusted the sling, and winced at the movement. "It's okay. I'm pale because I've been cooped up and haven't seen sunlight for days."

"Right. It has nothing to do with you still recovering." Christian wrapped an arm around her waist as they walked to the entrance.

Devan sat in front of a fire to the left of the registration desk while Christian signed them in. The decor ran toward rustic hunting and fishing cabin more than a castle. She hoped the rooms didn't boast plaque-mounted fish.

"We're set," Christian said. "Room nine. The desk manager gave me some information on the lake. This may be the place. She said there's a lakeshore trail that has views of O'Flaherty Castle on the island in the lake. She mentioned the cannon aimed at the castle."

Devan admired the view of the river from the window seat in the room. "Let's go see."

"After lunch. They've got a restaurant just off the registration area." He walked into the bathroom. "Nice tub."

Devan felt the blush redden her cheeks. "Is that all you can think about?"

Christian poked his head back into the room. "I'm thinking about a warm bath to ease your shoulder, especially if it's still raining after lunch. Besides, who couldn't keep her good hand off who last night?"

"A moment of insanity, I assure you." Devan grinned, shocked that she was joking with the scoundrel.

"Must I prove you wrong?" Christian lifted her into his arms and nibbled on her lips, trailing kisses over her jaw and down her throat.

As the heat spread inside her, Devan moaned. "Okay, okay. You win."

He set her back on her feet. "Do you want to rest a bit, or eat?"

"Let's have lunch. You're not going to distract me and leave me here while you check out the murder site."

"Okay, but if it's coming down hard, we'll rest some."

Devan waited in the hallway, looking at old photos while Christian set his tells.

"Do you really think someone's following us?" she asked. "This is an expensive place—surely no one would break in."

He shrugged. "I told you, I'm not taking any chances."

They sat at a table near the peat-burning brick fireplace in the restaurant. Several tables were full and three places at the bar were occupied. Devan scanned the individuals, especially the men. None looked like her attacker. She noticed trophies of fish hanging on the walls. The room had a homey feel to it and she began to relax.

The server took their order, then Christian reached for Devan's good hand.

"How are you feeling?" he asked. "The truth."

"I'm a little sore, stiff. I want to ditch the sling. Get some movement before it seizes up."

"After our walk, we'll do the mobility exercises the doctor gave you. Then you need to rest."

Devan polished off her sandwich and handed the prescription bottle to Christian. "Can you open this?"

"You must be feeling better." He pointed to her empty plate. "It's the most you've eaten in days."

"Their food's exquisite, even this lunch. I can't wait to enjoy dinner."

"That's good, because this place is the only food on the estate, unless you catch us dinner."

"Ha, ha. I'll eat fish, but I'm not touching slimy worms to catch it."

"No worms used here, Miss." The waiter refilled her water glass. "We're known for our fly fishing, hand-tied fly lures. Much cleaner and more skill involved. Perhaps, you'll have a go for your lady," he said to Christian. "Can I interest you in something else, dessert perhaps?"

Devan shook her head. "Maybe later. Thanks. My compliments to the chef. Best meal I've had in days."

"He'll like hearing that, I'll pass it along."

The rain had stopped, but the clouds threatened.

"Are you sure you're up for this?" Christian asked. Devan nodded.

They followed a trail that kept the lake on their right, then passed under an overgrown shrubbery tunnel. After thirty minutes, at a pace she could handle, the cannon came into view. Quiet permeated the area.

"This is it," Christian said. "Everything is the same. Except for the snow and ice. The cannon, the view of the castle on the island, even the low wall here." He walked around the cannon, leaned against the cool iron, and stared out at the lake. His voice drifted and his eyes glazed, as if in a trance.

"The fisherman may not be the one. Not enough power. The dagger's away, but the dragon blocks it. Hurled backward into the cannon. Christ, enough power to knock into this unforgiving hunk of iron, but not enough to bring my family back. Six months. I've lost them again."

Christian sagged. Tears fell onto his pale cheeks.

Devan steadied him. "Let's go back. You're whiter than I am."

"The grief, the guilt impale his soul." Christian rubbed his hands over his face, shuddering.

They retraced their steps, hand-in-hand, until they came upon a gravel road that veered off from the trail. To the left of the one-lane road, a two-story house sat behind iron security gates. Half a mile later, they came to a T-junction. Ballynahinch was to the left, and the main road several hundred yards to the right.

"I didn't notice this road when we drove in," Devan said. "Did you?"

"No. My eyes were drawn to the walled gardens and the castle. A killer could have taken this road, parked past the private house by the lake, and retrieved the body, all without coming into contact with anyone from Ballynahinch."

The rain that threatened during their walk broke with a flash of lightning followed by a distant boom. Drops pelted them. They rushed as fast as Devan could manage to the castle doors.

Once inside, Christian helped her out of her coat. "Let's get you warm and dry." He checked the undisturbed tell on the room door before using the old-fashioned key in the lock.

They rested until dinnertime.

"Ever wonder why he killed at this place?" Devan asked. "I mean, the first two sites were on sacred ground or near well-known monuments."

"Based on the grief I feel during the dream, I think the killer's wife and son died near here. Or he was here when he lost them." The smooth Irish lilt was back in Christian's voice, the tragedy he relived at the cannon no longer clinging to him.

Devan nodded. "You mentioned six months in your vision. I can do a search for deaths last June. I'll check around this area first, then widen the search if I come up empty."

"We can start that tomorrow."

After dinner, Christian and Devan chatted with the bartender about the area and any local legends. They learned of a horse-eel that lodged itself beneath the arched bridge on the river they had traversed on their earlier walk. The bartender explained that the monster became jammed under the bridge, causing the water from the river to stop. A local blacksmith fashioned a spear to pull the monster free, but the night before the man was to attempt it, a flood loosened the beast and swept it away.

"Do you believe the story?" Devan raised an eyebrow.

The bartender rubbed his chin. "I haven't seen it with me own eyes, but a local man, Martin, has seen a few strange things. Flying things in the night sky, stuff like that. I'm no judge."

Devan slid a glance to Christian. He shrugged and finished his pint.

"Do you think this Martin has seen dragons?" Devan rubbed her thumb over her dragon ring as they climbed the stairs to their room.

"Probably had too much to drink one night, made it all up to keep out of trouble with the wife."

"Still, we should track down the man. He might have some answers for us. This is the first mention of a possible dragon sighting."

Christian stepped into the room first, then motioned Devan forward. "Tomorrow is soon enough." He closed the door and slid the security bolt home. His mouth closed over hers and Devan couldn't think about dragons, or anything else.

The next day, Christian pulled the car into the long driveway of the Dan O'Hara Heritage Centre. The sun shone bright. The flowers still held raindrops from yesterday's storm. A farm tractor hitched to a twenty-seat trolley sat cockeyed at the entrance of the white-trimmed, lemon yellow two-story farmhouse.

A man with a full head of white hair leaned against the reservation counter. Devan thought he looked about sixty years old. The buttons of his sweater were misaligned over a wrinkled shirt. Gray trousers showed wear at the seams and mud splotches near his brown loafers.

"Can I help you, young folks?" Cornflower blue eyes twinkled and his voice carried the slow, heavy Irish lilt predominant in the West. "We have a tour starting in an hour. You can begin with the film presentation, or take a turn around the front garden to see the Crannog and Ring Fort." He gestured behind them to the entrance.

"Perhaps we can do the tour later," Christian said. "Rory, from Ballyna-hinch Castle, told us you've had some unusual sightings."

"And so I have." He extended his hand. "I'm Martin. And you are?"

"I'm Devan and this is my…Christian." She hoped she wasn't blushing.

"You're a Yank. You here to find your heritage?"

Devan's heart quickened. Did this man know something? Christian gripped her hand and squeezed. She recognized his attempt to steady her nerves.

"Something like that."

"Thought so. You've got the look of an Irish lass. The complexion. And a dreaminess in your eyes."

"We're researching for a book," Devan lied. "A compilation of strange happenings."

"You've come to the place for it. Ireland is full of myths and legends. And the West, more so than anywhere else." Martin led them to a cozy seating area across from the entrance. "If it's a story you're after, I've a few to tell."

"We're interested in any that might include dragons. Rory mentioned a horse-eel. Do you have other tales along the same thread?" Devan sat in a plush floral-patterned sofa near the empty hearth.

Christian dropped next to her. Martin took a chair across from them. He leaned forward, his elbows on his knees like he was about to impart the secret whereabouts of a pot of gold.

"There are stories of a large dragon-like sea serpent that travels the loughs throughout Connemara. Legend has the wingless dragon traversing the waters using underground rivers. Nobody's seen the creature for the last thirty years or so. Bogs are good for hiding eels and such."

"What about flying dragons?" Devan asked.

"Well, I'll tell ya, just like I told that book writer many years ago." Martin launched into his version of the time when he was returning home through the boglands and saw a disk hovering in the evening sky. The lights suggested the object was searching for something, but it didn't move like any flying machine Martin had ever seen.

"So it was a UFO, not a living, breathing entity." Christian squeezed

Devan's hand. "That's certainly strange, but not quite what we're looking for." They stood.

"Thanks for your time. We'll be on our way." Devan shook Martin's hand, disappointment in her voice.

Twenty Nine

Matthew felt Kiely's eyes bore into his back as he finished his meal. *"KIERAN, meet me by the lake. We'll leave from there."* He gulped the last of his tea and wiped his mouth.

Peter tapped Matthew on the shoulder. "What was last night about? What girl do you have your eye on?"

Matthew wondered if he should tell his friend what he'd found. No, better not mix him up in this, that way Kiely couldn't blame Peter. He waved his hand, dismissing the subject.

"No one special. I've got to run. See you later. Maybe I could help with GRAYSON."

"I'd like that. By the way, Grandmother's shooting darts at you. Better watch yourself."

Matthew shrugged, then retrieved his riding gear from the cubbies before leaving the dining hall. He crossed the inner courtyard and headed for the lake.

Kiely blocked his path. "Where are you going? You're not on patrol today."

"To visit my mother." Matthew stepped to the side. "KIERAN'S at the lake. I'm leaving from there. Problem?"

"You know no one's to fly alone." Kiely narrowed her eyes. "What are you up to?"

Matthew straightened his shoulders and tried to stop his knees from knocking together. "I'm flying direct, no stops. I've already cleared it with

Michael." He turned away so Kiely couldn't see the lie.

Damn, he should have checked with the new Ulster leader, but Kiely would know he'd lied if he went to find Michael now. It was better to continue the bluff and have his Kieran bespeak Michael's Seamus.

Once at the lake, Matthew strode to the whitethorn tree. He ducked behind, peeked out toward the clan compound to see if he was observed, then felt around the bole for the slender book. When his fingers didn't feel it, panic rose in his throat. His head whipped to the darkened hole. Where was it? Had Kiely found the book after he'd gone to bed? *Feck, feck, double feck.*

Sweat popped out of his brow. Matthew's fingers trembled, his breathing grew ragged.

Stop it, he chided himself, *Kiely doesn't know this hiding spot.* Sweeping the hole from side to side, then in a circle, his fingertips brushed the binding. It was jammed against the back. Had he done that last night? He wasn't sure.

He shoved the book inside his coat, then ran to Kieran at the water's edge. *"Let's go. Please have Seamus tell Michael that we're going to visit my parents."*

Kieran flew south at a steady pace until they crossed into County Meath, into dragon clan territory near Loughcrew.

"Kieran, bespeak Fionn as soon as we are close enough. I need to see my father right away. Tell him we'll be there in ten minutes. Ask Da to call Padrick. I have something I must show him."

"It is as ye requested. Clan Leader Sean awaits our arrival." Kieran increased his speed. *"What is wrong? Ye do not sit still."*

Matthew leaned forward and patted his compeer's neck. *"I'm fine, mo chroi. I have urgent news for my father and Padrick. No worries."*

Kieran landed in the inner courtyard. Matthew dismounted and rubbed his dragon's flank affectionately. He lengthened his stride, his boot heels tapping a quick staccato to his waiting father.

"Is Padrick on his way?"

Sean nodded. "What's so urgent? What's happened?"

"Everyone's okay that I know of. I'll explain soon." Matthew glanced around as several clan members preparing for patrol eyed him. "We'll need privacy. Where's Mum?"

"She's out hunting with BRIANNA." Sean lifted his arm to indicate the livestock pens.

They chatted about inconsequential things while waiting for Padrick. Matthew had just poured tea when Padrick knocked on the open door.

"Come in," Sean said. "Close the door."

"What's up?" Padrick raised an eyebrow at Matthew and sighed. "What's my mother done now?"

Matthew sized up Padrick. Yes, he was the young man in the photo album. The gray sprinkled throughout his hair showed the passage of time. He'd filled out in the shoulders and chest, wasn't lanky anymore. But the deep blue eyes, the set of his mouth, and the casual stance were the same.

"I found out something, quite by accident." Matthew pulled out the thin black journal. "Yesterday, Peter said Kiely had threatened him." Matthew relayed the details of his conversation with Peter. "It piqued my curiosity, so I searched Kiely's place for more information."

"You what?" Sean's rough voice shook as he rose and paced the room like a caged lion. "That was incredibly stupid."

"I know, but I found something about Erin, Padrick's fiancée—" Matthew started to explain.

"You know nothing." Padrick raised his voice. "Why would you stick your nose into something that happened over twenty-five years ago?" His eyes flashed hot and his mouth thinned. "Erin left me. Apparently she couldn't handle the secrecy."

"That's not true," Matthew interrupted. "It's all here." He handed the book to Padrick. "I found that amongst your mother's books."

Padrick thumbed through the pages, front to back. "It is Mother's writing." The thin volume was no more than fifty pages. Only the first half held writing. He looked up at Matthew.

"Start with page two," Matthew said.

The sunlight from the window behind Padrick slanted over the book as he bent his head to read. The only sound was the crinkle of paper as Padrick turned each page. When he reached the end, the color drained from his face. He cast tear-filled eyes down to the book in his trembling hands.

"What is it?" Sean stepped in front of Padrick, grabbing his shoulders.

"It's not possible. She can't be that cruel." Clouded eyes lifted from the book to Sean, then to Matthew.

"What's not possible? Who can't be cruel, Erin or Kiely?" Sean glanced at his son, but Matthew only shook his head.

The thin volume slid from Padrick's grasp and landed on the carpet. Sean scooped it up and quickly read the contents.

Padrick paced to the window and back. After three trips, he snatched the book from Sean's hands, shoved it into his jacket pocket, and whirled toward the door.

"Where are you going?" Sean broke out of his stunned stupor.

"Beaghmore." Padrick spit out the word. "To have it out with my mother, once and for all. To find Erin. To get to the truth." He could feel the blood rushing to his ears, the vein at his neck throbbing to the beat pounding behind his eyes.

"Wait." Sean glanced at his son, then rubbed his neck. "Calm down a minute. Think this through."

Padrick reached for the door handle. "She's interfered for the last time. I'm going to stop her, something I should have done long ago." He drew a strangled breath as the band of outrage tightened around his chest.

"Let him go, Da," Matthew said. "He has a right to his anger. And the truth. I'm sorry I discovered this."

"No!" Sean shouted. "Padrick, don't you see? If you go storming to Beaghmore, Kiely will know Matthew's part in all this. She'll have ammunition to have him tossed from the clan and to push for my removal as well. She'll use his breaking and entering against us."

"Mother's controlled my life for too long. Pulled the strings." Padrick yanked open the door.

"Please, hear me out. I'll help you find Erin, bring your mother to task. But what Kiely did happened over two decades ago. I need to protect my son, *now*."

Padrick closed the door. His shoulders slumped as he nodded. He sank into the couch, dropped his head into his hands, and groaned.

"What a fool I've been. I believed Mother when she said Erin couldn't live with the restrictions of the clan. I didn't trust Erin's love. I should've gone after her. I knew Mother's ambitions to be clan leader and for me to follow in her footsteps." Padrick rubbed his face. "Oh, God. Erin, I'm sorry."

Sean sat next to his friend. Matthew poured fresh tea for Padrick and his father, then slipped out the front door.

"You can't kick yourself for Kiely's scheming. You were what, nineteen, twenty? Hardly a match for a woman who'd been manipulating people for over a quarter century." Sean handed Padrick a mug. "I can put feelers out to my contacts in Dublin. It's the last place Erin was seen. If you give me her description—"

"That won't help. If Erin spotted someone watching her and disappeared all those years ago, she would've changed her appearance. Perhaps getting lost in a crowd of tourists or college students. That would be my guess." Padrick gulped his tea. "She could be anywhere after all this time. Not even in Ireland anymore. I'm not sure I'd recognize her if we passed each other on the street."

"What are you going to do?"

"I want to throttle my mother, and pry everything she knows out of her." Padrick held up his hand, forestalling Sean's response. "I need to think on it, do some remembering. Ferret out Mother's hired man. Then I'm going to find Erin."

"What about Meara?" Sean finished his tea and set the cup down with force.

"Of course I'll tell her. I've been honest with Meara from the start. She knows my feelings about Erin, my feelings about commitment. Believe me, she knows."

"Okay. You'll keep me informed? And let me know if I can help?"

"I'll be in touch." Padrick stood. "I won't do anything rash. I better get back, set up a couple days off. I'll let you know when, as we'll need an additional dragon and rider to fill in for me."

"No problem. Thanks, Padrick."

"For what?"

"Protecting my son." Sean clasped his friend's shoulder. "You'd have made a terrific father, still can be if you want."

"Not likely. Godfather to Matthew and uncle to Tess's brood suits me just fine. Besides, I wouldn't want to inflict my mother on any offspring." He managed a weak laugh.

"We'll figure out what to do about Kiely soon. I must get Roarke and Dochas partnered up to increase the clan strength. Then I can retire both Ronan and Kiely. That should help." Sean led him outside.

Matthew stood from the weathered porch chair. "I'm really sorry, Padrick."

"I'm not. I'd rather know the truth of it. Thanks to you, I'm on the right path. But you need to be careful around my mother. She's dangerous."

Sean pinched the bridge of his nose. "I may switch riders between counties. Someone I can count on to keep a low profile, stay out of trouble. Unlike my own son."

"Don't do that," Matthew said. "Kiely would be even more suspicious. She already thinks I'm up to no good. Almost caught me last night. If I'm replaced, she'll know I was the one in her house. Then she'll discover what I took."

"Kiely may already know it's missing," Sean said.

Padrick nodded. "I better get started, before Mother shuts up my only source for Erin's whereabouts. Send a replacement dragon and rider tomorrow. I'll be in contact." He gripped Sean's forearm. "Keep Matthew and Kieran here for a couple days. Make up some excuse."

"Don't worry about us." Sean smiled. "Without Kiely in charge, I have more control. I'll talk with Michael, keep everyone safe."

Thirty

As Declan flew west to Lough Gur, fury and remorse at what his mother had stolen from him invaded Padrick's thoughts. He tried to remember the day he brought Erin home to meet his family. The memory was hazy from the passage of time. He had wanted to tell her about his family, his obligations, and his destiny before he reached the clan compound at Beaghmore.

It had rained that day. Padrick's heart rate had matched the swoosh, swoosh of the wipers splashing soft rain across the windscreen as he debated the right words to tell the girl he loved about the clan and the dragons.

Padrick had wanted to explain before Erin got an eyeful. He'd turned over possibilities on how to start, and discarded ideas as fast as they popped into his head. How could he possibly have explained? Near the standing stones, he had tried. His words from so long ago came unbidden to him.

"That's Beaghmore. Six stone circles arranged in pairs, each with a cairn near the intersection. See that seventh circle, standing alone? The one studded with close-set stones? It's known as 'Dragons' Teeth'. They're from the Bronze Age and thought to contain *draiocht,* magic. My clan believes and shares this *draiocht.*"

Erin hadn't understood his hints. Before Padrick could spell everything out, she had seen his secret with her own eyes. He had berated himself for not finding the words to tell her, for being a coward, for her learning his secrets this way. His chest had felt like an anvil had fallen on him, crushing the air from his lungs. The same as he felt now, almost twenty eight years later.

Padrick blinked at Declan's deep rumbling inquiry. *"What are ye thinking?"*

"Just a memory, mo chroi. Before you were born." Padrick squinted into the afternoon sun and sighed as the memory faded. *"Land in the small courtyard. I need to talk with Meara, then we'll be away again."*

DECLAN backwinged, then landed with the slightest scrabbling of claws on cobblestones.

"Where have you been?" Meara asked. "You look like you've seen a ghost."

Several clan members glanced at him wide-eyed.

Padrick dismounted. "At Loughcrew. Listen, something's come to light and we need to talk. Privately." He nodded toward their house.

"Sounds serious. I'll brew tea." Meara led the way through to the kitchen. She set the kettle on the stove, then turned, taking an audible breath. "Tell me."

Padrick leaned on the counter, rubbed his face. *Christ. Where to start.*

"Matthew found something he probably shouldn't have. A journal, Kiely's journal from before I partnered DECLAN." Sweat beaded on Padrick's forehead. Anger sat like a molten rock in his stomach, ready to bubble and froth until it burst in his veins. He paced to control his feelings, and felt the slight shift of the tiny black book that held the heart-crushing words. "Here." He tossed the journal to Meara. "Read this."

Meara skimmed the pages, then looked up as Padrick removed the shrieking kettle.

"Are you after finding her then?" Her expression showed trepidation and fear.

"Yes. I thought Erin didn't want me, didn't love me. Couldn't handle the truth of who I am. That's not true." Padrick gathered Meara in his arms. "It doesn't change what I feel for you, but I need to…to make this right."

"And what about your mother?"

"For now, I'm hoping she doesn't know I have this." Padrick tucked the journal back into his coat pocket. "I'll deal with her. After."

"Do you know where to start?" Meara rubbed Padrick's chest, over his heart.

"I've stayed on somewhat friendly terms with Sullivan, Mother's go-to man from back then. I'll see what he knows, then head to Dublin."

"This Sullivan, is he still Kiely's boyo?"

"I'm not sure. But, he's my best jumping-off point." Padrick leaned his forehead against hers. "Sullivan, or Sully, lives near Carrick-on-Shannon now."

"Be safe." Meara kissed him, then stepped away. "I don't have to tell you how dangerous Kiely can be. And the clan is still dealing with four murders."

"No one knows that better. Sean's sending someone to fill in for me. You'll hardly have time to miss me." Padrick blew out a breath. "I have to know why."

"I know you do, that's what makes you who you are." Meara poured the untouched tea down the sink.

Padrick drew a deep breath before saying what he knew might hurt her. "On my way back here today, I remembered the first time I brought Erin home." He dragged a hand through his windblown hair and rubbed his neck. "I was nineteen and in love. Not very good at explaining. Erin saw TULLIA before I could prepare her. But after the initial shock, she seemed to take my life in stride. When she left so suddenly after midsummer, I was confused. Shocked. Now I know she didn't leave voluntarily." Padrick's stomach roiled at what his own flesh and blood had done. He clenched his hands into fists, his nails digging into his palms until the nausea subsided.

Meara studied the sink, the floor, anything but him. Padrick didn't blame her. He was leaving her to search for a ghost, for his first love, for the one person she understood he would give up just about anything for. He wanted to comfort Meara, but until he found Erin, he was in limbo.

Padrick walked out the door, not expecting Meara to follow. He slung a duffel over DECLAN'S saddle horn, then swung up into his riding harness.

"Take us to County Leitrim, Carrick-on-Shannon," he bespoke his compeer. Padrick saw Meara at the door, saluted her, then directed DECLAN aloft.

Once airborne and heading north, Padrick let his mind drift to Erin. Her stunned reaction to seeing a dragon for the first time. She had crumbled in his arms, but had recovered quickly, then barraged him with questions. She was one brave and strong woman. And Padrick's love for her had filled his heart, his soul, every fiber of his being.

The sun lowered through clouds as DECLAN landed in a low walled pasture. A light gleamed through the lone window of a stone cottage set behind a solid iron gate. Padrick dismounted. He opened the gate latch, stepped into the postage stamp-sized garden, and let the gate close with a clank that echoed like the slamming of a prison cell.

"Lord, I hope Mother's influence is over," Padrick muttered as he stepped onto the rickety wooden porch and away from the dragon magic. He rapped his knuckles on the door.

"Who's there?" a gruff voice asked, followed by a low growl.

"Padrick Nolan."

"Be off with you. I've nothin' to tell." Shuffling and banging noises echoed from behind the locked door.

"I need to ask you something."

"I said bugger off. I'll let me hound loose. I will."

"Sullivan, open the door." Padrick raised his voice. "Don't make me resort to dragon fire."

The door cracked open. Sully's lined face framed by wispy white hair popped through. His hazel eyes under wild bushy eyebrows peered at Padrick. "I've done nothin' to warrant a visit from the likes of you, boyo."

"We'll see about that." Padrick pushed past the man, not caring that Sullivan was at least ten years his senior. A gray wolfhound pup lay curled on a frayed rug beside the hearth. The peat fire glowed warm in the main room. Sparce funishings huddled near the fire.

Sully stared out into the red-purple dusk, closed the door, then slid the bolt home. "Ask what you will, then go. I want no trouble."

"I need you to tell me where you last saw Erin."

Sully sputtered, then shook his head. "I don't know what you're talkin' about."

"No?" Padrick advanced on the older man. "Let me refresh your memory. Kiely sent Erin away and had you follow her. I have proof." He held up the black book. "She wrote it all down. Now spill."

The pup whined as Sully moved to stoke the fire, adding another peat brick even though the room was too warm.

"I did odd jobs for Kiely, I'll admit. But I never touched that girl." Sweat beaded across Sully's forehead.

"Never said you did, but you followed her. I know it was you. I know you lost her in Dublin. I know Mother dismissed you."

The old man flushed crimson. He sat in a rocker near the window. The pup climbed into his lap and Sully stroked its head.

"She tell you?"

"Indirectly. Look, I'm not blaming you." Padrick sighed. "I just need to find Erin. Did you really lose her in Dublin, or was that a ruse?"

Sully stared at the low flames from the peat fire. Anguish, guilt, uncertainty, and finally resignation etched across his face. Padrick waited, his own anxiety churning in his gut before Sully spoke.

"That waif gave me the slip." Sully pressed his thumb to his chest. "I followed her to her dorm in Belfast, then crisscrossed over hell and back. County Down, Fermanagh, Antrim. I thought she'd gone home to her folks, or met with you in secret. She crossed into the Republic. I got nervous. Times bein' what they were back then. Not like nowadays. Anyway, she made it to Dublin proper. Blended in with the students at Trinity. That was about three months after she left Beaghmore."

"How long did you look while in Dublin?"

"Another month or two. But I couldn't find her. Had to report my failure to Kiely. She sacked me, told me to forget what I'd done, forget her and the clan."

"Why didn't you ever tell me? I thought you were my friend. All these years, all the times I kept in touch."

"I should have. No excuse. But your mum had me over a barrel. Threatened me and my family."

"How's that?"

"Said she'd turn me over to the Gardaí. Had proof I was IRA. My family woulda been disgraced, run out."

"But that's been over for years."

"Kiely keeps tabs on me, even now. I think she has one of the dragons watchin'." Sully shivered despite the oppressive heat from the fire. "I'd not be surprised if she knows you're here. Specially if you know about my part in Erin's leavin'."

"How did Erin seem? Before you lost her."

"I don't rightly know how Kiely got Erin to leave you, I was just following orders, but the girl was scairt. Lookin' over her shoulder, which I guess is how she spotted me. Seemed a bit tired, all that travelin'." Sullivan shrugged. "Not sure how I lost her. She was smart, sneaky, slippin' over the border." Sully pushed the pup away and stood. "That's all I know, honest. You best go. I've kept my mouth shut, but I can't start runnin' from Kiely now. Not at my age."

"I can protect you. Kiely's not in charge of Beaghmore any longer. She can't hurt you." Padrick wrote on a card he pulled from his wallet. "Call this number. Sean's my friend and clan leader. He'll settle you, either at Loughcrew or Lough Gur with me. Kiely never leaves Northern Ireland anymore. You'll be safe."

Sully left the number tucked under the shadeless lamp on the side table. He opened the door and clasped Padrick's arm.

"I'm sorry, lad. Be careful."

"I will. You, too." Padrick walked to the gate, took care to close it without a sound, and climbed aboard his black dragon.

"Did the elder know where to find your friend?" DECLAN asked.

"No. He confirmed what I already knew. He did indeed lose her at Trinity. We'll stop at Loughcrew for the night, then head to Dublin at first light. I'll check the university records, see what I can find out. Have Sean put me in touch with his contacts. I'm not holding out much hope. Erin disappeared so long ago."

DECLAN crooned reassurances that if Erin was alive, they would find her together and bring her back if that was Padrick's wish.

The next morning, over early morning tea and fresh baked blueberry scones, Padrick relayed yesterday's conversation to Sean.

"I'll check with some people," Sean said.

"Thanks. I'll be in Dublin." Padrick rose and pulled on his riding jacket.

"My contact can handle Trinity. Shouldn't you follow up on the other locations Sullivan talked about?"

"No. Those sounded like Erin trying to shake off her followers. Besides, I'd be able to spot some aliases she might have used back in the day. And, my computer skills are good enough to not draw any undue attention."

Padrick mentally called his compeer, walked outside, then mounted when Declan landed in the small courtyard. "I'll be in touch." He saluted as his dragon leapt into the air.

Meara rubbed the grit from her sleep-deprived eyes and threw back the covers from their bed. Padrick had only been gone for a day, but it felt like a lifetime to her. If he found Erin, would Meara lose him to his first love?

Why did Kiely keep that damn journal? Had she secretly hoped Padrick would find it and end his relationship with Meara? They weren't married in the eyes of the church, but they were committed to each other. At least Meara was committed. Padrick hadn't wanted the official marriage, said he had no good example to follow. She'd never gotten along with Kiely, but there had been no open hostility between them. She was a dragonrider after all, and a council member.

Meara showered, as much to wake up as to snap her out of her funk. She looked at her gaunt face, dark bags under her plain brown eyes in the semi-foggy mirror. She relaxed her brows, trying to smooth the worry lines branching over her forehead. To no avail. She felt old, older than her forty years.

"How am I supposed to compete with a young woman?" Meara said to her reflection.

Even though Erin would be older than herself, Padrick's age, his memory of her would keep her young and beautiful. A first love with the dew still fresh on the spring petals and the halo of perfection. And Padrick's time with Erin short enough that everyday flaws and ideosyncracies would never have surfaced. How could Meara measure up to young love's sweetness?

Meara reached for the anti-aging cream and slathered it on her face and neck, then applied makeup to conceal the worst of her rough night. Not much she could do to turn back the clock, but no one would see the worry she held close to her heart. Her priority must be the clan. Then she would deal with whatever Padrick learned. She snapped the cosmetic drawer closed.

"Damn you," Meara said, not knowing if she damned Padrick, Kiely, Erin, or herself.

She stepped into Padrick's office and looked over the schedule of dragon and rider pairings for the next few days. Work would drive away the uncertainty. With any luck, Padrick would be back later that day and Meara could send Colin and his dragon, LANDON, back to Loughcrew.

The shrill ring of the telephone pulled her from her thoughts. *Please, let this be him.*

"Meara?" The woman's voice held an edge of derision.

"Kiely, what can I do for you?" Meara scowled and snatched Padrick's pen from its holder.

"Put my son on the phone."

"Sorry. Padrick's out already. Can I pass along a message?" Meara tapped the pen on the corner of the desk.

"No. Yes. Have him call. It's important family business. Private. As soon as he returns."

"I'll tell—" Meara heard the distinctive click as Kiely hung up. Could she know already? Meara tossed the pen on the desk. Before she stepped outside, the phone rang again. She bit back a groan. Now what?

"Yes?" Meara remained standing.

"Meara?"

This time the questioning tone made Meara smile. "Hello, Tess. What can I do for you?" What a difference between mother and daughter. Her best friend and champion in all things Padrick. "Padrick's not here, if that's who you're after."

"Is Padrick...safe?" Tess whispered the last word.

"Yes, of course," Meara said. "He's fine. Helping Sean with something. Why?"

"Mum called earlier. She sounded furious. Wouldn't tell me anything, so I figured it had to do with my brother." Tess sighed. "If it was my Peter, I'd have had my ears blown off by Mum's wicked tongue."

Meara raised her eyebrows.

"Believe me, Mum has no trouble expressing her dissatisfaction that Peter didn't partner with a winged dragon," Tess continued. "Or that I didn't want clan life for myself. She still thinks that might be why ROARKE didn't choose Peter."

"You know that's not how each dragon chooses a compeer."

"I suppose," Tess said. "Anyway, I have other business to discuss. Earlier today, at the inn, Martin told me about a couple he spoke with yesterday. They asked about dragon sightings."

"Oh." Meara dropped back into the desk chair.

"Rory over at Ballynahinch directed the pair to Martin. He chatted with them for a while. Then they took off."

"Were they heading back to the castle?"

"Martin said no. They were driving off north when he started the next tour. He said the woman did seem a bit disappointed that he didn't know any stories of current flying dragons. I thought the clan might know what's up. Martin only told them what he knew, which is nothing. But—"

"Thanks, Tess. I'm glad you called. Should I have a chat with your innkeeper?"

"It's not necessary. I shouldn't have bothered you. Martin doesn't know about the clan. I'm sure the couple just thought he was a bit loose in the head."

"It's possible." Thoughts of Padrick and DECLAN alone, with a killer on the loose, thundered into Meara's head.

"But you don't think so?"

"With what's happened in the last six months, we can't take anything as coincidence." Meara heard the sadness in her own voice.

"You okay?" After several silent moments, Tess asked, "Is something wrong?"

"No, no. Just a thought. I'll have Braeden check into it." Meara stared at the duty roster. "Thanks for calling."

"I'll let you go, I know you're busy. My love to Padrick. *Slán leat, mo cara.*"

"*Slán agat.*" Meara held the receiver for a moment longer after Tess disconnected. *You best be safe, Padrick.*

Hours later, Padrick stretched his back from the uncomfortable chair in a small, hardly used library. He tugged his hair in frustration. Having bypassed the college's mainframe security, he searched thousands of student records for any hint of Erin. He tracked down student ID photos for several possible aliases. None looked like the Erin he remembered.

Padrick rubbed his tired eyes, blinking away the pinpoint stars, and spotted a curious entry. Lan O'Casey. Not quite his last name combined with not quite hers, more a play on each of their surnames. There wasn't a picture as the student attended for only the fall term. Records stated Lan emigrated to America with no forwarding address and no relatives. She vanished.

Was Lan O'Casey his Erin? Padrick threaded his hands through the sides of his hair, eased the tension in his neck, and drifted into another memory. It was as clear as if it had happened yesterday.

The midsummer's eve bonfires lit up the darkening skies over the stone circles of Beaghmore. Voices floated out of the stillness between musical sets featuring harps, flutes, and bodhráns. The céilí was in full swing. From great oak casks pumped dark stout and lighter ales. Tables creaked and groaned with platters of beef and lamb, potato and vegetable casseroles, fresh fruits and cheeses, and a myriad of desserts to tempt the most ardent sweet tooth.

Padrick touched his chest and the clan pendant his great-grandfather had given him on his sixteenth birthday. He wound his way through dancers and revelers in search of Erin. In the months since he introduced her to his family and the clan, she accepted the dragons as part of his life. Tonight, he wanted to start their lives together. Erin sat beside Sean, Padrick's friend, laughing and partaking of the feast. Padrick joined them. When the music slowed, Padrick and Erin danced near the firelight. The world felt steeped in magic as they stole away into the hush of dawn.

"My heart's lost to you," Padrick whispered in Erin's ear as he linked fingers with hers, linked his body to hers, allowed his soul to link with hers.

After their lovemaking, Padrick waited for his heart rate and breathing to return to normal, then removed the pendant from his neck and placed it around Erin's.

"This was my great-grandfather's. Riley was a dragonrider from the second generation of dragons that took humans as their compeers."

Erin opened her mouth, but Padrick pressed a finger to her lips.

"I want you to have this, to be a part of my life. To marry me. Say yes." He leaned over and feathered kisses over her cheeks.

Erin returned his passionate embrace. "Yes, I'll marry you. But…" Her brows drew together.

Padrick fingered the pendant resting between Erin's breasts. "If you're worried about the pendant, when I'm five and twenty and partnered with a dragon, I'll receive another."

A smile returned to Erin's face. "In that case, I accept the gift. If at any time you want it back, you only have to ask."

They made love once more before the sun broke over the horizon.

A shadow crossed between Padrick and the fading light of the library window. The librarian paced back and forth, huffing under her breath about closing time in fifteen minutes. Padrick shut down the computer, making sure he left no trace of his search. He exited the cozy confines of the library to continue his quest at an internet cafe.

Padrick ordered a mocha and sat behind a computer in the rear corner. His drink cooled as he checked flights to America over a one year period. No luck. He searched the missing persons records, and finally, death certificates. Several college-age women died during that time. One resembled Erin, but no jewelry was found on the deceased woman. Padrick's gift had never materialized, at least not that he could find. At midnight, with no solid leads, Padrick left, dejected.

What happened to you, Erin? Are you safe somewhere, or… His throat tightened and he squeezed his eyes shut on the only other possibility.

Thirty One

Devan faced Christian as he pulled out of the lot and headed away from Dan O'Hara's Heritage Centre and Ballynahinch Castle.

"Where to?"

"The next decent-sized town we come upon," Christian said.

"Why not stay at the inn we just left?" Devan readjusted her sore left shoulder.

"We asked a lot of questions. Questions specific to dragons. There's still one murder location to track down. And I'd rather put some distance between us and anyone following." Christian glanced at the rearview mirror then at her. "Whoever tailed us only has to talk up Rory and they'd know our next stop."

"Okay. That makes sense. But we're no closer to solving these murders. Or finding out about my heritage. I even forgot to ask Martin." Devan fiddled with her ring.

"I don't think he'd know anything about your ring or my pendant. He seemed a bit wobbly, if you catch my meaning."

They entered the town of Clifden, passed a gas station and two church-es before making their way onto the main street.

"Is this far enough?"

"I'd like to get farther, but if you're tired, this will do."

"Look." Devan grabbed his arm and pointed to a row of cluttered shops.

"What?" Christian squinted.

"The jewelry shop. There on the right. Let's see if they know anything about my ring."

Christian heaved a loud sigh, and pulled into a parking spot several doors down. They walked in to the melodious chimes of a sea bell, which echoed through the empty shop. Glass floor-to-ceiling display cases held gold and silver and precious stones in a myriad of patterns. Rings, pendants, goblets, dirks, headdresses. They browsed the cabinets, circling the shop until a deep, male voice broke their concentration.

"Hallo. I'm Jonathan. Let me know if you want to look at anything." The young man perched on a stool pulled up to a worktable filled with small boxes, a loupe, and spindles laden with gold and silver chains of differing gauges and designs. He bent his shaggy brown head to a lighted magnifying glass and a ring held in the cushioned jaws of a vice.

Devan watched in fascination until he finished mounting a deep blue stone in the center of twinkling diamonds, in the shape of a fiery five-point star.

"You have a wonderful shop here. Very unique pieces." Her gaze drifted over the display cabinets.

"We handcraft every piece."

"We?"

"My family. I'm the newest designer. You'll find no better quality anywhere. Is there something you fancy?"

Devan laughed. "I fancy everything."

A lightning quick grin flashed over the jeweler's face. He gestured toward Christian. "Perhaps for your companion's sake, we should narrow it down to one or two…dozen."

Devan couldn't help it; she laughed again. "Funny guy." She wiped a tear from her eye. "I have a ring that I'd like you to look at." She removed her ring and handed it over as Christian stepped next to her.

Jonathan studied the dragon insignia and placed the ring under the lighted magnifier. He turned it over and over. He mumbled the inscription.

"Excellent craftsmanship. Not ours, mind you. But excellent nonetheless. Sterling silver, ninety-two percent. Strong enough to weather long, constant wear. The inscription means loyalty…"

"Destiny and freedom," Devan finished.

Jonathan's eyes widened. "You speak the Gaelic?"

"No. I've already had it translated."

"Then what more can I tell you?"

"I was hoping you would know its origin."

"I'm not sure I follow." Jonathan turned back to her.

"This ring was my grandmother's. It came to me when my parents died." She waved a hand in the air. "Sorry, that's not important. My ancestors were Irish. This was the one part of their heritage that survived."

"Don't know what else I can tell you." Jonathan handed the ring back.

Devan slid the ring on her finger. "Have you ever seen another? Or this design on some other piece, such as a pendant or cup?" Christian pressed a hand to her back, but remained silent.

"Can't say that I have. And I would've noticed if the jewelry was in plain sight." Jonathan shrugged. "Part of the business. The artist in me always seeks beauty. And like I said earlier, extremely fine craftsmanship. Hold on, I think I may know who designed it. Or at least the ancestral family. O'Shea." He tapped a finger to his chin. "Kate O'Shea is the jeweler in the family now. She wouldn't have made this piece, as you say it belonged to your grandmother. But the overall design has the same characteristics as an O'Shea piece." He held out his hand. "Can I see it again?" She started to remove the ring. He shook his head and lifted her hand so she could see the ring. "Yes. It's the sweep of the wings. The tool employed to bring the wings to life."

Devan stared at her ring, unsure what he meant.

"Here." Jonathan pulled a hand-held magnifying glass from a box of other tools, then positioned the glass over her ring. "See the grooves that separate the bones and the wing membrane?" She nodded. "They are hand-made. Not cast."

Again, she studied her ring and looked back to Jonathan's animated face.

"Sorry. Part of my world. Knowing the competition." The jeweler grinned. "While I've never seen a dragon depicted in any O'Shea piece, the style is an O'Shea. I'm sure of it." He set the magnifier back on the workbench.

"Where can we find this Kate O'Shea?" Christian spoke for the first time.

"Oh, you're not a Yank." Jonathan blinked, then studied Christian for a moment. "Dublin?"

"Aye." Christian frowned.

"Kate O'Shea has a shop there, in the Temple Bar area."

Devan gasped, then turned it into a hasty cough when Christian tapped her back. She slid a quick glance at him and saw the slight jerk of his head. Was Kate the woman who couldn't wait for them to leave?

"Have you been to Kate's shop?" Jonathan's question interrupted her thoughts.

"I'm not sure. But when we return to Dublin, we'll look up her shop and ask for her," Christian said.

"You'll not be needing to ask for her. She's the owner and the only jeweler. Fiftyish with graying hair. I think she employs one or two college students as clerks, but they're young. You can't miss Kate."

Christian nodded, then turned toward the door.

"I have several dragon pieces that might be of interest." Jonathan's voice rose slightly to catch them before they left the shop. Hopeful. "I have a silver Celtic cross with a dragon's head. Let me show you."

He grabbed a set of keys from the hook above the cash register and skirted the counter to one of the glass cabinets along the side wall near the display windows. Devan glanced where Jonathan pointed.

And fell in love. The cross was simple with the side and bottom arms barreled like casks of fine whiskey. What caught her attention was the dragon head erupting from the top of the cross to hold the chain between the dragon's teeth. The piece didn't resemble her dragon ring in the least, but it called to her heart. Much the same way Ireland had when she'd first stepped off the plane and made her way outside the airport terminal. The calling was of home, of family, to the place where she belonged.

"Would you like to try it on?"

Devan couldn't get her throat to work, so she nodded.

Jonathan hooked the necklace around her neck and turned her to a wall mirror. "I can change the chain to any size you'd like. Even a thicker weave. Though it looks perfect."

Christian came up behind her, gathering her in his embrace. "It *is* perfect. A compliment to your ancestor's ring." He turned to Jonathan. "We'll take it, just as it is." He stayed Devan's fingers as she reached to unclasp the necklace. "Wear it, love." He kissed her temple then roamed down her cheek to her neck.

The jeweler coughed, then rang up the sale and handed Christian a small bag with an empty box inside.

"Thanks for all your help." Christian paid in cash.

"You're welcome. Come back anytime. And be sure to look up Kate when next you're in Dublin."

Christian guided her outside before she could say anything.

"That—"

"Shh. Not here." Christian looked through the windows, but Jonathan had disappeared. "We need to go."

"Is he on the phone? Do you think he's—"

"Let's just put some distance between us and this town." Christian ushered her to the Audi and skirted the front, glancing once more at the jewelry shop.

They drove out of town in silence. Devan fingered her necklace and glanced at Christian. His bunched jaw muscles had her swallowing her questions. His eyes flicked to the rearview mirror, then both side mirrors.

"We've picked up a tail."

She shifted to look behind them and winced at the sharp pain in her shoulder. A dark sedan trailed them far enough so she couldn't see the driver with any clarity.

"How do you know he's following us?" Devan turned back around.

"I saw him leaning against the wall, trying to act nonchalant. Not very adept. Limped to his car as we passed him."

"He what?" Devan bolted forward, then shuddered.

Don't be silly. He can't be the same one you tangled with days ago in Galway. They'd had no problems at Ballynahinch—at least not that she knew of.

Christian reached for her hand, interlaced his fingers with hers, and gave a light, reassuring squeeze. "Somehow he's tracked us. I didn't see him when we left the castle or the farm house."

"Have you spoken with Finley?"

"No. But now I've confirmed the attack wasn't random."

"Are you sure he's the same—"

"Aye. He's exactly as you described to Finley. Crew cut. Stocky build." Christian squeezed her hand once more before releasing it. "Nice eye for detail in the face of danger, by the way."

"Are you going to call Finley?"

Christian shook his head.

"Why not?" Anger rose at the thought her attacker would get away.

"If the Gardaí got involved, I'd lose the chance to find out who and why."

"Who and why, what?"

Christian didn't answer right away. Devan folded her arms across her chest and fumed in silence. They passed the entrance to Connemara National Park before she spoke.

"I have a right to know. I'm the one who was attacked."

"I've seen him before." Christian's voice sounded lost in thought. "With Logan. On the bridge."

"Who's Logan?"

"Nobody. Just…someone from my past." Christian blinked, then studied the rearview mirror. "This puts a different spin on things."

"Why?"

"Maybe I'm the target. You're just a tool to get to me." He glanced at her. "Only one way to find out."

"How's that?"

"Separate."

"What?" Devan's eyes widened. Hysteria bubbled in her throat. "You can't just leave me. Stranded all alone out here, away from anything."

"No, not here. In the next town or city we come to."

"So what?" She sputtered. "I'm just an inconvenience? What about what we've shared?" She balled her hand into a fist—vibrating with anger.

Christian grabbed her hand before she could use it against him. "Don't." The threat was clear in his sharp tone.

Devan jerked her hand free. So now she knew. She meant nothing to him, nothing but a means of getting the answers he wanted, nothing but a willing and warm woman to ease his physical needs. How could she be so stupid? Leave herself so vulnerable? It was almost as painful as her disaster with Rick, almost.

Devan glared out the window, trying to organize her thoughts and calm her growing fears. But the fears won out. She was in a car—his car—about as far away from Dublin as one could get and still be in Ireland. His homeland, not hers. Recovering from a violent attack. An attack that might be a result of her involvement with a man she barely knew.

Clenching her hands, Devan concentrated on stopping the tremors that had taken over her muscles. The harder she tried, the more she shook. She squeezed her eyes shut, inhaled, counted to five, then exhaled to the same count. One by one with each exaggerated breath, she relaxed her muscles. She opened her eyes to the warmth of the sun. Memories of her time with Christian flooded her mind. He never failed to act the gentleman, but what did she really know of him? She glanced at him. There was no way he was leaving her stranded. Not without a fight.

"This looks like a large town." Christian maneuvered the roundabout and exited in the direction indicated for Westport. "I'll find a hotel and get you settled." He parked at the Hotel Westport, unloaded her bag, and steered a silent Devan to the reception desk.

When the door to their room clicked shut, Devan shuddered and wrapped her arms around her body. She didn't turn to face him, didn't want him to see the hurt in her eyes.

"So that's it? Thanks for the vacation sex, but you're done?" She couldn't stop the hitch in her voice, but she kept the tears from falling. For now. "No problem. I'll get in touch with Finley. Explain—"

Christian whirled her around to face him, grabbing her by both arms. Devan winced.

"Is that what you think?" He loosened his grip. "Christ, Devan. I'm trying to do the right thing here. Trying to protect you."

"By leaving me alone? Vulnerable? So the brute can finish what he started?" A sob escaped. She shuddered.

Christian helped her to the edge of the bed and knelt before her. Devan gripped her hands together, twisted until her fingers tangled like the knots in her stomach.

"No. So I can draw him away." Christian scrubbed his face. "We need answers. So far, all we've got are more questions, more pieces to a puzzle, and…we're leaving more clues to who we are than I like." He pulled her hands apart and held one in each of his. "Someone has followed us. Since Dublin. It could be related to you and your ring. Or my pissing off Logan and it's his way of bringing me to heel. I need to find out which and stop it. Can you understand?"

Devan shook her head. "How does separating help?"

"When the bastard follows me, I'll deal with him. Get answers, my way."

"And if he doesn't? You'll be too far away. He could still use me as leverage." She pulled one hand free and wiped her moist eyes.

"I won't leave you alone for long. You'll be safe in this room. Don't open the door to anyone." Christian brought her hand to his lips. "If he doesn't follow me, I'll come right back. Figure out Plan B."

Christian rose and pulled Devan into his arms. He feathered a kiss to each cheek, then took her mouth in a searing kiss. His hips pressed into hers and she felt the hard length of him. "Does that feel like I'm done? You know perfectly well this isn't just sex. We're connected, linked. Your ring, my pendant." He ran his hands up and down her arms and kissed her, slow and deep, then released her. He stepped toward the door. "I'll be back."

"Why didn't you bring in your bag?"

"I saw the guy pull over just past the hotel. I wanted him to see only one bag. Make him think I'm moving on. Get him to follow me and leave you alone. Keep the door locked. This place is a fortress."

"Wait. How will I know it's you at the door?" Devan bit her lower lip. She could still taste him.

"I'll have a room key." Christian held up the plastic card. "Try to get some rest. You're going to need it." He raised an eyebrow and gave her a cocky grin, then grabbed the 'Do Not Disturb' door hanger and closed the door behind him.

Christian slowed when he drove past the gray-black Citroen sedan, a peat brick on wheels. He leaned over the steering wheel, and stared at the driver's side. It sat empty. Where could the man have gone? He hadn't seen him in the hotel, and he'd done a thorough search before leaving Devan alone. Should he return? Or circle the block looking for the bastard? At a stoplight, he spied the man's blond crew cut and burly frame push through the glass door of another hotel.

The blare of a horn brought Christian's attention back to the changing light. He honked back. Devan's attacker glanced his way. Christian grinned, then stepped on the accelerator. He watched the man through his rearview mirror trot-limp to his car. The attacker cut off a truck in his haste to follow. Christian wished he were back in Dublin, where he knew the streets and alleyways. But he'd make do. At least Devan would be safe.

Devan splashed cool water over her face and neck.

Calm down, he'll be back soon, she told herself. She stretched out on the enormous bed, propping several pillows behind her back. Her mind drifted once more to her first attraction to Christian.

Almost from the first moment, two weeks ago—had it only been a fortnight?—she'd felt both drawn to and intrigued by him. There was something in his lake-blue eyes, though only rarely, that spoke of violence. Perhaps a byproduct of his orphaned upbringing. She saw the part of him that was a dreamer as well, an unusual mix.

What Christian was, what he did to survive—though he'd never spelled it out—made her uneasy. All her life she'd believed in right and wrong, black and white, good and evil. Until she'd met him, she hadn't considered there could be so many shades in between. Nor had she realized she might be falling in love with a man who lived his life sliding in and around those shades.

But she was falling. Past experience taught her that what someone said and what that person felt could be two opposite things. She wanted more this time. She wanted shared feelings, shared emotions, shared passions. She wanted to take risks and make mistakes and do foolish and exciting things. Major steps away from her usual, shy style. And she wanted to feel safe, not hunted for someone else's thrills.

The main roadway through Westport narrowed to one lane. Christian checked his mirrors to ensure his quarry still followed. The peat-mobile was four cars behind. He drove toward the edge of town, noticed more cars between him and Logan's man. Another stoplight added more distance. Christian turned left and pulled to a stop on the side of the road. He watched the main road. One, two, three cars. A slight gap in traffic, several more cars, a long break, then the truck the attacker had cut off. No peat-colored Citroen.

What the feck? Did the attacker double-back?

"Christ." Christian peeled out and headed back to the center of town. "Goddamn. Hang on Devan. I'm coming."

Stuck behind a truck and horse trailer, Christian caught every red light. He honked, tried to go around, but with no road clearance, he settled for tailgating. By the time he returned to the hotel, he was seething. And worried.

Kelly swore. "Bloody eejit. He must have made you. The boss'll be pissed." When his target turned off the main road, Kelly veered into a short alley. He pounded his fist on the steering wheel, several times.

"Stupid, stupid. You're not thinking. The car's tracked. Besides, the chap was alone. He must have left her alone."

He reversed out of the alley and raced back to the Westport Hotel.

"I'll just grab her now. Head back to Dublin." He sped up at the thought of payback for all the trouble she caused him. Payback for his blasted knee.

Devan rolled her shoulders to release the tension and paced the plush white Berber carpet. She fingered the deep sapphire throw draped over the soft cream-colored duvet on the queen-sized bed. Her fortress might be upscale, but she felt like a prisoner. She was tired of not knowing what was happening, tired of being told what to do, tired of playing the role of helpless female. It was time to take charge of the situation and her life.

A knock on her door almost made her jump out of her skin. She clamped a hand over her mouth, stifling a shriek. Nice start to taking charge.

"Housekeeping." The high-pitched female voice sounded through the closed door. "Here to turn down the bed."

The scrape of a plastic key sounded in the lock. Devan ran to the door, twisted the deadbolt in place, then peeked through the Judas hole. The young, nubile blonde raised her hand to knock once more.

Devan couldn't see past the woman, but was spooked enough to not unlock the extra security.

"We're good here." She forced the words past the knot in her throat. "Don't need the bed turned down." She watched the perky, sun-kissed face turn and glance toward the end of the hall where the elevators were. The girl shrugged, then strolled in that direction.

Devan pressed her eye closer. She couldn't see anyone. But…was that a male voice she heard? She placed her ear against the cool, cream-painted wood. Nothing.

A bead of sweat trickled between her shoulder blades, and her shirt clung to her clammy skin. Should she wait here like a sitting target? She snatched her backpack and the room key from the dining table under the window. The setting sun drew her attention and she glanced down to the street. Way too high. She tiptoed to the door. Was that rustling on the other side? She couldn't tell. The harsh rasp of her own breath and the hammering of her heart pounding in her ears masked any other sound. The distorted area she could see through the eyepiece remained empty.

As quietly as she could, she unlocked the deadbolt while keeping an eye on the hallway.

"Go for it," she muttered as she gripped the straps of the backpack, ready to swing it like a mace. She whipped the door open and leapt out, swinging the bag at the sudden blur of motion in front of her.

Thirty Two

Devan's backpack slammed into the blond temple of the crouching figure, her attacker from Galway. She heard an *oomph* and felt the sting of contact sing up her arm. The man toppled. Devan didn't wait. She kicked at the beefy hand that tried to grab her ankle and ran to the elevator. She stabbed the down button repeatedly. Her sweaty finger slipped and missed. She tried again. On the third attempt, the button lit. While she glanced over her shoulder, the man rolled to his knees. His curses echoed to her. He gained his feet. The elevator door slid open. She dashed in, jabbed the lobby button, and prayed the door would close.

The clump, clump of the attacker's boots grew louder. As the door nicked shut, he rammed the metal door.

Sucking air in greedy gulps, Devan tried to calm her shattered nerves. Her eyes didn't waver from the digital numbers counting down. Perhaps she should have taken the stairs. Now she was trapped in a steel box like a corpse in a coffin. When the elevator door opened, she rushed out and collided with a solid male chest. She shrieked.

Somehow her attacker had caught up to her and was blocking her escape.

"Bloody hell, Devan." At the sound of Christian's voice, Devan backpedaled and lifted her head. He grabbed her arms. "What are you doing down here? I told you to stay in the room. What happened? You're shaking."

"He, he came for me." Devan's voice shook, but she was helpless to stop it.

Christian yanked her behind him and searched the empty elevator. "I'm sure the bastard's long gone by now. Come on. We can talk about this in the room."

"No." She pulled away. "Tried to get to me. In the room. Could still be up there. Or coming down." She spun around, scrutinized every man.

Christian guided her to an alcove between the elevator and stair door. "What happened?"

"I hit him with my backpack. Knocked him over. Escaped in the elevator before he could recover." Devan held up her bag as proof.

"Why didn't you just lock the deadbolt and call hotel security when you saw the guy? You did look through the peephole, right?"

Devan took several deep breaths to slow her galloping heart and regain her use of full sentences. "Of course I did. No one was there, at least not after the housekeeper left."

Christian glanced over his shoulder when the elevator dinged. A couple with two children entered and the door whisked shut before he faced her. "What housekeeper? I told the front desk you weren't to be disturbed."

Devan told him everything that happened after he left her alone.

"The woman must have been his accomplice." Christian shook his head.

"We need to talk. Things need to change." Devan's voice rose in volume as her fear subsided and anger filled her. "We stay together, or I tell the Gardaí everything."

Christian narrowed his eyes. "Fine, but let's do it in private. We're drawing a crowd." He nodded toward the reception desk and the gathered onlookers before pulling her into the returned elevator. "I need to check the room. Make sure nothing is missing. You'll be safe with me."

Devan gave Christian a withering glare.

When the door opened on their floor, he stepped out first, blocking her exit. He scanned the hall. "All clear."

Devan pushed past. "Don't do that."

"What?"

"Treat me like I'm helpless. I'm the one who's gotten away twice. I hurt the guy twice."

Christian held up his hands. "You're the one who bolted out of the lift.

Shouting, shaking, scared down to your lovely bones."

"Because I thought he…never mind. Let's just call Finley. I don't want a third encounter." Devan started to unlock the room door, but Christian stopped her.

"Wait." Christian crouched to inspect the card slot. "Looks like he tried to bypass the electronics. He broke something in here." Christian pulled a small zippered case from his inside jacket pocket, removed a miniature set of tweezers, and plucked a broken stub of plastic from the lock.

He held up his find, and squinted. "A demagnetizer. Wonder how he came by that. Doesn't matter. If he crouched here, it probably broke when you opened the door. I don't think he got in, but I'll check." He used his room key, whipped open the door, and entered crouched low. After sweeping the room from right to left, he turned back to her, his finger to his lips, and motioned her inside.

Devan stepped in, hugged the wall, then closed and dead-bolted the door.

Christian skirted the bed with its pillows propped against the wall and peeked into the bathroom. "He ghosted, I'm sure. But I'll call Finley if you want." She nodded. He placed the call using the room phone.

Devan paced to the window while he explained to Finley. The sun had set, leaving only darkness and the occasional flickering of a stoplight. The glass reflected Christian hanging up the phone. She wrapped her arms around her torso and gathered her thoughts. She needed to have it out with him, but Lord only knew she hated confrontations.

Christian broke the oppressive silence. "He couldn't have gotten to you with the deadbolt locked."

"I know that now. I panicked." Devan turned to face him. "What did Finley say?"

"He agreed with me. The guy wouldn't have hung around. Finley will talk with hotel security and the local precinct, but the arsehole is probably holed up somewhere. I'm to call if we see him or his car again." Christian's Irish became more pronounced.

Devan dragged a hand through her hair. The adrenaline rush of her escape left her spent. A pain in her shoulder made her realize she was slumped. She straightened, then arched her back. Did she have the energy to make her demands? She had to. She couldn't go through another attack.

"I'm sorry, Devan. I shouldn't have left you alone." Christian stepped toward her. Her head snapped up, along with a hand. He stopped.

"No. You shouldn't have. I told you." The words shot out in a staccato burst. "Your plan didn't work."

"Not true. When I left, he wasn't in his car. I was debating on coming back when I saw him exiting another hotel. Down the street." Christian spun toward the door. "Hell, I know where the brutal ape is. I can—"

"Forget it." Anger won over Devan's weariness. "Call Finley again. Give him the location. Let him do his job. We stick together. I mean it, Christian. Otherwise, I'll tell the Gardaí everything I know. Everything." She pinched her lips together in her sternest expression and hoped her threat would make him stay.

"I can get answers. I can stop—"

"How'd that work out so far? It's my turn for answers. From you." Devan stabbed a finger at him. "You know all about me. My parents dying. My ring. Why I'm here. Now it's my turn. Clearly, there are things from your past that have put me in danger." She walked to the door, and leaned against it. After folding her arms, she jerked up her chin. "You're not going anywhere until I know who I'm involved with."

Christian arched one eyebrow and lifted his upper lip in an amusing smirk. His dimple flashed. "You don't think I can get past you if I wanted?" The piratical look faded. He rubbed the back of his neck. "Christ, Devan. I outweigh you by at least four stone." He gestured at the table, then sat. "I wouldn't hurt you. Come, sit and I'll tell you what I can."

"All of it, Christian." Devan stayed where she was. "I jumped into this relationship—the physical aspect—too quickly. That's not like me. I know you grew up in an orphanage. Know you live, or have lived, on the edge of the law."

Christian opened his mouth, looked stunned. "How?"

"Your aversion to authority. Doctors, the Gardaí. Your knowledge of what, for lack of a better word, I'll call security." Devan ticked off each statement on her fingers. "You carry a large amount of cash, presumably so you don't have to use a credit card, and you don't have to use your real name. If Christian Riley is indeed your name." She stopped and waited.

"It is. At least that's the name I was given by Mother Superior. I don't know what my parents would have called me." He lifted a shoulder in a half-shrug. "The orphanage wasn't all that bad a place, but it wasn't all that great either. I survived."

"They didn't look for your family?"

"If they did, nothing ever came of it." Christian stood, paced the floor like a caged panther. "If we're going to get into all this, I need to move, breathe some fresh air. Let's take a walk."

"No. We need to have this out. Here and now. I need answers."

"To what? So far, you haven't asked any questions." He stopped at the table and sat again, leaned forward with his elbows on his knees. "I've already told you about my illustrious childhood. It's more than I've disclosed to anyone. What else do you want?"

"I want to know about this Logan character, and why he sent somebody after you. What you're involved in. How you learned all the security measures. Why you carry burglary tools. And while we're at it, how are you able to roam around the country with me for over two weeks?"

They stared at each other. The silence between them lengthened.

How much should Christian tell her? How much could he trust her? How much would she understand? Dammit, he didn't know what Logan was playing at. It could have nothing to do with him. After all, Logan's man hadn't made contact with him. But Christian knew Logan well enough, knew his tactics, knew he had his fingers in many pies. Devan deserved some answers. She'd been attacked. He may be at fault, may have dragged her into Logan's snare. No way in hell would he tell her everything.

Christian let out an audible sigh. "Sit down, Devan. As I said before, I'll tell you what I can." She started to protest. He held up a hand. "Take it or leave it. There are aspects of my life that I won't share, not with you, not with anyone." He gestured to the empty chair across from him. "Things that would put you in more danger if you knew. I won't be a party to that."

Devan shuffled to the chair and flopped down, huffing. Her whiskey-colored eyes stared daggers at him.

"You already know how I got my pendant."

She inclined her head.

"When I was just a wee lad, I'd weave fantasies of who my parents were, what adventures they were on that had them leaving me there. In that place. The day Mother Superior gave me my pendant, those fantasies gave way to the harsh reality that I was alone, on my own in this world." He brushed his chest where his pendant lay hidden. "I won't lie and say I didn't occasionally wonder what it would have been like to have parents, siblings, extended family. But I stopped living in those fantasies."

"You're not answering my questions."

Impatience simmered in him. "Do you want to hear this, or not?"

Devan rolled her wrist, signaling him to continue.

"I figured my life was what it was and I'd better start looking out for myself. Christian drummed his fingers on the table. "Up 'til then, I'd only hovered on the fringe of Logan's gang. I was several years younger than any of them, short and skinny as a post. Logan took me on, as a kind of sidekick. The swiping of sweets turned into picking pockets. I had nimble fingers and quick feet. Still do." He grinned, feeling a bit of pride creep in.

"There wasn't a mark I couldn't take down. My status in the gang grew by leaps and bounds. By the time I was sixteen, I'd ruffled more than a few feathers. I left.

"I'd been solo since day one. I cut ties and have been pretty much on my own. I built a life that suited, where I'd never have to trust in someone not to abandon me. Figured it was better to be self-reliant, then you always know where you stood.

"I like this life. I like my freedom just fine. I turned out okay. Maybe I live skirting the law some, but I don't hurt people. I'm not a drunken bum. I'm not a murderer."

"No one said you were. But I need to know more about you. Like, what you do now for a living?"

"I can't get into all that right now. It's not relevant. Anyway, I've been thinking. Logan's goon may not be after me. So far he's not come at me directly. He may not have known we were traveling together before he attacked you."

"You're the one who thought we'd been followed since we left Dublin."

"It was a logical assumption. Starting with the break-in at Ardmore and your father's cufflinks going missing. I can't say that I saw a tail, not until today. It's more likely Logan's after you for some reason. He has other… ventures, besides running his tourist-fleecing enterprise. More dangerous."

"You think we're back to my ring?"

"Yes." Christian breathed a sigh of relief. He'd keep her on this line of thought and deflect the rest of her questions.

Devan sat still for several moments. He could all but see the gears turning in her head.

"Why'd you first think Logan was still pissed at you? That was over ten years ago, unless… Are you still involved with his operation?"

Christ, the woman was like a dog with a prized lamb chop. He hadn't been part of Logan's crew since he'd left the orphanage. He'd been pulled in just the once. And he bailed when Logan had tried to hook him again. Christian washed his hands of that life.

Devan interrupted his thoughts. "I'm not an idiot, you know. Logan doesn't strike me as the wait-for-ten-years-to-settle-a-grudge type of guy. What does he want from you now?"

Christian saw the fury wash over her features.

Devan's eyes widened. "Am I your current mark?"

"Are you trying to provoke me, Yank?" Christian snarled. "No, you're not a mark. Not mine, anyway."

"I don't believe you." Devan spat the words.

Christian pushed away from the table, knocking his chair over. He ignored it and shoved his hands in his pockets. He paced and prowled until the anger from her accusation receded. Until the red haze in his eyes cleared. Until his thundering, boiling blood cooled. He felt her watching him. She stayed in her chair, silent.

He peered out the window to give himself time to steady his voice. "Logan tried to draw me back into the fold. Before I met you. Claimed I owed him. I felt guilty enough to capitulate for one stupid job. Then I got disgusted with his greed. I told him I was done, we were square. He didn't like that I stood up to him. We had words. I walked."

"Are you a thief?"

Christian spun toward Devan so fast she flinched. "You have no right to judge me. I did what I had to do to survive. I'll not apologize for my choices. Now I'm done dissecting my life." He snatched a pillow and the extra blanket from the bed, tossed them on the couch before stomping into the loo. He stuck his head back into the room. "By the way, I'd never hurt you." He slammed the door behind him.

Feck me. How'd he get tangled up with such an exasperating woman? He wanted to throttle her. He wanted to drive himself into her until neither of them had a functioning brain cell left between them. Until he'd purged her from his thoughts.

Christian scrubbed his hands over his face. Why was he so tied up in knots over a woman? Not just any woman, if he was honest with himself. He was certain she was the woman who shared his destiny. The woman he wanted in his life. He shook his head, groaned. Where had that little germ come from? And what would he do about it?

Lord, she stirred him up. Christian toed his shoes off, yanked his shirt over his head, and stripped the rest of his clothing. He twisted the shower valve all the way to cold, stepped in, and let the icy needles pummel his overheated body, his hot anger, his fiery confusion.

He'd just let her stew. Hadn't he told her more than anyone else? Opened himself up like an exposed, festering wound? Maybe he should see her safe with the Gardaí, and search for the answers on his own.

"Damn you, Devan. You've twisted me up, until I don't know if I can escape. Or want to." He snapped the water off. Then he remembered his vision of her and dozens of dragons. Devan in the path of a flying dagger.

Thirty Three

Padrick arrived home weary to his soul. The setting moon clouded over and rain fell in torrential sheets. While the magic kept him and DECLAN hidden from non-clan humans, Mother Nature's fury couldn't be stopped. Padrick slid off his compeer, hunched his head and shoulders as far into his riding coat as possible, and opened the barn-sized door to his dragon's warm, dry lair.

DECLAN shook off raindrops and trundled to his nest of hay.

"We need to oil your wing joints," Padrick said aloud.

I am tired, as ye are. The tending will wait until the full light of day. After I eat my fill. DECLAN circled his bed, folded his wings tight against his midnight black body, and curled into a ball the size of a eighteen-wheel lorry. He tucked his snout in his forelegs, breathed deep, and closed his lazy swirling eyes.

"Sleep well, *mo chroí*." Padrick rubbed his compeer's eye ridges, then slid the door closed with a soft click and headed for his own bed.

Padrick hung his wet coat on the peg in the mudroom off the kitchen and sat to pry off his boots. The overhead kitchen light blazed to life. Meara stood illuminated, mussed from sleep.

His boot thumped to the floor. "Sorry to wake you. I tried to be quiet."

"CARRIGAN awoke and let me know you and DECLAN were home. Safe. You're drenched. I'll make tea."

Padrick's second boot followed the first. He stood and made his way to her before she could reach the stove. He pulled her into his arms, embraced her, and held on. Held on until he thought he could speak without a quiver in his voice.

"No tea. I just want to lie down with you and sleep." Padrick stepped away, glancing at the damp he transfered to Meara's nightgown. "I'm sorry. I got you all wet." He wrapped an arm around her waist.

"Let's get out of these wet clothes, then you can tell me what you found."

He kissed her temple on the way to their room. "Later. When my brain's less cloudy."

Padrick dreamed of Erin.

His Erin, running, blending in as a student at Trinity, getting on an airplane, flying away from him.

The dream shifted.

Erin running again, but this time she was bleeding. Blood flowed from several gashes on her head and arms. Pain twisted her young features. Erin cried out as she stumbled and fell. Blackness surrounded her.

A steady beep, beep, beep sounded in the dark.

Erin's thin voice rasped. "Padrick, I love you. I'll always love you." The beeping slowed. "So sorry...I love you." Long pauses sounded between the beeps now. "Had. To. Hide. My. Love." Erin's words slowed, slurred. One beep echoed in the darkness. "Find..." A flat drone of a solitary buzz pierced the quiet. Then silence.

The ache in Padrick's heart spread until he couldn't move, couldn't breathe.

"Ye shall stay here." The insistent mental command from DECLAN collided with someone's frantic shaking of his body.

Padrick gasped, bolted upright, and clutched his pendant.

"Come back to me." Meara's panicked voice sounded far away.

The blood flowed again through Padrick's veins, pounded in his ears like the surf over rocky crags. He opened his eyes. Tears fell on his cheeks. Meara's face swam into view, retreated, then returned when the bedside light flickered on.

"I've got you. Breathe now. Slow, deep breaths."

Padrick tried to comply.

"Ye are alive. Stay. I will not leave ye. We are partnered." DECLAN'S frightened tone caused Padrick to shudder.

"I'm not going anywhere. Not without you," Padrick bespoke words of bra-vado he did not quite believe. He relaxed his fist but kept the pendant loose in his hand.

"Lord Almighty," Meara said. "What the hell was that?"

Padrick's throat begged for water, but he remained still another moment, waiting for his pulse to slow. He nodded to the glass on the bedside table and croaked out a weak grunt he hoped Meara understood. She retrieved the glass of water. Padrick reached for it, but his hand shook. She held it to his lips, allowing him to sip the cool liquid.

"A dream. Very vivid." Padrick swallowed. His voice grew stronger.

"I'll say. You stopped breathing. I think your heart stopped." Meara set the glass down and rubbed a hand over the back of her neck. "You scared the bejesus out of me."

Padrick scrubbed his cheeks, felt the clamminess. "I've never had a dream with so much detail before. At least I've never remembered details so clearly." He'd never forget the sudden, bitter cold. He drew a deep breath, filling his lungs, and told Meara what he had uncovered. Told her the two parts of his dream. Told her his fears.

The color drained from Meara's face. She sent him a pained look then broke eye contact. Her shoulders straightened.

"Kiely called yesterday, as did your sister."

Padrick sneezed. "What did my mother want?"

"She wouldn't tell me. Just wanted to talk to you. Said it was urgent, private. Do you think she found out that you know her secret?"

"I don't know. Perhaps I should have returned her journal. Or maybe Sully was being watched like he thought." Padrick shuddered and sneezed again.

Meara pushed back his damp, sleep-tousled hair and touched his forehead. "You're burning up. Could be from the dream, or you're coming down with something. I'll make tea. You rest."

Padrick heard her shuffling around in the kitchen, preparing the tea. He wiped the sweat that beaded on his forehead and upper lip. His cheeks were cool, clammy. Meara was right, he needed rest. He hadn't slept much since the discovery of his mother's treachery. Hadn't eaten much either. He pushed himself, harder than others. That wasn't smart, for himself or DECLAN. He immediately felt shame for disregarding his compeer's wellbeing.

"I am well, mo chroí." DECLAN's sleepy tone echoed in his mind. *"I will rest,*

as ye are. Then eat. I am famished. Ye must do the same."

"I shall. I'm sorry I've been neglecting you. Are you sure you suffer no ill effects? I need to oil your joints, check your wings and scales."

"This can be attended to later. I am tired now."

"Okay. I'll have Meara send someone to check on you later. Rest, a ghra."

Declan replied with a drowsy affirmation.

Meara returned carrying a tray filled with tea for two, a shot of Jameson, and toasted brown bread smeared with butter and honey.

Padrick sat straighter in the bed. "Can you have one of the youngsters check on Declan after he awakens? I'm afraid I've driven us both to the limit over the last two days."

Meara nodded, sat cross-legged, then set the tray on the bed between them. "I'll take care of it." She poured the tea, adding the whiskey to his. "This should knock out whatever is in your system."

He sipped, made a face, and shuddered as the smooth liquid warmed his insides. "More like knock me out."

"That works too. You need rest. We'll keep Colin and Landon for an extra day or two. Until you're well enough to sit your dragon and fly patrol."

"I need to get back to work. At least see to the scheduling. Keep my mind busy. We still have a killer to catch and the mystery couple to track down."

"I may have a lead on the couple." Meara handed him a thick slice of the toasted concoction. "That was part of your sister's call yesterday." She filled him in on her conversation with Tess and concluded with her idea of the couple's whereabouts. "Braeden knows Carrowmore best. I'll have him keep watch." Meara sipped her tea. "Drink up. The clan needs you better. I need you better."

"Who's paired with Braeden and Faolan today?"

"Carrigan and I will fly with them."

Padrick raised one brow. "He's still raw. Still mourning Mary's death. Be careful. His behavior may be unpredictable."

Thirty Four

Devan stared at the closed door. She'd gotten some answers out of Christian, but not all. She was sure she'd learned more than he'd intended. He'd skirted the main question: was he still involved with the dark side of the law?

She pondered for a moment, threaded her hands through her hair. She righted the overturned chair, grimacing at the twinge in her shoulder. She replayed his response to her last direct question. Christian spoke in the past tense when he talked of survival. If the thieving was in his past, why didn't he just say so? Unless he was still in the game?

Devan rubbed the ache building at her temples, fighting the weariness that always accompanied an argument. She heard the shower start and decided to change for bed while he was occupied. The man infuriated her, fascinated her. She liked his complexity, his moods, his intensity, his deadly dimpled grin. She appreciated the difficult choices he'd faced, and that he'd managed to survive.

Her temper faded. What right did she have to judge his past? He hadn't done that with her. Granted, she had never walked on the wild side of anything, unless she counted her tormented relationship with Rick. Her only contact with the law before Ireland had been when the New York cop had called about her parents' accident.

Devan decided she wouldn't apologize for needing more from him. They were in this, whatever it was, together. He'd just have to accept that and treat her as an equal.

When the water stopped, Devan scurried into bed.

"Coward," she whispered as she turned off the bedside lamp and clamped her eyes shut.

With his bag still tucked in the boot of his car, Christian redressed in his underwear. No way was he sleeping naked on the couch, and he would be on the couch. The rawness of his feelings toward Devan required distance. For his own sanity, and hers.

Christian entered the darkened room, could just make out the lump in the bed before he settled himself on the too-short couch. Punching the pillow into submission, he drew the blanket over his bare chest. He prepared for a long, sleepless night. Rain pattered against the window and he dropped like a stone into the dream. The same dream he'd had just before he met Devan. The fourth murder.

It was early morning, just past dawn. He skirted past one whitethorn tree and halted short of the stone circle. The figure emerged from beneath another tree and walked to the center of the upright stones. He crept forward. The figure spun to face him.

"What are you doing here?" Her eyes narrowed. "Haven't you done enough?" He didn't answer. "What, no quick retort? You come to my place of remembrance. For what? To assuage your guilt?"

Anger and pride forced his unsteady hand to pull the dagger from its sheath at his belt. His vision wavered. One moment the blonde stood before him, hands on her hips, mocking him. The next, his lovely wife held his prematurely-born son wrapped in a light blue blanket. Blood streamed from a nasty gash on her forehead, soaking her dress and turning the blanket a dreadful crimson-brown.

He staggered. His legs had gone rubbery. His lungs burned, desperate for air like a firestorm craved oxygen.

"A knife?" Her voice slashed the vision of his family to shreds. "You are a coward. What have I or the clan ever done to you? You're the one who killed my last remaining family."

"No. It was an accident. Some stupid Yank driving on the wrong side of the road." His voice sounded like sand rolling over glass. He shook his head to clear his grating voice as much as to emphasize the denial.

"Maybe. But you're the one who insisted she be with you, even when she was so close

to term. She told me she wanted to be near her doctor. Not with you on the other side of Ireland." He heard the venom spit from her sorrow and anger.

"I just wanted her to be proud of me. To see what my new project involved."

She pointed a finger at him. "Selfish. You're as much to blame as the tourist. It may have been an accident, but it's your fault she was in the car with you." She glanced up as a shadowy dragon swooped down to land between them.

"Now," his mind screamed. "Before the creature transforms completely and kills you." He stood, unable to wretch his gaze from the apparition. He gulped air. The image of the dragon grew in density. The gray shadow changed to iridescent burgundy. It stood on scaly hind legs, thick as oak trunks. Spikes erupted from the top of its triangular head. A red forked tongue flicked between gleaming razor teeth. Sapphire eyes whirled under lowered ridges. The bat-shaped wings extended from its back, hiding the woman. Its chest, devoid of diamond-hard scales, lay exposed.

He tightened his fingers around the jeweled handle of the dagger, flipped it until he pinched the tip of the blade between his thumb and forefinger, drew back his arm, lunged forward, and hurled the dagger. He braced his legs to absorb the dragon magic. The dagger passed through the still shimmering body of the dragon, and embedded into the woman's chest.

Wave after wave of power buffeted him. He staggered. Wild and fiery, it tore through him, drove him to his knees. He gasped and fought to lift his head.

Christian awoke face down on the couch with his heart thundering in his chest. The storm thundered over the hotel room and rain beat on the lone window. His legs were weak, nearly gave way as he got to his feet. He stumbled to the loo.

"Damn."

He splashed cold water on his face and neck, then headed back to the couch. The clock by the bed read quarter past three. Maybe he could catch a little more sleep. As he lay back, he thought he should have expected the dream after the emotional battle raging in him about Devan. But this vision of the fourth murder had been different—contained more. He'd have to think about it in the morning. There was no way he wanted to continue the dream tonight. He closed his eyes and prayed for undisturbed sleep. The pounding of a headache increased, matching the rhythm of the bodhrán drums.

Dragons and their riders flew over the grassy mounds and landed in a clearing to the south during the ceili. An enormous bonfire took up the mound closest to the Celtic cross and standing stone. The dying sun sank in the West, adding its warm red glow to the flames of the bonfire. Dragons and humans formed a ring around a small knot of people and the famous stone.

His vision drew in until the flames illuminated a tall, burly man with red hair and beard leaning toward Devan. A kindly matron threaded her hand through the man's bent arm. They turned as two dragons, one a forest green and the other a midnight blue with silver wings, were led by a man with salt-and-pepper hair through the outer circle of people and dragons. The crowd quieted until the only sound was the beating of a single bodhrán. His heartbeat matched the drum—boom, boom, boom.

In an instant, he felt a desire for power, the control of that power, so swift his knees almost crumpled. A cry of anguish and loss escaped his lips. All eyes turned to him. Exaltation surged in his blood. Tonight he would get his family back, his wife and newborn son. He looked down at their bodies. Bodies he had unearthed. Bodies he had prepared for this sacred moment by cleaning and dressing them in the finest clothing he could buy. They lay lifeless now, but he would bring them back. It was his destiny.

He raised his head and saw nothing but anger and disdain in the faces that looked at him. The path lay open to the Yank and her companion who would give their lives for his family. He seized his dagger. A chorus of voices reached him, shouting at him to stop, pleading with him, begging him.

"For my family," he whispered and sent the dagger whirling toward his intended victim.

Christian yanked himself out of the second dream and into the hazy light of dawn. Fear tripped in his heart. Cold tore through him, driving him from the couch to his knees. Christian felt something rip from him. He choked out a gasp as unspeakable pain pulsed through his body.

Struggling for breath, he leaned against the couch. It made sense he would dream of the attempt on Devan's life. He'd had his share of nightmares, but never one this intense. Never one where he'd actually felt pain. He could still feel it as he gritted his teeth against the sharp stabs in his chest. He clutched his pendant and knew not only his and Devan's lives were at stake, but his honor, and his soul.

When the pain dulled, Christian staggered like a drunk back to the loo, and turned the shower on hot. He was freezing. He bent his head, splayed his hands wide against the tiled wall, allowing the spray to assault his whole body, clear his head, and hopefully push away the last wisps of the dream. With his eyes closed, all he saw was the dagger sailing toward Devan. Over and over and over.

He opened his eyes and snarled. "Not going to happen. I won't let it."

"What won't you let happen?" Devan asked.

Christian swore, one vicious oath. Good thing he was braced or he'd have jumped at the sound of her voice.

"What are you doing in here?" He heard the anger and impotence he felt from the dream and last night's encounter creep into his voice. He couldn't stop it. "I'll be done in a minute and get out of your way."

The shower curtain whipped open. His hands still on the wall, his profile to her, he turned his head.

"You're an ass," Devan said.

Christian lifted an eyebrow. "Naked here."

"I've seen you naked before. That isn't what makes you an ass, or maybe it does." Devan gestured to his erection.

He watched the flush rise from her neck to her cheeks and continue to her hairline. "Care to explain?"

"Testosterone. Male ego." Devan turned her head away from him.

Christian grinned as he shut off the water. His little spitfire was shy. He found the notion satisfying. For all Devan's book smarts, she was still a touch naive. He could use that to deflect the questions he hadn't come clean about last night.

"Yes, I'm all male. You haven't complained, 'til now." Christian grabbed a towel and wrapped it around his hips. He shook his head. Water sprinkled from his hair. Droplets clung to the sink and hanging mirror. The terror of the dream had faded.

"Listen." Devan returned her hot glare to his. "I thought I made myself clear last night. We're in this together. I'll not be kept in the dark, shielded by the big, strong man. I'm capable."

Christian held up his hand like a stop sign. "Never said you weren't. But we're in Ireland, I'm Irish—"

"As if I could forget."

Christian narrowed his eyes and lowered his brows at her interruption. "I meant that, even though it's the twenty-first century, Irish men, our culture, dictate men take care of and protect women."

"Did you steal from only men?"

The question caught Christian off guard. He opened his mouth, closed it. Then said, "No."

"How's that caring for women?"

Christian leaned his hip against the counter, crossed his arms. Devan hadn't let last night's argument go. And that realization brought the last dream back into his thoughts. He frowned. "As I explained last night, I was young. I did what I did for survival."

"When you were older? What then?" Devan's lower lip quivered. She bit it, but didn't lower her gaze.

Christian was impressed with her courage. She was obviously angry and a little fearful, but she didn't back down. "I parlayed my skills into another line of work. More lucrative." He half-shrugged.

"More against the law?"

"No. Not in the way you're thinking."

Devan tilted her head. "What am I thinking? For Christ's sake, just tell me the truth so I can understand."

"I progressed from lifting wallets to lifting…more valuable items. Almost got caught by the Gardaí when I was twenty-two. I wised up. Took my skills to my former marks and offered a service. I'd provide them a layout of their security holes." Christian waited a beat for Devan's response. When she said nothing, he continued. "I didn't have the computer background to fix their systems, so they took my findings to their security company. When the fixes were in place, I'd attempt another theft. Until I couldn't break in."

"Okay, I get the picture. Why didn't you just tell me you're in security?"

"Because I'm not exactly legit. I don't have a license. My clients pay me cash. They don't ask questions and I don't explain how I know specifics about their valuables." He finger-combed his wet hair. "There is some risk. If I get caught, they don't know me, have never seen me, haven't paid me."

"Oh. Well, I'm not the tax man. I won't give away any of your secrets." Devan left the loo.

Christian followed her out and noticed the sway of her slender hips and that her sleep shirt barely covered her bum. His body tightened with desire. With lust he told himself, only lust.

"You never answered my earlier question," Devan said.

"Which was?"

She turned and faced him. "What won't you let happen?"

Christian gestured for her to sit, then paced. "I had another dream. Two dreams."

"Another killing?" Devan straightened in her chair. Her attention focused on him.

Straight out guts, Christian marveled. He nodded. "Yes, the last murder. And an intense version of one I had before. Yours."

Thirty Five

Christian recounted his dreams. His breathing had eased during the retelling of the first one and had spiked again with the second.

"We're close to the answers. I feel it," Devan said. "Let's find the last murder site. Did you see other landmarks, besides the stone circle and the tree?"

Christian closed his eyes. "There's a single track road. I see a plateau with a wedge-like tomb. From my angle in the dream, it looks like the top stone is suspended in mid-air, surrounded by a smaller stone circle. Horses graze in an adjoining pasture."

He opened his eyes when he heard movement. Devan retrieved her guidebook from her backpack and flipped through the pages.

"Anything else?" she asked.

He cocked his head, trying to picture the scene. "To my right, about one hundred meters, is a pile of stones. About the size of a barn, fifteen meters or so in length and four meters high. That's all I can see. No opening, just a mound of stacked river rocks. It's raining, early morning. I can't hear anything over the storm and the beating of my heart. Until the snap of the branch."

Devan continued rifling through her book. "Sounds like a megalithic site. That would be consistent with the first two murder locations, and with the fourth victim—"

"Mary," he supplied.

"Yes, what Mary calls her place of remembrance. A cemetery of sorts." Devan halted, bent her head to the opened pages, nodded, then showed him the book. "I think this could be the place."

Christian took the book from her and studied several photos. One showed a portal dolmen one meter in height surrounded by a chain-link fence holding back a small mountain of stones.

"Listoghil," he said. "Yes, this could be inside the stacked stones in the dream." He flipped the page and saw several smaller tombs: portal dolmens and wedges. He returned to the previous page. "Carrowmore Bronze Age Cemetery, County Sligo." Christian rose. "Looks like we have our next stop. I need to get my bag, change, then we can go. I'll be right back."

Outside, Christian hurried down the street to the hotel with the revolving door. He hadn't called Finley again last night, so he'd check out his hunch. He didn't see the attacker's peat-mobile parked in front, but he wanted to follow up anyway. The desk clerk shook her head at his description of Logan's man. Christian searched the adjacent car park. No luck. Retrieving his bag, he returned to the room to the sound of Devan warbling some raucous version of *Whiskey in the Jar* in the shower.

The corners of Christian's mouth curved up. Perhaps he could join her. He wondered if she was finished thinking him an arse. Time to find out. He stripped, then slipped into the shower. Devan's eyes were closed, her head tipped back. Water sluiced the shampoo from her hair. The pose forced her breasts forward. He dipped his head and captured a nipple between his teeth. Devan yelped, and would have stumbled if his hands at her waist hadn't held her steady.

Christian raised his gaze to Devan's and watched her eyes darken as he skimmed his hands up her ribcage to the sides of her breasts. She sighed as her eyes closed. He lowered his head again, sampled her, savored her, saturated himself in her. He knelt and traced his tongue down her glistening torso.

Devan moaned deep in her throat, and grabbed the back of his head as he swirled kisses over her quivering stomach. Then lower. He didn't think he could get any harder, any larger, but he did.

His tongue flicked over her sensitive nub, slipped into her moist heat. He inhaled her sweet, musky scent of desire, and groaned. Water rained over them. Steam filled the room. He kneaded her hips, the tops of her thighs, as her fingers threaded through his hair drawing him closer. When he thought he'd go mad if he didn't have her now, he stood, swung her around, and pressed her back against the tile.

"Tell me you want this. Want me as much as I want you." His voice was husky with need.

"Yes, I want you."

Christian hooked one of her legs around his hip. He kissed the underside of her jaw, her chin, the corners of her mouth. His tongue traced her bottom lip, sucked it in as he plunged into her. Her warmth surrounded him, soothed his fiery need to hurry. He set the pace with slow, deep strokes, quickened only when her nails dug into his shoulders. Their moans echoed, turned to gasps. He whispered kisses over her face. His heart beat as fast as hers. Devan tightened around him, milked him as he climaxed and reverently called her name.

When Christian caught his breath and could feel his toes, he stepped back. The water had gone cold at some point. He reached behind and shut it off.

Devan shivered.

Christian pulled her into an embrace and held her while he reached past the shower curtain for a thick, fluffy white towel. He wrapped it around her, knotted the end at the valley between her breasts.

"I'm sorry I left you yesterday. I care about you. More than I have anyone. I need to protect you. Can you understand?"

Devan nodded, then started to speak. He pressed a finger to her lips.

"My methods weren't the best, I understand that now. I've never had to look out for someone else. Trust someone else. I'll do what I must to keep you safe."

Again, she tried to speak. He shook his head. "Let me finish. You were right. We're in this together, we're a team. More than lovers. We stick together. Trust each other." Christian lowered his finger and kissed her. "Are we okay now?" He stepped back, grabbed for his own towel, and wrapped it around his hips. "Crap. I didn't mean that…" Christian felt heat rise up his neck, burning his cheeks. He waved his hand between their bodies.

"I know what you meant." Devan chuckled. "If I was still mad," she mimicked his hand motion, "this wouldn't have happened. I mostly forgave you last night. After I realized I couldn't expect you to confide in me about everything in your past. I was being unfair. I was scared. But, no more secrets in our shared quest. No more talk of separating to protect me. Understand? Or I'll make good on going to the Gardaí."

"Your eyes darken dramatically when your Irish temper rises." Christian held both her hands in his and pulled her against him. His grin flashed and she shook her head. He lifted her hands to his mouth, kissed the palm of one, then the other.

"We understand one another." He pressed his lips to hers. Tasted her, treasured her, and tormented himself.

In the long moments it took to cross to the bed, Christian's thoughts whirled like waterspouts across a windy lough. Not only lust. No, this was more, much more. He was in trouble, serious trouble. He laid Devan down amidst the rumpled sheets. Her body vibrated against his, she moaned in his ravenous mouth, and he realized he didn't mind this kind of trouble.

For an hour Christian let himself drift with her, wrapped around her like a shield. He would do his best to protect her, even if she balked. His stomach protested its emptiness, long and loud.

Devan snickered. "Guess we should get going. Get you fed. I'm hungry myself."

He nipped her neck, the sensitive skin below her earlobe. With an exaggerated sigh, he began roaming his hands over her body. "So demanding. I'll do my best to quench your hunger."

She batted him away. "Different hunger. Besides, your stomach growled, not mine." She looked at the bedside clock. "We should be checking out soon, unless you want to stay another day."

"No, let's get to Carrowmore while we still have daylight."

They dressed and packed after deciding to find a diner away from the hotel.

Christian kept an eye out for the peat-mobile. The late morning held the remnants of the storm from the previous night. Gray clouds streaked across the sky from horizon to horizon. Rain fell, slowed to a drizzle, then picked up its intensity.

At breakfast, Devan mapped their route to Carrowmore. Once they were on the road again, she grew pensive.

"You're quiet," Christian said. "What are you thinking?"

"I'm hoping for answers. This is the last murder site. What if we don't figure this out?" Devan raked a hand through her hair, in a gesture Christian now recognized as either frustration or nervousness. "I know we need to confront Kate O'Shea about my ring, but what if she won't talk? She wasn't exactly honest with us."

"One step at a time. We gather information like pieces of a puzzle, then assemble them until we have a clear picture. We've already recognized patterns. Don't get discouraged. You're exceptional with the information. In all the time before I met you, since the dreams began, I've accomplished nothing. Look how far we've come."

"I forgot, you've lived with all this much longer than I have. I just feel we are so close, yet still miles away." Devan rolled her neck and shoulders and sighed.

"How are you feeling? Physically?"

"Better. My shoulder aches some, but the range of motion is improving every day. I'm sure the weather adds to the discomfort."

"You don't get rain in California?" Christian glanced in both side mirrors.

"Not as much as here, and not usually this late in spring." Devan craned her head around. "I think you missed our turn."

"Just making sure we haven't picked up a tail."

Christian exited at a small juncture, pulled into the petrol station, and watched for other exiting vehicles. They sat in silence, except for the light pattering of the rain on the roof and the intermittent swish, swish of the windscreen wipers. Satisfied, he headed back to their desired exit. "We're clean, so far."

"You're very good at the double-oh seven," Devan said, shaking her head.

"The what?" He raised his eyebrow.

"Cloak and dagger, you know. Detective stuff. Private Investigator. I meant to tell you yesterday—"

"Not good enough to keep you safe."

"That's not fair. We had no reason to suspect we were being followed. Once my dad's cufflinks went missing, you did all that sleuthing so we'd know if someone broke into each room." Devan ducked her head and gave him a sheepish smile. "Besides, I'm partially to blame for yesterday. I would have been safe if I hadn't panicked and left the room at the first sign of trouble."

"You wouldn't be in trouble if not for your involvement with me."

"We don't know that for certain. The guy came after me, not you. I'm on the side of my ring being the cause. The question is, why? Is this Kate involved?"

"We'll find out. When we get back to Dublin, Logan and I are going to have a face-to-face. I'm getting answers." He checked the rearview mirror before taking the single lane road the roundabout indicated for their destination. "At least this will make a tail easier to spot. Unless the guy changed cars."

"Why do you say that?"

"I didn't see his Citroen in the car park this morning."

"You couldn't have looked too closely when we drove past."

"No. I checked the lot this morning before I retrieved my bag." Christian held up a hand at her open mouth. "I would have called Finley if it had been there." He wouldn't have, but he'd let her think so.

"Really? Or are you just saying that to placate me?" Devan folded her arms across her chest.

"Probably. Anyway, the car wasn't there and I haven't seen anything suspicious since we left the hotel."

She glared at him. "You should have told me."

"I just did." He pulled into a car park adjacent to a white cottage. The lot held one other car, a bold blue touring car.

"We obviously need more work on trust." She grabbed her camera from her backpack. "Let's play tourist. Find the murder site."

The light rain stopped and a slight breeze tickled Christian's nose with the sweet, damp smell of fresh grass. They entered the cottage that had been remodeled into a visitor center. He held the door for a family of five to exit. They paid for a self-guided tour and headed out the back door to view the cemetery.

"We could have asked the docent about the stone circle." Devan oriented her map as they passed through a gate. "You really don't like people in authority."

"I didn't want to draw any undue attention to us. Besides, the place is over there." Christian pointed forty-five degrees to their left.

Devan's gaze followed his finger. "That's fairly close to the cottage and road. What time do you estimate the murder took place?"

"Morning, just after dawn. It was storming. But I don't think it would have mattered. This place doesn't appear to bring in a crowd at any time. The center doesn't even open 'til ten a.m."

They passed the whitethorn tree with its branches full of colorful prayer ribbons. The grass, still wet from the recent rains, muffled their steps, but the clouds lay scattered to the east.

Devan snapped pictures as they approached the stone circle. "Do you remember anything else from the dreams?"

Christian circled the outer perimeter, then made his way between chest-high stones to the inside. At the second whitethorn tree, he crouched, fingering several ribbons, much as the fourth victim must have before she died.

Grief slammed into Christian, sucking the air from his lungs. His vision wavered black with tiny pinpoints of light. He heard his name called over and over as though from a great distance. Was that Devan?

Someone solid tackled him to the ground. The action pumped a measly gasp of breath into his starved lungs. Christian's chest compressed toward his backbone several times, his head was tilted back, his nose pinched closed, and warm air forced into his lungs at a steady rate.

He coughed and blinked to clear away the blackness. A blurry face lifted away and he could make out Devan's elfish features. Her ruddy cheeks blew out air, her whiskey-colored eyes wide and wild looking.

"Damn you, Christian." Tears fell unheeded as Devan rocked back on her heels. "Don't you leave me. Don't you stop breathing. Don't you dare die."

Thirty Six

"Dragon magic." Braeden, mounted on tan FAOLAN's spiky neck, shouted to Meara as she flew on CARRIGAN. "Do you feel that?"

Meara nodded, circling her finger in a spiral. She pointed to an open area between the stone circle and a small portal tomb. Braeden scanned the area. The murderer could be here, back to the scene of the crime, back to where he murdered Mary. He directed his dragon compeer straight down, not as his friend and flight leader indicated. He heard Meara curse, but didn't care.

FAOLAN pulled up sharply from his dive. The dragon back-winged so hard it flattened the grasses and scattered rain drops as they landed. Braeden's head snapped forward then back. He couldn't hear anything, except his blood roaring in his ears.

Before Braeden slid down, Meara yanked him from his riding harness.

"What the bloody hell are you doing?" Meara's tone could have frozen hell itself. "You could have killed yourself and your compeer. Is that what you want? Is that all Mary meant to you?"

Braeden growled and freed himself from Meara's grasp. "The killer's here. Mary's killer. I'm going to end this now." His heart beat so frantically he thought it would rip from his chest.

"No," Meara hissed. "Think, damn you. I know you're torn up about Mary, but you felt the dragon magic. Who possesses dragon magic? Dragonriders, or potential dragonriders. Not the killer."

Braeden looked at her through a haze of red. He couldn't seem to catch his breath. He rubbed his chest over his heart, and touched his pendant.

"Calm yourself, Dragonrider," FAOLAN'S deep rumble reverberated in his mind. *"CARRIGAN's rider is correct. This magic is fresh. Not remnants from our dead clan members. We shall exact our revenge. I promise. This is not the assailant."*

Trapped between FAOLAN'S bulk at his back and Meara with CARRIGAN blocking his path forward, Braeden slumped against his compeer. The red haze receded as he steadied his breathing.

"If it's not the killer," he said to Meara, "and I'm still not convinced it isn't, then who?"

"The clan leaders and I have been searching for a woman, a Yank, with a clan ring in her possession, and her companion. The ring probably contains residual dragon magic."

"Why have you kept this secret? The rest of the clan has a right to know." Braeden stomped away from her, then returned. "What now?"

"I want to get a feel for the situation. Find out why they're here. Quietly. Without exposing the clan or the dragons. Can you handle this?"

Braeden nodded. As Meara outlined her plan, he thought about Mary and his loss. He'd go along, but if the persons wielding the dragon magic so much as twitched wrong, he'd have FAOLAN rip them apart. No way was he going down without a fight. Not like the others, not like his sweet Mary.

"Stick close, compeer," Braeden bespoke his dragon. *"In case."*

"CARRIGAN and I will be with ye. I will not let anything untoward happen."

The two dragonriders strode from the back of the portal dolman. They approached the stone circle and heard strangled cries.

Meara leapt forward. "What's going on here?"

The woman kneeling over the man spun to face Meara and Braeden. She sprang up, feet splayed like a boxer's, arms bent, ready to defend. Her eyes narrowed.

"Nothing. My friend just blacked out for a second. He's fine," she said.

Meara held up her hands, palms out. "We didn't mean to frighten you. Just offer assistance."

"What do you sense?" Braeden asked his dragon *"Can you tell if they are friend or foe?"*

"I sense no hostilities toward ye. I believe ye indeed startled her," FAOLAN bespoke.

The woman's gaze darted above his head. Her eyes widened as she let out a startled gasp. She backed up a step, tripped over her companion's prone body, and landed on her arse next to the man. He groaned.

"Who…who are you?" The woman's gaze stayed locked at a point several meters above Braeden's head. "Dragons," she said, and tried to crawl away.

"What?" The man struggled to sit. He reached into his right boot.

At a flash of metal, Braeden leapt forward. He didn't have a weapon, only his own hands and his dragon. He knocked the woman away and pushed the man onto his back. Braeden straddled his chest, brought both hands to the man's throat, and squeezed.

"Murderer." Braeden spat. "You'll not get another chance."

The man flailed, trying to dislodge his grip. He gagged, cried out.

Meara begged Braeden to stop. She pulled his shoulders, but he bore down.

No way was he stopping until Mary's murderer was dead. Dead by his own hands. Red haze clouded his vision again. The man bucked to break his hold. Braeden pressed his thumbs harder on the man's windpipe.

"Stop, Braeden." FAOLAN's voice penetrated Braeden's fury *"That is not what your mate would have wanted. Stop now. Do not force me to remove ye."*

"He killed Mary, he killed AALYSIA," Braeden shouted. Tears fell in rivulets down his cheeks, landing on the man's puce-colored face. "And the others. I'll kill—"

"No!" FAOLAN bugled a note and a growl.

At his dragon's command, Braeden let go. He turned, bewildered eyes seeking his compeer.

Talons gripped his shoulders. FAOLAN plucked him from the ground. Braeden thrashed. "Put me down. Don't you understand? He'll kill us all."

Christian coughed, drew a ragged breath into his flaming throat. Someone helped him to a sitting position. He groaned. He felt as if he'd been hit by an axe. Dizziness swamped him. He clenched his eyes shut to keep from being sick.

Scurrying noises mixed with grumbling. When a hand gripped Christian's arm, he opened his eyes. The world tilted, swayed, bounced, then steadied. Devan leaned white-faced against the tree, holding her arm, and an older woman knelt before him.

"Here," the woman said. "Small sips."

Water trickled into his mouth. Christian forced himself to swallow it. His throat burned. He pushed her hand away, rolled to his side, and retched. Molten flames seared his windpipe. He concentrated on breathing through his nose. Small breaths at first, then deeper as the burning eased.

"I'm sorry. My friend is grief stricken. His wife died several weeks ago. He thought you were the killer." The woman moved back.

Christian lay on his side, mind fuzzy. The wet from the grass seeped into his shirt, and he shivered. Who was this woman? He closed his gritty eyes. What happened to Devan? Had they hurt her? That thought brought anger, fear, and adrenaline. He rolled to his knees, crouched on his heels, ready to spring. He gasped as pain shot through his head and throat.

"I'm right here." Devan touched his cheek.

He opened his eyes. His vision frayed, then cleared. Devan knelt in front of him, blocking his view of the other woman.

"Who?" Christian croaked.

Devan turned to the woman but still caressed his face. "Who are you?"

"I'm Meara. Are you Devan Fraser?"

Devan's hand stiffened then fell from his face. "How do you know my name? Who's he?" Devan pointed behind the woman.

Past Devan's head, Christian noticed a man suspended in the air by a dragon's front talons.

"Are you dragonriders?" Devan shifted to help Christian sit, then looked expectantly at the woman.

"You can see the dragon?"

"I see two. A pale green one and the sandy-tan one holding your friend. Now answer my questions."

Meara held up a hand. "Better to have this discussion with Sean, the clan leader. In private. We are too exposed here. We can transport you."

"We're not going anywhere with you. Nor with that raving lunatic." Devan's tone heated. "He almost killed my…my friend. Who's Sean? And how's it possible, real dragons?"

Christian took her hand, intertwined his fingers with hers, squeezed. He hoped she understood his silent message. These could be the very people they'd been searching for, but he didn't want her to reveal too much. Not until they knew more. Devan glanced at him, half-smiled, and nodded before returning her glare to the woman.

The woman noticed their joined hands. She pointed to Devan's other hand. "We heard you've been asking about your ring, a family heirloom. May I see it?"

Devan curled her fingers into her palm, keeping her ring on her finger.

"Over my dead body," she whispered for Christian's ears only. She tilted her head in the direction of the two dragons and the struggling man. "Shouldn't you do something about your friends first? They're likely to attract attention."

"No one except other dragons and riders can see them, unless the dragons reveal themselves. But I do want to leave. Braeden needs to calm down. He's too riled up in this place where his wife was murdered. I shouldn't have brought him. It was too soon." Meara's eyes took on a vacant stare.

Christian squeezed Devan's hand to get her attention. When she looked at him, he thrust his chin in the direction of the parking lot.

"We have company." His voice rasped. "Let's get under cover. I'm too unsteady to take on anyone else."

Devan whipped her head toward the cottage. She blanched. Her hands shook before she clenched them.

Meara came out of her trance. Her gaze fell on the man with the blond crew cut trampling the grass in their direction. "Friend of yours?"

"No." Devan's voice shuddered. "Are you sure your friends aren't visible or audible? He's heading this way."

"Trust me. The dragon magic will keep them hidden. That can include you as well, if you come with me. Right now."

The intruder was gaining on their position, but they were crouched low, next to the whitethorn. Christian hoped they hadn't already been spotted.

"Where?" Devan broke into his thoughts. "My life is in our car. We can't leave it."

"We'll come back for it, I promise."

The tan dragon launched into the air from its powerful hind legs. It swooped gracefully, the man held rigid in one of its front claws. No sound emerged, even with the downbeat flattening the grass below. The green dragon edged closer to them, hunched down.

"Climb her foreleg. I'll bring your friend." Meara shoved Devan to the dragon. "No one can see you, you're within range of the magic." She helped Christian stand, then cupped her hands.

Christian staggered against the dragon, missed the woman's hands, and saw Logan's man slip through the stones, not two meters from him.

The man halted, swung his head from side to side, narrowing his eyes as he searched the circle.

Christian felt the dragon shift away from him. He turned his head in time to see Meara vault onto the dragon's neck. He sank back to his knees.

He couldn't lose Devan, but he couldn't protect her in his current condition either. She would be better off with the dragonriders, the woman anyway. He lifted his gaze to Devan and saw her start to slide out of the saddle. Her face was flushed, her fists clenched, her mouth set in angry lines. Meara shook her head.

Christian tried to smile and wave them away. His heart lurched at the thought of being separated from Devan. Before he turned back to face the man, he felt a large taloned claw circle his chest under his arms and lift him into the air. He grabbed the talon and held on.

"Where could that bitch and her lover have gone?" Christian heard the man mutter. "They couldn't just disappear. Their car's still here, the tracker's still in place. The old guy said they headed this way."

Christian watched in surprise as he was pulled out of the stone circle and away. He wasn't sure his stomach would handle it if the dragon decided to fly. He closed his eyes and swallowed hard. His head ached and his throat still burned. The claw around his middle held him secure, but gentle. When he no longer heard the man grumbling, he opened his eyes. They were at least fifteen meters in the air, banking away from the cemetery, and his stomach threatened to revolt.

What have we gotten ourselves into? Have we gone from the pan into the fire? Dragon fire?

They flew a short distance to a recently-plowed field. No buildings stood nearby. The dragon set him down and landed in one smooth motion. Christian sank to his knees in the boggy ground.

Devan slid from the dragon's neck and rushed to him. "Are you okay? Meara said that was the fastest way to escape. Did the dragon hurt you?"

Christian shook his head and immediately regretted the motion. The dizziness returned. He held his head to keep it from rolling off his shoulders and landing in the muck.

Meara approached and cleared her throat. "I'll have Braeden and Faolan bring your vehicle. We should go."

"Wait." Christian lifted his gaze. "The car has a tracker. I heard the guy say it was still intact."

"A tracker?" Meara asked.

"An electronic device that sends a signal…never mind." Christian waved a hand. "That's how the guy followed us. I need to destroy it. Or he'll be able to find us again."

"No way. The guy will recognize you," Devan said. She turned to Meara. "Can't we just wait until the guy leaves, then you can take us back to our car?"

Meara shook her head. "We need to leave. Our absence will be noted if we don't check in soon."

"We can't just leave the car. The visitor's center will close soon." Devan peeked at her watch. "In ten minutes. Any cars left in the parking lot will be suspicious. We've already had to involve the Gardaí twice with this guy. They are sure to know our vehicle."

Christian nodded. "Devan and I need to get to a hotel, preferably in a decent-sized city. I can destroy the tracker." A plan developed in his clearing mind. "How close are we to the car park?" He stood and scanned the area. They had flown across the road and landed on a slight rise beyond the suspended rock monument from his dream. He pointed to the portal dolmen in front of him. "We can return to our car by way of that monument. It's part of the tour and we won't look suspicious."

"Are you well enough?" Devan shivered. "I don't relish another encounter with that man."

Christian surveyed the cemetery grounds. "He's heading farther away. I say we go now, before he returns to his car."

"Sligo is the closest town," Meara said. "There are several hotels on the main road that should suit your purpose. We'll fly overhead. Pick you up outside of town."

"Why can't we drive to wherever we're going?" Devan stood hipshot with her arms crossed.

"Because no one outside the dragonriders is privy to our location. Sean, our leader, will explain everything." Meara nodded across the road. "No time to waste."

"How will we find you?" Devan asked.

"We'll track you. When you leave Sligo, head southwest on the N4 toward Dublin. Since you can see the dragons, we'll land in a suitable spot and go from there."

Christian took Devan's hand and hiked toward the car park.

"Do you trust them?" Devan asked.

"Not the boyo." Christian reached tentative fingers to his tortured throat, brushed the skin, and cringed at the bruising.

They crossed the road and hustled into the car.

"Holy shit! Can you believe dragons are real? I mean, I know you saw them in your dreams, but, wow!"

To their left, the dragons launched into the cloudy early evening sky.

"I'll give the woman, Meara, some leeway, because I think this dragonrider thing is the break we've been looking for," Christian said.

"Agreed. She could have left you back there. I thought…" Devan shuddered. Her lips trembled.

Christian reached for her hand, squeezed. "I know. No one was more surprised than I to be saved by a dragon." He focused on the road, but kept his hand in hers. "They know about your ring. Not my pendant, so I am expendable."

Devan shook her head. "No you're not. Not to me."

He smiled, brought her hand to his lips, kissed it, and the tight band around his heart loosened. "Thanks. But what I meant was, we have an advantage they don't know about. We need to keep my connection, my dreams and my pendant secret. Until we understand the situation better, find out what they know, and what they want."

This time, Devan kissed his hand. "We stick together no matter what. They don't separate us."

Christian agreed. They drove into Sligo as dusk fell. "Look for a blue Audi like mine. I'm going to transfer the tracker. Let that gobshite follow someone else for a while."

Devan grinned. "I like your style. I hope it causes all kinds of trouble for him."

"Should clear a path for me with Logan when we get back to Dublin." Christian turned into a modest-sized hotel car park. "Let's see." He spotted another Audi, but it was a later model. He hoped Logan's man wouldn't notice and pulled in beside it.

"What does a tracker look like?" Devan hopped out her side.

"Not sure, but it's probably attached to the undercarriage. Otherwise, I'd have seen it. Away from the heat and vibration of the engine." Christian crawled on his back under the driver's door. "Can you get me the torch in the glove box?"

"Torch?"

"Light, handheld."

"Oh, flashlight." Devan opened her door and reached in. She brought it to him.

Christian swept the undercarriage. He methodically searched under the driver's side from front to back. "Bloody, bleeding, bollocks." He reached under the bumper below the boot and dislodged a magnetic disk the size of a bottle cap. He held it up for her, before placing it in the same location on the other car. Then he searched his car once more.

"What are you doing?"

"Checking for a back-up. If I was tracking someone, I wouldn't use just one. Too easy to have it fall off." Christian didn't find another tracker, so he handed Devan the torch, and indicated she should get in. "The eejit only placed one. Let's get out of here, in case he's close by. I don't want to pass him and have the tracker show us stationary at this hotel." He drove down several side streets and headed out of town on a different road.

"Why can we see the dragons? Do you think it has something to do with my ring and your pendant?" Devan worried her ring around her finger.

"Not sure, but their leader needs to answer our questions, before we reveal anything more about ourselves."

Twenty kilometers southeast of Sligo, they saw the two dragons in a field near the road. Christian pulled over and stopped the car. Devan turned to him. He cupped her face in his hands, brushed his lips over hers, and smiled.

"Together, or not at all. Remember our advantage," he said.

Devan nodded and Christian saw trepidation in her eyes, but also determination. He kissed her again, quick and strong. They exited the car. He searched the road in both directions, but could see no car lights.

Meara dismounted. "You'll both ride with me on CARRIGAN. Braeden and FAOLAN will take your car. It's free of the tracker?"

"Yes." Christian helped Devan mount the pale green dragon, then scrambled up behind her. The tan dragon clutched Christian's car in its talons and lifted off, its wings beating furiously.

Meara climbed the dragon's foreleg and sat in front of Devan. "Hang on to me."

Christian's arms surrounded Devan and gripped a leather strap attached to the back of the riding saddle.

CARRIGAN launched in the sky as the sun dropped below the horizon, plunging them into night.

Thirty Seven

The dragons flew southeast, passing over small, lighted villages. Nothing so large as Cork or Galway, and most definitely not Dublin.

Since they flew only about a hundred feet above the ground, Devan made out rolling landscape dotted with stone walls for fencing. The wonder of what was beneath her competed with the wonder of Carrigan's wings lifting them up and over the hills. The dragon's sinuous body was covered in large, jewel-toned scales, smooth as glass. Gossamer wings fanned out to catch the updrafts.

Devan's raincoat was not keeping the cold wind away and she shivered. Christian tightened his arms around her. She leaned back into his warmth and realized how cold he must be since he had lain on the wet grass at Carrowmore. Yet his embrace warmed her.

Her fingers relaxed during the short flight. They flew straight and level, rising only when the land below dictated. The dragon banked left, circled lower, and she grabbed Meara's waist.

They circled a grove of trees on a hill. As they descended, Carrigan veered away from the trees. Lights from the farmhouses lit a central cobblestone courtyard, where the dragon landed with a slight bounce.

The tan dragon, Faolan, deposited Christian's Audi on a single-track dirt road next to a wood and stone barn. Then it landed in a grassy area adjacent to them.

Meara climbed down first, sliding to the dragon's foreleg before landing on the cobblestones. Devan followed, her sore shoulder jarring on impact. Christian landed next to her. She took his hand and held tight.

The front door of a two-story house stood open. The light inside back-lit a tall, broad-shouldered man with one arm around the waist of a woman whose head came to his chin.

"Meara." The man's gruff voice echoed in the shadows. "FIONN bespoke of your adventure. And guests." He stepped aside and gestured into the warmth of the house. "Please, come in. *Fáilte.* I'm Sean and this is my wife, Aisling. Make yourselves comfortable. I'm sure you have questions. I just need a quick word with Meara." His staccato rush warred with the soft lilt of his accent. He ducked his head as he strode past them to the pale green dragon and Meara. The young man named Braeden approached, his head hung down.

Devan watched for several heartbeats, then followed the woman with Christian into the house, and the sitting room to the left. They sat on a couch facing the entrance while Aisling wheeled over a tea cart with four cups on saucers, a platter of assorted cookies, and a decanter that held a dark gold liquid.

Aisling held up the teakettle. "Cream? Lemon? Whiskey?"

"Whiskey, straight." Christian fingered his throat. "Long, confusing day."

Devan nodded. "Tea with a splash of whiskey, thanks."

As Aisling prepared their drinks, Devan noticed they were in a library. Floor-to-ceiling built-in shelves lined the main wall. A rolling ladder attached to the ceiling stood at one end. They sat in one of two couches facing one another in the center. The room boasted a large picture window that overlooked the courtyard. Another door stood opposite the door they entered. Devan wanted to wander the room, examine the knickknacks, get another glimpse of the dragons. Her palms itched to browse the books, learn about their hosts. She stayed rooted next to Christian.

Aisling handed them each their drink. Christian released Devan's hand to steady the lead crystal whiskey glass.

Footsteps brought Devan's attention back to the door as Sean crossed the threshold. The other two dragonriders were not with him. Wanting to see the two dragons launch into the night sky, Devan glanced to the window, but it only reflected the room.

Sean took his place across from them with formidable gravity. Devan estimated him to be close to fifty, with his red-orange hair and trimmed facial whiskers sprinkled with gray. He briefly held her gaze with his clear, bottle-green eyes. He accepted a cup and saucer from his wife with a smile that crinkled the corners of his eyes.

Aisling set the cookies on the table between them, then sat next to Sean. An awkward silence weighed heavy as the two couples sized up one another.

Sean noticed Christian's neck. "I am sorry for the misunderstanding with Braeden. I humbly apologize."

"Misunderstanding?" Devan sputtered. "He almost killed Christian. That man shouldn't be allowed…"

"He's been through a lot the past few weeks," Sean said. "As Meara tried to explain." He pointed to himself and his wife. "I'd like to start fresh. Sean O'Shea, Tuatha Dragon Clan Leader and rider of red FIONN. Aisling, rider of gold BRIANNA. You are Devan Fraser and Christian—"

Devan saw Christian narrow his eyes. "*Just* Christian. You obviously know about us."

"I understand your reluctance, your distrust." Sean sipped his tea. "We only know you've been asking after a ring. A dragon ring with a Gaelic engraving. I'll answer whatever questions I can."

"What can you tell me about my ring?" Devan set her cup and saucer down on the table with a snap.

Christian interrupted. "Are you related to Kate O'Shea? Did one of your ancestors craft the ring?"

Sean looked from Christian to Devan and back. "Yes, and yes. Kate is my sister. We've had a jeweler in the family for generations. I don't know if they crafted your ring."

"How is it possible?" Devan asked. "The dragons, I mean. I thought they were myths. And why are we able to see them?"

Night sounds penetrated the silence. Sean nodded as though he had come to a decision. "The thing about myths, if you reach down deep enough, you'll pull out the truth. Legends exist because they have their core in fact." He nibbled a cookie. "Let me ask you something. What does a modern, intelligent, American woman think of the existence of dragons?"

Devan reached for Christian's hand. "Until I came here, I believed in what I could physically see and touch. Dragons fascinate me, always have. But I live in the real world. Now my belief system is in tatters. We've seen them, flown on them." She shook her head. "Forgive me. My brain is spinning at the implications. If dragons exist and can be kept hidden from a whole island of people, then it follows that magic must also exist."

"You already know that *draiocht* or magic exists, in your heart, in your Irish blood. It's only a matter of letting your mind catch up. The dragons are magic and use magic. So do humans. Our Celtic ancestors knew this, coveted their abilities." Sean sipped from his tea, then set his cup down. "Modern civilization drove the magic back into the earth. The magic continued to exist. It just needed an outlet. When our people were dying almost to extinction with the Great Famine of the 1840s, highly intuitive, sensitive people opened their minds and hearts to the magic. The dragons of Éire partnered with these individuals. Generations of dragons and riders have ensured the survival and prosperity of Ireland. To communicate, a talisman was crafted. Your ring is one."

"Is this why I saw the two dragons at Carrowmore? Why haven't I seen others? There are more, at least your two."

"Yes, Fionn and Brianna. There are more. But we'll talk of the whole clan later. I'm not sure why Carrigan and Faolan chose to show themselves to you. Your ring could be one reason. Need could be another. I understand the emotions were running high at the cemetery, Braeden's and your own." Sean inclined his head, then shifted his gaze to Christian. "You were injured before Meara and Braeden found you."

Christian remained silent. He squeezed Devan's hand and clenched his jaw.

"Meara said she heard Devan begging you to breathe, to live. You lay on your back, on the wet grass." Sean lifted his hands, palms up. "Look, no one's going to hurt you. Either of you. I can't answer your questions if I don't understand what has happened. How you are tied with each other."

"Devan and I are a team. That's all you need to know," Christian said, his tone rough. "We've had trouble. I won't leave her. I'm sure your rider mentioned the man who has been following us. You talked long enough."

Sean sighed. "She did. Why were you being followed?"

"I'm not sure," Christian said.

"We thought it was because I had been asking about my ring," Devan said.

"But you don't think so." Sean directed his comment to Christian.

"I've seen the bloody gobshite in Dublin. Before I met Devan. He works for a…less than scrupulous man. Twice he's gone after Devan. Never when I'm around, the coward. I'll do what I need to, to protect her from anyone with less than honorable intentions."

"Point taken." Sean leaned back. "Neither of you seem too shocked about the dragons. Why is that?"

"Perhaps the reality hasn't sunk in yet." Aisling spoke, her soft voice breaking the tension between the two men.

Devan hid a yawn behind her hand. The adrenaline and excitement of flying on the dragon was ebbing.

"It grows late." Sean stood, helping his wife to her feet. "Just one more thing. What drew you to Carrowmore? And have you been to Ardmore in County Waterford as well?"

Devan gasped.

Christian squeezed her hands. "I have had dreams or visions of those places. We investigated." He lifted a brow. "That's all I'll say on the matter for now."

"Okay, we'll discuss this further tomorrow. Please be our guests. You will be safe. I promise."

Christian helped Devan from the couch.

Sean lightly touched their joined hands, his voice dropped to a whisper. "There are things that come to us whether we ask for them or not. Do you believe in power? Not the kind that comes from muscle or position. The kind that comes from inside a person? That power is in both of you. I feel it as surely as I feel you both now." He dropped his hand and the whisper strengthened. "Aisling will show you to your room. Sleep well." He nodded, then left them in Aisling's care.

"I must retrieve our bags," Christian said.

"Of course." Aisling stepped to the stairway at the entry. "Devan and I will wait here."

Christian strode into the growing darkness. When he returned, Aisling led them up the worn oak steps, turned left at the landing, and opened the door to a bedroom at the end of the hall.

"Goodnight," Aisling said. "My husband is correct. You each emanate power. Together it is quite formidable."

Christian ushered Devan into the room and closed the door. She sat on the edge of the pillow-filled bed, rolling her shoulder to relieve the twinge before lifting her gaze to him. Devan played with her ring and thought she heard murmurings, not outside the room, but in her head.

"You're tired." Christian placed their bags on a two-person, chocolate brown fabric chair next to the window. "We both are. Let's get some sleep so we can think more clearly for the morning interrogation."

Devan retrieved her sundry bag and pajamas and headed for the en suite. When she came out ready for bed, Christian kissed her forehead, grabbed his own gear, and followed suit.

They lay in bed, listening to the house settle around them. Christian tucked her against his side. Devan rested her hand on his chest, over the steady thump, thump of his heart, over his pendant.

As Devan's eyes drifted closed and she inhaled Christian's warm masculine scent, she heard the whisper, *"Could she be the one?"* Before she could question it, sleep overtook her. And she dreamed of flying on the back of a dragon.

Sean shut himself in his office. He pulled the clan archives from the locked bottom drawer of his desk and was thumbing through them when he heard the knock.

"Come in."

The door opened. Aisling poked her head in.

"Our guests are settled." His wife cocked her head. "It looks like I'm heading out before dawn for patrol and to confer with Meara about Braeden's mental state. Do you need anything before I'm off to bed?"

"No, I'm just browsing through the records." Sean grimaced. "Thanks for tackling the situation with Braeden. That's more your specialty, and it frees me up to deal with our guests. I know one or both of them are hiding something." He held up his hands. "I know, gently. We don't need a Yank and her possessive friend spilling their ale about a clan of dragons and riders."

"You'll do fine," Aisling said. "On another matter, did Matthew have any problems with Kiely when he returned to Beaghmore this morning?"

"So far, so good. He checked in after his patrol. Said he was minding his own business and staying away from Kiely. That includes not hanging around Peter. He's concerned for his friend, though. I may need to have Michael check on the lad." Sean sighed and ran his thumb and forefinger over his mustache. "I hate getting in the middle of family dynamics."

"I'll leave you to your work. Wake me when you come to bed, *a ghra*." Aisling closed the door.

Sean toyed with his pendant and stared at the ink on the pages until the words blurred. What were his guests keeping secret? He saw the wariness come into the young man's eyes when the Yank reacted to his question about Ardmore. The boyo didn't trust easily.

But Sean hadn't lied about the power he felt from them. He just didn't know if they were on the side of good or evil. They could be the clan's salvation, or its downfall.

Thirty Eight

Devan bolted upright in the unfamiliar queen-sized bed as screams echoed in her head. The stillness and sudden silence disoriented her. Was it all just a dream? She speared her fingers through her short brown hair, spiking it in clumps away from her face. Christian stood, a dark silhouette against the predawn gray, looking out the lace-covered window.

Not a dream then, as everything came rushing back. She wasn't safe at home in California. She and Christian were in Loughcrew, guests of the Tuatha Dragon Clan Leader. She hadn't believed dragons existed in the twenty-first century, not until yesterday when she'd ridden on one.

Piercing cries for help shattered her thoughts. She clamped her hands over her ears and cried out.

Christian ran to her side, turned on the bedside lamp, and gathered her to him. "What is it, *a ghra?*"

As she curled into his soft T-shirt, the wail in her head froze her blood.

"Pain, oh pain, so much. Please make it stop." The discombobulated voice sounded young, yet old-fashioned English. Similar to the murmurs she heard upon her arrival last night that asked, *"Could she be the one?"*

Before she could ponder further, another cry assaulted her until she lay limp and battered. Tears streamed from her eyes as she sucked in lifesaving oxygen in greedy gulps. She felt her heart skip a beat, then thud like a runaway thoroughbred.

"I'm here." Christian tightened his hold on her. "What happened?"

She drew a deep breath. Feeling safe in his embrace, she waited for her galloping heart to slow. "I'm not sure. I heard screaming, cries for help. But only in my mind."

Christian stroked her mussed hair. "I experienced something too—another dream. In it, a small gray dragon was being tortured. Could that be the screams you heard?"

"Yes, it's possible. The tone sounded young, like a child." She wiped her eyes. "I know we met Sean, this clan leader, for the first time yesterday, but we must help whoever is injured. We can't do that on our own."

"Agreed. We'll tell Sean, but keep it to this incident. Don't mention my other dreams or my dragon pendant." He looked at her with concern. "Can you walk?"

She nodded and they hurried hand-in-hand to their host's room at the end of the second floor carpeted hall. Christian knocked.

Terrified screams of agony and cries of despair invaded her mind. She collapsed.

Through hazy, tear-filled eyes, she saw Sean, his red hair askew, bent over her. Christian lifted her into his arms.

"What's this?" Sean asked, although he sounded as though underwater.

Christian sank into a blue and white striped couch facing a fireplace glowing with the yellow-orange of a peat fire.

She nestled in Christian's lap as a headache pounded behind her eyes.

"Do you know what happened?" Sean asked Christian.

"Some. I think it's still happening."

Regaining control, Devan wiped the tears from her cheeks. She rubbed her chest, hoping the tightness would ease.

Sean perched on the edge of a couch across from her. "How can I help?"

"She's hearing screams of pain, in her head. A dragon, young by the sound of it."

Sean frowned. "How do you know it's a dragon?"

Christian kissed her forehead before answering. "I had a vision. The gray dragon—except maybe it's not a dragon, as it doesn't have wings. Anyway, someone tried to kill it. The beast used its claws and teeth to keep the attacker away." He held up his hands. "Don't ask. I couldn't see the attacker."

Devan gripped Christian's hands in hers. "The dragon's hurt. We must hurry, it grows weaker."

Sean stood and paced the sitting room. "We have one Tuatha gray dragon, a newborn called GRAYSON. He's at Beaghmore, the clan compound in Northern Ireland. Do you know where he's being held?"

"In a barn," Christian said. "In the dream, I heard animals and smelled leather and hay."

"Get dressed. We'll leave when you're ready," Sean strode to the adjoining bedroom. "I'll call Padrick, my second in command. His mother's dragon birthed GRAYSON and we may need Padrick's help to control both his mother and her dragon."

Five minutes later, Devan watched as dawn broke fiery orange over the forest to the east. She sat sandwiched between the two men on FIONN, Sean's cherry-red dragon's, neck. The baseball diamond-sized dragon beat his translucent wings in powerful strokes and lifted skyward, heading north.

The wind swept tears from the corners of her closed eyes. She shivered behind Sean, not all from the cold. FIONN'S wings rose and fell in a steady cadence. She felt the smooth, jewel-toned scales flex as the powerful muscles beneath worked to keep them aloft. Flying adragonback, open to the elements, was worlds apart from being confined in the belly of an airplane. It was scary and…exhilarating.

Several times during the flight, she heard GRAYSON'S muddled cries of pain. She tightened her grip on Sean's waist, leaned toward his ear, and told him of the pleas. Far below, the multihued green and brown fields flew by. Would they arrive in time?

Sean turned his head, shouting above the wind. "Try to communicate with him, using your mind. Tell him you hear him, that help's on the way."

Devan focused her thoughts. *We're coming, help's coming.*

The dragonet's panic lessened. The cries for help were tinged with gratitude and one word: *Hurry.*

Leaning forward, she relayed the command.

Within minutes several stone circles appeared, nestled at the base of a grassy bog. The sun broke through the swirling mists. FIONN flew to the opposite side of the bog where a valley lay open, forming another clan compound. FIONN landed in the courtyard nearest the barn. Christian jumped, lifted Devan off, then they rushed to the barn with Sean.

Devan used telepathy to reassure GRAYSON. *"We are here, little one. Are you okay?"*

"Where are ye? I cannot see. It is dark, like the deepest of night." The unusual communication grew stronger as Devan neared the barn. *"I cannot move, I am tethered."*

Sean tugged open the weathered barn door. They scrambled down the center aisle, peering left and right into hay-strewn, but otherwise empty stalls.

Christian skidded to a halt. "He's not here. Is there another barn? Smaller?"

Sean nodded. "Of course, the infirmary." He headed back outside. She and Christian followed. A smaller building sat attached to the far side of the barn. Sean yanked the door handle, but the door didn't budge.

Christian pulled Sean away and kicked the door. On the second attempt, it swung inward. Splinters flew from the shattered frame.

"I hear something. Is that ye?" GRAYSON bespoke.

Devan continued her thoughts, soothing the dragonet.

The scrape of metal against wood arose from the room. Christian and Sean rushed in first. Devan spun around as shouts emanated from the clan compound behind the barn.

"I'll handle this one." Sean manhandled a dark-haired young man from the room. "Help the dragonet."

Devan nodded, crossing the threshold as Christian opened the lone stall door.

Crouched against the back wall, a gray, wingless creature moaned. Chains anchored into the wall held two quivering hind legs. Thick rope bound the forelegs to the hind legs, like a frog readying to jump. The spiky tail lay forced against the wall. A burlap sack covered the dragonet's head, his protruding jaws tied closed with a hank of rope. Blood from several gashes on the underside of the body and from between the neck scales seeped into the hay-covered floor.

She removed the rough sack, mindful of other potential injuries hidden from view. The triangular head lifted at her touch

"Shh. I'm here now," Devan said aloud. "I'm going to remove the rope from your snout."

The dragonet swept his head to look from Devan to Christian, then shied away, snorting. *"No. Do not let HIM touch me. The dark-haired man bound me, hurt me."*

"It's okay. He's not the one who hurt you. Don't move now. He's going to cut the ropes and free you from the bindings."

Grayson's blue eyes whirled, frantic.

Devan crooned reassurances as she examined the four knots holding Grayson's jaw closed.

Christian pulled a knife from his boot, sawed the rope binding one foreleg to a hind leg.

"Ohh. Please, my leg."

She stopped Christian's hand. "Careful, he's injured. Look." She pointed to the claw where the thumb would have been. "I think it's torn."

Christian nodded. "I'll get something to stabilize it and find the key to these shackles. Be right back." He left her to deal with the other bindings.

Her fingers worked knot upon tight knot. Once untangled, she threw the rope in disgust and murmured comforting words over the savage rope burns.

"Thirsty." The thought echoed in her mind.

She found a water bucket in the corner, dipped the ladle in, and poured the liquid down Grayson's parched throat.

"Here's something to bind the injury," Christian said as he returned. He handed her torn cloth strips and two pieces of splintered wood. Fitting a key to the lock, he opened the iron shackles. "Should use these on the bloody, sadistic bastard that put them on you."

At his newfound freedom, Grayson tipped his head toward Christian and blew a puff of warm air that ruffled Christian's black hair.

Gently, Devan stabilized the injured claw. "Can you move?"

The dragonet extended his legs, lifting his body from the crouch of forced captivity. He groaned aloud. His brows creased downward. His eyes swirled faster.

The instant the damaged foreleg touched the ground, pain shot like a lance into Devan's head.

"Oh, oh. The pain. It hurts."

Instinctively she rubbed GRAYSON'S eye ridges. "I know, but we need to get you out of here. Can you bear the pain a little longer? We'll get you comfortable soon, I promise."

GRAYSON hobbled out of the stall and into the fresh air. Emerging from the building's shadows, Devan spotted Sean talking to the dark-haired man from the barn and an older couple. Furious, she marched up to the group with Christian and GRAYSON in tow.

Sean focused on GRAYSON, then seized the man's scratched arm. "Peter, what have you done?" Not waiting for an answer, he spun to face the old woman. "Kiely, as GRAYSON'S protector, you must have known about this."

Kiely shook her head then her face filled with rage as she rounded on the young man. "How could you? I gave him into your care so you could bond."

Peter rubbed his bloody lip. "He's defective. He's n-not a real dragon."

A roar split the air. Devan and Christian reached a hand to GRAYSON'S shoulder, both soothing and stopping the dragonet from rushing Peter.

"I'll n-not have him," Peter said. "You p-promised me I'd be a dragon-rider. I c-can't, he has n-no wings."

Devan spoke, yet kept her hand on the gray dragonet. "He may not fly, but he is a true dragon. I can hear him, just as I hear FIONN soothing him now. Other dragons as well."

Sean raised his right eyebrow. "Have you always heard all the dragons, not just GRAYSON?"

"No...." She thought of the murmurs she'd heard once she and Christian landed at Loughcrew. "I take that back. I have heard them. I just didn't know what I was hearing. It was whispers before, snippets of thoughts. Now it's as if a stiff breeze has blown the mists from my mind. Everything is clear—words, thoughts, feelings."

"Amazing," Sean said as his gaze locked on the silver dragon ring on her right hand. "The legend is true then. The One who wears the clan ring can hear all dragons." He turned to Christian. "What about you? You said you saw GRAYSON being attacked."

Christian nodded. "I told you I have visions. I've seen dragons before." He glanced past the injured dragonet to Devan.

She gave a slight nod.

Christian pulled a leather cord from under his shirt. Sunlight glinted off the attached silver disk. "I believe you know what this is, as you've one yourself. I saw it this morning."

Sean stepped closer to Christian. "Yes, I do. All dragonriders have one. It helps us communicate with our dragon and empowers us to keep Ireland and its inhabitants safe and prosperous. Where did you get yours?"

"It was found with me at the orphanage, where I was abandoned twenty-seven years ago."

Kiely stumbled back. "That can't be."

Christian's gaze alighted on the old woman.

Sean spun around. "What do you know of this?"

Before Kiely could respond, the white-haired gentleman with her inclined his head. "May I see the pendant, young man?"

Christian's eyes narrowed. "Come here, as I'll not take it off. It's the one clue to my identity."

The man approached Christian, examined the dragon-embossed disk, and squinted at the Gaelic words engraved on the back. He studied Christian then extended his hand in greeting.

"I'm honored to meet you. I'm Ronan, your grandfather."

Christian blinked then retreated a step, only to encounter Grayson's bulk.

Devan muffled a gasp when she noticed the twins of Christian's deep blue eyes alive in Ronan's weathered face. The color drained from Christian's cheeks. She squeezed his icy hand to keep him from pitching forward.

Sean stared at the two men for several long seconds. "Uncanny. I didn't see the resemblance before. A good blend of Padrick and Erin."

"What about me and Erin?" A man with salt-and-pepper hair approached. He flicked a glance at Kiely. "Mother," he said, his voice filled with contempt. Then he turned to Sean. "What's going on? Your call said Grayson's in trouble."

Grateful for the momentary distraction, Devan stepped forward.

"Grayson needs medical attention."

"We'll care for him," Kiely said.

Padrick scrutinized the injured dragonet, then glared at Kiely. "No, you've done enough."

"He'll be transported to Loughcrew to receive proper care. Peter will go as well, to answer for his crimes," Sean said to Kiely. He shifted to face Padrick. "Let me introduce you to Grayson's rescuers. The young lady is Devan, the Yank who heard his pleas for help. She can hear all dragons."

Padrick nodded in her direction, but Devan saw it was her companion that held his attention.

Sean clasped Padrick's arm. "This is Christian. He envisioned the attack." Then his voice softened. "Padrick, meet your son."

Both men's eyes widened as revelation dawned. Padrick reached out and Christian stumbled back, holding onto Devan. In unison, father and son shook their heads and whispered, "My God."

Thirty Nine

Christian groped for Devan's hand. "I need to get the bloody hell outta here."

Sean stepped between the newfound father and son. "I'm sorry. We'll handle this in private, at Loughcrew." He turned to Padrick. "Can Declan transport Grayson?"

Padrick nodded, his eyes never leaving Christian's bone-white face.

"Ronan and Kiely can bring Peter," Sean said.

"No, they stay here. I don't want to be near Mother just yet." Padrick's jaw clenched, the muscle bunching and easing. "Peter can ride with me."

Sean acquiesced, then addressed the injured dragonet. "Grayson, black Declan will carry you to a new home. One free of harm. Is this okay?"

"Fionn, stress the safety with Grayson. I don't want a startled, wiggly dragonet," Sean bespoke his compeer.

Grayson's eyes whirled fast and he whimpered as he craned his neck to see Declan approaching.

Devan placed her hand gingerly on Grayson's raw snout. "He wants to know how the dragon will pick him up. Do you have a harness that won't cause further injury?"

Padrick rubbed his chin. "A large wheelbarrow might work, with some padding."

"I need a word with Michael before we leave," Sean said. "See to it." He grabbed Peter and boosted him up on Declan's back. "Stay here. Do not cause any more trouble."

Christian stood motionless as Padrick headed to the barn. He felt numb, adrift, as if he was detached from his inert body and watching a tragic play. Devan crooned encouragement to the wingless dragonet. GRAYSON's soft moan mingling with Devan's strained breaths brought him back. Padrick and Devan were trying to load the injured dragonet into a black metal wheelbarrow lined with wool blankets. With GRAYSON's injuries, the dragonet floundered and made the task all but impossible.

"Be still, GRAYSON," Christian said. "We shall lift you into the carrier."

The dragonet quieted. His only motion was a slight trembling Christian hoped was from nerves, not pain.

"Devan, keep the wheelbarrow from tipping. Guide us." Christian positioned himself beside the dragonet and motioned Padrick to the opposite side. They bent, linked arms under the scaly gray body, and pressed to a stand. The dragonet was small and wingless, but his body was solid. Both men grunted under the weight.

"Stay there." Devan adjusted the wheelbarrow. "Steady now." She rolled it into place. "Okay, lower him slow and easy."

Christian's arms shook with the strain. Sweat beaded on his forehead and dripped into his eyes as they settled the dragonet. On GRAYSON's sigh, Christian broke contact with Padrick. He wiped his brow.

"DECLAN will take it from here. Thanks." Padrick nodded to Christian, then vaulted into the riding harness on his dragon's back, with Peter behind him.

GRAYSON curled into the blankets and raised his head to Devan's hand. She stroked his eye ridges, soothing him until the whirling of his eyes slowed.

"We'll be flying next to you on red FIONN." Devan hunched to catch the dragonet's attention. "If you get scared, just let me know. I'll be with you."

GRAYSON huffed air out his snout, ruffling Devan's hair. She laughed. Without a word, Christian guided Devan to where FIONN waited. Sean finished his animated discussion with Ronan, Kiely, and another man, then returned.

Sean inclined his head toward DECLAN. "They're ready. Let's go before we draw a crowd. Michael will handle the clan here at Beaghmore."

Christian whipped his head toward the buildings and central courtyard. The three riders Sean had spoken with intercepted several people with curious looks on their faces.

Sean climbed to his place between FIONN'S neck ridges and leaned down to help Devan. Christian boosted her into the riding harness, then scrambled up behind her. Sean lifted his fist in the air, pumped it twice, and FIONN launched into the morning sky.

After two strong wing strokes, Christian glanced at the black dragon keeping pace off their left side. The dragonet's body was snug into the makeshift carrier. His head slithered over the edge, looked down, then up to them. His blue eyes whirled faster, his neck ridges bristling in a frantic wavelike pattern.

Devan's body tensed against Christian's arms. He whispered in her ear. "He'll be fine. Tell him not to look down."

She nodded. A moment later, GRAYSON'S head disappeared into the black wheelbarrow.

The rest of the flight proceeded without incident, allowing Christian to think. How could Padrick be his father? Who was this Erin, and where was she? Why did she dump him at the orphanage? Padrick had been completely taken by surprise. Christian couldn't have misread that response. Now he wondered what to do about the sudden appearance of his father, his grandparents. Tension and anger radiated from him in waves that were almost visible.

Christian's head pounded with a vicious ache at his temples and the roaring in his ears increased. He closed his eyes, slowing his breathing to ease the viselike band constricting his heart.

Devan snuggled into his chest. Her brisk American accent softened as she told him everything was going to be okay and they'd get through it together. He didn't have her confidence in the situation, but his breathing leveled out and the tightness in his chest eased. FIONN banked right and Christian opened his eyes as they descended in a wide, slow circle.

DECLAN settled below them, placing his delicate cargo in the center of Loughcrew's small courtyard, before landing in the larger one. FIONN circled lower and lower, waiting until DECLAN folded its wings against its body, then FIONN landed alongside the black dragon.

Padrick held GRAYSON'S tormentor against his dragon. Both men were red-faced as though they had been arguing. Sean dismounted and helped Devan to the ground. Christian followed.

A half-dozen people spilled out from the large, single-story stone building across the courtyard from Sean's house. Shouts broke out. Five dragons emerged single-file from a gigantic earthen mound at the far end of the clan compound.

Sean raised his hands. "Enough! Go about your tasks. There will be a general meeting this evening. I'll explain then." He propelled Peter to the single-story building butted against his house.

Devan ran to GRAYSON. Christian waited until the crowd dispersed before heading to the wheelbarrow, and Padrick. He couldn't wrap his mind around it—Padrick, his father.

The two men reversed their earlier process, lifting the dragonet clear.

An elderly man leaning on a carved shillelagh ambled to them. He doffed his wool cap, his bald crown gleaming in the morning sunlight.

"I'll get this young'un settled into a lair, sir. Tend to his wounds."

"Thank you, Timothy." Padrick clasped the man's hunched shoulder. "See that he gets porridge with small chunks of lamb. I'm not sure when he last ate, so we'll start slow. Sean will want an update. Give us an hour."

"Aye." Timothy offered a gnarled hand to GRAYSON'S snout. The dragonet pulled his head back, his eyes swirled faster, and his brow ridges raised. "Easy boy. I'll not hurt ye."

Devan comforted GRAYSON. "He'll take care of you. I promised I'd get help. You can trust him." She glared at the old man until he nodded.

"I'm a caretaker, I treat all the dragons here at Loughcrew. You can both help me settle the young one." Timothy peered at Padrick, one brow raised.

"Ten minutes," Padrick said to Devan and Christian, his voice husky. "Then meet us at Sean's place, the front parlor." He strode away.

Timothy led them to the dragon mound, chatting nonstop with Devan as Christian followed in silence.

Jumbled thoughts roared in Christian's head, much as the River Liffey roared in full spate through Dublin after a mighty rainstorm. He rubbed his temples, hoping to ease the pounding. At the warm, coppery taste, he realized he'd bitten the inside of his cheek.

Bloody, buggering hell. He needed to get away, back to his own life. He couldn't think here. Not with the expectations he saw on Padrick's face. He was a man, grown. He didn't need a damn father, not now. Where was the bloody eejit during his turbulent youth?

Christian sighed and stopped at the threshold of a vast circular chamber. Eleven smaller, mushroom-shaped lairs branched off in a clock pattern. Air cooled his pounding head, and he knew they were underground, at the center of the earthen mound.

Devan and Timothy led GRAYSON left into the lair. Other dragons rustled in the fragrant hay. GRAYSON was settling, too.

Devan will be safe here, Christian thought, the dragonriders will protect her.

"Go ahead, lass," Timothy's voice echoed. "Don't keep the clan leader waiting. This one is in good hands."

Devan mumbled something that Christian couldn't hear, then stumbled through the lair opening and straight to him. She came into his arms, held him tight. Her trembling reminded him he couldn't walk away from her.

Sean paced before his desk, scowling at the bowed dark head of his best friend's oldest nephew. What punishment should he mete out? He'd tried to think on the flight from Beaghmore, but his mind kept reliving the moments he learned of Padrick's grown son. And the stunned look on Padrick's face. Not to mention the young man, Christian.

Clearing his throat, Sean focused on Peter. "What should your punishment be?"

Peter jumped at the sound of Sean's voice. "I d-don't know." He intertwined his fingers, twisting and untwisting. "That b-beast attacked me. It should be d-destroyed."

The office door opened and Padrick entered. His eyes narrowed, his brows lowered, and a frown formed. "Don't spout that bullshit, boyo. GRAYSON was under your care. I know your parents raised you better than what your behavior today suggests. Why did you abuse GRAYSON?"

Peter looked at Padrick then Sean; tears welled in his eyes, his cheeks flushed. "He was n-never going to grow w-wings. He was p-punishment for Grandmother d-disobeying the clan leader. S-she didn't want him, w-wouldn't even look at him. I know she w-wished him gone."

Sean opened his mouth, then shut it. He shook his head. "Did Kiely tell you to maim or kill GRAYSON?"

Tears fell down Peter's cheeks. He wiped them away. "S-she didn't say the w-words, but I knew. I w-was looking out for the clan."

"Peter." Padrick knelt in front of his nephew. "You are positive Kiely never said to kill GRAYSON?"

Peter nodded, a sob escaped. "If he could n-never fly, he w-wasn't a true d-dragon. I'd n-not be a rider." He hiccupped.

Sean rested a hand on Peter's shoulder. The young man lifted his gaze. Sean saw confusion in Peter's tear-filled slate-gray eyes.

"Your grandmother did you a disservice." Sean sighed. "Kiely couldn't guarantee you'd be a rider. Each dragon chooses its compeer. No one understands what each dragon takes into consideration when choosing. This is why each dragon matures for a year before partnering."

Peter's eyes widened. "S-so, even if he had w-wings, he m-might not have c-chosen me?"

"That's correct. I'm sorry, son." Sean squeezed Peter's shoulder. "I need to talk with your uncle now. I want you to go to the main hall, have the cook fix you breakfast. Wait for me there. Do you understand?"

"Y-yes, Clan Leader." Peter's voice strengthened as he stood up with Padrick. He shuffled out the door.

Sean peered at Padrick's troubled face. "Where are our guests?"

"Helping Timothy get GRAYSON settled. I didn't think you wanted them underfoot while we dealt with Peter. They'll be in your parlor soon." Padrick rubbed the back of his neck. "Peter's a good lad, under normal circumstances. A fine hand with the cattle. I'd like to take him to Lough Gur. I want Sully there as well. Keep him from Kiely's wrath when she finds out

I've spoken with him. I'll have Sully mentor the boyo, if that's okay."

Sean nodded. "That works. Keeps Peter away from GRAYSON. For what it's worth, I believe the lad was truly confused on his action being wrong. I require your word he'll be closely supervised."

"You have it." Padrick clasped Sean's forearm. "My plan will benefit both Sully and Peter. They'll be away from Kiely's influence."

"I'm going to call Aisling, she's with Meara." At Padrick's raised eyebrow, Sean said, "I think the Yank and your son are going to figure heavily in the clan."

Padrick's mouth fell open, his eyes widened.

"Before GRAYSON'S incident this morning, I was to meet with them," Sean continued. "Explain more about the clan, the dragons. Get some answers. They've been to Ardmore. Maybe the other murder sites as well."

"Do you think…my son murdered…?"

"No." Sean's voice was adamant. "You may not have noticed earlier with all the commotion, but they both exude dragon power. Not from absorbing the residual from murder victims, either."

Padrick let out a heavy breath. "Thank God."

Sean picked up the phone, paused before placing the call. "Are you going to be okay? Long-term?"

"I'll have to be. I have no choice."

Sean nodded. "Give him some time. Yourself, too." He pushed buttons as Padrick departed.

"Meara, I need you and my wife to bring ROARKE and DOCHAS here to Loughcrew," Sean said into the receiver.

"Is everything okay?"

"I'll explain when you arrive."

"We're on our way."

Sean hung up, grabbed several volumes of clan history from his desk, took a deep breath, and strode into the parlor. His guests waited on one side of the room. His best friend, Padrick, eyed the six-foot lanky frame, shoulder-length black hair, and blue eyes of the young man that was his son.

"I'm sorry to keep you waiting." Sean sat in the same spot as last night, then placed the books on the coffee table. "GRAYSON all settled?"

"Yes." Devan ran a hand through her hair, spiking it up away from her face. She and Christian crossed to the facing couch. "What's to be done with the young man who attacked him?"

"He'll be dealt with. And kept away from GRAYSON. He was misled...." Sean raised his hands, palms up.

Padrick sank into a side chair. "I'll be taking responsibility for my nephew. Kiely, my mother, really messed with his head."

"Thank you both for what you did for GRAYSON," Sean said. "But I need you to explain your visions. Why you were at Carrowmore?" He pinned Christian with his stare.

Christian massaged his throat. He glanced at Padrick, then down as Devan clasped his hand, and linked their fingers. "The visions, dreams—"

Devan interrupted. "We'll tell you about the dreams after you tell us how the dragons are kept secret."

Sean reached for one of the volumes. "Last night, I did some research in the clan histories, looking for your ring. There was nothing. At least nothing written. I do remember stories from *seanachais*, my grandfather being one." At Devan's raised eyebrow, he explained. "Seanachais are storytellers. Anyway, I remember a legend that says the wearer of the clan ring can hear all dragons. That appears to be the case."

"So each rider can only hear his or her own dragon?" Devan twisted her ring around her finger.

"Yes. That's part of the magic. The dragon magic is quite old. It consists of three components. Telepathy, transparency, and enhancing the ley of the land. Our talisman, the pendant, allows each rider not only to communicate with his or her dragon, but also to stay invisible within a ten meter radius of the dragon, especially while flying adragonback." Sean replaced the book.

"How many dragons and riders are there?" Devan asked.

"Until recently, thirty-two. One for each province, twenty-six in the Republic and six in Northern Ireland. The clan doesn't differentiate between nations, we are sworn to protect all of Éire." Sean shifted his gaze to Christian. "Over the past six months, four dragons and their riders have been murdered. What do you know of this?"

"First off, until two weeks ago I'd never been outside Dublin. And I wouldn't have left if not for meeting Devan." Christian fingered his pendant. "About the time you claim your first dragon and rider were killed, I began having dreams, visions, whatever."

Christian squeezed Devan's hand and held her gaze. She nodded. He took a deep breath, then addressed Sean.

"They were jumbled, confusing. In each, a person seemed to be caught off guard. A dagger was thrown. A dragon materialized out of nowhere, landed in front of the person, more a shadow than whole. The dagger passed through the dragon and embedded into the person's chest." Christian rubbed his own chest, caught himself and lowered his hand. "The dream shifted locations. Each dead body was placed in front of the same carved rock."

Padrick leaned forward, elbows on his knees. "How many?"

"Four." Christian cleared his throat. "Four distinct murders. Devan figured out the murder sites and that the bodies were placed at the entrance to Newgrange."

"What made you think the killings were real, not just nightmares?" Sean asked.

"Until Devan, that's what I wanted to believe they were. Then I read each victim's obituary. There was no good reason for anyone in their midtwenties to have died, let alone four in a six month period."

Devan helped him explain. "My ring, his pendant, the dreams, and the reality of four people dead, the same four from the dreams, were too much of a coincidence. We decided to investigate. See what we could make of it all. And hopefully learn more about my ring and my ancestors." She hopped up. "I have a letter from my mother's grandparents, the Gallaghers. It was in the box with the ring. I'll get it." She hurried from the room.

Sean rose, paced to the picture window and back. "Tell me more about the visions. Details."

Christian coughed. "Can I have something to drink?"

"Of course, sorry," Sean said. "Aisling will surely string me up for my abysmal manners. I'll be right back." He looked pointedly at Padrick, then turned on his heel and left.

When Sean returned, wheeling a full cart, the room had lapsed into a stony silence. Christian watched the confusion and hurt play across Padrick's features. Devan returned with her box and placed it on the table.

"Scones and tea." Sean lifted the basket and placed it on the coffee table, breaking the tension. "What do you take in your tea?"

"Cream, please." Devan reached for a blueberry scone. "I'm starved."

"Just tea," Christian said.

Padrick stood. "I should check on Peter."

"He's fine," Sean said. "Peeling potatoes for supper. Here." He handed him two mugs.

Padrick set the tea in front of Devan and Christian. He returned to the cart and filled his own cup as Sean sat. For several moments, the room was silent, except for the sounds of breakfast being wolfed down.

Devan dusted off her fingers and opened the mahogany box that sat in her lap. She pulled a folded paper out, unfolded and smoothed it, cleared her throat, and read aloud.

"My Dearest Brinna,

We understand what a hard decision this has been for you. You must believe we are and always have been so proud of you. Our choice in life is not for everyone. Our destinies are tied to the Clan and to Ireland, but your destiny is in your hands and you are the only one to decide what you're going to do about it.

We hope you and Patrick will be happy in America. May all your dreams come true. Know too that you are both always welcome home here, either for holiday or to stay. Please keep in touch often, as we will miss you terribly.

This ring is part of your heritage. Keep it safe. As one day your children, or children's children, may feel the pull of their destiny and return to Éire to fulfill it.

God bless you. Love, now and forever. Ghra, anois agus go deo.

Mum and Da"

After Devan finished, she looked at Sean. "The ring and letter brought me here. To find my heritage, my destiny."

"Gallagher, either Patrick or Brinna." Sean stroked his beard, then grabbed the bottom volume on the table. He thumbed through the brittle pages, then paused, his finger tapping halfway down the page. "Brinna, daughter to Graeme and Siobhan Murray. Married Patrick Gallagher, from outside the clan, and left for America after World War Two." He flipped back and forth several pages. "No record of either Graeme or Siobhan requesting another ring or pendant. In fact, no mention of a clan ring. The records don't specify different talismans at all."

"So I have riders in my past." Devan sat back from her perch on the couch's edge. "I wonder why my grandparents felt they needed to get away from Ireland?"

Padrick wandered to the bookshelves. "There was a time in clan history where relationships with non-clan members were strongly frowned upon." He stopped and faced the seated trio. His eyes glazed over and his voice lowered to a whisper. "Some still hold to that prejudice."

Christian stared at Padrick.

"Yes," Sean said to Devan. "It appears you have found your heritage. As for your destiny—"

Forty

A commotion outside brought all in the parlor to their feet. Christian heard Devan suck in a breath, then reach for his hand, interlacing their fingers. She stood still, eyes unfocused.

"Four dragons have landed. Carrigan and three others I haven't met." Devan blinked, and the veil lifted.

Sean ushered Devan and Christian from the room and outside just as Aisling and Meara stepped to the house. At Aisling's raised eyebrows, Sean answered her unspoken question. "She heard the dragons. Recognized Carrigan but not the others."

"What else?" Aisling inclined her head toward Devan and Christian.

"I'll explain inside."

Two dragons, one silver blue and the other forest green, rocked and wobbled on their hind legs into the smaller courtyard. Their triangular heads thrust forward, sweeping side-to-side. The neck ridges bristled in time with the frenzied swirling of their deep blue eyes.

Christian stood mesmerized. Devan squeezed his hand tight and pulled him toward the two dragons. They were smaller than pale green Carrigan and the gold dragon still in the outer courtyard.

"This is Dochas." Devan reached for the lowering silver blue head. "And—"

"Roarke." Christian spoke the name as it formed in his mind. His free hand clasped his pendant under his shirt. Feelings of joy suffused him— warmth, tenderness, unrestricted affection, and instant respect. "I heard him in my head."

Devan smiled at him. "I know. Amazing, isn't it?"

"A bit disconcerting as well." Christian released their joined hands and reached for ROARKE'S eye ridges. He rubbed first one then the other.

Thank ye. They have itched something fierce on the flight here.

Christian barked out a laugh. The trepidation he felt from the earlier conversation lessened. He knew he'd have to tell Sean and the others the details from his dreams. Just not everything.

Behind them, a throat cleared. "Come, we have much to discuss. DOCHAS and ROARKE need to rest." Sean motioned them back inside.

"Ho, Clan Leader," Timothy hailed from near the dragon lair entrance. His shuffling gait quickened with the thwack, thwack of his walking stick striking the cobblestones. "You wanted an update on the drake."

"Can you settle these two in empty lairs first? Then meet us in the parlor." Sean indicated the house with a wave of his hand.

"Aye," Timothy said. He looked over DOCHAS and ROARKE, then clicked his tongue against his teeth. "Beautiful. Let's get you both down for a rest, aye?"

Devan and Christian moved to the side and watched the caretaker lead the two dragons to the earthen mound.

Ye shall do well. Speak the truth. I will be with ye. ROARKE'S voice jolted Christian. He watched as the dragon craned his neck over his shoulder and stared at him with slowly whirling eyes almost the same color as his own.

Devan reached for his hand again. "We can do this. Together." Several moments passed, and she squeezed his fingers.

Christian nodded. They followed the four dragonriders into the parlor and sat on the same couch vacated only minutes before. Somehow the interrogation he had dreaded earlier seemed bearable now.

Sean inclined his head toward the door, then spoke to Aisling and Meara. "Earlier this morning, Devan and Christian woke me in the wee hours with a problem." He recounted GRAYSON'S pleas for help, the rescue, and the apprehension of Peter. He looked from Christian to Padrick and spoke of Christian's pendant.

Padrick approached Christian, pointing to his chest. "Do you mind?"

Christian pulled the pendant from his shirt. He hesitated a moment, then looped the leather cord over his head and handed it to Padrick.

"I am still with ye." ROARKE'S voice sounded husky from sleep. *"The talisman brought ye to me."*

Padrick sucked in a breath. "I haven't seen this since the night I asked Erin Casey to marry me." He held it close to his heart for several moments. Meara stood behind him and put her hand on his shoulder.

Christian stared up at the man he resembled so much. He swallowed, pushing his fear away. "What happened?"

"My mother." Padrick returned the pendant. "She's a believer in the caste system. Erin didn't come from a clan family, or a noble one. She was a commoner, Scots Irish. I met her at university. We fell in love." He shook his head. His face was haggard. Dark half circles bruised the skin under his eyes. "My mother drove Erin out of my life after that midsummer night céilí. I was young and stupid. I believed Mother's lies."

"What happened to Erin?" Devan asked. "After."

Padrick rubbed his face, pinched the bridge of his nose, a wider, longer nose than Christian's.

"My mother had Erin followed. I don't have all the details, but Erin managed to evade Mother and blend in with students at Trinity. I'm not sure after that." He held Christian's gaze. "I never knew she was pregnant. I swear. If I knew, I'd have…I'm not sure, but I'd never let her go through it alone. I loved her. I'm sorry." He half shrugged in defeat; his shoulders slumped along with his head.

"Maybe there's more information about her at the orphanage." Devan rested a hand on Christian's arm. "Mother Superior gave you the pendant. Perhaps there was something else left behind. Something not suited for a ten-year-old."

Padrick glanced at Devan. "It's worth a try."

Sean started to speak, but Timothy knocked on the frame of the open doorway.

"Pardon me, Clan Leader. You wanted an update." He removed his cap and folded it neatly in his gnarled hands.

Sean nodded and gestured the elderly man to the chair vacated by Padrick.

"The young'un is strong. Good thing. I've cleaned and tended near a half dozen gashes and his raw snout. The worst injury is a torn metacarpal joint on his right foreclaw." Timothy shifted his gaze to Devan and Christian. "I've stitched and rebound the claw for healing. He should stay off it for a week or two, but it should heal proper." His eyes returned to Sean. "Severely dehydrated. He'll need watching so he doesn't gorge himself. He's asleep now. Along with the other two."

"Thank you." Sean rose. "We are indebted."

Timothy pushed up from his seat. "Nigh, Clan Leader. 'Tis my privilege. I'll have my grandson Niall check on him when he arrives from school."

"That'll be fine. Have him come see me if he has any questions."

Timothy made his way out. The only sound was the front door clicking shut.

"Where's Peter now?" Aisling asked.

"In the main hall. Cook has him peeling potatoes for the community dinner. He'll be fine for a while." Sean motioned Padrick to sit. "We have other things to discuss. Christian was about to tell us more of his visions."

All heads turned.

Devan and Roarke's faith mixed with the confusion that bubbled over in Christian's mind.

Just give them the facts of each murder. You don't need to tell them about your unique vantage point. Lord, he was knackered. Christian rubbed his neck. He half smiled as Devan slid her hand into his. Her warmth radiated up his arm and gave him courage.

Christian took a deep breath. His gaze stayed on Sean as he recounted the details of each dream. After he was done, no one spoke for several long moments. The retelling of the dreams wasn't so bad, yet he hadn't explained the very visceral responses and emotions he experienced during them. Or when he and Devan had visited each murder site.

"Where are you during the dream?" Sean asked.

Feck. Christian didn't want to get into the semantics. He wasn't sure they wouldn't hand him over to the Gardaí. Long lost son of a dragonrider or not, he didn't know much about these people. He shrugged and tried an impassive look.

"Can you describe the killer?"

"No."

"Do you have any kind of a feel for him? Why he's killing?"

Double bloody feck. If Christian explained the killer's state of mind, they'd know he was tapped into that rat bastard somehow. Yet, every emotion he had during the dream could help bring the killer to justice. The sooner the better, before the killer could make good on the one dream that might be a premonition. The one dream that nagged at his conscience, awake or asleep. The one dream that involved Devan. He needed to protect her.

Christian took a sip of his tea and grimaced at the bitter, cold brew.

"Devan figured out each of the murder sites. At each location, I.…" He swallowed the lump that suddenly stuck in his throat and closed his eyes to quell the panic that threatened to overtake him. Devan squeezed his hand. "I experienced the murders from the killer's point of view."

At the sound of gasping, Christian opened his eyes. Aisling's hand covered her mouth, her gray-green eyes large as a euro coin.

Sean leaned forward. "Tell me."

Christian told the rapt audience his theories. "I think the first murder was an accident. The killer went to Ardmore to memorialize a lost loved one. Devan and I believe it's his wife." Christian wiped his upper lip. "He got a taste for the killing, or the power. When each dragon and rider was killed, I felt a blast of power engulf me. Each growing in intensity. He's trying to harness that power. Also, each murder site means something to him. At the second, he's assuaging his guilt over the loss of his newborn baby. We believe his wife and baby died near the third murder site."

Christian shifted to Devan. "We haven't had a chance to confirm this, or look up the names of who may have died near Ballynahinch Castle around that time. The last murder reveals the most. The woman he killed was related to his wife. He argued with her in my dream. That's why I can confirm he was mourning for his wife and baby. A tourist driving on the wrong side of the road killed them in a car accident. The wife was pregnant."

"Mary's brother-in-law?" Meara choked out a sob, then collapsed on the arm of Padrick's chair. "He's the murderer? Why? What does he gain from all this?"

"What's his name?" Sean asked Meara.

"Robert Smyth. Spelled with a 'y'. Last I heard, he still lived at their flat in Dublin. I don't have the address. Maybe Braeden knows."

"I'll get my contact with Dublin Gardaí to check." Sean strode to his office door, then turned around. "We need to prepare the clan. Introduce Devan and Christian. There's much to figure out."

Devan turned to Padrick. "I understand why the first murder was a surprise, but why couldn't the others be prevented?"

"We tightened our security after Conor and DONOVAN were killed, but we didn't know what we were up against," Padrick said. "It wasn't until Shannon and TARA were found murdered that we knew it wasn't random."

"I noticed Meara didn't have a mobile phone. Do they not work all over Ireland?" Devan raised her brow.

"No. The dragon magic interferes with mobile devices. We can't use them around our dragons. The land lines work fine."

Sean returned. "My contact will let me know."

"We were discussing the limitations with the magic and modern technologies." Padrick nodded toward Devan. "Maybe we have an answer."

"No!" Christian jerked Devan closer to him. "She needs to go home now. To America."

"What are you talking about?" Devan pulled away. "I'm staying. I just found my heritage."

Sean and Padrick stared openmouthed at Christian.

"The killer won't stop until he's killed her." Christian's voice wavered. "I've seen the dagger aimed at her heart."

"NIGH." ROARKE'S voice reverberated in Christian's mind in harmony with the startled cries from the four dragonriders.

Sean recovered first. "You've had a dream that hasn't happened yet? A vision?"

Christian nodded.

"We can protect her," Padrick said.

"Because you've done such a bloody bang up job with your own clan members." Christian spit out the words. "No thanks. She'll be safer away from all this."

"I'm already involved in all this." Devan waved her hand, encompassing the humans in the room and the dragons without. She held Christian's face between her hands. "You felt the connection with Roarke. I saw your expression. It's the same for me with Dochas." Her hands gentled into a caress. "Even before. With Grayson. We're both captivated. It's what we've been heading toward since we met."

"But, the killer—"

Sean broke the tension. "We have an advantage we didn't have before. Two, in fact. You've envisioned the attempt on Devan. So we can figure out the where and when and protect her. And Devan can hear all the dragons. Communication will be almost instantaneous, which was not the case previously." He shifted his focus to Devan. "We'll need to test your abilities and limitations."

Devan nodded then spoke to Christian, stroking his cheek with her left hand while her right dropped to his chest. "I understand this is a lot to take in at once. Lord, I'm still reeling myself. But this is what we're fated to do. I can feel it."

Christian frowned. First they helped rescue a tortured dragon, then he met his father, a man who knew nothing of his existence and had obvious issues with his own mother. Now the clan leader and these others want him—for what? To be a dragonrider? A visionary? All to stop a killer. He could help capture the killer, but at what cost? Devan's life? He wanted her safe.

"*Ye shall partner with me,*" Roarke bespoke him. "*Nigh harm shall befall the lass. Dochas and I shall protect her. I promise.*"

Christian blinked, amused at Roarke's arrogant tone. He held Devan's hand against his chest. "I told you before I wouldn't let it happen. We'll need to devise a foolproof plan, or I'll find a way to get you out of Ireland."

Devan glared at him. The ringing of the phone in Sean's office broke the stare down. Sean left to answer it. No one spoke. The tick, tock of the clock on the fireplace mantle dominated the silence.

Sean returned. "My contact went to Mr. Smyth's flat. He knocked, no answer. Without more substantial evidence for a search, that's all he can do for now. They'll keep a watch, but can't spend too much time. Maybe we'll get lucky and the Gardaí will apprehend him. Tell us your vision."

Christian related his dream, never relinquishing Devan's hand beneath his, or her gaze.

"Beltaine," Padrick whispered. "At the dragon partnering and oath ceremony. That doesn't give us much time."

Forty One

"That gives us less than two weeks to prepare. I'll need Michael here right away." Sean made a quick call from his office, then returned to the couch.

"What's this ceremony?" Devan asked. "Why not just postpone it?"

"Magic has responsibilities. Each May, on Beltaine, the clan renews their sworn oath. The dragon magic and the magic of all Ireland must be rejuvenated. There are several ways to accomplish this. Dragons and their riders acquire their magic by flying over dragon lines." Sean paused at the blank looks from both Christian and Devan.

"The ancient Druids believed the earth itself was like the body of a dragon. They built their sacred stone circles upon power nodes of this body. These stone circles are aligned with dragon lines or ley lines. Stonehenge is the most famous. Ireland has many. Lough Gur, Beaghmore, and Loughcrew, to name a few. This is why the clan lives near these prominent stone circles. Each dragon must cross a ley line once every seventy-two hours, or their magic will begin to fracture."

"Oh." Devan's eyes widened.

"Similarly, earth's magic must be replenished. The Celtic holidays are the catalyst. Beltaine, the ancient fire feast, is the most powerful. Each time the bonfires are lit without the clan reaffirming their oath, a little more of Ireland's magic slips away. Too much has slipped away in the past, so we take our vow seriously."

"What about changing locations, somewhere safer?" Christian asked.

Sean shook his head. "This ceremony must take place at the Hill of Tara. The magic is exceptionally potent there. It is where Lia Fáil, the Stone of Destiny, resides. Each new dragonrider takes their first oath touching Lia Fáil."

"Either the killer is well-versed in Celtic dragon lore or he was mighty lucky," Aisling said.

"Why?" Devan looked at the matronly woman seated next to Sean.

"All four murders took place on days with significant meaning in Celtic folklore. Each dragon and rider pair was killed at or near sacred stone circles or monuments."

Devan shook her head. "We only saw Grace O'Malley's stone castle ruins on Ballynahinch Lake."

"Ballynahinch Lake is close to the stone circles at Roundstone, near the coast."

Silence permeated the room.

"All that talk is well and good," Christian said, "but at some point Devan and I need to return to Dublin. We have lives to get back to. We've already been traveling for over two weeks." He waved a hand at Devan. "She's an American. She can't just hang around indefinitely."

"You're correct," Padrick said. "She'll need to petition for dual citizenship if she's to become DOCHAS's compeer. Just as you'll need to wrap up your affairs in Dublin to be ROARKE's."

"Whoa." Christian shoved to his feet. "I never agreed to any of this. Only that I'd keep Devan safe. The dragon can partner with someone else, someone from your clan."

'Nigh. I have chosen ye. There is nigh other.' ROARKE mentally chastised Christian.

Devan smiled at him. "I guess he put you in your place."

"Son—" Padrick stood.

"I'm not your son," Christian interrupted, "biology notwithstanding. I grew up in an orphanage and you never knew I existed."

"I've explained this." Padrick rubbed the bridge of his nose. "We need to check out the orphanage. Find out what happened to Erin."

Christian glared at Padrick. "I can do that on my own. I don't need you. I won't have you dictate my life."

ROARKE growled in Christian's mind. *Nigh more on your own. I am your compeer. Ye dare defy—"*

A warbled shriek sounded at the front door, followed by other strained bellows. The oak door burst into flames. Everyone raced to the entryway. Aisling and Meara ran past Christian. Devan followed them to the kitchen.

Sean grabbed a glass flower vase from the entry table and threw it toward the fire. The small amount of water hissed, but had little effect on the flames engulfing the wood. Padrick shouted for everyone to back up, then rammed the burning door with his shoulder. On his third assault, the hinges gave way and the door toppled to the porch outside.

The three women returned with pots of water to throw on the flames, extinguishing the fire. Smoke and the acrid scent of burned cloth and singed flesh stung Christian's nose. He watched openmouthed as Padrick stumbled back.

"Christ, man, what were you thinking?" Sean patted the smoky remains of Padrick's shirt.

ROARKE stood outside with DOCHAS, peering at the smoldering wreck on the porch. FIONN, DECLAN, and several other dragons were scrambling over the cobblestones toward them. DECLAN nudged ROARKE with his snout. His eyes whirled like a pinwheel caught in a hurricane.

"What the bloody hell?" Christian regained his voice.

"Ye defy the fates, your destiny," ROARKE bespoke in Christian's mind. *"I will not be denied my choice of partner."*

"I wasn't denying you," Christian said aloud as he rubbed his neck. "I was talking with this one." He pointed at Padrick.

ROARKE'S eye ridges arched, his lip curled baring his teeth, then he snarled.

"Disrespect." The word bounced around inside Christian's head, tinged with anger and hurt.

Christian held up his hands in surrender. "I meant no disrespect. We are not yet partnered. I…there are things I must take care of first. Alone." He turned to Sean. "How can he hear me?"

Sean lifted one shoulder in a shrug. "Each dragon partnership is different. Some are closer than others, but all dragons share a strong emotional bond with their rider. Dragon riding is in your blood. You wear a clan pendant."

"My great-grandfather's." Padrick's voice sounded hollow, laced with pain. He leaned against the wall holding his arm close to his body. Half his shirt was burned away. "He was of the second partnering. His pendant must have nearly the same strength of magic as the Yank's ring." He jutted his chin to Devan.

Meara stepped toward Padrick and draped a wet towel over his flaming red shoulder. "I need to tend this. Honestly, why did you try that stunt?"

"The flames would've sent the whole place up. We can replace the door and the porch easier than the whole house. ROARKE doesn't have enough control yet." Padrick shuddered.

"Why not just wait for us to douse the fire?" Devan asked.

"Dragon fire burns faster, hotter than a regular fire. I didn't know how much time before it caught something inside." Padrick's voice softened as he patiently explained.

Meara led Padrick back into the parlor. Aisling emerged with a first aid kit and followed them.

At ROARKE'S indignant snort, Christian and Devan sidestepped the burnt door. They strode toward the two young dragons. Christian intended to chastise the unrepentant ROARKE.

Sean watched the united pairs, both human and dragon, for several moments before turning to check on his friend.

Meara finished spreading salve on Padrick's shoulder and lightly placed gauze over the burns. "You should see a doctor."

"I'm good." Padrick took both her hands in his. "It feels better already. Thanks."

"You've had a busy day, all of you." Meara stressed the word 'all'. She squeezed his hands. "Give yourself and him time. You're both still in shock. As we all are."

"I wasn't trying to push." Padrick frowned.

"We're quite a bit for a non-clan member to take in," Sean said. "The two of you will work it out, but we have a lot to do to get Devan and Christian prepared for dragonrider responsibilities."

Padrick nodded. "You can count on me, Clan Leader."

"I know. Christian was right, they must return to Dublin." Sean held up his hand to forestall interruptions. "You can check on the dagger set and help Devan with her paperwork. I'm positive she's decided to stay, even before meeting DOCHAS. You should have seen her this morning. She was fabulous. Strong and compassionate even when she didn't fully understand her talent."

"Sorry I missed it," Aisling said, handing Padrick a blue chambray shirt.

"She was the same at Carrowmore." Meara helped Padrick shrug into the borrowed shirt.

Sean leaned forward. "They're in love with each other. That's an advantage for us. If ROARKE doesn't convince Christian, Devan will. But I think it was a *fait accompli* when human saw dragon."

"That's good. I'd hate to have to kick my son's arse before I got to know him." Padrick half-smiled. "While I'm in Dublin—"

Sean winked when he heard Devan arguing with Christian as they entered the parlor.

"It's my life, my choice. I have no one, nothing for me back in the States. I'll need to go back to settle my affairs, sell my parents' house, that kind of thing, but I can do that after…" Devan spread her hands toward Sean and the others.

"It's not just you now, remember." Christian captured her hands and tugged her to him. "We're in this together. Your rules. I'll not risk your life."

She leaned up and kissed him. "Have faith. We're going to stop him from killing anyone else, ever."

Sean cleared his throat.

Devan blushed and tried to pull away, but Christian held her close.

"Michael, the rider I was talking to this morning before we left Beaghmore, will be here soon," Sean said. "We have a lot to discuss. I'll need to introduce you to the clan members at Loughcrew tonight at supper." He raised an eyebrow and gestured for Devan and Christian to have a seat. "You have decided to join us, yes?"

Devan agreed. Christian followed with a reluctant nod as they resumed their positions on the couch.

"Tomorrow or the next day you can go back to Dublin to start sorting out your business. Padrick will go with you."

"We can handle it on our own." Christian narrowed his eyes, first at Sean then Padrick.

"You'll need to be here for training in less than a week. Padrick can help with Devan's paperwork."

"What kind of training?" Devan raked a hand through her hair.

"Flight and care of dragons, use of the magic, your duties and territories." Sean rolled his wrist and hand. "We should have a plan ready for Beltaine. I need to test each of your abilities as well."

"I think you'll find we're quick studies." Devan grinned. Christian looked abashed.

Fionn rumbled a laugh in Sean's mind. *'Roarke and Dochas are debating the proper etiquette for breathing fire. Seamus and Michael have arrived.'*

"Clan Leader," Michael said from the parlor entrance. "What happened to your front door?"

"An overzealous young one." Sean rose to greet the new arrival. "There is much to discuss."

Sean filled in Beaghmore's leader on the events of the past several hours. He stressed the need for discretion relating to Christian's dreams. "We'll introduce them to whoever is in attendance tonight." Sean checked his wristwatch. Time enough to explore the other pressing problem. "How is Kiely?"

Michael wiped his palms on the thighs of his trousers. "She was fuming. I'd say shocked, but we're talking Kiely here. No doubt she's scheming how to work this to her advantage." He gave Padrick a sorrowful look. "Sorry."

Padrick waved the apology aside. "I know her. I may have put blinders on for too long, but not anymore." He faced Sean. "She won't take a dressing down and being caught unaware about Grayson well. She'll seek retribution. We'll need to be careful."

Forty Two

Kiely paced Tullia's empty lair. "Where does that damn upstart Sean get his nerve?" She pounded her fist into her hand, punctuating each word. "Like I can't handle my own grandson. Or take care of my compeer's offspring." Her words sounded a staccato burst in time with the hard slap, slap of her boots on the tile floor in front of the dragon's raised hay bed. "I'll teach Sean to respect his betters."

She came to a sudden halt. Her eyes widened. "That's it. I'll take over the Northern clan. Separate out the six counties." She grinned. "I'll need to oust Michael and Seamus, he's Sean's man anyway. Kick out Matthew, Maggie, and their dragons. They can rejoin the Republic at Loughcrew or Lough Gur, I care not which. Move Ryan and Quinn to oversee County Tyrone. At least Northern Ireland will be safe from murderers. And Sean's abysmal leadership."

Her decision made, Kiely swept out of the lair to implement her plans. She ran into Michael climbing onto a saddled Seamus. "Bloody, bleeding yes-men," she mumbled under her breath, then raised her voice. "Where is everyone?"

"Out on patrol." Michael inclined his head toward an approaching Tullia. "Where you both should be. Is there a problem?"

"No. Nothing you could help with." Kiely turned to her compeer, clearing her plans from her mind. She didn't want Tullia to pick up on her thoughts until she'd had a chance to feel out Ryan. He was young and impetuous. If she approached him about his dragon being the next to breed, he'd agree. He certainly had his eye on Darcy, and Quinn would fly Aileen well. They were sure to produce the normal two eggs. Maybe even—

"I'm off to Loughcrew for a meeting." Michael interrupted her thoughts.

"Of course. Sean beckons, everyone jumps." Kiely waved her hand. "Don't let me or the worries of Northern Ireland stop you."

"What is troubling ye? Surely the young, wingless one is cared for," Tullia bespoke Kiely.

"Not to worry, mo chroí." Kiely stroked her dragon's chest. *"I'm just frustrated with all the inaction on the clan leader's part. He's all meetings and endless discussions without resolutions. You and I shall keep Northern strong, safe."*

"It is nigh our responsibility alone. Ye take on too much. All of Beaghmore compound strives for this." Tullia dipped her head. *"Are ye ready? I am yearning to spread my wings and fly."*

"Let's both feel the wind upon our faces, blow our troubles free." Kiely pulled herself up to her saddle on Tullia's neck and gave the command to take flight.

It was late afternoon by the time Tullia landed back at Beaghmore. Kiely had mapped the bare bones of the rebellion in her mind.

"Time for step one." Kiely settled her compeer and checked Calhoun's lair for Ronan. Her husband had been remote and not a little angry with her since Sean's visit after Grayson's hatching. The same day the clan leader had stripped her as leader of Beaghmore.

When she saw Ronan and Calhoun had not returned from patrol, she sighed in relief. The man was clearly controllable, but in his present state... Kiely let the thought dissipate. She'd put her plans in motion, then explain to her recalcitrant husband. He would not be able to stop her.

Kiely strolled out of Calhoun's empty chamber and into the cavernous center of the Beaghmore underground dragons' lair. Ryan and Quinn were lodged directly across from Calhoun's new sleeping quarters.

Damn inconvenient having Tullia's and Calhoun's lairs away from us, Kiely thought.

Once she had control over Northern again, she and Ronan would regain possession of the leader's house. Tullia and Calhoun would own the private lairs that were their due. Ronan's attitude must surely improve then.

Kiely saw Quinn's shiny teal-colored tail whip back and forth across the lair opening. She knocked on the frame of the open birch door.

Ryan faced her, oil pot in one hand, rag in the other. "Kiely." He nodded. "What can I do for you?"

He continued oiling his dragon's wing joints as Kiely closed the door with a soft click. "I'd like to discuss an idea with you."

"Okay."

"How would you feel about QUINN and AILEEN being the next dragons to mate?"

Ryan stopped tending to his compeer. QUINN blew out a soft snort as his neck ridges waved with interest.

"The Clan Leader's decided?" Ryan's lips turned up in a quick grin.

"I've decided. For Northern. Sean would have us decimated by this murderer in the time it would take for him to finish mulling over every variable."

"But—"

Kiely interrupted. "We need to act now. Before all our young, strong dragons and riders are past their prime or killed."

"Sean hasn't agreed to this, has he?" Ryan's brows lowered.

"No. He won't acknowledge the danger. We need to insulate ourselves, keep the clan strong with riders from within. He's looking outside. Even at a bleedin' Yank." Kiely's tone was laced with disgust.

"I'm listening." Ryan inclined his head.

Kiely explained her plans for the six counties. Ryan nodded. A gleam lit his eyes as she enticed him with the promise of dragon mating.

"QUINN and AILEEN would pair well," Ryan said. "I have courted Darcy for a spell. The dragon pairing would help seal our relationship and influence Darcy to accept my marriage proposal."

Kiely smirked. Step one of her plan was falling into place. Once she had Ryan's loyalty secured she'd have to gather the remaining Northern riders and explain her position. Then there would be six riders and dragons against three. Two, if she could pull off this coup before Michael and SEAMUS returned from Loughcrew. Matthew would be the most problematic. Too bad he hadn't been summoned to Loughcrew along with Michael.

"Not a word to anyone," Kiely said. "I'll let you know when we're ready to act."

Ryan didn't respond. His gaze was focused on his compeer. The dreamy half smile softened his features.

Kiely let herself out of QUINN's lair, pleased with herself. "I'll have QUINN and AILEEN breed quickly, then another pair." She glanced around to make sure no one heard. "The sooner we have a dozen dragons in Northern, the sooner we can hold off any retaliation from the Republic. Or a murdering bastard."

Ryan stroked more warm oil into QUINN's joints, his mind on the lovely Darcy.

"Would ye break with tradition and your oath to ensure my mating with AILEEN? Fall under TULLIA's compeer's rule?" QUINN bespoke Ryan.

"No, a Storin. I needed her to believe it so, only to learn more of her plans." Ryan soothed QUINN's bristling neck ridges. *"Are Matthew and KIERAN within speaking range?"*

QUINN mentally sent an inquiry. *"Nigh. I cannot hear him."*

"Keep trying. We must warn him. I need to keep up the ruse with Kiely. Matthew can inform the Clan Leader. Let me know when you've made contact." Ryan put away the oil and cloth. *"I'll check on Kiely."*

Ryan entered the communal dining hall when his compeer's excited voice sounded in his mind. *"I bespoke KIERAN. He and his rider will relay the plot. They are turning toward Loughcrew and will bespeak FIONN and the Clan Leader as soon as they are near. AILEEN and her rider are returning here."*

"I hope Matthew and KIERAN reach Sean quickly. Kiely is already speaking with the other dragonriders." Ryan narrowed his eyes.

Matthew directed KIERAN to attempt contact with FIONN. *"It's a long shot as we're still too far away, but Da and FIONN might be on patrol."*

KIERAN's strong downbeat faltered and his neck ridges bristled. Matthew lurched forward at the sudden change in speed. KIERAN righted himself and glided for a brief moment, then stroked a hard downbeat, resuming his steady flight.

"What happened? Are you okay?" Matthew gripped his saddle strap.

"I attempted to bespeak FIONN, yet another answered. A human female. She is known as Devan. She urged us to come quickly. She will speak to the Clan Leader. We must hurry."

"This woman is with my father? She heard you and responded?" Matthew pressed his knees tight to KIERAN'S sides and leaned close to the now calm neck ridges.

KIERAN'S wings beat strong and quick, matching Matthew's pulse. The land sped past as the pair pressed for more speed.

"Excuse me," Devan interrupted Sean. "I have just heard from a dragon named KIERAN. Trouble is brewing in the North."

Sean opened his mouth, then snapped it closed. He blinked and cleared his throat. "Sorry. Your talent's a bit disconcerting. Please tell us."

"Apparently," Devan said, facing Padrick, "your mother is planning to cede Northern Ireland's six counties from the clan."

Padrick looked gut-punched. No one spoke for what seemed like hours, but was probably less than twenty seconds.

"What?" Sean croaked.

Devan related the small amount of information KIERAN had told her.

"She'll try it tonight," Michael said. "While I'm here. If she thought Ryan was on her side, Matthew and Maggie would be her main obstacles. With your son on his way here, Maggie would be easy to subdue."

Sean sprang from his chair. "Let's go. Aisling, can you stay with Devan and Christian?"

"I'm going." Devan rose and pulled Christian to his feet. "We're going."

"I don't have time to argue." Sean glared at her.

"No, you don't. I can communicate your wishes to the other dragons."

Sean glanced at Padrick and Meara. Padrick nodded.

"Fine." Sean bit off the word. "A show of force it is."

Devan and Christian followed the riders outside.

FIONN bugled a fierce note from his crouched position in the small courtyard. DECLAN, CARRIGAN, and two other dragons—a gold and a bronze—waited in the larger courtyard.

DOCHAS, followed closely by ROARKE, stormed from the dragon lair hidden under the earthen mound. They tottered from right hind leg to left, sapphire eyes whirling, tails slashing the air.

Sean faced the two young dragons. He spoke aloud. "No, you are not going. You may have chosen your compeers, but I'll not lose them because of an accident in our haste. Devan and Christian must learn to fly properly. There is no time now. They can ride with me on FIONN."

Devan stepped forward. "You agreed to a show of numbers. Christian and I have ridden both CARRIGAN and FIONN. We can do this."

"As passengers, aye. Not as dragonriders, alone. Besides, DOCHAS and ROARKE are not strong enough to keep up with the others," Sean insisted.

"BRIANNA and I, along with Matthew and KIERAN will fly with them," Aisling said. She laid a hand on Sean's arm. "We may need them."

Sean stared at his wife a moment, then turned to Devan. "Can you direct your mind to a teal dragon named QUINN? Ask him for an update."

Devan closed her eyes and concentrated on QUINN's name.

A surprised mental voice answered. *"I am QUINN. Who are ye?"*

Devan quickly explained who she was and asked Sean's request for an update of the happenings at Beaghmore. QUINN responded that his compeer had Kiely in sight, talking with several other riders. Devan relayed QUINN's reply to Sean.

"Have QUINN tell his rider we are on our way. Keep an eye on Kiely, but don't try anything foolish." Sean shook his head. "This is why you need to ride with me. How are we to communicate if something comes up while we are flying on two different dragons?"

"FIONN can tell me. I'll tell FIONN when QUINN contacts me," Devan said, then relayed Sean's instructions to QUINN.

"Slow and cumbersome."

"Only as slow as thought. Better than without me. Besides, DOCHAS and ROARKE insist they can keep up with you."

Sean instructed Devan and Christian where to sit on saddleless dragons, then mounted FIONN. The others were perched on their compeers. Sean pumped his left arm twice and his red dragon launched into the air. DOCHAS and ROARKE lumbered three steps, then leapt, wings beating fast.

Less than five minutes into the flight, a young man on a brown dragon joined them. Devan recognized KIERAN'S greeting.

FIONN flew in the lead with Padrick's DECLAN and Meara's CARRIGAN on his right. Michael's bronze SEAMUS flew on the left. The formation reminded Devan of an arrowhead. DOCHAS and ROARKE, flanked by Aisling's BRIANNA and Matthew's KIERAN flew about fifty feet behind the leaders.

Twice QUINN updated Devan on Kiely's actions. Devan relayed the information to Sean through his compeer.

As the large stone circles came into view, Devan recognized the clan compound from earlier that morning. Lord, had it been less than twelve hours ago?

"TULLIA's compeer and other humans are surrounding FLANNA and her rider." Alarm colored QUINN'S tone. *"Ryan requests guidance."*

FIONN's reply sounded in Devan's mind. *"We are at the stones. Is CALHOUN's rider with the humans?"*

"Nigh," QUINN answered.

"We are here. Have Ryan ready to protect FLANNA's rider." FIONN led the flying wing in a low skimming pass over the compound.

A deep rumbling emanated from DOCHAS'S throat. Devan heard the other dragons' answering growls.

"Land in a containment circle. Do not allow anyone to escape," FIONN bespoke.

The dragons broke the arrow pattern, realigned into a hovering circle wingtip-to-wingtip, and landed before Kiely and the humans could scatter.

"CALHOUN approaches," QUINN reported. *"The dragons are curious. They emerge from their lairs."*

A sandy-haired man stood protectively in front of a willowy, dark-haired woman. She stared wide-eyed, trembling at the sight of the circle of dragons. The man said something Devan couldn't hear.

Kiely spun to face Sean, who climbed down from FIONN, his eyes roaming the faces of Kiely's cohorts. His expression grew hard as granite and his lips compressed in a frown drawing his brows low.

The people in Kiely's group ducked their heads and shuffled a few steps away from Kiely, then stopped as they encountered the dragon circle.

"Kiely, you are hereby relieved of dragonrider status," Sean said. His words were clipped, yet clear.

"You cannot stop me." Kiely spat.

"What the bloody hell is going on here?" Ronan pushed his way into the circle.

Sean turned to face him. "Your wife was trying to stage a coup."

"Arrogant bastard!" Kiely shouted. "I'm protecting this clan. Keeping it pure. You...." She stabbed a finger at Sean, her face livid. "You do nothing. Allow four dragons to be murdered. Then, you bring in outsiders, a Yank." She smirked at Devan. "You insult the clan by allowing them on dragon-back. Taking away the privilege from our own."

Sean stepped toward her, but Ronan reached a hand out halting the clan leader.

"Enough, Kiely," Ronan said. "Dragons choose their own compeers." He turned a weary frown to Sean. "I am sorry, Clan Leader. It is my fault for allowing her prejudices to go unchecked. I should have kept a closer watch after GRAYSON hatched. She hasn't been herself."

Padrick snorted, then dismounted. "Mother has been out of control for a long time." He pulled a thin black book from the inside of his riding jacket. "Do you know about this?"

Ronan squinted at the book in Padrick's fingers. He shook his head.

"That's mine." Kiely narrowed her eyes. "Where did you get it?" She whirled toward Matthew. "You thief. You took it when you broke into my office and house. I'll hand you over to the Gardaí." She faced Sean. "You're through."

Sean turned to Padrick. "In private." Sean's gaze swept Kiely's group. "Ryan, please guide Maggie and FIANNA to their quarters. Keep them safe."

"Traitor," Kiely hissed.

"No," Ryan said. "You were the one who wanted to break up the clan." He led the shaken Maggie away.

"You others." Sean pointed to the Northern riders. "Go with Meara and Aisling to the dining hall. I'll be with you shortly."

The remaining Republic riders dismounted. Padrick squeezed Meara's hand. She nodded at his whispered words, rounded up the recalcitrant Northern riders, and headed to the sprawling building in the center of the compound.

"Michael, the use of your office please," Sean said.

"The parlor would be less crowded." Michael inclined his head.

"Thank you." Sean waved a hand for Ronan and Kiely to precede him. "Devan, Christian. This involves you as well."

Devan glanced at Padrick, then twined her fingers with Christian's and followed.

Sean spoke briefly to Padrick before falling into step behind.

When the group reached Michael's parlor, Kiely whirled around and grabbed for the black book. "I'll have my property back."

Padrick lifted it out of her reach. "I know what you did, and I think Da will be keen to know what a selfish, conniving shrew you are."

Ronan sighed. "What now?"

"It was a long time ago," Kiely said. She lifted her chin. "I was looking out for the clan, keeping it strong."

"Like you're trying to do now?" Sean stepped between mother and son. "Sit down, everyone."

Kiely glared at Padrick, then Sean.

"Before I let Padrick have his say, I'll have mine." Sean raised his hands to hold off any interruptions. "As I said outside, Kiely is relieved of all rider duties. We are shorthanded, but the clan will *not* divide. We protect Éire as a whole, all thirty-two counties. I don't want to hear another word about the Northern Six. We have bigger issues to deal with and frankly," his gaze held Kiely's, "I'm shocked that you'd threaten one of our own."

Sean faced Devan and Christian. "DOCHAS and ROARKE have selected. The oath and Chosen Ceremony will take place on Beltaine as scheduled. We have much to prepare in a short amount of time. Devan is a direct descendent of dragonriders. As is Christian." Sean waved his hand to Padrick.

Padrick held up the thin black book. "I recently came into possession of Mother's journal." He looked at his father, then his son. Padrick bowed his head, opened the cover, and read his mother's words.

"It was so easy. The tart has no backbone. She won't ruin

my son's chance for clan leadership. I've seen to that. Erin bought the whole story of Padrick sowing his oats before he settled down with a dragonrider of my choosing. I told her it was clan law and she fell for the lie. I will never allow my son to take a bride that doesn't belong to the clan. Besides, I framed the chit's father. Told her he'd go to the gaoll if she came back."

Padrick flipped through to the last passage and read again.

"Five months have passed and still no sign of the chit. Padrick has left Beaghmore for Lough Gur. He won't listen to reason. Thinks I drove off his precious Erin. If he only knew."

When he finished, Ronan's face looked ashen, Kiely's furious, and Christian's impassive.

"I've been trying to track down Erin, but…it's been close to twenty-eight years." Padrick clenched the book until his knuckles turned white and the book shook. "Christian, I realize I don't know you and this is a lot to take in. I'll not pressure you, but I hope we can learn to be…at least friends. We'll be working together and due to the special circumstances, the clan must rely on each other." He pinched the bridge of his nose. "I am in agreement with Sean, the clan must come first. We pledged an oath. We honor that oath and our dragons. But I will continue my search. Alone, if I must."

Christian stared icily at Kiely, but said nothing.

"I am sorry, Son." Ronan fumbled with his hands in his lap. He lifted his eyes to Padrick. "I didn't know of this. I should have. We all have our faults. I was blinded by love, but no more." His voice rose in strength. "I will do as you wish, Clan Leader. Be that abdicate my position to oversee Kiely, or…" He lifted one shoulder and sighed.

"No stepping down." Sean slapped his hands on his knees. "Kiely must be watched, but Michael will do that for now."

Kiely gasped.

Sean glared at her. She bowed her head and he continued. "We need to get through Beltaine. Then we can implement my plans for more dragons and riders. Ronan, please take Kiely home. Stay there until Michael and I come."

Ronan dipped his head in acknowledgement, then dragged Kiely out the door.

Sean stood and walked to the large picture window. He stared out for several long, silent moments, then turned around. He steepled his fingers, tapped his lips

"We are presented with an opportunity. We know who the killer is and where he'll strike next. We just need to lay a trap."

Forty Three

Christian wished he could escape. The discussion went on and on, round and round with no firm decisions. He was beginning to agree with Kiely's earlier assessment of Sean's penchant for talking everything to death.

"Michael and I need to deal with Kiely and her misguided followers. Why don't you both get some fresh air? Check on DOCHAS and ROARKE. I'll have FIONN let you know when we're done. We'll have a brief meeting in the dining hall before we all head back to Loughcrew." Sean rolled the stress from his neck.

Sean and Michael headed toward the sprawling single-story hall. Padrick and Meara walked in the direction of the lake, talking in hushed tones. Devan eased her hand in Christian's as they strolled in the late afternoon's hazy warmth. They made their way to the three stone circles they flew over earlier. DOCHAS and ROARKE followed.

At the entrance of the farthest circle, between the two bigger stones, Christian gathered Devan in his arms. He rested his chin on top of her head and breathed in her scent, a light, breezy smell mixed with her citrus shampoo. He sighed and closed his eyes. *Home.* He felt an unfamiliar tug on his heart at the thought that this woman could be the one thing he'd never dared wish for—a home, a shared life, a family.

"Ye are mine as well," ROARKE bespoke the words in a reverent hush.

Devan tightened her hold. "FIONN says we should come back now. He's not happy that we're outside the clan compound boundary." She leaned back, her shoulders hunched and her head dipped as if she were a scolded child, then she straightened up and smiled.

Christian lowered his mouth to hers. He wanted to share a light moment with her, but the kiss grew intense as the events of the day and his feelings swamped him. When he broke contact, they were both breathing heavily.

He grinned. "Let's ride."

"Do we dare without Sean's permission?"

"Let's be adventurous. Live outside the rules while we can."

They mounted ROARKE and DOCHAS and flew back to the cobblestone courtyard nearest the dining hall. After dismounting, they walked hand-in-hand toward the low building.

Padrick waited at the entrance, frowning. "You shouldn't wander by yourselves."

"We weren't alone, DOCHAS and ROARKE were with us," Christian said.

"You haven't been trained in the dragon magic. Anything could have happened to you, or the dragons."

Christian dipped his head. "Sorry. Thought the stones were clan property."

"No. They are a well-known archeological site, open to the public. Magic keeps the compound hidden, but you're exposed unless within ten meters of the dragons." Padrick raised a brow. "No matter, this time. FIONN watched over you. Come, Sean is waiting."

They entered the dining hall. A dozen people sat at a long, rectangular table in the middle of the room. Kiely and Ronan were not among them. Sean and Michael stood to one side, talking to the young woman who was the focus of the attack. Several of Kiely's cohorts lowered their heads. The rest of Beaghmore's inhabitants stared openly at Devan and Christian.

Christian hoped it was because of his and Devan's new rider status, but saw the speculative glances from Padrick to himself. How had he gone from living a solitary life to caring for a woman, a Yank at that, to having an immediate family? A crazy one, to be sure. His mind whirled at the changes that were thrust on him in just one day.

Sean clapped his hands twice, interrupting Christian's thoughts. He explained the events and conclusions reached that day. His succinct words left no doubt who was in charge. When he finished, he nodded to Michael, then ushered the non-Beaghmore riders outside. The group mounted their dragons and headed back to Loughcrew.

Exhaustion seeped into Christian as they flew. He closed his eyes and swayed with ROARKE's beating wings. He jerked awake when he heard ROARKE in his mind.

"Do not rest. Ye must stay awake. We are almost to Loughcrew. Ye held up well this day. I am proud ye are my compeer."

"We have not undergone the ceremony."

"The human ceremony is nigh but a formality. We are already partnered. It has been destined."

Christian decided not to question ROARKE further. When they landed at Loughcrew, dusk had settled over the compound. The setting sun cast abstract shadows across the hilltop.

So different from Dublin, he thought. Would he ever get used to the quiet? Would he miss the life that he knew? Surely, not the Gardaí. Another thought surfaced. What did these people do for money? He'd have to find out before he joined them. He slid from ROARKE's neck and trotted to the silvery-blue DOCHAS to help Devan down.

"I shall rest now. Go with the Clan Leader." ROARKE trudged toward the dragons' lair with DOCHAS in tow.

"Sleep well," Christian said.

Devan patted down her windblown hair. "That was interesting. I hope the meeting here goes better. I'm exhausted. How are you?"

"I'm bloody tired of being on display. Can't wait to get back to Dublin. Even if it's only for a few days. Maybe all the curiosity will die down by the time we're needed back here."

"Are you unhappy?" Devan's eyes widened. "I mean, partnering with ROARKE?"

"No, actually, that's been…I don't have the words to describe it. Illuminating. Warm. Comforting." He shrugged and his lips lifted in a half smile. "About my family—" His smile disappeared.

Devan caressed his cheek and he allowed himself a moment to lean in to her warm palm and accept her strength.

"You've done wonderfully so far. I'm here for you."

"Thank you." Christian tilted his head and pressed a kiss to her palm. "I'm counting on you to help me through this gathering tonight. I just want to be alone with you. Me without all this baggage."

"You're still the same person." She chuckled. "Just with a few screwed up family members and skeletons in the ol' closet. Welcome to life, like the rest of us."

"I think you have the better deal." He frowned. "Sorry. I know you loved your parents and are essentially an orphan yourself now." He rubbed the back of his neck, careful to avoid the bruising running along his throat. "I'm tired, confused. I used to fantasize about my parents and now I've come face-to-face with my father and his family. I've learned my grandmother is responsible for my mother disappearing and leaving me at the orphanage. What am I supposed to feel now?"

"You don't have to categorize these feelings. And you definitely don't have to censor your thoughts and words with me. We're in this together, remember?"

"Let's get this meet-and-greet over with so we can…talk. Alone."

Devan tucked her arm in his. They headed to the communal dining hall and the raucous noises spilling from inside.

The room was a hive of people sitting or standing in groups around rows of rectangular tables. Sean, Aisling, Padrick, and Meara were at the circular head table at the far end from the massive double entry doors. Conversations stopped and heads turned when they crossed the threshold. Sean motioned them to join him. Devan squeezed Christian's arm. He took a deep breath, then strode with her to the clan leader's table, ignoring the open stares and whisperings from the crowd.

Sean stood. "Settle, please." He never raised his voice above a conversational volume, but the room silenced immediately. "The Tuatha Dragon Clan welcomes two new riders, Devan Fraser from America and Christian…" He glanced at Christian.

"Riley," Christian muttered. Padrick gasped audibly, but didn't comment further.

"Christian Riley from Dublin. They will partner DOCHAS and ROARKE in the Chosen Ceremony on Beltaine." Sean raised his glass. *"Fáilte."*

"Fáilte." The crowd welcomed them, lifting glasses in salute.

"Dílseacht. Fáil. Saoirse." Sean placed his right hand over his heart. The crowd rose and mimicked the clan leader. Christian and Devan scrambled to their feet. Each word rang distinct through the hall.

Sean motioned for everyone to be seated. Rustling followed, then he held up his hands for attention and the room quieted.

"Much has happened in the last twenty-four hours," Sean summarized their encounter yesterday with Meara and Braeden, the early morning attack on GRAYSON, and the meeting between the pair and the dragons. He skimmed over Kiely's attempted coup, finished by announcing Devan's ability to hear all the dragons and described Christian's visions.

Murmurs rumbled through the crowd. Someone yelled, "How do we know he's not the killer? Infiltrating the source to wipe out the entire clan?"

Sean scanned the room. "His dreams have provided the clues that led us to the killer. One vision shows the killer's intended next victim and location."

"He could be lying." The deep voice echoed in the hall. Christian glanced around, trying to find his antagonist.

One of the beefier men pushed back his chair and lunged toward Christian.

Padrick stepped between them. "Not when the next target is Devan. The one person who can not only hear, but communicate with all the dragons."

"They could be in it together."

Sean rested a hand on Padrick's arm, then addressed the audience. "Devan has agreed to act as bait, to draw out the killer. We have until Beltaine to devise a plan."

"He could still be the killer," persisted the hostile voice.

"Would one of our dragons choose to partner a murderer? Use your brain." Sean huffed. "Now there's work to be done." His tone brooked no further argument.

Everyone returned to their seats. The evening meal was served and people tucked into their food. Conversations resumed. Christian ate like a man starved while Devan nibbled and pushed the food around on her plate.

"You must be tired," Aisling said. Concern laced her words and her gaze drifted between them. "I'll take you back to the house if you'd like."

"Thank you," Devan replied. She folded her napkin and placed it next to her still-full plate.

"Rest well," Sean said, then mouthed 'thank you' to his wife.

Aisling led them to the same suite they'd shared last night. Before everything in Christian's world had spiraled arse over teacup, like how his insides rebelled when ROARKE swooped to a landing.

Christian sank on the bed as Devan scooted into the en suite. He kicked off his shoes and removed his socks. He unbuttoned his shirt, but left it on.

Sean's words echoed in his mind. They were to belong to the clan, become dragonriders. Only if he kept Devan safe from a murderer—a grieving, desperate madman with knowledge of the dragons and their power. Again, Christian marveled that he'd been dragged away from the life he'd known, away from the carefully constructed solitary existence that kept him from wanting too much.

Devan stepped into the room and froze. Her gaze travelled from his, down his exposed torso, past his black jean-clad legs, to his bare feet, and back. "You wanted to talk?"

He stood, crossed to her, and cupped her face in his hands. "Another form of communication." He wove his fingers in her hair, held her mouth to his, and plundered. More, he wanted more.

Her hands skated over his chest, pushed the shirt off his shoulders. Her short, unpainted nails scraped down his stomach to the snap of his jeans.

He gasped, breaking the kiss and covered her hands with his. "Too fast. Let me undress you." His voice shook and he paused to bring it under control. "I want, I need—"

"Shh. I understand." Devan lifted her hands up to his face, rubbed his stubble, and brought her lips to his in a soft, sweet meeting.

Christian took his time undressing her and laid her on the bed. His cock leapt at the sight of her long, slender legs and arms, her flat, pale stomach. He peeled out of his remaining clothes and joined her. Propped on his elbow, he gazed at her trim body. He followed with his hands, then his mouth.

The tension grew to an ache deep in his groin. With his pulse thundering, his heart pounding, he took her. Hard, deep, and fast. No longer able to keep the pace slow, he let his body take what it wanted.

She spasmed around him, purring his name over and over. He came growling, teeth clenched, jaw tight. Again, the word home echoed in his mind, over and over. Could she be the one thing he craved all his life, yet never possessed? His eyes met hers. "Devan."

Forty Four

Devan's name, whispered in Christian's mellifluous accent, surprised her. With trembling fingers, she traced the path of his dew-slicked spine. So much had happened to the two of them in the short time they'd known each other. Perhaps she was confusing the shared experiences—and stupendous sex—for love, but she didn't think so.

Love. She let the word drift through her mind. Yes, she was in love with this man. This complex, isolated, and sexy-as-hell Irishman.

The next morning dawned gray and bleak. After a hasty breakfast, Devan and Christian watched as first Dochas then Roarke flew low over the stone-walled field, cornered a black-faced sheep, and ate it with gusto. Devan's stomach threatened to revolt.

"My fast is broken with the tasty morsel." Dochas's smug thoughts flowed in Devan's mind.

She shuddered. *"I'll stick to cooked food, thanks just the same."* Dochas gave the mental equivalent of a draconic shrug and continued chewing her meal.

After the dragons finished, Devan and Christian mounted them under Sean's watchful eye.

"We'll measure you for harnesses before you leave for Dublin. They should be ready when you return." Sean swung into his own riding harness.

Padrick and Meara mounted Declan and Carrigan. Peter rode, stone-faced, behind his uncle. The group flew in an abbreviated formation to Lough Gur, the clan compound in County Limerick.

When Dochas and Roarke landed in the outer courtyard, Devan gasped. She turned to Christian. "Remember, the drive after the first night when my dad's cufflinks went missing, I told you I heard something that sounded like voices?"

"Yes." Christian helped her down from DOCHAS.

"We must have driven past here. The road couldn't be more than thirty minutes west."

Sean approached, his eyes narrowed, worry lines etched his ruddy forehead. "Are you hearing all the dragons at the same time? How are you not bloody stark-raving mad?"

Devan shook her head. "It's more…a jumble of whisperings, like the wind whistling through a forest, but no clear words." She shrugged. "I can hear DOCHAS clearly, of course. ROARKE, FIONN, GRAYSON. The dragons I've been around. DECLAN and CARRIGAN, as well. It's hard to explain."

Sean rubbed his chin. "We'll need to test your limits. Distance. Relative knowledge of each dragon. That sort of thing."

"Also, we'll need to come up with some protocols," Padrick said. "To not overwhelm you, or confuse the dragons."

"We are not confounded with the Ring Wearer's communication," DOCHAS bespoke Devan. She relayed the dragon's words, grimacing at the title bestowed her.

"Still," Sean said. "We'll need to understand this gift in order to best use it." He led them to the communal dining hall and introduced them to the dragonriders they had yet to meet. Other people who worked or lived with the clan were also introduced.

"Sully." Padrick clasped the older man's forearm. "Glad you accepted my offer. This is my nephew, Peter. Your new charge. Come, I'll fill you in." He led both Sully and Peter outside.

Braeden, the lunatic who attacked Christian two days ago, stood next to Meara. He dipped his head and mumbled an apology. Meara led him away.

The small number of clan members at Lough Gur kept the meeting brief. Sean, Devan, and Christian left the hall and made their way to their dragons.

"Were the murder victims from here?" Devan asked.

"Yes, all four." Padrick joined them, carrying a duffle. "Lough Gur is home to Munster and Connaught clan members. Eleven dragons and riders, plus support personnel at full strength."

Sean rested a hand on Padrick's shoulder, then spoke. "We've been filling in with dragon and rider pairs from the other provinces. We're flying thin. DOCHAS and ROARKE, and the two of you, will be assigned to counties here after the Chosen Ceremony. We'll still be shorthanded—"

"More so with what Kiely did, yes?" Devan glanced at Padrick.

"Yes." Padrick shoved balled hands into his coat pockets. "Mother doesn't think past her own wants. Michael will have to look after her as well, hindering those in Ulster."

"After Beltaine, I can implement my plans for growing the clan." Sean released his grip from Padrick.

"Why was nothing done after the first murder?" Christian asked.

"DOCHAS and ROARKE were originally bred to replace Kiely's and Ronan's dragons," Sean said. "After the first two dragon pair deaths, I decided that DOCHAS and ROARKE would fly their counties. At that time, we didn't know we were dealing with a serial killer. Before I could schedule a mating flight, the killer struck again."

Devan held up her hand, incredulous. "You schedule the breeding of dragons?"

Sean nodded. "The female dragon reaches fertile maturity at five years. The mating flight is…very intense." When neither Devan nor Christian spoke, Sean explained. "Intense sexually for the mating dragons' compeers and other nearby humans. Normally, the flight happens on Samhain, the first of November. Gestation lasts three months. The female is not able to fly for long periods in the last month. Once the two eggs are laid, they incubate for six weeks, hatching at the spring equinox. Both male and female share the incubation duties. The female dragon spends most of the time near the eggs to provide a constant temperature of forty-one Celsius, or about one hundred and six degrees Fahrenheit. Any significant drop would leave the eggs nonviable."

Padrick picked up the explanation. "When the dragonets hatch, the rest of the clan assists in the care and feeding of them. At six months, the wing membranes are strong enough for flight. The dragonet can then feed itself from the smaller herd animals, but an older dragon must still keep a watchful eye on the young one. With the rapid growth, the dragonet needs daily oiling of its joints. Otherwise, it loses the ability to fly. So a person is responsible for each dragonet."

"Now I understand the need for scheduling," Devan said. "GRAYSON, was he…?"

Sean rubbed his forehead, above the bridge of his nose. "He was from an unauthorized breeding. TULLIA and CALHOUN were both well past breeding age. That may be why there was only one egg. And the reason he's a drake. Perhaps the egg temperature varied too much. We just don't know for sure."

"After the first two murders?" Christian caressed ROARKE'S snout.

"The normal mating season had passed. I wasn't sure if a mating flight in the dead of winter could impact the eggs, or even if it would be successful," Sean said. "There is so much we don't know, never questioned, never needed to question."

"And now?" Devan asked.

"We'll be experimenting." Sean pointed at DOCHAS and ROARKE. "These two still had not chosen their compeers. The murderer killed the third dragon and rider pair. Then, most recently, Mary and AALYSIA. That's where we stand now."

"So much tied in with Celtic holidays. The dragons, the magic, the murders," Devan said.

Sean nodded. "We better get back to Loughcrew. There are tasks to be started before you head to Dublin."

They mounted their dragons. Sean gave the signal for flight and FIONN leapt into the dark, cloud-filled sky. DECLAN followed, then DOCHAS and ROARKE.

"Padrick desires ROARKE to fly behind and to the Clan Leader's right. DOCHAS, the same but to the left. I shall fly rear guard," DECLAN bespoke Devan.

Devan was beginning to differentiate between each of the dragons. She relayed the instructions to ROARKE and DOCHAS. When the two young dragons flew into position, Padrick nodded and pumped his right fist twice. Black DECLAN dropped back and settled into the final point of their flying diamond.

She mulled over everything she'd learned about the dragons and her telepathic abilities. Not for the first time, Devan wondered how Christian's dreams fit. Was there something special with his pendant? It looked identical to the clan leader's. Maybe his mother had visions and had passed the phenomenon to her son?

The flight between Lough Gur and Loughcrew took twice as long as Loughcrew to Beaghmore. Stone walls crisscrossed fertile fields. Ruins and narrow paved roads mixed in haphazardly.

Tomorrow, Devan would take the first step toward dual citizenship. After Beltaine, she would have to go back to America, at least for a quick visit, see to her parents' house. Perhaps she'd sell it. She shuddered. No, she couldn't lose her only tie to her parents. She'd lease it. The decision felt right and she breathed a sigh of relief.

When they landed, the stooped figure of Timothy waited.

"Come with me, young 'uns." Timothy motioned to her and Christian. "I'm to measure ye for a proper-fitting harness." He turned toward the barn. "I'll no' need the dragons, just the two of ye." Christian and Devan followed.

The measuring consisted of sitting on various-sized horse saddles thrown over a mock-up of a dragon's back. Leg length, stirrup size, and backside width all had to be considered. After half an hour each, Timothy released them. Christian shook his legs as he walked outside, doing what looked like a jig.

Devan giggled.

"What?" Christian frowned. "I've never been on a horse, let alone a dragon before all this. It's bloody uncomfortable. These saddles feel wider than ROARKE's neck."

"Because it sits on the dragon's back, not on the neck. Do you remember riding on FIONN? The saddle was just in front of his wings."

"Right." Christian smoothed the front of his jeans. "I like riding on ROARKE's neck better. Less rubbing in awkward places." He grinned and winked.

Forty Five

As Christian descended the stairs with Devan, Padrick waited in the parlor, teacup in hand.

"Morning," Padrick said. "Sean was required elsewhere. Thought we'd get an early start for Dublin since we'll need to drive."

Christian narrowed his eyes. "You're already shorthanded. We can do this on our own."

"I can quicken Devan's application process." Padrick sipped his tea. "Besides, I have other business in Dublin."

"I don't want you butting into my affairs. My life, the way I've lived before meeting any of you, is none of your concern. You may be my father, but I don't need a Da, understand?"

Padrick's jaw clenched. "I won't interfere in your business dealings, unless those ties endanger the clan. But Erin, and what happened to her, *is* my business. I *will* investigate. With or without you. I'm damn bloody good at ferreting out the facts." He placed his half-empty teacup on the side table with deliberation and spun on his heel. "I'll drive Sean's lorry. You can follow in your own damn car. Devan, you'll need identification, your great-grandparents letter, and death certificates for your mother's parents." He stalked out.

"I'll be right back." Devan rested a hand on Christian's arm. "He just wants to help." She didn't wait for a response, but darted up the stairs.

"Ye must calm yourself," Roarke bespoke. *"Declan's rider can get ye back to me quicker. Remember, there is much to learn and little time before the Chosen Ceremony."*

"This is all new to me," Christian responded. *"I've built a life before all this. There are things I need to handle on my own. I don't expect you to understand. The clan is all you know."*

"I understand we are destined to partner. Together we shall protect Éire and the clan. Including DOCHAS and the Ring Wearer. That is what is important." ROARKE chastised him.

Christian sighed and rubbed his aching forehead.

Devan returned. "Ready?"

"We're going now. I don't know how many days we'll be away," Christian bespoke. *"I shall be with ye."*

Christian embraced the warm, soothing mental touch. He scooped up Devan's backpack and small duffel, then headed outside, and stowed them in the Audi's boot.

They followed Padrick to the outskirts of Dublin. Padrick found a car park one block from the U.S. Consulate General building and pulled in. He approached Devan's side of the car.

Padrick held up a briefcase. "I have the forms you'll need to fill out and copies of Graeme and Siobhan's birth, marriage, and death certificates. Also, Brinna's and Patrick's birth and marriage documents. What do you have?"

She frowned. "Just my passport, birth certificate, driver's license, the letter, and a handwritten family tree. I never expected to need anything else."

"We'll see what else is needed. I'll help with anything I can. Sean knows a solicitor here in Dublin if we need assistance." Padrick looked past her to Christian. "Shall we meet you somewhere? Give you time to handle some personal business?"

Christian wanted time alone to hunt down Logan and settle that business, but he didn't want to leave Devan. She could take care of herself. But he didn't trust Padrick not to plead his case for a father-son reconciliation.

"I'll look after her, don't worry." Padrick handed him a card. "Here's my mobile number. Call in an hour. We should have a better idea of where we're at by then."

"I thought you couldn't use mobile phones?" Devan raised a brow.

Padrick glanced around the car park and lowered his voice. "Only around the dragons and the clan compounds. Once we're a few kilometers away, we can."

"You want me to come with you?" Christian squeezed Devan's hand.

She smiled and returned the pressure. "Divide and conquer. The more we accomplish apart, the quicker we can get back to Loughcrew. You have more to wrap up here than I do. I'd slow you down." She leaned over and kissed him. "Be careful."

"You too. Stay together." Christian directed his next comment to Padrick. "Don't lose sight of her. We don't know where Logan's man is, but it's a fair bet he came back here after we ditched him in Sligo. An hour."

Devan got out of the car and Christian drove away. He watched her from his rearview mirror until he could no longer see her. From the car park, he drove straight to his flat. He needed leverage to deal with Logan. Christian had one ace to play to ensure Logan and whomever he worked for would back off. He'd kept the insurance as a precaution. Now he'd use it, for Devan.

At his flat, Christian checked his tells, found all intact, then entered and double-locked the door. He strode to the bedroom. The book on his nightstand was still hanging a thumbnail length over the edge and the single strand of hair he'd left on the bedspread hadn't been disturbed. He played a complicated tattoo on the checkerboard-patterned bedpost and a door popped open in the oak headboard. He pulled a metal box from the hidden compartment, stuffed most of his cash reserves in his jeans pocket, scooped up the manila envelope, then re-secured his hidden vault. He packed a bag of his personal items. After he and Devan survived Beltaine, he'd arrange to have his bed and remaining items moved to Loughcrew. No, that was wrong, Lough Gur. He sighed.

"Looks like you're going to be stuck with dear old dad after all. Unless you can persuade Sean to relocate you and Devan to Loughcrew," he murmured aloud. "Deal with that later. Let's get through the next ten days."

"All shall transpire as destiny dictates. Keep safe." Roarke's mental voice startled him.

"Easy for you to say, the destiny stuff anyway. I'm going to make sure Devan and I won't be bothered anymore. You…you won't communicate any of what I'm about to do

with anyone, right?"

"Ye are my compeer. I trust ye. Nigh, I shall not communicate with another of your dealings."

"Thanks."

Christian stole a quick glance around his flat, then locked it and reset his outside tells. He left his car in a parking garage near the tourist section of O'Connell Street, within easy access.

He found Logan in the second pub he searched.

"Christian, my lad." Logan waved him to a seat in the booth. "Where've you been? I could've used you for a sweet job. Surveillance."

"The one you put your blond, flat-topped, bloody eejit on?"

Logan's mouth opened, his eyes widened. He stammered. "How? What do you know about Kelly's job?"

"Just that he fecked it up." Christian leaned forward. "Tell me."

"That's my business," Logan said. He drank half his pint in one swallow. He recovered enough to lower his voice, lacing it with a threat. "Where's the woman? You deliver her to me and I'll forget your disrespect. Maybe cut you in on the finder's fee."

"You seem to forget, I don't answer to you anymore." Christian shoved the manila envelope across the dark oak table. "Call Kelly off. That's if you even have control over him. Know where he's hiding?"

Logan looked at him, face impassive. "I always know where my people are."

"Did he check in after he lost her in County Sligo?" He smirked at Logan's narrowed eyes and lowered brows. "Didn't think so."

Logan poked the envelope. "What's this? You want the full take for the bitch?"

Rage surged through Christian. He fisted both hands under the table until his nails dug into his palms. "No, you goddamn fecking shite. That's your orders, your incentive shall we say, to end the job here and now."

Logan froze for a moment, then burst out laughing. "You had me for a second there, boyo."

"I'm not slagging. The job's done. Give me the client's name and contact number. Get control of your henchman." He paused to let his words sink in. "Then you're going to forget you knew me."

"I don't think so," Logan said, then peeked into the envelope. "Bloody shagging hell. What have you done?"

Christian inclined his head. "Nothing yet. That's a copy. Originals—"

"I'll kill you, you fooking bastard."

"I die, that sees daylight now. And you'll never see another sunrise. I promise."

"No one'll ever find your bloody body." Logan hissed the words at Christian. "You come into my place, think you can drop this on me, and just walk away? You're the eejit." He lifted his head, ready to nod to his barman.

Christian leaned across the table, the blade taken from his boot pressed to Logan's gut. "Don't. You'll be dead before he can get from behind the bar." He moved the tip slightly, cutting skin. Logan gasped. "Now, client name."

"No name. Only a number," Logan said. With trembling hands he picked up his mobile and scrolled through several screens. He rattled off a number.

Christian repeated it. "What did he look like?"

"Blond, academic type. Tight with the funds." Logan dropped his mobile to the table. "What's the bitch to you?"

"None of your concern," Christian said. He didn't want to draw Logan's curiosity. This insurance would only go so far. He cocked his head to the envelope. "That stays between us, unless you renege. I better go. Someone's waiting for me." He tucked his blade into his boot, then eased out of the booth. "I don't make idle threats. Forget you ever knew me."

Christian strode out, his heartbeat thundering with each step. He crossed the street and watched the pub door from the shop windows as he continued down the block. When no one emerged before he rounded the corner, he let out his breath.

Pulling an earpiece from his pocket, Christian inserted it in his left ear. He heard a string of inventive cursing from the bug he planted under the lip of the pub table. He glanced at his watch, then called Padrick's mobile phone.

"Where are you?" he asked when Padrick answered.

"About to meet with Sean's solicitor friend. There's some paperwork

Devan needs from America. The solicitor can work with her lawyer there. There's another timing issue. She can fill you in when we're done."

"Okay. I'll check us in at the Gresham. How many nights?" Christian positioned himself to see the pub entrance.

"At least two. Should we meet there?"

"Yes, at the pub." He disconnected and swore as he spotted one of Logan's runners enter the pub.

A high-pitched voice came through the bug. "What's up, boss?"

"Find Kelly. Check his hidey-holes. I want him here." Logan raised his voice. "Yesterday."

Christian heard glass shattering and feet running. He grinned and decided to stay another half hour in case Kelly turned up, then he'd head over to the Gresham. His boyhood chum might know about his flat, but no way he'd look for Christian in the posh hotel.

The runner, a young, filthy street urchin, bolted through the door, scanned the immediate area, then headed away from Christian.

The receiver crackled in his ear. "Kelly, you bloody gobdaw. Where are you? The job's changed. Check in with me ASAP." Christian heard flesh connect with wood, then, "This ain't over, boyo. No one threatens me. Not and lives."

Christian rubbed the back of his neck. "Dammit, Logan. Don't make me bring the wrath of hell down on your head." After an uneventful twenty minutes, Christian zigzagged through Temple Bar, blending in with tourists. He kept Logan's pickpockets in sight, then headed north across the Ha'Penny Bridge, when he was sure no one followed.

In the opulent lobby of the Gresham, he requested a two-room suite and checked in under an alias. No sense tempting fate where Logan was concerned. He slid into a booth in the pub with a view of Upper O'Connell Street to his right. Straight ahead, the mirror behind the bar showed the only entrance.

Devan and Padrick arrived as a uniformed server placed a perfectly foamed Guinness in front of Christian. He signaled for two more, sipped, breathed a sigh of relief to see Devan, and felt the sharp edge of tension relax.

"Trouble?" Christian asked when he saw Devan's furrowed brows.

She shook her head. "A minor detail. I have to go to the American Embassy to extend my stay. I only planned to stay a month, but—"

"That's next week," Christian said. "So…."

"More paperwork. I'll need to show I have enough funds to extend my trip, give an address of where I'll be staying. The dual citizenship substantiates the extension. At least for a while. The lawyer, er…solicitor, will expedite things, but I may need to return to America if the application is delayed."

Christian's chest tightened. "When?" He exhaled the word.

"After Beltaine." Devan reached across the table for his hand and squeezed. "We'll handle it, if and when. I have confidence in Sean's friend. I have an appointment tomorrow, late morning."

"Okay." Christian released her hand when the server appeared with two more pints. "We'd like to see a menu."

"Yes, Sir." The woman left and returned with three leather-bound menus. "I'll give you a few minutes."

Christian scanned the lunch list and wondered at his reaction when he heard Devan might have to leave. *Slow down, Riley,* he berated himself. *You don't have a claim on her. Or she on you.* But he knew different. She owned him, mind, body, and heart.

His eyes watered as he gulped his Guinness.

The server broke into his rising panic. "What can I get for you?"

Devan and Padrick ordered. Christian couldn't speak, so he pointed in the general direction of the lunch special. The server gathered the menus and retreated.

"Are you okay?" Devan asked. "You're pale."

"Fine. Just hungry." He cleared his dry throat and sipped his stout. "I'll go with you tomorrow."

She glanced first at Padrick, then back to him. "What about the orphanage? I thought you two should find out what you can about your mom. I'll be safe at the Embassy."

Fury washed over him. "You think I give a goddamn about what happened twenty-seven years ago?"

Devan flinched.

"Sorry." Christian pressed his fingertips to his eyes, then stole a quick peek at the startled look on Padrick's face. "I need to make sure you're safe—" He shut up as the server delivered their food.

When she left, Christian held his hand out, palm up. He held his breath until Devan placed her hand on top, then he interwove their fingers. Padrick scooped up half his sandwich and crunched down.

"I confronted Logan." Christian held her gaze. "He's lost control over his man. Doesn't know where he is. I can check on all the other stuff later. After Beltaine."

Padrick kept his eyes on his plate, saying nothing.

"We'll discuss this after lunch." Devan pressed her palm to his, half-smiled, then released his hand.

They ate in silence. Christian never tasted his food. After paying, he led them to their suite.

Padrick broke the silence. "I have some clan business to attend to. I'll be back later."

Christian gave Padrick a room key. "Be watchful. I'm not taking chances with Devan's life. Make sure you're not followed."

Padrick nodded, then left. Christian shut and locked the door. He gathered himself, preparing to defend his position with Devan, and turned to face her.

Devan tossed her folder of papers on the coffee table in the center of the suite. When she lifted her head, her lips were pinched together, her eyes darkened to near black.

"I'm a grown woman. I can go to the American Embassy on my own. You can't protect me all the time. Besides, you said you admired my spirit, my guts."

"I do, but this bastard attacked you." Christian took a tentative step toward her. She narrowed her eyes and he stopped. "You've hurt him. I know what type of men Logan hires. I heard the bloody fool's anger when we disappeared at Carrowmore. He's not finished with you. No matter what Logan dictates. It's why he hasn't checked in with him."

"He wouldn't risk the Gardaí would he? There's bound to be security at the Embassy." Devan tugged her hair. "You can drop me at the entrance. Then go to the orphanage. How's that?"

Christian paced to the window and back. "I'll think about it. That's the best I can do."

"All right. I need to work on this paperwork. Where's my backpack?"

"In the car. Stay here. I'll go get our bags. Have a look around." He turned for the door. "Don't open the door. I have a key. I shouldn't be more than thirty minutes." He opened the door, scanned the hallway, and left, securing the door behind him.

Christian strolled out of the hotel toward the Millennium Spire, keeping a wary eye for any of Logan's cronies. He backtracked twice and window-watched. Satisfied he wasn't targeted, he retrieved their baggage and returned to the hotel.

When he entered the suite, Devan strolled out of the bedroom to the right, drying her face and hands.

She studied his face. "You and Padrick need to find out what happened to your mom. Please Christian, work together on this. You both need to understand, get closure."

"I said I'd consider it. Don't push me."

Devan fisted her hands on her hips. "If everything goes according to plan for the Chosen Ceremony, we'll be with the clan for a long time. That includes your father. The sooner this is settled, the better. For both of you. I can't begin to understand what it was like for you not growing up with a mother and father, but I know the anguish of losing my parents. I'd give just about anything to have more time with them. You've been given a gift. Share this time with him, learn about your mother."

"And if she's dead? What then?"

"You deal with it. Together. I'll be here for you as well."

"Perhaps I'm not as strong as you are," he muttered under his breath, then cursed himself at her expression. Feck, she heard him say.

Devan wrapped her arms around his neck and feathered a kiss over his lips. "Oh, Christian. You're stronger than you know. You've survived far worse. You've pulled yourself out from within a criminal organization. You've helped uncover a murder spree."

"Because of you."

"No." She shook her head. "I may have been a catalyst, but you were already on the path. You're not the rough and tumble thug you pretend to be."

Christian raised a brow. "Shall we test that theory?" He didn't wait for her response. He ducked out of her arms and scooped her over his shoulder. She shrieked, then laughed as he strode to their bedroom.

Forty Six

Two hours later, Christian watched as a grim-faced Padrick entered the suite.

"Were you followed?" Christian peeked out the door before closing it and throwing the security bolt.

"No." Padrick heaved himself into a chair. "Just received some disturbing news."

What?" Christian sat next to Devan on the couch opposite.

Padrick dropped his head into his hands. "The daggers used to murder our dragons and riders are special."

"Special how?" Devan's eyes widened as she scooted to the couch's edge.

"Magic infused." Padrick's words drifted to a whisper as he pushed his hands through his hair.

"You mean, residual magic from the murdered dragon?" Devan asked.

Padrick shook his head. He opened his briefcase and placed a heavily wrapped object on the table between them.

Christian unrolled the cloth, exposing a jewel-handled dagger. He whistled softly. "The murder weapon from my dreams."

Devan leaned over to look.

"One of them," Padrick said.

She gasped and jerked away. "I never…of course the murderer would have more than the one."

"He's used four. Out of a set of six. At least that's what my contact tells me."

Christian gripped the handle and lifted the dagger away from the cloth.

He ran his index finger the length of the blade to the tip. He felt it then, something powerful. Dark and powerful.

"Christ Jesus." He dropped the dagger back into the folds of the cloth and set it back on the table. Devan reached for it. He stopped her. "Don't."

"Too right." Padrick slipped the bundle into his case. "It's been woven with a spell—some type of control over the dragons. Sean will need to investigate."

Devan shuddered.

Padrick rose on unsteady feet. "I'm going to check in with him." He grabbed his case, stepped inside his bedroom, and closed the door.

At half-seven room service arrived with supper. The trio ate in silence, lost in their own thoughts.

"You can drop me off in the morning, then do your business at the orphanage," Devan said to Christian.

"I haven't agreed. Besides, he can go on his own." Christian lifted his chin to Padrick.

"They won't give me any information," Padrick said. "I've tried. Their records aren't electronically accessible either. You'll have to go. They're required to provide you with all information that pertains to you."

"Fine." Christian pointed a finger at Devan. "You'll stay at the embassy until we return."

She shrugged. "The place will probably be crawling with Gardaí."

"I don't care. Logan's man wants you dead." Christian narrowed his eyes. "Promise, or I'll be on you like foam on a pint."

Devan chuckled and nodded, then disappeared into the bedroom.

"How serious is the threat?" Padrick asked.

"Let's just say, I'd like her completely surrounded by the bleeding Gardaí and I've run on the wrong side of the law enough to be thrown in gaol myself." Christian rubbed his neck. "I know the type Logan employs and this guy is off his leash. I want her well hidden until I can deal with this eejit. The sooner we're out of the city, the better."

Padrick slapped his thighs, then rose. "You don't have to handle all this yourself."

"I won't bring this kind of trouble to the clan. I'll neutralize Logan and handle his wayward henchman." Christian stood. "Let's get in and out tomorrow so we can concentrate on stopping the killer." He strode into the bedroom.

Devan ignored him as she prepared for bed.

Christian closed the door behind him with a snap. "I don't appreciate being put on the spot like that." He peeled off his shirt and tossed it on the vacant side chair.

"Someone had to notch a chink in the wall between you two." She threw her hands in the air. "For God's sake, you're both hurting—two sides of the same coin. Honestly. Men." She stalked to the bed, flipped the cover to the end, and crawled in.

"Do me a favor. Let me handle my own business."

"Back at you." Devan punched her pillow, rested her head, then shut her eyes.

He stared for several long moments, shook his head, and retreated to the loo. "Stubborn woman."

"Pot, kettle."

What the bloody hell had he gotten himself into? He shut the door and leaned over the sink counter. The woman didn't understand how he felt about his childhood. Could never understand the stab of pain every time he was passed over by a Mum and Da who held hands, but shook their heads at his presence.

The gash of watching other boys and girls skipping in front of smiling new parents as they made their way out of the bleak, gray stone walls of the orphanage. The tears that leaked down his schoolboy face, knowing he wasn't good enough. Was never going to fall asleep to the loving singsong voice of a bedtime story.

"Stop it." He fisted his hands and smacked the marble countertop—once, twice, three times. "That's over and done with. You can't go back. Move forward or die." He finished in the loo and quietly opened the door.

Devan sat up in bed, her arms wrapped around her bent knees. "Sorry. I shouldn't have pushed." She peeked at him. "All the cloak and dagger stuff is getting under my skin. Hopefully not literally." She grimaced.

Christian knelt next to her, unwrapped her arms, and kept her hands in his. "There's a lot going on. I have to rat out someone who used to be a friend. My only friend. I knew it would end this way, but…"

"You hoped otherwise."

He nodded. "I'll do what I must to keep you safe. For the first time in my life, I care about someone other than myself. It's a new experience." He kissed her knuckles. "I'm bound to make mistakes, but I'd rather you be mad at me than dead because of me."

Devan tipped his chin up until he held her steady gaze. "I'm forced to repeat myself. Back at you, boyo." She slipped into a mediocre Irish brogue.

Christian laughed and drew her into his embrace. "Ah, lass. 'Tis a bawdy accent ye have. I find it quite stimulating." Wanting more, he shifted to bring her under him as he pressed his lips to the curve of her neck.

In the morning, they left the hotel separately. First Devan and Padrick, then Christian. He saw no one that stood out. After a quick surveillance down O'Connell Street, he joined Devan and Padrick in the car park.

At the American Embassy, Christian warned Devan to stay inside until he and Padrick returned. He watched her present the guard with her passport and enter before he drove away.

The trip to the orphanage took fifteen minutes, all in stony silence. Christian stopped at the iron gate that kept the dreary, rundown buildings of his youth from encroaching on the solid middle-class citizens. He rang the buzzer and watched Padrick's expression shift from curiosity to anger to something he couldn't quite comprehend. Perhaps remorse.

The crackle of the intercom startled him. "Good day. May I help you?"

"Christian Riley to see Mother Superior."

"Do you have an appointment?"

"No." He took a deep breath. "I used to be…I grew up here. I need information."

"I'm sorry, the previous Mother Superior has left the bounds of earth and is with her holy father. We don't have a replacement, but I'm sure someone can help. Please drive to the administration building to the left." The intercom buzzed once, then fell silent. The iron gates creaked inward.

Christian followed the road as directed. He shuddered and narrowed his eyes when he caught sight of the two-story dormitory. He parked and shot a quick look of warning to Padrick, then exited the car.

A bald, black-robed man stood at the administration entrance. He held out his hand. "Mr. Riley?"

Christian nodded and briefly shook his hand.

"I'm James." He looked at Padrick with milky gray eyes, then back to Christian, bushy black eyebrows raised.

"My father."

"Oh." James mumbled something and led them to an office. "How may I be of assistance?"

Christian explained what they were searching for and gave a brief timeline of his years at the orphanage. He showed his identification.

"I'll check our files." James stood. "Please make yourselves comfortable. This may take some time, as I'll have to check the archives." He exited, plunging the sparse room into cold silence.

Devan sat through the bureaucratic paperwork necessary to extend her stay for another month. She hoped Sean's solicitor friend could work a miracle to get her dual citizenship processed in record time. She thanked the woman behind the desk and asked where she might find a decent cup of coffee. The American staffer smiled and directed Devan to the garden café attached to the right of the embassy building.

She strolled through the low iron gate and sat at a table overlooking Elgin Road. A slender, elven-faced woman with shoulder-length copper hair and pale blue eyes took her order. Devan looked over her paperwork, then stuffed it into her backpack when her server placed an over-large mug of steaming coffee in front of her. She inhaled the aroma and sighed.

"I'm all for 'when in Rome', but I'd just about give my firstborn for this marvelous cup 'o joe." She sipped as the server giggled.

When she was alone, Devan pulled out Christian's phone and called Padrick. "I've wrapped up here. What about you guys?"

"We're waiting for someone to dig up the file from their archives," Padrick said. She heard Christian's voice, then Padrick recounting her words.

"Stay there. We'll be done as soon as we can," Christian said loud enough for her to hear.

"I'm having coffee at the café attached to the embassy. I'm fine here. Take your time." She heard a door squeak open, and another voice.

"Better go. Looks like he found the records." Padrick hung up before she could respond.

She tossed the phone in the front pocket of her backpack and sat back to savor her coffee.

"The records we have are sketchy," James said. He sat behind the desk, opened the battered folder in his hands, and squinted at the frayed and yellowed pages. "There's an account from one of the sisters that speaks of a basket with a newborn boy left at the side gate. Late March of that year." He flipped to the second page. "One potential adoption ten years later. Returned after sixty days. Several others, none lasting more than a fortnight. Middle-of-the-road academic marks. A fair amount of mischief. Punishments." He looked up at Christian and grinned. "Sounds like me at that age. Before I found my calling."

Christian said nothing.

"Anything about the mother?" Padrick's steepled fingers tapped his lips.

James shook his head. He turned over another page and held up a worn, letter-size envelope.

Christian gasped. Padrick and James both looked at him.

"That's the envelope Mother Superior pulled my pendant from. She gave it to me before I went to live with the couple who were to adopt me. They brought me back, but I got to keep my pendant." Christian's cheeks warmed and he lowered his head. After several heartbeats, he heard paper crinkling.

"There's a letter," James said.

Christian jerked up his head.

James skimmed the brittle paper. "From your mother." He handed the letter to Christian. Padrick stood behind Christian and read over his shoulder.

My Dearest Riley,

If you are reading this, then it hasn't been safe for me to come back for you. Happy 18th birthday, my sweet boy. I'm sorry I wasn't there to see you grow to a man. I can only hope you've turned out to be as fine as your da. He has no knowledge of you, and I'm sorry for that. I just didn't see any way to keep both of you safe.

I know this will be confusing for you, but please believe that I love you with all my heart.

Your paternal grandmother never wanted your da and me to fall in love. You see, we are from vastly different beliefs. I am from a Catholic Scots Irish family. Your da's family is very influential. Protestant. We met at University. I'm on scholarship, he's not.

Anyway, your grandmother can get word out to the right people and my family and I would just disappear. She's threatened such a thing if I ever contact your da. I must protect my family and your da, so I ran. I've been followed everywhere.

When I found I was pregnant, I wanted to contact your da, but I couldn't. I was still being watched. I hid amongst the students at Trinity.

I gave birth to you two nights ago. You are so beautiful—just like your beloved da.

Tonight, I saw some of your grandmother's hired muscle searching for me. I don't think she'll ever ease up. My only thought is to give you a chance at a better life, not being on the run with me. I don't know any other way. I'm sorry.

This pendant belonged to your da. He gave it to me the night you were conceived, the night he asked me to marry him.

Please know I love him and you with everything I am. I'll gladly sacrifice my life for yours. I hope someday you can forgive me and that you will find your da. Maybe, when that day comes, the reasons for my running will be over.

All my love,

E.N. This is who I think of myself, though I can't use your da's name.

p.s. I'll keep you in my heart and hope to come back into your life as soon as I can guarantee your safety.

Christian's vision grayed on the edges. He squinted, tried to focus on his mother's words. Black spots drifted in front of his eyes.

"Christ. Breathe, Son."

A hand pushed Christian's head between his knees. Another pulled the letter from his numb fingers. The movement forced a breath into his starved lungs. After several breaths, the tight band around his chest eased and the spots disappeared. He blinked and rubbed his face, surprised and mortified to find his cheeks wet.

"Bloody hell." Padrick's voice rasped. "Sorry, Father."

Christian lifted his head.

"No bother." James waved a hand in the air in dismissal. "I take it you knew none of this?"

Padrick shook his head. "Suspected. This confirms what I've recently learned, but raises more questions." He touched Christian's shoulder. "You okay?"

Christian could only nod.

"You must have left before your eighteenth birthday." Padrick's gaze softened. "Wonder why they didn't name you what Erin wanted?"

"My guess?" Christian pushed the words past the painful knot in his throat. "To keep me safe. In case your mother found out Erin was pregnant. Probably used Christian for the Catholic leanings of the orphanage and Riley as a concession in case she came back for me."

Padrick turned to James. "Anything else?"

"Sorry, no."

Christian flushed when he remembered they were not alone. "I'd like to keep this." He indicated the letter Padrick was carefully folding.

"Of course. It's yours. Should have been given to you before you left." James handed Padrick the envelope.

"I departed in a hurry, well before I turned eighteen." Christian stood on shaky legs. "We better go. Devan's been alone too long."

Christian thanked James and made it to the car before he leaned against the driver's door and gulped fresh, cool air.

"Hey," Padrick said. "Maybe I should drive."

Christian held up his index finger. He needed a moment to collect himself and steady his battered system. He started to speak, but couldn't think what to say. Turning away from Padrick's sad gaze, he tried to steady his shaking hands. At a loss as to how to control his conflicted thoughts, he shook his head and pushed away from the Audi.

Dear Lord. His mother loved him. If he hadn't left early, he'd have known all this ten years ago. What could have happened to keep her away so long? He couldn't play the 'what if' game. No, he was who he was regardless. He'd grown up in these circumstances. The only change would have been if his mother hadn't left him.

Forty Seven

Devan closed her eyes and savored the last sip of her coffee.

"Ma'am." A gruff voice interrupted her.

She opened her eyes to find a hulking man standing before her. The blaze of the morning sun cast a halo around his head and shadowed his features. A black circular, flat hat perched low over his forehead contrasted with the reflective yellow rain slicker emblazoned with 'Gardaí'.

"Come with me." His menacing tone raised the hairs on the back of Devan's neck.

"Is there a problem, Officer?"

A beefy hand clasped her arm and yanked her to her feet. "No problem if you come quietly." A silver blade glinted against her ribs. "Don't do anything stupid."

Devan bobbed her head once. Her tongue cleaved to the roof of her mouth. She swallowed hard several times before she had enough moisture to un-stick her tongue. "I'll j-just pay my b-bill."

"Slowly, or I'll gut you here and now."

She pulled euros from her pocket, scattering coins and loose items over the table. Risking furtive glances around her, she saw the streets were empty. No one to help, she thought. She grabbed her backpack, hoping for a chance to escape. The man crowded her, preventing her from swinging the pack. She peeked at his face as he propelled her away from the café. Once out of the direct sunlight, his face came into focus. The same face as her attacker in County Galway.

Devan breathed in through her nose for an eight count, held her breath for a moment, and breathed out through her pursed lips for another eight count. She repeated this until an idea sparked a glimmer of hope. Would the dragons hear her? she wondered.

"Dochas, Roarke, I'm being attacked. Same guy from Galway. Leaving the embassy grounds. Away from the highway. He's dressed as a Gardaí. Armed."

Devan stumbled on a raised bit of sidewalk and broke off her mental shouting. The tip of her attacker's blade bit into her side, below her ribs. She gasped and muffled a sob at the stinging pain.

Christian drew a deep breath. "Let's get out of here." Padrick nodded and got in the passenger side.

They were stopped at a light in thick traffic when Christian heard several frantic voices.

"Must help the Ring Wearer," Roarke bespoke.

"He has her. The Gardaí. Not a true Garda." A female voice warbled.

"I see her. I shall protect." A deep male voice sounded confident.

Christian jerked, gasped, then leaned on his car horn. "Feck. He's got Devan."

The attacker yanked Devan down an alleyway.

"Ring Wearer, I am above ye. I am too large to enter your space," a deep male voice bespoke her.

"Who?" Devan could only manage the single thought. Her abductor dragged her roughly down the narrow, trash-lined alley.

"Declan, Padrick's compeer. Are ye injured?"

"He cut me a little." Devan fought the urge to look up.

"Padrick and his son are on their way. I must have more room. In a dragon length, the passage opens into a courtyard. I'll take care of him."

She stumbled twice more. The knife jabbed deeper each time. Warm blood oozed down her side. She swayed, lightheaded.

"Clumsy bitch." The abductor gripped her arm tighter as they stepped clear of the alley. "Keep up or I'll—" He shrieked. His fingernails carved deep gouges from her biceps to her wrist as he was pulled away. The knife clattered to the ground. "Fucking bloody hell. Let go. I'll fuck you up."

Devan, breathing heavily lunged for the knife and kicked it away. She turned around, stumbled, and saw black DECLAN crouched on his hind legs. The dragon's front claws pinned the man against the dragon's chest.

The Gardaí hat lay on the ground and the man squirmed and twisted to see what held him. He glanced up, then his eyes darted from side to side. "I know you're there. Show yourself. Who or what are you?" When he couldn't dislodge DECLAN'S claws from his shoulders, he sputtered and spit out profanities between mewling cries.

DECLAN'S whirling sapphire eyes slowed. *I shall hold him for Padrick. Unless ye desire I bite his head off?"*

A screech of tires and slamming of doors drew Devan's attention to the alley entrance. Christian led Padrick at a full run. They skidded to a halt.

"Christ, you're bleeding," Christian said. "What has that bloody fecking eejit done to you?"

Devan looked down and saw deep red blood seep through her shirt and puddle on the pavement. Her head swam. Christian's voice grew distant. Her legs trembled first, then the rest of her body. She melted toward the concrete.

Christian caught and scooped her into his arms. "You'll be all right, *a ghra*. I've got you."

She snuggled into his chest. "He…"

"Hush now. I'll take care of that fecking eejit. After I get you out of here."

"No. Call Finley. DECLAN must…out of sight." Devan's voice faltered.

"Do not fash, Ring Wearer," DECLAN bespoke her. *"Nigh but the clan can see me. To be sure, he can feel my claws, mayhap even catch a glimpse of my talons."* DECLAN gave a mental shrug.

Devan heard threats tinged with confusion from her attacker. She cleared her throat and forced the words out. "Please. More trouble impersonating Gardaí. Keep clan hidden." A hazy blackness clouded her vision, nausea threatened to overwhelm her. She lowered her eyelids.

Christian held Devan tighter. DECLAN pushed the attacker forward and to his knees. Padrick slipped his belt free, looped it around the man's chest, pinned his arms to his sides, and notched the belt tight.

The assailant ranted. "Who the hell are you people? What kind of beast works for you? You're dead. I'll kill all of you."

"Shut your bloody hole," Padrick snarled. He pulled his mobile and waved it at Christian in a silent question.

Christian held up one finger. Once DECLAN leapt clear into the sky above, he strode to the assailant and kicked him to get his attention.

"Kelly, you've been a bad boy. Logan's pissed." Kelly's eyes widened. He struggled to free his arms. Christian continued. "Yes, I know who you are. You fecked up. You're probably safer with the Gardaí than with Logan." Christian stepped away and nodded to Padrick.

Within five minutes a police car and an ambulance blocked the alley entrance. Two Garda approached.

"What have we here?" The female Garda flipped open her notebook. Her male partner scooped up the fallen Gardaí hat.

Padrick stepped forward. "This bag of shite assaulted this woman." He inclined his head to the knife several feet away. "With that. I don't believe he's one of you fine Gardaí."

The conversation halted as two medical personnel wheeled a gurney down the narrow alley.

Christian laid Devan down. "Fecking eejit stabbed her." He spat the words through clenched teeth.

The trussed up attacker groaned. "Keep him and his beast away from me. Something unnatural is happening here." His voice rose in a whine.

Christian took a step toward Kelly.

"I'm Garda O'Neill." The male Gardaí moved to intercept Christian. "My partner, Garda Collins. You need to calm down."

"The hell I will. This arsehole has attempted to snatch her before." Christian reached toward his inside coat pocket.

O'Neill withdrew his solid oak truncheon from his belt. "Stop."

Christian froze. He held up his hands in front of him. "I'm getting Sergeant Finley's card from my wallet. He's from Galway."

"Nice and slow." O'Neill focused on Christian's hands.

"Don't trust him." Kelly swayed from side-to-side. His eyes bulged. "A beast attacked me. With claws the size of that rubbish can over there." He tilted his head toward the gray rectangular receptacles lined up like soldiers on parade.

Both Garda ignored him.

Christian handed Finley's card to O'Neill. "Call him, there's a report on file."

"What about what he's saying?" Collins pointed to Kelly. "What beast?"

Christian shrugged. "I don't know what he's going on about. We saw him shove Devan into the alley. We followed, and Padrick grabbed him. There was no one else around."

"No, no." Kelly wailed. "Something huge clutched my shoulders. I couldn't see, only scaly claws, but I felt something warm and solid against my back. From the middle of this open courtyard."

Collins turned her attention to Kelly, her notebook open and pen ready. "Did you attack this woman?"

Kelly clamped his mouth shut and lowered his head.

"Your names?" O'Neill, his phone to his ear, asked Christian.

"The woman is Devan Fraser. I'm Christian Riley. That's Padrick Nolan." Christian walked back to the gurney.

Garda O'Neill relayed the information through the phone and nodded. "He's dressed as one of us. Yes, Sergeant. Stab wounds. Not sure, hold on." He spoke to the medical team. "Is she going to be all right?"

The medic starting an IV answered. "Three wounds, deep. She's lost a bit of blood. We'll need to take her in. Determine if the blade nicked any organs."

Christian rubbed Devan's cold hand. The color from her cheeks had leeched out, giving her a gray pallor. "Hang in there." He turned to the medic. "Can we get her out of here?"

The medic nodded. "Bloomfield Hospital."

Christian tossed his keys to Padrick. "I'm coming with you." The medic frowned, but relented.

"Mr. Riley." O'Neill approached the gurney.

"You know where I'll be." Christian continued holding Devan's hand as the medics wheeled the gurney to the ambulance.

At the hospital, Christian paced the five-meter square waiting room. The place was making him claustrophobic. A doctor had wheeled Devan to be examined, shutting the door after giving Christian a terse command to wait. The minutes ticked by. He willed someone, anyone, in medical scrubs to come in. A half-hour turned to an hour. When the door opened, Christian pounced.

Padrick stepped back, hands held in front of him. He scanned the otherwise empty room. "No word yet?"

Christian shook his head. "I don't like that it's taking so long."

"Is she in surgery?"

"Don't know." He narrowed his eyes at Padrick. "Is the Gardaí satisfied?"

"Yes. That bloody fool was ranting incoherently when the Gardaí took him away. O'Neill and Collins will be here soon to get Devan's statement. I think Sergeant Finley is coming." Padrick pressed a finger to his lips. "You need to calm down. The tension is rolling off you in waves. You won't help Devan if you get tossed in gaol yourself."

Christian rubbed his neck, then scratched his scalp vigorously. He breathed in and out to a count of ten. His thoughts spun in circles. He needed to deal with Logan. He couldn't leave Devan.

'Declan's compeer is correct. Ye must calm yerself. Declan protected the Ring Wearer before further injury could incur,' Roarke bespoke.

'How do you know? Devan could be seriously hurt. She was so—' Christian's mind screamed.

'Declan has kept me informed.'

'How?' A new thought intruded. Christian turned to Padrick. "I was able to hear not only Roarke, but Dochas and Declan. How is that possible?"

Padrick shrugged. "I don't know. Perhaps your love for Devan and her need for you."

"You didn't hear Dochas or Roarke?"

"No, only my compeer."

"ROARKE says DECLAN is keeping him updated." Christian stared at the closed waiting room door. "How is that possible? I thought there was a distance limit."

"The Ring Wearer is the conduit." ROARKE'S voice held reverence.

"Are you hearing Devan now?" Christian rushed the thought. *"Is she okay?"*

"I feel her pain. And weariness, but she does not bespeak at this time."

Christian glanced at Padrick. "ROARKE says—"

Padrick interrupted. "DECLAN related it. This is good news."

"How?"

The door opened and a bespectacled, gray-haired doctor in sweat-soaked green surgical scrubs entered. "Christian Riley?"

"How is she?" Christian forced his voice to stay calm, though his heart raced.

"Ms. Fraser was lucky. The knife missed all her organs. A nick on one of her ribs. There's some internal bleeding, small. It'll stop on its own. We cleaned the wounds and sutured them. She'll be sore and bruised for a time. We gave her antibiotics to keep the risk of infection to a minimum."

"When can I see her?"

"She's being moved to a room now. I'll have the nurse let you know when Ms. Fraser's settled."

Christian breathed a deep sigh of relief.

"Thank you," Padrick said. The doctor nodded and opened the door. Garda O'Neill and Collins entered.

"How's Ms. Fraser?" O'Neill asked.

Christian clenched his fists. "That bastard's lucky he didn't hurt her more seriously."

Padrick wrapped an arm around Christian's back, resting his hand on Christian's shoulder, and squeezed.

He shrugged off Padrick's gesture. "I should've been with her. This wouldn't have happened."

"Not true." Collins' soft tone caught Christian's attention. "From what Sergeant Finley relayed, this Kelly Dunkirk was hell-bent fixated on Ms. Fraser. Any idea why?"

"No." Christian ground his teeth. "What's the eejit saying?"

"Just more gibberish about some beast with talons like a dragon," O'Neill said.

"We need to get a statement from Ms. Fraser and you." Collins flipped her notebook open. "Let's start with you, Mr. Riley."

"I told you already."

"You just said you should have been with Ms. Fraser. Did you have plans to meet?"

"Yes. She had an appointment at the embassy."

"Which embassy?"

"American. We were to pick her up after concluding some business."

"What business?"

Christian waved his hand dismissively. "Personal. Of no consequence."

"We'll determine the relevance." Collins scribbled in her notebook.

A red-haired nurse entered. "Mr. Riley, Ms. Fraser is asking for you. She's in room 22. Right this way." She narrowed her eyes at the two Gardaí. "You'll need to wait here."

O'Neill sputtered but didn't stop Christian from following the nurse out the door and down the hall.

Devan lay reclined on a stack of pillows. Some color had returned to her face, but Christian noticed the lines of pain around her eyes and mouth. He pulled a chair closer to the bed and sank into it. She held out her hand, palm up. He gripped it tight.

"Thank you for coming for me." Her unsteady voice tormented him. He brushed her knuckles with his lips.

"Christ, Devan. You could've died." He closed his eyes and breathed in the cloying smell of antiseptic.

"Seems I'm a lot of trouble."

"Damn right you are." Christian opened his eyes. Devan's lips curved into a slight smile. He grinned back. "Listen, the Gardaí want a statement." He reiterated his version and told her they knew about the incident in Galway. "I wouldn't be gobsmacked if you get a visit by Sergeant Finley."

"What about Declan?"

"No problem. They believe Kelly was spouting nonsense. Crazy."

She grimaced.

"You're in pain. I'll get the nurse." Christian rushed to the central desk outside her room. "Ms. Fraser's hurting. Can you give her something?"

The nurse joined him in the room. He hovered as the nurse inserted a full syringe into the IV tube. She adjusted the flow rate, then wrote in Devan's chart.

"She'll sleep now," the nurse said. "I'll inform the Gardaí. She'll be here through at least tomorrow. Perhaps you should get some rest yourself."

Christian shook his head. "I don't want her to be alone when she wakes up. Can you have the gentleman who waited with me come in?"

"Is he family?"

"He's my father. Devan and I are…yes, he's family."

The nurse pursed her lips, waited a heartbeat, then nodded and exited.

Several minutes later Padrick entered. Christian pulled him to the window, away from the door and prying ears.

"I need you to stay here. Protect her. I told her what I told the Gardaí, but don't let them talk to her alone."

"Where are you going?"

Christian lowered his voice. "To stop these attacks once and for all. And to put a scare into the killer."

Forty Eight

Padrick sputtered. "What?"

"I know Kelly's boss, Logan. I have something that will put Logan out of business. Permanently." Christian shoved his fists into his pockets. "Logan gave me the killer's phone number. It seems Robert Smyth used Logan's services to keep track of Devan. I'm going to leave a message for him."

"Saying what?"

"The trail ran cold, he'll need to pony up more money. Whatever. I want him angry so he'll make a mistake, be off his game come Beltaine. I'll nose around. Do you have Smyth's address?"

"Sean does," Padrick said. "But we have no solid evidence for a search."

"I don't need evidence." Christian's tone sharpened. Padrick gasped. "Call Sean. I want to get this rolling while Devan's here under the Gardaí's and your protection."

Padrick pulled his mobile from his pocket and punched buttons. He spoke quietly.

Christian sat next to Devan. "I'm going to take care of this. Padrick will be here. I shouldn't be too long." He leaned over and kissed her forehead. She stirred, but remained asleep. "Rest, *a ghra.*"

Padrick handed him a scrap of paper with an address scrawled on it. "Be careful. Stay in touch with Roarke. And call at the first sign of trouble."

"This won't be dangerous, not for me. Stay with her." Christian rested his hand on Padrick's shoulder then strode from the room. He detoured to the side stairs avoiding the waiting room and the two Gardaí.

Christian drove back to the city center and stashed his car at their hotel. He went to the bank and retrieved one of two manila envelopes from his safety box. He addressed it to the Assistant Commissioner, Dublin Metropolitan region. After wiping any fingerprints, he dropped it at the Gardaí headquarters in Phoenix Park.

He returned to the Temple Bar district where Logan hung out to collect the daily take from his team of pickpockets. When he spied the same street urchin from yesterday, he placed the first call.

"Hello. Dublin Metro Gardaí. How may I direct your call?" A woman's shrill tone echoed in his ear.

"Assistant Commissioner, please." Christian exaggerated a west county brogue into an untraceable mobile phone.

"Is A. C. Byrne expecting your call?" The woman sounded bored.

"No' exactly. I 'av a tip for 'is ears only. 'Tis he there?"

He heard a booming male voice in the background. "Get me the Commissioner. Now. I've got a bleeding keg of dynamite." The woman's tone changed as she mumbled an apology into the phone.

Christian smiled. "No problem. He got me message." He hung up, waited ten minutes, then called Logan.

"I warned you to get control of Kelly. The Gardaí have him now. He's singing like the proverbial canary." Christian watched the pub door as four Gardaí converged on Logan's location. He heard his ex-friend swearing through the phone. When the first Garda entered the pub, Christian spoke again. "I don't make idle threats."

Christian kept the line open as boots scrambled over the pub's hardwood floor and several shouts and grunts echoed through the line. He heard Logan's panicked words.

"What the bloody hell are you doing? I pay good scratch not to be rousted like this. I'll have your arses."

"Logan Walsh, I am placing you under arrest on the charges of extortion and money laundering, for starters."

Christian ended the call. He hailed a cab, then placed one more call. "Your hired man, Logan, has been stringing you along. He has the Yank." Christian hung up to the sounds of sputtered indignation.

After riling up Robert Smyth, he gave the driver an address down the block from Smyth's flat, north of the Liffey. Christian strolled to the corner park, buried his knife in the bushes, and watched. He'd learned to never carry a weapon during a break-in; the punishment if caught was quite stiff. Across the street, the primary school's bell shrilled and students flooded down the steps of the brick schoolhouse. Laughter and children's voices rose in excitement as clusters of navy and white uniformed bodies scattered in every direction.

Two boys of about eight entered the key-coded building where Smyth lived. Christian snagged the door before it shut and slid around the corner, out of sight. The two boys never looked back. When he could no longer hear the boys, he made his way to the stairs and climbed to the third floor. Smyth's flat was on the far end.

Christian pulled out his tools. He pressed his ear to the door and knocked. No sound emanated from the flat. He scanned the hall, then set to work picking the locks. On the last click, he slowly twisted the knob and quickly entered, shutting and re-locking the door behind him.

He stood in an open living area with the kitchen to his left. To his right, a couch and coffee table overflowed with books and papers. Beyond the seating area, a sliding door led to the balcony and the fire escape.

Christian scanned the book titles and noted Smyth's interest in Celtic mythology, photography, and witchcraft. He rifled through the papers with notes on dates, places, and what appeared to be incantations. He left the papers exactly as he found them. An end table held a lamp, but nothing else. Where were the daggers? He wandered down the hallway and into a room that was furnished for a baby.

His gaze drifted to a tiny crib with a plain white dress laid inside, to a rocking chair draped in a woman's pearl-buttoned jumper. Below the talc scent of baby powder laid the sharpness of paint.

The hand-painted mural caught his attention. Fanciful Irish landscapes covered the walls. Loughs, stone circles, Celtic crosses, and peat bogs encompassed the room. Saint Declan's Well, Poulnabrone, Ballynahinch Lake, Carrowmore, Newgrange, the Hill of Tara. And in the sky, above the murder sites, dragons. Dragons of every color and size.

"Bloody hell," Christian whispered. He crossed the room to look at what appeared to be burn marks on the walls.

"What are ye doing?" ROARKE bespoke, startling him.

"I'm in the flat of the killer." Christian mentally answered ROARKE.

"Is he there?"

"No. But there's something quite interesting here." Christian reached a hand to the mural above Saint Declan's Well. He squinted his eyes and traced a slash in the chest of a dragon depicted perched above the two openings of the sacred stone well.

"Tell me what is so interesting."

Christian described the mural and the painted dragon with a gash in the wall plaster. He followed the scenes around the room. His eyes narrowed on the stone monument of Poulnabrone and the similar gash accompanied by a burned area about a quarter the size of the dragon. At the depiction of Ballynahinch Lake, the gash and burned area covered more than half the painted dragon emerging from the ice encrusted blue lake.

A burned-out hole showed above the stone dance at Carrowmore. He knew the mural once showed a dragon hovering above the whitethorn tree in the place the hole now occupied.

Christian turned to the images of Newgrange and the Hill of Tara. The grass covered mound of Newgrange stared back at him, intact and without burns. At Tara, multiple burned-out holes surrounded the hill where the Stone of Destiny stood. Leaning in for a closer look, he described the scenes to ROARKE. Christian heard the click of the flat door opening. He swore silently and dashed into the cupboard.

"What is happening?" ROARKE bespoke.

"He's home," Christian whispered in his mind.

"Kill him." ROARKE'S tone sparked and Christian imagined flames spouting from the dragon's snout.

"With what? He's got magical daggers. I don't carry weapons when I'm...scouting." He shuffled farther back, burrowing among clothing. *"Can't talk now."*

Footsteps stomped, growing louder as they neared the nursery. The rhythm blended with Christian's frantic heartbeat. He held his stance, and his breath, ready to pounce if Smyth entered. Maybe he could surprise him, overpower him.

"Goddamn that Logan and the idiots he has working for him. He can't do one simple task, keep watch on the American and her companion while I—" A door slammed, cutting off the rest of Smyth's words.

Christian took a breath and eased out of the cupboard, out of the nursery, and into the hall. Across from him, the loo stood empty, but the last door down the hall was closed. He tiptoed to the door, pressed his ear against it, and heard nothing. He tested the handle and found it locked. Not knowing what trap might lay beyond, he retraced his steps and exited the flat, quickly and quietly.

Christian took the stairs two at a time and slipped out of the building. He sauntered down the now empty street to the park and retrieved his knife from its hiding place, replacing it in his boot. He scanned the street. His gaze shifted to the windows on the third floor of Smyth's building. Nothing moved.

"I'm out. On my way back to hospital. Has Devan communicated to you?"

"Nigh. The Ring Wearer is asleep."

"Good. Don't mention my excursion to anyone. I'll explain to Sean and Padrick later."

"As ye wish." ROARKE sounded petulant.

Christian flagged down a cab and returned to their suite at the Gresham. He packed clothes for Devan, then drove to the hospital. When he entered her room, Padrick started out of his chair, his finger to his lips.

"Has she been asleep the whole time?"

Padrick nodded. "The Gardaí have ducked in several times. O'Neill asked for you."

"If you're okay here, I'll check in with them. Then I have some information for you and Sean. We'll need privacy."

"Not here, too many walls with ears. Can it wait?"

"Yes. I'll be right back." Christian found the two Gardaí pacing the waiting room.

"Where the hell did you disappear?" Garda O'Neill sputtered. "You weren't supposed to leave before we took your statement."

"I gave you my statement at the scene. I have nothing to add."

Sergeant Finley strolled through the open door. He removed his hat and the two Gardaí snapped to attention.

"Sir. Garda O'Neill and Collins," O'Neill said. "This is—"

"We've met." Finley held out his hand. Christian shook it. "Mr. Riley. I understand Ms. Fraser's attacker has been apprehended." He glanced at the two Gardaí, then back to Christian. His tone softened. "How is she?"

"The fecking eejit nabbed her at the embassy, stabbed her several times. Luckily, he didn't hit anything vital. The nurse gave her something for the pain. She's asleep."

"Why don't you go back to her," Finley said. "I'll come get you after I talk with O'Neill and Collins."

"But…he left hospital." O'Neill reached a hand to stop Christian. "Without answering our questions."

Christian turned back to Finley. "I went to the hotel to bring Devan fresh clothes, not ones bloody and cut to shreds."

Finley raised a brow. "I'm surprised you left. Who's with Ms. Fraser now?"

"My father, Padrick Nolan. He was with me when…earlier."

"Mr. Nolan gave his statement." Finley didn't phrase it as a question. His eyes narrowed on the two Gardaí and his lips thinned.

Collins stepped forward and answered anyway. "Yes, Sir." She hastily retreated.

"I'll only be a moment, Mr. Riley. Go be with Ms. Fraser."

Christian nodded, glared at O'Neill, then left. When he returned to Devan's room, she was awake and Padrick was plumping her pillows.

"Sergeant Finley's here." Christian rubbed his chin. "He's having a word with Garda O'Neill and Collins, then he'll be in. Do you remember the statement I gave O'Neill?" Devan nodded. "If you aren't up to talking, we can postpone Finley's visit."

"No," Devan said. "I don't want it to look like I'm hiding anything."

"No one will think that." Christian sat in the chair next to the bed and held her hand. "You've been through hell."

"The sooner I give my statement, the sooner I can put this behind me, and the sooner we can get back to the clan and ROARKE and DOCHAS." She smiled a crooked smile, but he could see she was hiding her pain.

"The nurse says you'll be here overnight. I brought you a change of clothes." He motioned to the bag he left on the table by the loo. We've got a few days. You need to heal up before you can ride Dochas."

A light knock sounded at the door and Sergeant Finley entered. "Ah, I see you're awake. Are you up to telling me what happened?"

Christian squeezed her hand, a subtle reminder.

Padrick cleared his throat and held out his hand. "I'm Padrick Nolan."

"Yes, Mr. Riley said you're his father." Finley shook the offered hand, while Padrick's brows rose. "I'm Sergeant Finley from Galway. I met your son and Ms. Fraser when they had a spot of trouble a week or so ago." His gaze took in Padrick, then shifted to Christian. "There's a strong resemblance."

Padrick glanced at Christian, then stepped toward the door. "Think I'll grab a bite in the commissary. Can I get you something?"

Christian and Sergeant Finley shook their heads.

"Let's get this statement over with and then, Ms. Fraser, I promise to let you recover in peace." Finley pulled out a pocket notebook and a pen. "Can you tell me what happened today?"

Devan spoke in short bursts. She began at the café and finished with collapsing in Christian's arms. She didn't mention Declan.

"As ever, Ms. Fraser," Finley said, "you're retelling is concise. I am truly sorry for the troubles you have had in my country. Now that your attacker is in custody, I hope the rest of your stay is uneventful." He closed his notebook and slid it into his shirt pocket, along with his pen. "Mr. Riley, take good care of her."

"I will. Thanks for handling Garda O'Neill and Collins." Christian rose and shook Finley's hand. "No disrespect intended, but I hope to not need your services again."

Finley chuckled. "None taken. Good evening."

Christian sat back down and breathed a sigh of relief.

"What aren't you telling me?" Devan asked.

He gazed at her pale face and the noisy machines. "Not here. It'll keep until we get back to the hotel. I only want to explain it once." He shuddered. "You need to rest. Close your eyes. I'm not going anywhere."

Devan's eyes widened. "That bad?"

Forty Nine

Robert hissed after the female voice on the answering machine told him to leave a message. "I must see you, Bridget. Call me. I need a stronger spell. Time's running out." He slammed the phone down and sank into the uncluttered corner of his couch.

"I can't rely on having the American woman and her companion for the switching of lives. Damn Logan. Where's he hiding? Maybe he has the pair. I'll kill the conniving bastard." Robert leapt up, paced, then stopped and drove a fist hard into the papers piled on the coffee table. They scattered to the floor.

He yelped and sucked the first two knuckles of his fist. "Damn Bridget. She's holding out on me. Haven't I paid her a fortune? What more does she want, my soul?" He snorted. The sound echoed in the empty space. He stormed to the icebox and opened the lone beer. He gulped half, then rolled the bottle over his abraded knuckles.

"Think, dammit. You don't have much time." Robert turned and faced the mess of his notes and research books. He tilted the bottle to his lips and polished off the strong ale, then tossed the empty container in the sink. The glass shattered. He didn't care anymore. Not without his Anne and RJ.

The ring of the phone broke his despair.

"Hello," Robert snarled.

"It's me." Bridget's voice rasped through the receiver. "You can't leave that type of message. My family would disown me for helping you. I told you last time, anything stronger would be too dangerous. It could kill you."

"Already dead without Anne," he mumbled.

"What? Did you say something?"

"No. What you've done won't be strong enough. I've tested the daggers. Their spells are barely more than the previous ones. I must have stronger spells. I'll do anything. Just tell me what you need. I'll get it."

"You don't understand. These types of spells take a piece of you. What I've done already...I can't help you further."

"Wait. Please," Robert begged. "What about a sacrifice, a blood sacrifice." The gypsy gasped. He rushed on before she hung up. "I've been reading that spells can be increased when cast with a blood ritual."

"I...I don't know."

Robert shoved papers aside, looking for his notes on the obscure paragraph. He found the crumpled scrap. "Listen to this. 'Protection incantations may be enhanced, strengthened with the combination of a blood ritual performed in a properly cast circle and the anointing of an artifact'."

"But these haven't been protection spells."

"So what. It should still work. The daggers are the artifacts. This will be my last chance. My only chance to protect my family." Silence lengthened between them until he thought he'd lose her help. "Please try."

"I'll need to do some research. Give me a couple days."

"No more or it'll be too late," Robert said, then whispered, "Thanks." He dropped the receiver in the cradle and fell to his knees, surrounded by books and notes.

"Anne, my sweet Anne. It won't be long now. You'll be with me. You and our son. I promise." Tears streamed down his cheeks. He wiped them away, furious at his weakness.

Robert rose and straightened his scattered notes. He needed to keep it together for just a little longer, then he'd have Anne and RJ back. Everything would be okay. He'd be a better husband, an attentive father. A few more days. He could manage.

Organization, he thought. I must be ready when Bridget calls again.

He'd research the blood rituals. He glanced in the direction of his books, yet saw only gray nothingness. The clock in the hall chimed the half-hour. The room grew dark.

He knew he should eat, keep up his strength. No, there was no time to waste on such trivial matters. He'd eat his fill when he had his family back. He stood, rooted between the kitchen nook and the living room.

At the sixth chime, Robert absently switched on the side table lamp. He stared glassy-eyed at the books and papers stacked on the coffee table, wondering what he should be doing. His mind flitted, thoughts appeared then shredded like a fine mist over a lough.

Anne's face swam before his closed eyes. Yes, he'd concentrate on his love for his wife. He must find the answers to bring her back to him.

The daggers are the key, he thought. Anne's love is the strongest magic of all. Her wedding gift must be enough to capture the dragon magic.

He shuffled to his bedroom, throwing switches to light his way. Anne's vanity table held her hairbrush, her pots of lotions and makeup, her perfume. He spritzed the air with her scent and saw an apparition of his beautiful wife sitting at the upholstered bench in her midnight blue nightdress. She brushed her long, golden tresses. Her innocent smile crinkled the corners of her eyes.

The longer he watched, the more substantial her form. Then she spoke the last words she'd said to him in this room. "My love, I have all the time in the world to watch you at your work. I'd feel better here in Dublin, with the doctor close at hand." She stroked her delicate fingertips over the swell of her belly. "You'll only be gone a week. Besides, I'll distract you from your work."

"No," Robert wailed. She began to fade. His vision shattered. "We didn't have enough time together."

He wiped his moist eyes and stared at the photographs of his wife covering the vanity mirror. The largest photo was his favorite. Anne's green eyes twinkled and her grin hinted at a favorite joke shared only moments before. She sat on a blanket in the middle of a meadow filled with spring blooms. Her cobalt sundress competed with the deep blue of the vast sky.

His heart lurched at the memory of the day he took the photograph. May first, Anne's birthday, and the day he asked her to marry him. His life was perfect then. He dropped his gaze to the oak and blackthorn display box he'd left on the bench seat. His fingers trembled as he opened the lid.

Two daggers remained nestled in the velvet-lined case. He lifted both of them and felt the awkward balance from the gemstones. They weren't typical throwing knives, but the small, colorful stones held the dark magic Bridget infused in each blade. He had learned to control the direction and blade rotation to achieve his desired goal.

Robert crossed the two blades, spoke of his love and promise to Anne, then kissed each dagger before replacing them in their slots.

It was destiny. He'd get his family back on Anne's birthday, the anniversary of his proposal, Beltaine. May first would be his last chance to return his family to his side. Two daggers, two lives exchanged for his Anne and RJ, all on one fast-approaching day.

Fifty

Christian watched over Devan as she slept. When Padrick returned with a sandwich and coffee, he accepted them with alacrity, then sent Padrick to the hotel to rest. There was no sense in both of them guarding Devan and not sleeping.

The nurse came in every two hours. She checked on Devan and tutted over Christian's refusal to leave. At half-seven, Devan stirred. Christian blinked his grit-filled eyes, sat up in his chair, and squeezed her hand. She rolled toward him and moaned.

"Easy now. You're in hospital." Christian boosted Devan farther up on the pillow. "You were stabbed. Do you remember?"

"I do now." Her eyes dropped to the chair, then rose to his face. "Did you sleep here? Where's Padrick?"

Christian sighed and rubbed a hand over his chin, scratching his stubble. "Yes. I sent Padrick to the hotel."

"You should have gone, too. I don't think I woke up all night."

"Nope. Once the medicine kicked in, you were out. How are you feeling?"

"Sore." Her stomach rumbled. "Hungry. Do you think I can have some water? My mouth is so dry."

Christian poured water into a plastic cup, dipped in a straw, and held it for her. She sipped several times then nodded that she was done, licking her lips.

"Will you tell me what you found yesterday?" she asked.

"You were correct about the orphanage." He rested the cup on the side table and sat again. "There was an envelope in my file. It contained a letter from my mother. She…she hoped to come back." His throat closed.

"Oh, Christian." Devan clasped his hand.

"She named me Riley. She loved Padrick, and me." Tears swam in Devan's eyes. "Don't cry, not for me. She did what she did to protect us both. We don't know a lot more, but we'll put your research skills and our efforts into finding out what happened. After Beltaine."

"What about—"

The door opened. Padrick and a nurse carrying a tray entered.

"Your breakfast, Ms. Fraser." The nurse frowned at Christian. "The night nurse said you wouldn't leave. You'll need to step out while I examine the patient's wounds and change her dressings. I won't be long." She glared at the two men until they departed.

"How is she?" Padrick handed Christian a steaming cup.

He sipped strong tea before answering. "Sore and full of questions."

"What have you told her?"

"A bit about the letter. We were interrupted."

Padrick arched a brow. "Have you seen her doctor?" Christian shook his head.

When the lift down the hall pinged, they turned. Several medical staff emerged carrying clipboards and headed their way.

Christian stepped forward. "Are you here for Devan Fraser?"

The carrot-topped young woman in a white doctor's coat eyed the two men. "You are?"

"Devan's family." He continued to sip his tea. "I'm Christian and this is Padrick. Sergeant Finley vouched for us yesterday. How is she? When can she get out of here?"

The doctor checked her clipboard. "Yes, the sergeant authorized the two of you. I'm Doctor Maguire. I'm going to examine Ms. Fraser, then I'll assess her condition. Excuse me."

Christian handed Padrick his tea and followed the doctor into the room.

"I need to examine my patient in private." Her tone matched the fiery temperament hinted at by her hair color.

Christian stood inside the door with his arms crossed. "She's been attacked. Twice. I'm not leaving her alone with anyone I don't know. Sorry, nothing personal. I'm sure Finley noted my excessive stubbornness."

"But her injuries—"

"I've seen her naked."

Devan blushed. "It's fine. I prefer him here." She winced and blew out a sharp breath.

The exam lasted less than ten minutes. The doctor wrote a prescription for a five-day course of antibiotics and cautioned Devan on excessive activities until the wounds healed. She said Devan could be released that afternoon if she had no problems keeping food down.

Christian walked Dr. Maguire out as Devan started eating. "Thanks." He shook the doctor's hand. "I'm sorry for the attitude, but she's important."

"I understand. Make sure Ms. Fraser doesn't overdo. She'll need to have the stitches removed in ten days." Christian nodded and the doctor left.

Padrick held out Christian's tea. When Christian shook his head, Padrick tossed the cup into a nearby rubbish bin. "When's she being released?"

"In a few hours, if she has no trouble."

Padrick's face drained of color. "Trouble?"

"Keeping her breakfast down. Abrupt actions could start internal bleeding, pop stitches." He gripped Padrick's shoulder. "Come on. She asked after you." Padrick flushed pink.

Devan placed her empty cup on the tray. Only the scrambled eggs remained untouched.

"Do you mind?" Christian grabbed her fork. "I'm starved." She waved at the plate. He ate the eggs in three heaping bites.

"You should get a proper breakfast. The doctor said they'd check on me in an hour or two."

Christian started to object, but Padrick stepped forward. "I'll sit with her. There's a decent cafeteria downstairs."

"No sudden movements," Christian said. "Don't even get out of this bed. Promise me."

"Yes, Sir." Devan saluted. "Boy, you sure are bossy when you don't get enough sleep."

Christian gripped her chin and kissed her hard and fast. "You could have died." His gaze held hers. "Troublemaker," he whispered. This time his lips captured hers in a slow, soft, soulful kiss. He stepped away and nodded to Padrick.

Devan waited for Padrick to get comfortable in the chair. "Christian told me Erin left a letter. How are you?"

"Angry, sad, shocked." Padrick raised pain-filled eyes as he reached for her hand. "Confused, relieved. So many feelings. Anger and hurt top the list. The letter confirms what we know from Mother's diary. Erin wrote of her love for me, for Christian." He closed his eyes and took a deep, shuddering breath. "She named him Riley."

"He told me." Devan laced her fingers through Padrick's.

"He wouldn't know, but Riley was my great-grandfather. It's his pendant I gave Erin. She remembered." Tears leaked down Padrick's cheeks. His voice roughened. "Oh, God. Did Erin sacrifice her life for me, for our son?" He lowered his head and wept.

Soft voices fell silent as Christian opened the hospital room door. He clutched a small bouquet of posies from the gift store, as if he were a schoolboy with his first crush.

Devan's eyes widened and a grin split her face. He ducked his chin. Her "thank you" nearly made him blush the same crimson as the crinkly paper around the flowers.

Padrick cleared his throat. "I'm going to check on something." He shuffled out the door.

"Is everything okay?" Christian glanced at the shut door.

"He's hurting. He loved your mom very much, still does." Devan buried her nose in the colorful blooms, then lifted her head. "He blames himself for not trusting in their love. For not going after her. For all the years lost, with Erin and you."

Christian rubbed his neck and walked to the window. He kept his back to her. "I don't understand how he could have let her go. If he really loved her, he should have done whatever it took to be with her." His voice lowered. "I would have."

"You should talk with him. Remember, he was not yet twenty, just a boy really. He was still influenced by his mother and by society's views."

"He may have been young, but he was a man grown."

"You can't compare your dad to yourself at that age." Devan's voice caused him to face her. "You grew up quick, he didn't. His mother and the clan isolated him. You can't blame him for something out of his control."

"My head understands all that, but…"

Devan held her hand out to him. He gripped it hard, sank into the chair, then twined his fingers with hers. "You'll figure it out. As I said before, you've been given a gift. Not what you ever expected, but you have a family now."

Christian lifted their joined hands and brushed a kiss over the top of her hand. "You, too."

The door opened and the nurse entered. "Any problems, Ms. Fraser?" She glanced at the machines and made notations on her clipboard.

"No. Does that mean I can be discharged?"

"When Doctor Maguire signs the release paperwork. I'm afraid you'll need fresh clothes, we had to toss yours."

Christian nodded to the bag by the loo. "I brought some last night."

The nurse disconnected the heart rate monitor and Devan's IV. "Very well. I'll let you get dressed. Take it slow, no sudden movements." She pursed her lips. "I'll hunt down the doctor."

"Thank you," Devan and Christian said together.

"I can fly the Ring Wearer home. Or have DOCHAS *come for her,"* DECLAN bespoke Christian.

"DECLAN wants to fly you back to Loughcrew, or have DOCHAS come get you," Christian said. "I told him the jostling of the flight might open your wounds."

"I heard, at least DECLAN'S side of the conversation."

The drive back to their hotel was uneventful, but Christian remained vigilant nonetheless.

Once inside their hotel room, Devan asked, "Aren't we leaving for Loughcrew? I thought you had important information for Sean?"

"I need to check on one thing first," Christian said. "You should rest. We'll leave in the morning. My information can wait." He raised an eyebrow at Padrick.

"Tomorrow will be soon enough," Padrick said.

Christian helped Devan to the couch. "I'll be back in an hour. Are you hungry?" She shook her head. "Then we'll order room service when I get back. Just rest." He kissed her forehead, then closed the door behind him.

He made his way to Grafton Street. When Christian didn't see any of Logan's crew working the tourists, he checked Logan's known hangouts. He slipped into the pub in the Temple Bar district and ordered a pint. The barman started building his Guinness.

"Logan around?" Christian asked.

The beefy hand on the tap stilled for a brief moment. "Haven't seen him."

A thin, reedy voice at the end of the scarred oak bar mumbled. "Heard the Gardaí scooped him up yesterday." The dark-haired man stayed bent over his half empty shot glass. "Bloody good riddance, I say."

"Shut the hell up." The barman growled. He finished building the Guinness, then placed the foamy pint in front of Christian. "I remember you. You an associate of Logan's?"

Christian curled his lip. "An acquaintance. Has anyone else been asking for him?"

The barman glanced toward the end of the bar, pressed his lips together and remained silent.

Christian sipped his stout. "Perhaps a blond, scholarly-looking fellow? The guy's a snitch. He gave up Logan to the Gardaí."

The barman's eyes narrowed, but he didn't confirm or deny. Christian shrugged, finished his pint, laid euros on the bar top, and sauntered toward the door. He watched the reflection in the window as the barman reached for the phone by the register.

Christian hid a smile as he left. If Robert Smyth returned looking for Logan, he'd be in for a rude greeting. Logan and Kelly were guests of the Gardaí.

Christian vaguely wondered who would fill the gap in Logan's absence, then shook his head as he walked away from Logan's world. He kept a steady lookout for anyone tailing him, but saw no one. He entered the Gresham behind two Gardaí and loitered to make sure they weren't there for him.

On the drive the next day from Dublin to Loughcrew, Christian exited the main roadway twice and doubled back to ensure they weren't followed. They met Padrick at a predetermined location and followed him on the narrow, single-track dirt road to the clan compound.

As they neared, Christian heard ROARKE'S excited mental shout. *"Finally, ye have returned."*

For the first time in two days, Christian remembered he heard other dragons in his head during the attack on Devan and while at the hospital.

Bloody hell, he thought. Was that what Devan had to deal with all the time?

"When you were attacked, I heard DOCHAS and DECLAN, not just ROARKE." He glanced at her pale profile. "How do you keep sane?"

Devan chuckled, then gasped and tightened her arms around her stomach. "I don't hear every thought of every dragon. At least not now. Before the incident with GRAYSON, I heard murmurings. Since meeting DOCHAS, I only hear the other dragons when they are communicating with me directly."

"Makes sense. How come I could hear DOCHAS and DECLAN?"

"That's a question for Sean."

Christian parked by the barn, in the same spot that Braeden's dragon had deposited his Audi a little over a week ago. Had only such a short time passed? It felt like he had known Devan for months. He helped her out as Sean approached, concern etched on his face.

"Padrick told me what happened." Sean's gaze traveled over Devan. "Should you be out of hospital so soon?"

Devan showed him a weary smile. "The doctor cleared me. I won't be climbing Croagh Patrick, but I'm not dying. Besides, we don't have much time before Beltaine."

"We need to rethink using her as bait," Christian said. "I lit a fuse under the killer and I found out some information that will make our stopping him harder."

"Let's go inside." Sean waved to his new front door. Padrick joined them. Once everyone settled in the parlor, Sean turned his attention to Padrick and the cloth-wrapped dagger he laid on the coffee table. "What did you learn about the daggers?"

Padrick relayed his information about the magic spell placed on the dagger and confirmed his contact's belief the set contained six daggers total. "The spell was designed to penetrate dragon scales, then absorb and harness any encountered magic."

"That corresponds with what I found." Christian rose and paced to the picture window overlooking the courtyard. A chill swept over him and he shivered. His neck hair stood on end.

Ye did correct. The only better action would have been if ye had killed the Clan Slayer," ROARKE bespoke Christian.

"I may have put Devan and the clan in more danger. I don't know if I could kill someone. That would make me just like the murderer."

"Nigh!" ROARKE roared. *"Ye are protecting lives. Not just dragons and riders, but many other humans. Everyone we strive to provide a better life for. We swear an oath to protect and defend the inhabitants of Éire. If more pairings die, all suffer."*

"Stop the killer, yes. Murder him, no." Christian shoved his hands into his pockets.

He turned to Sean. "Devan's attacker worked for an old friend of mine from the orphanage. Logan operates on the shady side—running scams, pickpockets, extortion, anything for the right price. Robert Smyth hired Logan to track down Devan and keep a close watch over her."

"Why?" Sean asked.

"Logan didn't ask, didn't care. Robert provided a photo of Devan in the library at Trinity College, and plenty of money."

Devan gasped. "The killer was there?"

Christian nodded. "Apparently. Logan described him to me. Blond, early thirties, bookish."

"I remember." Devan tapped a finger to her lips. "He was talking with the guide before I asked about the Gaelic on my ring."

"That's all fascinating, but what did you find as to the daggers?" Sean leaned forward, resting his elbows on his knees.

"Logan didn't know Smyth's name, just a phone number." Christian sat next to Devan. "Yesterday, I called him. I told him Logan was holding out on him, keeping the woman from him. I wanted to rile him. He was furious. When Smyth went looking for Logan, I stole into his flat."

"You broke in?" Sean frowned. "You could have been caught. My Gardaí friend is keeping a light surveillance."

"I wasn't spotted. I'm better than that." He glared at Sean, then shrugged. "The killer is into witchcraft. He had books and papers filled with dates, places, spells. That's not the clincher, though." He took a steadying breath, then described the mural in the nursery. He left nothing out.

Sean and Padrick muttered curses.

"Before I could search for the daggers, Smyth returned." Christian ducked his head. "He locked himself in the master bedroom. I never looked in there." He cleared his throat. "Sorry. The mural drew my attention."

Sean waved his hand in dismissal of Christian's apology. "Can you give me more details about the burn marks?"

"The burns escalated in size and depth. There wasn't a burn mark at Saint Declan's Well, only the knife gash. At the second murder site, the burned area accompanied the gash. By the fourth site, a burned-out hole was in the wall. The two holes at the Hill of Tara were not much larger than at Carrowmore." Christian shook his head. "I don't know about unnatural, but the scene felt…incomplete. Like he's still experimenting."

Devan closed her eyes and blew out a shuddering breath. "If the daggers can penetrate dragon scales, what are we going to do?"

"I don't want you used as bait. I'd prefer you weren't even there."

"I'm partnering with DOCHAS." She dragged a hand through her hair and glared at him. "I'll be there, same as you."

Padrick broke the stare down. "He has two daggers left. I know who his second target is."

"Who?" Sean asked.

"Christian and ROARKE." Padrick held Christian's gaze.

Christian remained impassive, cursing silently.

When Christian didn't respond, Padrick continued. "It makes sense. Two young dragons that haven't yet formed the tight bond with their human compeers. The magic is strong but unpredictable with young dragons. Devan and Christian both exude dragon magic, even before the Chosen Ceremony."

"If the killer somehow felt the magic that day at Trinity, then he must have felt it from you too." Devan's eyes widened. "You knew." Christian shifted his gaze away from her. "Damn you. I'll take every precaution, but you're in just as much danger as I am."

"I'm not recovering from multiple stab wounds."

Devan narrowed her eyes. "You could be."

Fifty One

Devan went to the side table and poured herself a glass of water. "If the daggers can penetrate dragon scales, what chance do we have of stopping them?"

"In the previous murders, each dragon and rider were alone," Sean said. "This time the entire clan will be there."

She sat back down. "That could be more dangerous. The killer has more people and dragons to target."

Padrick shook his head. "Smyth will need the strength of the younger dragons. That still leaves the two of you as the most likely targets. He's already felt your power. He'll hone in on the familiar."

"For the Chosen Ceremony, we'll be in a circle around the Stone of Destiny. The two of you, with your dragons, will be in the center," Sean said. "I've asked my Gardaí friend for a couple of Kevlar vests."

"I still don't like putting Devan in harm's way." Christian paced to the window. "Why must the ceremony take place at dusk? It'll be harder to keep a lookout, especially with the bonfire."

"The magic is strongest then." Sean poured himself a drink, waving the Jameson bottle. Padrick and Christian shook their heads.

"My point exactly," Christian said. "If the spell on the dagger draws the magic to the killer, why give him the chance to harness all that power? Won't we still have partnered with the dragons if we do this earlier? We'll be more protected and we can stage a faux partnering to capture the killer."

Sean sipped his whiskey. "I'll look into the clan records, but the ceremony always took place at dusk. We won't have the same vulnerability issues because the dragons will not waste time materializing. I have to believe our numbers will prevail."

"Sean and I will work out the placement of dragons and clan members and estimate where Robert Smyth might approach," Padrick said. "In your dream, can you identify what's behind the killer?"

Christian shook his head.

"No matter." Sean waved a hand. "We'll assume he'll approach from the car park next to the church."

For two days, Sean tested Devan's telepathic skills. He checked for distance as well as communicating with the dragons she had yet to meet. Her range seemed to be the entire Emerald Isle, once she could form a mental image of each particular dragon.

Devan longed to fly DOCHAS like Christian flew ROARKE, but Sean was overprotective. On the second day, he stretched her patience to breaking.

"Sean, I need to practice flying. I promise to be careful. My wounds are healing." She rubbed the bandages below her ribs to ease the itching.

"I wanted you one hundred percent, but I know we don't have the time. Okay." Sean acquiesced. "At the first hint of pain, promise you'll stop. The Chosen Ceremony is simple, not overly physical. Go ride with DOCHAS."

She grinned.

Padrick assisted her with harnessing DOCHAS. The silver-blue dragon shifted from hind leg to hind leg.

"What's the matter?" Devan bespoke DOCHAS.

"The harness chafes."

"Where?"

DOCHAS lowered her snout, flicking her two-pronged tongue above her right foreclaw. *"There."*

Devan ducked under DOCHAS's raised foreclaw. *"I'll loosen the strap and pull the harness farther down your body."* She turned to Padrick. "I think DOCHAS has grown since she was measured. Only one more adjustment remains on this harness."

"We found the same with ROARKE yesterday. Timothy is making new ones for Beltaine." Padrick helped her tug the harness lower and cinched the last buckle. "That'll do for today. Up you go." He schooled her on the best way to mount.

"Where are Christian and ROARKE? And DECLAN, for that matter?" Devan huddled in her raincoat.

Padrick leapt behind her. "Practicing flyovers at the Grange Stone Circle near Lough Gur. We're on our way there now." He gave her the command for taking off, then saluted Sean, who had emerged from his office.

DOCHAS beat her wings twice, then leapt into the thickening rain.

"Through rain and sleet and snow and ice," she muttered, wiping a gloved hand over her stinging brow.

"What?" Padrick leaned forward and spoke in her ear.

"Nothing." Devan turned her head so he could hear. "Guess you fly in all kinds of weather."

Padrick chuckled. "You get to where you hardly notice."

Lightning split the sky to their left. Thunder rumbled like an approaching train.

"Have DOCHAS land in that pasture to the southwest, away from the buildings," Padrick shouted as he pointed.

Devan instructed the dragon. DOCHAS circled low over the rocky field, hovered over a small clearing, then twisted her wings, dumping the air beneath and landed. The dragon hunched down pressing her belly to the ground. Padrick and Devan slid off. DOCHAS extended one wing and they huddled underneath the silvery membrane.

"Sorry about that," Padrick said. "The forecast didn't mention thunderstorms until tonight. It's the only weather we avoid, if possible. Harness buckles are great conductors."

"Another reason to fly without it." Devan shivered, then smiled at Padrick's puzzled expression. "Christian was sore last night."

"I guess he's had no reason to ride a horse in Dublin town. What about you, have you sat a saddle in America?"

"Once or twice. I'll work as hard as Christian, but he's obsessed with protecting me. I'm sure he's pushing himself. Besides, Sean made me promise not to overdo."

"You know Christian very well. I warned him to ease into the flying.

But the truth is the clan needs the two of you and your compeers now. Six months ago." A shadow darkened Padrick's blue eyes. He blinked twice and it was gone. "We can't change fate…or bring back the dead." He half smiled. "So we press forward."

"The jagged light has stopped. We can continue," DOCHAS bespoke Devan.

"The storm—" Devan began as DOCHAS lifted her wing.

"Yes, we should continue our flight. Come." Padrick led her to the stirrup and boosted her into the harness, then climbed aboard and settled behind her.

DOCHAS launched into the air. The rain slowed to a mist as they approached County Limerick.

Padrick leaned forward. "DECLAN informs me ROARKE and Christian are practicing dismounting drills near the small stone dance, next to the Grange Stone Circle. They are awaiting us."

Devan nodded, then bespoke her dragon. *"You know where to go, love?"*

"Aye. I have black DECLAN in view. I shall land within the circle. Show how agile I am." DOCHAS sounded smug.

"Just be careful. I'm still recovering and the clan doesn't need you or Padrick hurt."

DOCHAS snorted. *"I had nigh problem earlier."*

Devan rolled her eyes, but didn't comment further. A black smudge in the cloudy sky grew larger and more distinct as they approached. She recognized DECLAN hovering above the rolling green landscape past a gray, storm-colored lake. DOCHAS flew within five feet of DECLAN and hovered.

Christian jumped from his perch on ROARKE, landed briefly on his feet, then rolled twice and came up in a crouch in front of his dragon's chest.

Devan gasped when she saw the knife in Christian's hand. "What the hell are you doing?" She shouted from her perch.

"Practicing defense." Christian looked up as the silver-blue dragon landed in the stone circle. DOCHAS folded her wings and crouched. As Devan and Padrick dismounted, Christian sheathed his knife in his right boot.

Devan walked through a gap in the stones and stopped in front of him. "Is that part of the prescribed training?"

Christian shrugged. "I'll be ready for anything." He caressed her face, from her cheek to her chin. Then brushed a light kiss over her lips. "How was your flight?"

"Wet and illuminating."

"Care to explain?"

She ran a hand through her hair, shedding raindrops. "We had to land quickly, flew too close to a lightning storm."

His eyes widened. "You didn't get hit, did you?" He ran his hands from her shoulders to her hands. His gaze followed.

She shook her head. "Just wet. I need better rain gear."

Padrick cleared his throat. "Let's get you caught up." He explained the intricate flight pattern that allowed all the ley lines to be crossed to focus the magic. "Mount up, both of you. Watch Christian and ROARKE. Then it'll be your turn."

They mounted, Padrick once more ensconced behind her. Christian and ROARKE flew the complicated sequence, weaving above the upright stones to form an invisible knot pattern. When they finished, they hovered next to DOCHAS. Christian gave her a cocky grin as ROARKE blew out a puff of white smoke. Padrick nudged her and she beckoned DOCHAS forward.

Forty-five minutes later and after missing the same intricate loop three times, Devan needed a break. DOCHAS landed near the small stone circle. ROARKE glided to rest nearby as Padrick slid off the dragon.

Christian sauntered over. "Relax. You're doing great."

"How many tries before you got it right?" She narrowed her eyes at him.

"I didn't keep track."

Padrick snorted. "He had it in his second attempt."

Devan sighed at Christian's wicked laugh.

"This is the most complicated pattern you'll learn," Padrick said. "They are similar for all the stone dances, but the number of standing stones dictates the complication of the knot pattern. The Grange Stone Circle is the largest in the Republic."

"Do the dragons know the pattern?"

"Aye, but the magic is strongest when you work together, with your mind and the dragon's physical flight." Padrick pushed away from the rock he leaned on. "Come, let's go again."

Devan shrugged off her raincoat. "I'll try alone. Can you and DECLAN just watch from above?" Padrick nodded, then mounted his compeer. DE-

CLAN launched into the air. She strolled to Christian and handed him her coat. "Keep your thoughts to yourself. Both of you."

Christian raised a brow, then burst out laughing. "Guilty."

DOCHAS took off and hovered over the northernmost stone, the tallest one.

"Okay, love. Disregard ROARKE. Let's do this." Devan wove the knot in her mind and sent the pattern to her dragon, one pass at a time.

When they completed the flyover, a surge of elation flowed through Devan, and something more—magic. She shouted and pumped her fist high above her head. Then grimaced at the pull of her stitches.

The next day, Sean presented Devan and Christian with protective vests. She complained the vest restricted her movements, but Christian was insistent.

"You wear this vest or I'll tell Sean to ban you from the ceremony. I'll put you on a plane back to America."

"You wouldn't dare." Devan huffed. "We're in this together."

"I'm not taking any chances with your life."

Sean peeked his head into the parlor. "Ready for a dry run?"

Padrick and Aisling were already on their dragons in the outer courtyard. Sean nodded and they mounted. At the clan leader's signal, all five dragons leapt into the cloud-filled morning sky.

Devan's nervousness increased as they swept the rolling green pasture southwest of a stone church and graveyard, away from the road. Sheep scattered, bleating their cries in the slowing rain. Their black faces, a sharp contrast to their white bodies, lifted toward the dragons. Colorful paint splotched their hindquarters.

The dragons skimmed the field and landed in a loose circle around a three-foot, upright stone in the center. All the riders dismounted and climbed the slope.

"There is a car park beyond. My guess is Smyth will come from there." Sean gestured from the immense whitethorn tree at the side of the church, past the grassy knoll of the Mound of Hostages, to the hill on which stood the Stone of Destiny. "We will form a ring, human and dragon, around Lia Fáil. You will both face me with your dragons behind you. Devan between

Lia Fáil and the Celtic cross. Christian on the other side." They positioned themselves as Sean indicated. "I will conduct the ceremony. Then I will pledge my oath with my hand on Lia Fáil. Each human clan member will step forward and repeat the oath. Aisling will start, concluding with Meara. Christian, you will swear your oath, then Devan. Your dragons recite the words with you. Padrick will finish. Then you will mount your compeers and fly the magic-focusing knot pattern."

Sean motioned to the adjoining grassy mound. "I'll lead the clan into a circle around Teach Cormaic and start the bonfire. Once assembled, we finish with a final oath."

"Won't the bonfire be visible to anyone on the road?" Devan asked.

"No, the magic will keep us hidden from anyone outside this ringed earthwork."

Padrick turned to Christian. "When do you think Smyth will attack?"

Christian shut his eyes. "In my vision, I see the glint of the dagger in the flames of the bonfire around Devan." His voice faded to a whisper. "After the ceremony."

Fifty Two

Robert threw the spell book in disgust. For two days, he had read and reread every spell in the multitude of books scattered throughout his living room. He ate only when the pounding headache from hunger drove the written words from his mind. Likewise, he slept wherever he slouched when his eyelids wouldn't stay open any longer.

Nothing. He could find no stronger spells to harness the dragon magic.

His mind flirted with the notion that perhaps the dagger wasn't the talisman after all. He remembered the bright flash of Mary's necklace pierced with his dagger, but waved the thought away. The other victims hadn't worn jewelry, had they? He couldn't recall.

Robert was wasting time chasing this thought. The daggers must be the key to his success. And Anne's love. Hadn't she said the greatest magic was love? Anne would have known about the dragons and their magic. Why else would she have given him the dagger set? His love for his family must prevail.

The shrill ring of the phone interrupted his memories.

Bridget spoke without preamble. "I've found no more about the blood ritual. But I ran across an obscure passage in my grandmother's scrolls."

Robert grinned, his previous sour thoughts of the gypsy forgotten. "When can we cast the spell? What do you need from me?"

"Tomorrow, midnight. At Newgrange. I need some special items. You'll need to supply their blood. Have you kept up with the reformation spell as I instructed?"

"Yes, every month like clockwork since last September. Believe me, I want my family returned to me whole, not deteriorating. How much blood?"

"Ten milliliters from each of you should be enough. Break them up in half. Can you get that?"

Robert thought of Anne's half-liter stored at the blood bank in case of complications from the pregnancy. This certainly qualified as an emergency, but he had none from RJ. Perhaps he could substitute some of his for his son's. He knew they were the same blood type because he had donated to try to save his son's life. He'd have to steal what he needed. There would be too many questions if it all went missing.

"Yes," he whispered. "Anything else?"

"The daggers and an iron sheath for each, to protect the spell from dissipating." She hesitated. "I can't guarantee this will work, but blood is the most powerful binding agent for spells."

"I must try." Robert hung up before whispering, "This is my last chance."

He rushed to his bedroom and fell to his knees in front of Anne's vanity. "My love, I'm so close. I can feel it. This is going to work. You and RJ will be back with me on your birthday. Just a few more days. I love you, sweetheart."

The oak and blackthorn box called to him. He opened it and gazed at the two gleaming jewel-handled daggers. "Iron sheaths, those I'll get tomorrow. Tonight I have an appointment with the blood bank."

He closed the box, rose, and glanced at the bedside clock. "Supper first. Then the little matter of retrieval." He rummaged in his closet until he found what he was searching for.

Dressed all in black, Robert entered the nursery. Baby powder wafted from the bassinet. He smoothed the white satin of the christening gown that lay atop the cheery blue blanket. Blinking, he bent to sniff Anne's jumper wrapped over the back of the rocker, then lifted his gaze to the mural. He ran his fingers over the burn holes on either side of the stone sitting atop one of the grassy mounds at Tara.

"This time, I will succeed. I will resurrect you both. I promise. Our love will prevail."

Robert strolled into the side entrance of the hospital. The blood cache was in the rear, away from the bustling emergency room. All was quiet. His soles slapped against the linoleum floor. At the end of the hall he slipped on the white lab coat he had bought at a second-hand store, and smeared grease over the security camera lens. Satisfied he wouldn't draw anyone's attention, he strolled the length of the hall once to make sure no Gardaí came running.

He stopped at the designated door and peeked into the rectangular window. No light penetrated. He jiggled the knob. Locked. He scanned the empty corridor, then withdrew a glasscutter and cut a circle in the windowpane. He reached in and unlocked the door. Keeping the lights off, he switched on his hand-held torch.

Once inside, Robert booted up the computer. He found the password taped to the underside of the keyboard. In moments, he had the cold storage location of his wife's blood. He cleared the computer's search history and shut it down.

Voices and muffled footsteps passed in the outside hall. Robert crept to the door and peeked out. Whoever it was had gone. He replaced the glass circle, anchoring it with strips of translucent medical tape. He locked the door and made his way to the back room, with its dozen floor-to-ceiling walk-in coolers.

Robert found Anne's sample and took it to the blood-drawing room. He grabbed a half dozen five-milliliter purple-topped vials and two extraction needles. He withdrew two vials from Anne's half-liter packet. Then he applied a rubber tourniquet to his own arm using his teeth, found a vein, and filled the remaining vials. He labeled them, gently encasing each in foam wrap, and placed them in his lab coat breast pocket. He cleaned up the evidence, returned Anne's blood to the cooler, and slipped out.

Thunder woke Robert from his light doze. The muted light peeking in from the curtained window didn't reveal the time. He rubbed the sleep away, wincing as the tape pinched the bend in his elbow.

"One step closer, my love. I'll sacrifice anything to have you and our son back." He rose and checked the vials in his icebox, then went to clean up.

He retrieved one of the daggers and placed it in his jacket breast pocket.

At the second knife shop Robert visited, he found iron sheaths to fit his daggers. Once back home, he prowled the flat, restless to complete this next step. Outside, the spring storm threatened to erupt in wild fury.

Robert rechecked the vials, the newly sheathed daggers, and his notebook of incantations. Once, twice, three times. He paced between his books and the icebox. Sighing, he entered the nursery. Two new dragons needed to be drawn to test the spells. He sketched them above the blackened holes, near the upright stone.

Not bad, he thought. Anne was the artist, but his drawings would suffice. He found his paint jars and took his time painting the dragons. In his mind, he saw one blue and one green.

At ten p.m. Robert could stand it no longer. He packed the vials in an ice-filled cooler, then slipped his notebook, the daggers, and a torch into a rucksack.

With the storm raging, the drive to County Meath took longer than expected. The windscreen wipers barely kept up with the determined rain. Lightning shot across the sky, white heat against boiling gray clouds and obsidian and purple sky. The deafening roar of thunder penetrated the cocoon of his car and drowned out his swearing.

Robert passed the locked visitor's entrance to Newgrange and turned instead onto a side road, passing several homes. At the late hour, no one was awake. He pulled up to the fence that separated the road from the monument and cut the motor. Lightning forked again, illuminating the white quartz facade of the earthen mound. The rain pelted his car and sounded like firecrackers. He hoped the storm wouldn't interfere with the casting of the spell.

When Bridget pulled up behind him, Robert grabbed his umbrella, rucksack, and the cooler from the passenger seat. The clouds and rain obscured the moon and stars. He fished through the bag, pulled out his torch, and switched it on. The beam faltered, then disappeared. He slapped the torch against his leg until the beam erupted through the dark.

He helped Bridget ease past the metal s-shaped gate. They crossed the grass to the entrance of Newgrange. Neither spoke.

Bridget set down her bag. It clanked as she rummaged. She knelt next to the entrance stone and drew a pentagram surrounded by a circle using white chalk. She placed a disc-shaped ceramic bowl in the center of the pentagram, then lit a fat, stubby candle at each tip of the pagan symbol. The flames flickered and hissed in the rain, but continued to burn.

She turned to Robert, her face shadowed in the crazed light. "Place one dagger, unsheathed, in the sacrificial krater."

"The what?"

Bridget pointed to the ceramic bowl. "Krater."

Robert did what she asked, careful not to step on any drawn lines.

Bridget knelt before the krater, facing the entrance stone. Her black hair clung to her body in soggy ropes. "Now, your wife's blood and a dash of yours." He retrieved Anne's two vials and one of his. Bridget gave him a smaller, engraved pewter bowl. "Mix the blood in here. Kneel opposite me." He took his place after mixing the blood, and handed her the bowl.

"Hold the dagger parallel to the krater, one edge facing up. At my signal turn the blade over." She recited an incantation under her breath, then held the blood-filled bowl above the dagger with both hands as an offering. "Repeat after me." She closed her eyes.

"On this night of raw power, I offer the blood of my beloved to anoint this sacred artifact. I willingly give a piece of myself, so my family might be returned to me through the dragon magic. Infuse this dagger with the power to pierce dragon hide, to seek out the dragon magic, and bind said magic. On this night of raw power, with this blood sacrifice, I call to the dark goddesses to grant my solemn desire."

Robert repeated the incantation. After three repetitions, Bridget poured the blood over the upturned blade edge. She signaled and he turned the blade over. She poured the remaining blood over the second edge.

"Sheath the dagger," she said. Robert complied, placing it in his breast pocket. Bridget lifted the krater now filled with the poured blood, whispered another incantation, then handed the krater to him. "Drink."

Robert raised a brow. At Bridget's stony look, he tipped the krater to his lips and drank. Pain exploded in his head, his stomach. His blood surged hot in his veins until he thought he would erupt. He gasped and nearly dropped the krater. He fell to his side, curled in a ball, moaning and clasping his head to stop the unbearable agony.

Bridget grabbed the krater, wiped it clean with a cloth, and placed it back in the center of the pentagram.

"What the bloody hell have you done to me?" Robert choked out. His head pounded with each word, matching the beat of the rain. He squeezed his eyes shut.

"I told you you'd have to sacrifice something."

"That was a hundredfold more intense than the previous spells, perhaps a thousand times." He raised his head, barely opening his eyes.

"That is the price of a blood ritual." The moment spun out, crackled like the lightning against the night sky, then swirled like the screaming wind. Bridget reached a hand toward him but stopped before touching him. "You'll need to repeat the ritual for your son. The sooner the better, before the power of the storm dies."

Robert rolled to his knees still clutching his head between his hands. Bile rose in his throat. He swallowed. Tears fell unheeded. "Give me a moment," he croaked.

When he thought he could stand without his head falling off his shoulders, Robert retrieved the second dagger and remaining vials of blood. Could he withstand another assault? He wondered if it would work. The blood wasn't even RJ's.

Together they repeated the ritual and spell casting. Again, he collapsed after drinking the blood. This time he lay curled in the fetal position while Bridget extinguished the candles and packed away her supplies.

"I hope you get what you desire. I can't help you any further." She left him in the center of the pentagram.

The storm slowly abated. Robert wished the rain would cool his overheated body. Time passed. It could've been minutes or hours. He didn't care. His mind filled with fear. And finally hope.

"I love you. I'll bring you back. I promise." He repeated the mantra over and over.

As dawn lightened the sky, he rose. Robert gathered the empty vials and stowed them in the cooler, then stumbled to his car with his rucksack. His umbrella and torch lay forgotten against the entrance stone.

He drove home without remembering the ride. Inside, he staggered to the nursery. He wanted to test the power, but wasn't sure if that would void the spell.

"Just one," Robert said to the empty room. He withdrew one dagger from its protective sheath. He punctured the wall at the chest of the freshly painted green dragon. Flames leapt up the wall. He was knocked backward and the dagger clattered to the floor.

"Holy Mary and Joseph." Robert scrambled to the dagger, scooped it up and shoved it into its sheath, then ran to the loo. He whipped towels off the rack and soaked them in the tub, praying he'd be in time to stop the nursery from burning.

Fifty Three

Beltaine dawned cool and clear. The clouds from yesterday had long since blown away, so the light fell luminescent on the stone dance. A breeze whistled up from the pastures and lough that comprised the Tuatha dragon clan compound.

Christian hiked the tallest hill that made up the Loughcrew Cairns, Cambane East. He made his way across the rough, slippery ground. At the top, he surveyed the green rolling fields, stone circles, and ring barrows leading to a kerbstone-ringed mound that dominated the top. He circumnavigated the monument, wanting to peer into the dark, iron-gated passage, but he hadn't brought a torch. He continued around until he came upon an intact stone circle.

Christian stood still, absorbing the serenity of the beginning of his new life. A new life that he knew would be anything but peaceful. He had awoken from his disturbing vision and needed time alone to sort out his feelings. Just over six weeks ago he'd been content. Then he'd met Devan and his solitary life had been tossed away liked an empty tourist wallet. Not only had she infiltrated his life, she had burrowed into his mind—and his heart.

She brought out feelings of protectiveness and unselfishness. Christian didn't like it. He had a family now. A father that over the last week or so, again because of Devan, he'd come to not really know, but at least respect. He avoided his grandmother, but he wished to know his grandfather and his aunt and cousins. Now he had the dragon clan.

Thoughts of Devan brought the Yank clearly into his mind—her tousled, spiky hair, her whiskey-brown eyes half closed with pleasure, her sharp American accent defused by her laughter and soft sighs while he had loved her last night.

Christian knew he should return to the compound below. There was bound to be plenty of work in preparation for the Chosen Ceremony that evening. He breathed the crisp, clean air. His gaze shifted away from the sunrise as a silver-blue dragon crested the hilltop and landed outside the stone dance.

Devan slid from the dragon's neck and strode to him. "Are you okay?"

"Couldn't sleep. How'd you find me?"

She took his hand, stepped closer. "ROARKE said you were restless." She lifted her face to his, searched for a moment, then kissed him. "We're going to stop Smyth. He may have magic daggers, but we have dragons, more than three dozen clan members, the drake, and your insight. He won't catch us off guard, not like his other victims."

"I still don't like you being his target."

"If Padrick is correct, so are you."

"I'm not recovering from injuries." He caressed her cheek. "And I know my way around a knife."

"Sean's planned for every possible contingency. Everyone is on edge. Come, let's help them." She pulled him toward DOCHAS. "We have a full day to prepare."

Christian helped Devan into the riding harness, then sat behind her. DOCHAS ran two uncoordinated strides, unfurled her wings, then swooped down the grassy embankment toward the clan compound. Christian's stomach rose to his throat at the short free fall.

When DOCHAS landed near the lake, Christian jumped from the dragon and lifted Devan down. He raised a brow in question.

"She wants a bath," Devan said. "ROARKE will be here shortly."

Christian helped unbuckle the riding harness. ROARKE landed nearby as the silver-blue dragon waded into the deep blue depths. They removed ROARKE'S harness and grinned as he joined DOCHAS in the lough. Concentric circles rippled from the two playful dragons and lapped the rocky shoreline.

"FIONN says all the dragons will bathe. We are to find the harness crafter, Timothy, to get our new harnesses." Devan's eyes took on the faraway look that Christian recognized as the telepathic communication with a dragon. She blinked once and refocused on him. "Let's go."

"What about the dragons?" He looked at the splashing water.

"They'll dry off in the sun. Timothy needs us for the finishing touches."

They found the old-timer hovering over several riders seated in the communal dining hall. Leather straps lay spread in front of the riders. Cloths ripe with the musty scent of sheep oil littered the table as Timothy demonstrated the proper softening technique to a lad of about eight.

Timothy glanced up, a smile spread over his crag-lined face, and his green eyes twinkled. "Aye, I see FIONN relayed my request." He tilted his bald pate toward another table, empty of riders but full of new straps. Two saddles sat on the bench closest to the entrance. "These are your compeers'. I'll show ye how to work them. They require softening 'afore they can be used, otherwise they'll chafe."

Christian and Devan spent the morning working on their riding harnesses and saddles. After a brief lunch, they oiled their sun-warmed dragons' wing joints and cinched on the softened harnesses. She rolled her head side to side and stretched her back. He massaged her neck and shoulders.

"I think Sean had Timothy keep us busy," Christian said.

"It worked." Devan purred under his hands. "I need a long, hot shower. Care to join me?"

They exited the dragon lair mound and headed toward Sean and Aisling's house.

"I'm going to talk to Sean about a private flat if we need to stay here much longer. I haven't shared living space since I was sixteen." Christian opened the front door, climbed the stairs to the guest room, and shut the door behind them.

Devan kicked off her shoes. "Padrick said we were needed as dragonriders right away, so we'll probably be sent to Lough Gur after the ceremony." She peeled out of her oil-stained T-shirt and jeans.

Christian followed suit, entered the loo, then turned on the shower. They stepped in.

"Are you okay going to Lough Gur? You and Padrick seemed to reach some sort of truce."

Christian shampooed her hair, tilting her head into the hot spray to rinse before answering. "I'm working on it." He pressed his body to hers, and gently nipped her lower lip before soothing it with a kiss. They washed, then distracted each other until the water ran cool against their overheated skin.

As he finished dressing, a knock sounded on the door. Devan continued drying her hair.

"Come in," Christian said. Sean entered, carrying two brown paper-wrapped packages. Christian shot the clan leader a subtle look. "If we're going to be staying here in Loughcrew, Devan and I need our own place."

"I'll arrange it, but you'll be moving to Lough Gur within the week."

Devan appeared and Sean handed each of them a package. "Your outfit for the ceremony." Christian raised a brow. Sean continued. "It's custom. Everyone will be wearing the same. Another advantage."

She ripped open her package and held up toffee-brown riding pants, a pale green long-sleeve button-up shirt, and a wax-coated brown thigh-length riding coat.

"The shirts are loose-fitting to accommodate the Kevlar vests," Sean said.

"How do you know our sizes?" Devan held up the trousers.

"From Timothy's measurements." Sean turned to Devan. "My wife has some boots she'd like you to try on for tonight. She's waiting for you in our bedroom."

Devan's cheeks turned bright pink. "I'd have bought my own pair in Dublin, if I'd been thinking clearly."

Christian tossed his unopened bundle on the bed. He cupped her face with his hands. "We'll get a pair for you in a few days, when you see the doctor." He kissed her and rested his forehead on hers. She sighed, nodded, then left the two men.

"What's the problem?" Christian leaned toward the still open door and watched as Devan walked down the hall.

"There's still some suspicion you two are in cahoots with the killer."

Christian spun toward the clan leader.

Sean rubbed his neck. "Padrick and those I trust most will be shadowing you both for your protection. At least until we apprehend the killer."

"I don't want anyone else at risk. It's bad enough Devan's the primary target. Can't you have the naysayers not attend?"

"That will only splinter the clan. Everyone participates. The magic demands it. Our oath swears us to protect Éire. Dragonrider will not harm dragonrider. It goes against everything we believe."

"We've already seen what one misguided human can do to a helpless drake," Christian said. "People can be cruel. Especially when they are scared. Swearing an oath doesn't guarantee safety. You and Padrick look out for the clan. I'll keep myself and Devan safe." He shook Sean's hand. "We'll be ready."

Sean glanced at his watch. "We leave in half an hour."

When Devan returned, Christian remained silent. They redressed in the new outfits with the Kevlar vests under their shirts.

"I'll be right behind you." Christian ushered her to the door. He slipped his knife into his boot.

Fourteen gleaming jewel-toned dragons gathered on the two courtyards and the nearby pasture. GRAYSON stood in front of FIONN, trembling inside an under-the-belly netting and metal bar contraption. Scores of plastic and wood crates filled with supplies lay scattered next to each dragon.

Christian and Devan joined the similarly dressed riders in a circle around Sean. The kitchen staff, Timothy, and several others Christian hadn't met dispersed from a meeting with Aisling. Each mounted a dragon. Timothy climbed on DOCHAS's back. No one mounted either ROARKE or FIONN.

Sean gave the dragonriders their position in the flight formation. "Riders, mount up. Dragons, ready your cargo."

Christian boosted Devan into her saddle in front of Timothy, then grinned and strode to ROARKE. The other riders scrambled onto their compeers.

The dragons straightened from their crouch, grasped their packages in their foreclaws, and watched for Sean's signal. FIONN grasped the metal bar from GRAYSON's netting and settled the drake against his chest.

Excitement and tension filled Christian. This would all be over soon, one way or the other. He'd protect Devan no matter what.

"Ye both shall be saved. I shall protect ye. Tonight we embrace our destiny," ROARKE bespoke.

"Of course." Christian mentally reassured his soon-to-be-compeer. He buried his thoughts of what he was willing to sacrifice.

Half an hour after arriving at the Hill of Tara, a white, open-sided canvas tent the size of a rugby pitch stood erect on the south side of the hilly mound area known as Teach Cormaic. Trestle tables were set with dinnerware, musical instruments sat in a corner, kegs were tapped, and the kitchen staffs from all three clan compounds were busy preparing immense platters. Wood lay stacked high inside a man-made rock circle in the center of Teach Cormaic.

As the sun slipped to the edge of the horizon, thirty dragons gathered in a circle. Their riders took their designated places around Lia Fáil. Christian reached across, squeezed Devan's hand, then stood ready on his side of the sacred, upright stone.

From the sanctuary of the church, Robert watched the dragons arrive. He'd been ensconced inside with his precious Anne and RJ for over two hours. His car was parked well away. He noticed the old man stationed by the car park under the whitethorn tree, but disregarded him.

The people scurried about, readying for a party. Robert spied his brother-in-law, Braeden, in the crowd, but paid him scant attention. Instead, Robert closed his eyes and opened his senses to the dragon power.

When he felt the same surge he experienced at Trinity, he smiled and opened his eyes. He peered through the window. Standing with the tall, black-haired Irishman from the library was the American woman. Both wore the same clothing as the others.

"Soon, *a Storin*," Robert murmured to the motionless, seated figure of his wife. "The two who will sacrifice for you are here."

At dusk, the dragons and humans gathered in a circle around the upright stone on one of the hills. Robert gathered Anne in his arms and nudged open the side door leading to the graveyard, close to the crowded grassy mound. He propped her slightly decayed body against a Celtic cross at the edge of the cemetery. Without glancing at the hill, he rushed back to collect RJ. He placed his newborn son's body, dressed in his christening gown, in Anne's arms.

The restoration spell had worked, but three months had elapsed from their deaths until Robert had found Bridget and tricked the spell out of her. Once he uttered the words, the ravages of death ceased. Yet, in those months, the decaying had been considerable. The rotting flesh made his stomach revolt. He gagged, then shifted to bury his nose in his bent elbow. His eyes watered.

"The magic will restore you to your full beauty, my love." Robert crouched in the growing shadows and waited for the bonfire to be lit.

Sean's voice echoed in the cool dusk air. "*Fáilte*. We, the Keepers of Éire, gather on this day, Beltaine, to celebrate the partnering of dragon ROARKE to Christian Riley and dragon DOCHAS to Devan Fraser.

"We, of the Tuatha Dragon Clan, bear witness. We shall honor and support these partners to the best of our abilities. We shall make welcome Christian and Devan." Sean turned to Christian, a warm smile on his lips.

"Christian, place your right hand on Lia Fáil. In your left, take your clan pendant as bestowed on you from your mother, Erin, and your father, Padrick, and from Padrick's great-grandfather, Riley. Please repeat after me. "I, Christian Riley, swear to protect and nurture Ireland and all its inhabitants, to the best of my ability. To utilize the dragon magic from my partnering only for good in the service of Éire. To care, assist, and nurture my compeer, ROARKE, in his likewise endeavors. From this day, I swear my allegiance to the Tuatha Dragon Clan."

Christian repeated each sentence. He heard ROARKE's oath in his head and felt his pendant heat in his hand. His heart seemed to swell in his chest as he finished.

Sean turned to Devan. "Devan, place your ring-clad right hand on Lia Fáil. With your clan ring as bestowed on you from the death of your parents

Meghann and Joseph Fraser, your grandparents Brinna and Patrick Gallagher, and your great-grandparents Graeme and Siobhan Murray. Please repeat after me." Sean repeated his earlier words, substituting Devan's and DOCHAS's names. She repeated the oath.

Sean held one of Christian's and Devan's hands in each of his, then raised his voice. "As Tuatha Dragon Clan Leader, I task each member here to act as mentor and friend to ROARKE and Christian and DOCHAS and Devan. To pledge their oath to uphold the partnering of these two dragon and rider pairs. To rededicate our lives in the service of Éire, with an 'Aye'."

A mixture of human voices mumbled, said, or shouted, "Aye."

Christian and Devan mounted their compeers and directed them to take to the darkened sky. Devan and DOCHAS flew the complicated magic pattern. Christian and ROARKE followed, nearly dragon tail to dragon snout. When they completed the circuit, the two dragons landed. Christian helped Devan down and they returned to their places at the stone.

Sean raised his voice. "Tuatha Dragon Clan, prepare for your *geall*, your promise." He placed his right hand on Lia Fáil, held his pendant in his left hand, bowed his head and spoke the three words on the back of the clan pendant *"Dilseacht. Fáil. Saoirse."* He dropped his hands and stepped back.

Aisling stepped forward and repeated the oath. Each dragonrider in turn followed. After Meara, Christian intoned his promise. ROARKE's jubilant tone echoed in his mind. Devan followed and Padrick completed the oath.

When all had promised, Sean led the circle of alternating humans and dragons in a figure eight to their places around Teach Cormaic. He stepped forward. A hush came over the crowd, then they chanted in unison, *"Ni neart go cur le cheile.* There is no strength without unity."

At a signal from Sean, each dragon's chest puffed up and spewed forth a burst of fire at the stacked wood. The fire leapt into the dark sky, casting an eerie glow over the surrounding hills. A whoop went up from the white tent as several children and adults ran across the uneven grass toward the bonfire.

In the press of swaying bodies, Christian lost sight of Devan.

Fifty Four

When the bonfire roared to life, Robert gathered Anne and RJ in his arms. He skirted the hill behind the bonfire and climbed the grassy mound that held the Celtic cross and standing stone. Dragons and people milled around the bonfire.

Robert propped Anne against the cross and repositioned RJ in her lifeless arms. The rot of the decomposing bodies assaulted his nose. No amount of Bridget's magic could hold back the ravages of death. Crouching down, he turned toward the fire and his two targets. He let his eyes adjust to the darkness, broken by the occasional flame as a gap appeared in the crush of humans and dragons.

He squinted until he saw the American woman. Her Irish companion stood several meters from her, looking toward the church. Robert pulled both daggers from their metal sheaths on his belt. He sent a silent plea to whatever god would listen and kissed one dagger. A dark-cloaked figure crossed between him and his first sacrificial victim.

A shriek rose from the crowd. To the left of the American, a woman pointed in his direction.

"She's…she's dead!"

"Ach, her flesh is fallin' away." A second cloaked figure staggered away, retching.

Braeden stumbled toward him, shrieking. "Murderer. I'll kill you." He spun around, trying to dislodge the talons of a tan dragon that lifted him into the air.

Humans and dragons scattered like dried leaves on a sudden breeze.

When the path to the American woman cleared, Robert stood, aimed, and hurled the first dagger with all his strength.

At the sound of the scream, Christian whipped around. He caught the glint of a dagger in flight, then Devan across the ringed bonfire and knew he'd never get to her in time. He shouted for her to drop, even as he dashed toward the assailant.

Though time seemed to slow, he couldn't get between her and the dagger. Several riders leapt onto their dragons, while others grabbed children and ran. A flight of dragons arrowed into the safety of the sky. He lost sight of ROARKE and DOCHAS in the melee.

Devan turned to look at him. In that moment, the dragons' wing strokes fanned the flames. A glint of silver tumbled to emerald, then silver, and blood red ruby as the dagger hurtled toward Devan's heart.

At Christian's shout, chaos erupted. Devan glanced over. In that split second, she saw the killer in the exact spot she'd partnered with DOCHAS.

Devan caught a flash of ruby red, shiny silver, then a deep blue the same color as Christian's eyes when his desire intensified, head straight toward her. She stood rooted to the spot, mesmerized. In those brief seconds, her mind replayed the first moment she met Christian, the tenderness he showed the first time they made love, and her utter terror when Christian collapsed while reliving a dream.

A gray blur flashed in front of her, spinning her around. She crumpled to her knees as pain shot through her ribs. She wrapped her arms around her middle and muffled her screams.

"Tis the Wingless One. I could not protect ye." DOCHAS's sorrowful tone cut through Devan's miasma of pain and fear. *"The dagger is tainted with a poisonous magic."*

Devan crawled in the direction GRAYSON fell. As she neared the gray mass, her hand slipped on a dark, wet patch of grass and she sprawled face first. She scrunched her eyes shut, spit out copper-tasting grass and mud, pushed back to her knees, and prayed he was still alive. When she reached GRAYSON'S heaving side, the dagger was buried in his neck, between two diamond-shaped scales. Blood gushed.

"Help! GRAYSON is injured," Devan bespoke her compeer and any other dragons that might be listening. *"The dagger's stuck in his neck."*

"The harness crafter and the healer come," DOCHAS bespoke Devan.

"Hurry. He's not moving." She stroked her savior's eye ridges with a blood-stained hand. A foul stench emanated from GRAYSON'S torn neck.

Silence engulfed her in the red and orange-tinged shadows that danced against the blackness of night.

The deathly silence was broken by an anguished shout of "No!" Christian searched wildly and then realized he had cried out. He turned back to the killer and gripped the worn bone handle of his own blade.

"I must save my family. They're all I have. Without them, I'm dead." Smyth waved a hand at the decomposing bodies of his wife and son propped against the cross. He threw the second dagger.

Christian closed the distance. He could only hope the Kevlar vest had protected Devan where he'd failed. Where the hell were DOCHAS and ROARKE? He had just enough time to change his angle to the killer. The jewel-handled dagger embedded in his left shoulder with a sickening thud. Excruciating fire radiated down his arm and across his chest. His fingers went numb, his body jerked to escape the blaze searing his left side.

"No! No, I must have the dragon power. It's my last chance," Smyth cried. He stumbled toward Christian, arms outstretched. The distance between them closed rapidly as he screamed his intent to strangle the magic from the injured dragonrider.

Christian squinted against the pain and nausea, took aim with his right arm, and threw his blade. It was so quiet he could almost hear his knife slicing through the thick night air. His legs gave way and his vision dimmed. The pain from the blade embedded in his skin and muscle and sinew burned hot like lightning. He sank to his knees in the cool, damp grass, then toppled over.

"Devan, save Devan," he mumbled as strong hands clutched him. *"Where were you? Is DOCHAS with Devan?"* Christian bespoke his compeer.

"Stay with me. I was nearly trampled by the hordes when the blasted female shrieked. Could not get to ye or the Ring Wearer." He heard ROARKE'S thoughts faint in his mind, then nothing at all.

Devan, a ghra, I need you. Need you to help me with my da. Need you in my search for my mum. Please be alive. I love you. He repeated the last three words over and over in his mind as he struggled against the heavy darkness that held him tight.

Through her tears, Devan thought she saw GRAYSON'S side rise with a breath, but wasn't sure.

Sean knelt at the drake's head. "GRAYSON, can you hear me? Devan is here. Speak to her if you can hear me."

"Please, GRAYSON." She pleaded in her mind as she lightly stoked the drake's side. *"You saved my life."* She focused her thoughts on her compeer. *"DOCHAS, help me with GRAYSON."*

Sean gripped the handle of the dagger then yanked his hand away. "Devil hellfire."

"I've got it, Clan Leader," Timothy said, dropping his shillelagh. "Hope it didn't sever a vein." He wrapped a cloth around his palm, bent down and pulled the dagger from GRAYSON with a quick jerk. Blood, almost purple in color, flowed from the wound.

"Aaah. It burns, it burns. Help."

Devan shouted in relief. "He's alive. He says it burns." She looked up at Timothy, then Sean. "Oh God, where's Christian?" Ignoring her own injuries, she shoved to her feet.

Someone rolled him onto his back. Christian groaned. Murmuring voices drifted in his consciousness. He blinked and batted his right hand at the shadowy figure hovering over him.

"Bloody fecking hell. Come to finish me off, have you?" The thought of dying cleared the last vestiges of darkness from his head.

"Lie still." Padrick ripped Christian's shirt open. "The dagger is buried deep. Your skin has turned black already. The dagger's magic-infused. I need to remove it, but I can't tell if it's pierced a major artery."

"Just be quick about it." Christian clenched his teeth.

"You could bleed to death."

"That would be better than being burned alive. Hurry." His breathing sounded harsh in his ears.

Padrick pulled on his riding gloves and whispered a quick oath. "Here goes."

Searing pain tugged Christian's shoulder. He yelped, then bit his lower lip to keep from crying out again. He tasted copper. Warm blood gushed from his shoulder. Pins and needles tingled into his fingertips as the numbness dissipated. He closed his eyes and hoped Devan was alive.

Padrick pressed his gloved hand hard against the wound. "I need some help over here," he shouted.

"The Ring Wearer and the Clan Leader approach," ROARKE bespoke, cutting through Christian's pain. *"The Wingless One is injured."*

"What of the killer?"

"He is of nigh consequence. Do not fash yerself." ROARKE's tone held disdain. *"The poison must be purged."*

Christian opened his eyes when soft hands caressed his face. Devan leaned over him. He opened his mouth, but no words escaped.

"Hush." Devan brushed his hair from his forehead. "Looks like you don't know your way around every knife." She returned his earlier words with a slight smile on her lips, but it didn't reach her worry-filled eyes.

"ROARKE—" He cleared his throat, trying to pull moisture into his mouth. "ROARKE said poison."

"I heard. Timothy and Meara are mixing a potion to draw it out." She brushed the hair from his eyes. "Hang on."

Sean dropped down beside Devan. "I see the dagger missed the vest. Help's coming."

"What about Smyth? Where is everyone?" Christian struggled to sit up.

Strong hands held him in place. "Stay still." Padrick's rough voice sounded to his left. "We don't need the poison spreading."

"Smyth's dead. Your blade struck true," Sean said. "Roarke and Declan are guarding him. Michael is gathering the rest at the tent."

"Grayson?" he asked Devan.

"Saved my life. The dagger pierced his neck, but he's awake." Her face took on the abstract look of telepathic communication. "He's relishing Dochas's attention. I think he's smitten."

"Dochas is destined to be my mate," Roarke bespoke. *"As the Ring Wearer is for ye."*

He mentally groaned. *"Please tell me you didn't send that thought to Devan?"*
"Nigh. That task I left for ye."

Padrick interrupted his mental communication. "Here come Aisling and Meara."

"I'm going to see to Smyth and his wife and child," Sean said.

Christian raised his right hand to Sean. "In my dreams…he was distraught and confused. He loved his family. They were his whole world. Can—" Words failed him.

"What are you asking, Son?" Padrick asked.

Christian closed his eyes and took a deep breath. "Leniency. A clan burial or whatever you did for the four murdered dragonriders." He opened his eyes and stared at his da. "I have to know a murderer can be forgiven." His breath hitched. "I thought he killed Devan. I didn't just want him stopped. I wanted revenge. I'm the same—"

"No you're not," Padrick whispered. "You were defending the clan. Ireland, Devan, yourself."

"Padrick's correct," Sean said. "But I'll take your wishes under advisement." He stepped back. "Let my wife tend you now."

Padrick shifted to let Aisling kneel beside Christian's injured shoulder. She stirred a bowl containing a sour-smelling mixture. Christian wrinkled his nose and swallowed as bile rose in his throat.

"Here." Meara handed Devan a mug. "For medicinal purposes." She cocked her head toward him.

Devan raised his head and tilted the mug to his lips. Christian swallowed a thimbleful of Jameson that warmed his chilled body. He managed a wobbly grin, drained the remainder of the mug, then nodded to Aisling.

"This will hurt, but not as bad as the dagger, I'm thinking." Aisling spread sticky, cold goo over the wound. Christian hissed. "Sorry, I need to make sure I get this everywhere the blade penetrated." She packed more around his shoulder and manipulated the wound to work the cure into the bone-deep cut.

Christian gritted his teeth and cursed vehemently inside his head. He clenched his eyes shut.

"You're doing great," Devan murmured in his ear.

He growled as a cool cloth was placed over his forehead.

"Okay, here's the tricky part." Aisling prodded his shoulder. "We need to burn out the poison."

His eyes flew open. "What!"

"It's the only way to counteract a blood-binding spell."

"And if you don't?" Christian croaked.

"The poison won't spread because of the poultice, but you'll lose the use of your arm. Permanently."

Devan stroked his cheek. "Timothy has just finished with GRAYSON. He seemed to tolerate it okay."

"He has scales to protect him from being burned alive." Christian knew he sounded petulant, but didn't care. He hadn't survived the killer's attack only to die during the cure.

The fire will rid your body of the poison. It will no' consume ye. I will control it, ROARKE reassured him.

"You'll provide the fire? You burned down Sean's door! Thanks, mo chroi, but how about a more-experienced dragon?" Christian heard ROARKE huff.

Aisling spoke. "FIONN will do the honors. Ready?"

Christian nodded. Aisling moved away. Padrick and Devan stayed, each holding one of his hands. A narrow stream of blood-red fire bathed his wound, then he turned his head away from his shoulder and held Devan's steady gaze. Heat licked into his wound, down to the bone. The pain wasn't as bad as the dagger had been.

After several seconds, Roarke snarled. *"Enough. The wound is pure."* Christian imagined a stream of fire emanating from his compeer, but couldn't see Roarke to know if he was correct.

Devan repeated Roarke's words aloud. The dragon fire abated. Aisling applied a salve, several plaster strips to close the gash, and a pressure dressing.

With Devan and Padrick's help, Christian sat up and shivered as the chill air hit his exposed chest. Padrick shed his coat and wrapped it around him.

Roarke snarled again as voices, heated in argument, closed in on them.

"Da? Mother?" Padrick shielded Christian from them. "What do you want?"

"To see the boyo," Kiely said. "Heard he was hurt. Heard he killed the dragon slayer."

Padrick shifted, ready to stand. "Now is not the time. If you want to help, then assist Michael in re-gathering the clan."

"Come, Kiely." Ronan took her arm. "Let him recover in peace." He nodded to Christian and lifted his lips in an apologetic smile. Kiely snorted and stomped toward the milling crowd.

Murmurs wafted on the night breeze from the direction of the tent. Soft dragon keening blended with the rougher human tones.

Christian grimaced as Padrick helped him to his feet. He closed his eyes and swayed before Devan wrapped an arm around his waist and pulled him against her side. He leaned down and brushed a kiss on her cheek. He tasted her salty tears. She hadn't cried until now. Lord, his Yank was tough and he loved her.

Fifty Five

FIONN lowered the wooden pallet holding the bodies of the Smyth family on the ground in front of the entrance stone at Newgrange. Robert and Anne lay side-by-side with their newborn baby tucked between them. Dragons and their riders gathered in a semicircle around the stone.

Sean stepped forward to speak, but Christian cleared his throat. "May I?" Sean waved him to continue. Devan squeezed his hand.

"I know this is strange, providing a clan honor to a murderer," Christian started. Several people murmured their ascent. He waited a beat, then continued. "Through my dreams, I came to understand—though not condone—Robert Smyth's actions. He was a tortured and broken man after his family was ripped from him. His mind snapped, along with his sense of right and wrong. That doesn't bring back the four riders and dragons he killed. Nothing will. As the Keepers of Éire, we need to forgive and begin to heal, both as individuals and as a clan. For the benefit of all Ireland."

Christian gazed at his new family. "Let us start by letting Robert Smyth's soul join his family. Let us forgive the actions of a crazed, yet all-too-human man. Let us ride on the wings of honor."

Sean clasped his clan pendant and the others followed. "*Bealtaine do Soul teacht ar na síochána.* May your soul find peace."

"*Síochána.*" The dragonriders spoke together as dragon fire engulfed the bodies.

When the dragonriders landed back at the Hill of Tara, a sorrowful tune played within the crowded tent.

"Take a walk with me?" Christian asked Devan. She nodded and weaved her fingers with his. They strolled in silence up the grassy hill, keeping their gazes on the uneven ground. Wind stirred the flames of the still burning bonfire like dancing ghosts.

Christian halted in front of Lia Fáil, the Stone of Destiny, and prayed Devan's destiny was intertwined with his until the day he died. He captured her hands and tugged her to him. A not-quite painful burn danced under his bandaged skin, but he ignored it and gazed into Devan's eyes. A cloud drifted past the moon, casting her face into shadow.

The softness of her features and the knowledge of her strength added power to the words he spoke. "Until I met you, I'd never let myself think about what I wanted beyond the life I led. Never let myself trust anyone. I didn't think about long term, especially not with anyone else. I've never wanted forever."

He took a steadying breath. "Devan, *a ghra*. I love you."

The moonlight peeked through and a ghost of a frown touched her mouth. He squeezed her hands. Before she could gasp, he loosened his hold, brought each to his lips, and dropped a string of kisses along each bent knuckle.

She smiled now, a smile that lit her eyes like firelight warms a snifter of aged brandy. "Christian—"

His heart stuttered, then thundered to life. "Tell me I didn't muck this up with you? My past? Killing Smyth?" He searched her face. "I'll turn myself over to the Gardaí."

"No." She cupped his cheeks. "I'm in love with you, too."

Devan pressed her lips to his. Christian slid his palm along her neck, tipped her mouth closer, and took the kiss deeper.

"What does ahh graw mean?" Devan stumbled over the unfamiliar words. "You said it when you told me you loved me."

"It means 'my love'." His brogue thickened. "'Tis the first time I've called anyone that. I like it." He hugged her tighter to his side.

"I like it, too. And your sexy accent."

"You've the accent, *a ghra*. Remember, you're in Ireland."

"I'm not likely to forget. What other Gaelic words do you know?"

"Several. I'll teach you." Christian nuzzled her neck as he guided her back to their new family.

When they were halfway to the milling crowd, dread flowed through Christian, stealing his breath as he heard ROARKE's apprehensive tone. *"The poison flows in the Wingless One."*

An Deireadh

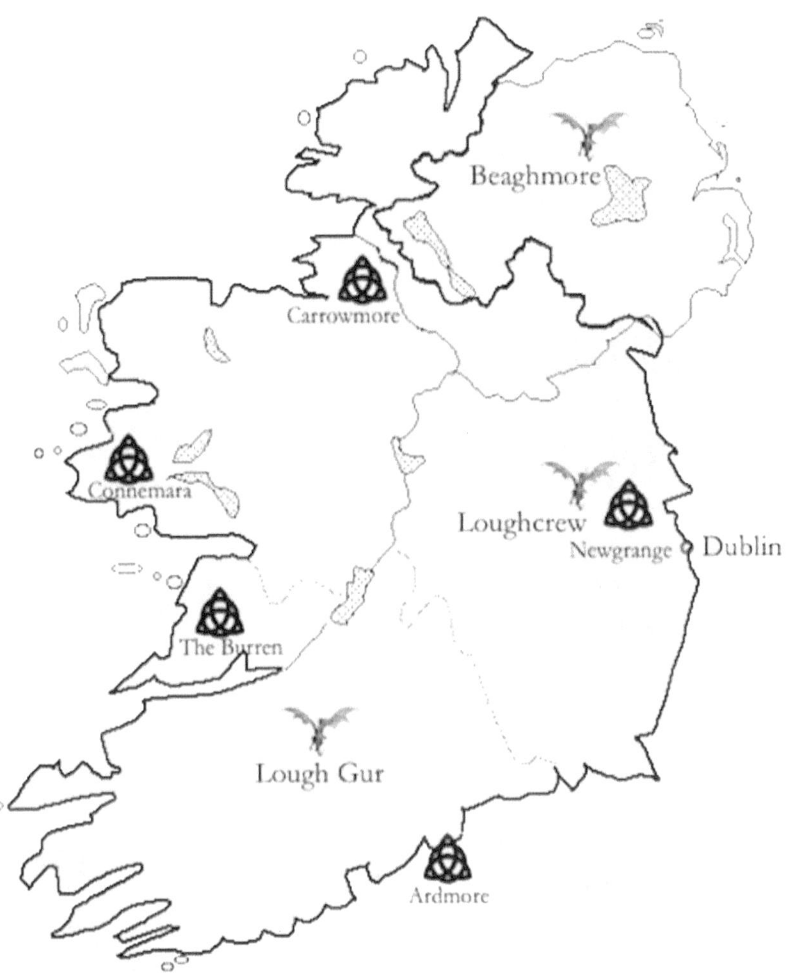

Beaghmore
Carrowmore
Connemara
Loughcrew
Newgrange
Dublin
The Burren
Lough Gur
Ardmore
= Dragon Clan Compound
= Murder Sites

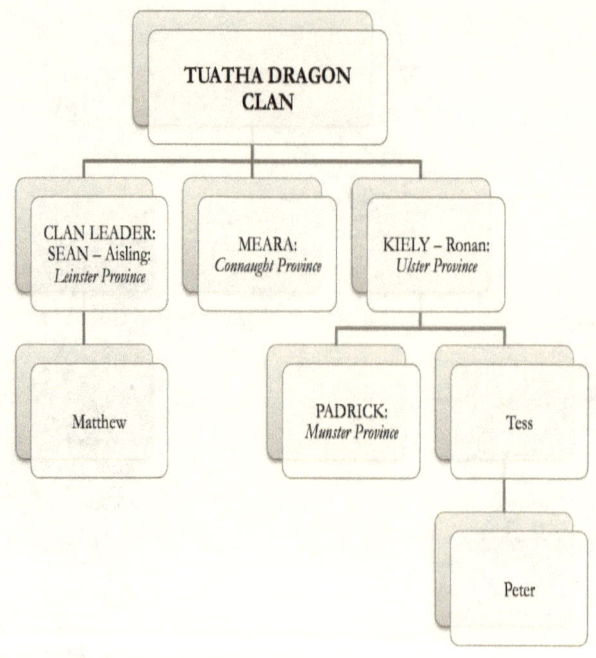

MAIN DRAGON CLAN CHARACTERS ONLY

Riders and their Dragons — only those named in the story

Rider	Dragon	Province	County
**Sean	FIONN	Leinster	Dublin
Aisling	BRIANNA	Leinster	Wicklow
Aiden	SEBASTIAN	Leinster	Wexford
Liam	RORY	Leinster	Kilkenny
Colin	LANDON	Leinster	Laoise
Daniel	LORCAN	Leinster	Louth
Moira	AEDNET	Leinster	Meath
*Padrick	DECLAN	Munster	Kerry
*Meara	CARRIGAN	Connaught	Mayo
Braeden	FAOLAN	Connaught	Leitrim
*Kiely	TULLIA	Ulster	Derry
Ronan	CALHOUN	Ulster	Antrim
+Michael	SEAMUS	Ulster	Tyrone
Matthew	KIERAN	Ulster	Monaghan
Ryan	QUINN	Ulster	Cavan
Maggie	FIANNA	Ulster	Donegal
Darcy	FLYNN	Ulster	Armagh
Keira	AILEEN	Ulster	Fermanagh

Murdered Rider & Dragon

Rider	Dragon	Province	County
Conor	DONOVAN	Munster	Waterford
Shannon	TARA	Munster	Clare
Dylan	TIERNEY	Connaught	Galway
Mary	AALYSIA	Connaught	Sligo

** = Tuatha Clan Leader

* = Province Leader

+ = Temporary Province Leader

Glossary

A Caras: A clan or family unit
A Ghra: My Love / ahh graw
A Storin: My Treasure
Across the foam/ pond: Across the sea
An Deireadh: The End
Bespoke: Telepathic communication between dragon and rider
Biscuits: Cookies
Bloody: Expletive attached to all manner of things
Bodhrán: An Irish frame drum / bow-ran
Boot: Trunk of vehicle
Boyo: Variation on the word boy
Bugger it: General purpose expletive used to express displeasure
Céilí: Party / kay-lee
Compeer: Partner
Craic: Gossip or chatter / crack
Croagh Patrick: St. Patrick's Mountain or St. Patrick's stack
Cupboard: Closet
Dia duit: Hello / dee-a gwith
Dia's Muire duit: Hello in return / dee-as mwir-a-gwith
Dilseacht: Loyalty / deel-shockt
Dochas: Hope
Draiocht: Magic
Eejit: Idiot
Éire: Ireland / AIR-reh
Fáil: Destiny / fall
Fáilte: Welcome / fall-sha
Fash: Worry
Feck: Fuck
Fooking: Fucking
Fortnight: 14 days
Gaol: Jail
Garda: Title for police officer

Gardaí: Police / Gar-d-i

Geall: Promise / Gy-al

Ghra anois agus go deo: Love, Now and Forever

Gobdaw: Slowwitted person

Gobshite: Asshole, shit

Gobsmacked: Stunned

Half seven: 7:30

Jumper: Sweater

Knickers: Underwear

Lift: Elevator

Loo: Bathroom

Lorry: Truck

Máistir: Master

Mo chroí: My heart / Muh kree

Ni neart go cur le cheile: There is no strength without unity / nee hyart guh curr leh kay-lay

Nígh: No / h-ea

Of an age: Close in age

Ogham: Medieval alphabet used to write the early Irish language / OH-am

Plaster: BandAid

Publican: Bartender

Rucksack: Backpack

Saoirse: Liberty or Freedom / sear-sha

Seanachais: Storyteller / san/a/khes

Shite: Shit

Six and Twenty: Twenty Six

Slagging: Making fun of

Sláinte: Cheers / sloynta or sloyn-cha

Slán Leat: Goodbye / slawn lath

Sweet: Dessert or candy

Tapadh leat: Thank You / tapah lat

Torch: Flashlight

Tuatha: A tribe or family group, like a clan / Too-aha dai

Windscreen: Windshield

Acknowledgements

Where to start? This story would not be the best I could tell it without some talented people. First and foremost, I am honored and humbled by the care and nurturing, yet tough love of my critique group: Marlene Dotterer, Lani Longshore, and Ed Miracle. They helped me cut the excess, develop believable characters, and learn this craft. These three are fantastic writers all.

Next, the insightful teachings of Julaina Kleist-Corwin's Monday *Polish Your Fiction* class and my classmates' helpful comments. Paula Chinick for allowing me to bounce ideas around and work out the ramifications of my characters' actions.

Many thanks to my Beta readers: Kay Hutchings-Cook, George Cramer, Anthia Felt, Susan Hamrick, Anne Koch, and Cathe Norman. I hope you enjoy the finished product.

For putting up with all my cover ideas and changes, thank you to graphic designer extraordinaire, Christine McCall. Rosa Sophia, my editor, helped keep my punctuation and content clean. Any errors are mine alone. Vi Carr Moore for giving of her editing skills so freely. And Patricia Marshall for her expertise in formatting.

Of course, I would not have met most of these people without joining the California Writers Club Tri-Valley Branch. A special thanks for the close friendships cultivated with some of the best human beings I have had the pleasure of sharing my writing journey with.

Thanks to my friends and family who put up with me living in my story world for over four years, I appreciate your support. And Jules for hounding me to keep writing and to pursue my dream of visiting Ireland.

A special shout out to the wonderful people I met in my wanderings through Ireland. I encountered many gracious people from all across your wonderful island. I thank you for your interest in me and what I was there to accomplish. Sláinte.

As a writer, I would be remiss if I didn't acknowledge the authors that have given me the opportunity to delve into their worlds. While too numerous to list here, I must honor the memory of my favorite author,

Anne McCaffrey. Her *Dragonriders of Pern* series opened my mind to the possibilities of the imagination. *Tapadh leat, Máistir Seanachais* (Thank you, Master Storyteller). May your golden wings continue to carry you into readers' hearts.

About the Author

Jordan Bernal grew up in the heart of Silicon Valley, San Jose, CA. She spent most of her career in the high-tech industry as a product coordinator/technical writer and earned her bachelor of science degree in business entrepreneurship.

Her enduring love of fantasy, especially dragons, inspired her to write her debut novel, *The Keepers of Éire*. She is currently the vice-president of California Writers Club Tri-Valley Branch and credits her growth as a writer to her critique group, open mic nights, and various writing classes she has attended.

Jordan lives in the Tri-Valley region of Northern California. She enjoys reading, photography, and spending time with Roarke, her Pomeranian.

For more information on Jordan's current projects, visit www.jordanbernal.com.